I0784994

ARC VERSION VERSION ONLY

Original Ebook/Print Cover: Carol Marques Design
Editing, Proofing, backgrounds, & Formatting: Dirty Sexy Words/ Storm shield Editing/Little Tailfeather Publishing
Cassandra's logos: Pretty in Ink Creations/Artlogo
Goosebusters Alpha team: Kat Silver, Becky Ross, Erica Taryn
Duckhunters Beta Proofing: Jackie LH, Chilly G
ARC Team(s): Cassandra's Claws
Sensitivity Readers: Brit Mason, Gail Jericho
Translation Consultant: Mo Jacobs
Legal Services: Joshua Farley, esq.
Images/Fonts: Depositphotos, Shutterstock, Canva, & Photoshop

No GenAI was used within this book. All errors and greatness are by an ADHD muppet.

RISE OF THE **3** RESISTANCE

LOVE THE WAY YOU LION

INTERNATIONAL BEST SELLING AUTHOR

CASSANDRA FEATHERSTONE

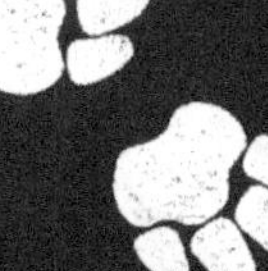

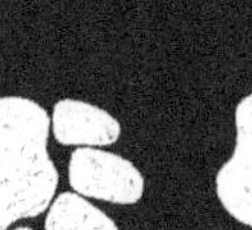

Content Information

This is a *paranormal whychoose romance with poly elements*—our FMC, Delilah, **will** make choices, but it will be to protect her peace and her family. She will make more choices throughout the series, so don't worry that you've been 'RH baited.' It's coming, I promise.

There are many situations included that are intended for <u>mature audiences (18+)</u>.

In these books, there may be instances/references (be they small or lengthy) that could trigger some individuals such as:

- liberal use of appropriate consent
- Mention off-page of dubious consent situations
- group scenes
- MMF, MM, MFM, MF, MFMMM, FF, FFM, FFMM, relationships and more throughout series
- emotional abuse by mates
- physical abuse (off-page) by mates
- alphahole/possessive MMCs

- cinnamon roll MMCs
- multiple POVs— including ones beyond the MCs
- unhinged MMC
- unhealthy coping mechanisms
- selfish, narcissistic mates
- boundaries being crossed
- BDSM
- raw sex
- traumatic childhood
- alcohol use and abuse
- threats of bodily harm
- death
- body modifications
- fancy genitalia
- mating bites/marks
- androids and building androids
- bullying (in person and on social media)
- PTSD
- blood
- emotional abuse from outside poly group
- body dysmorphia
- adult language
- pop culture references
- literary references
- emotional manipulation
- power play
- adorable nicknames
- physical intimidation
- rough sex
- markings/tattoos
- family dysfunction
- Community of various poly families
- animal companion
- brief mentions of non-body positive dieting culture

- very liberal re-imagining of history
- morally gray secret organization that monitors mercenaries/dimension
- official corruption
- name calling
- occasional misogyny
- exhibitionism
- hand necklaces
- adult bullying
- magical kinks
- impact play
- elitism
- bribery
- corpses
- drama
- physical threats to FMC and others
- species-ism
- pregnancy (no loss)

No sexual practices in this book should be taken as safe or appropriate for real life application.

Content information is important and I don't ever want to harm a reader with inaccurate information.

A Note To My Loving Family Members and Friends...

THANK YOU FOR SUPPORTING ME BY BUYING MY WORK.

TO THOSE OF YOU WHO AREN'T HEEDING MY WARNINGS: I SEE YOU.

I STILL DON'T WANT YOU TO TELL ME ABOUT IT, ESPECIALLY AT CHRISTMAS IN FRONT OF THE YOUNG'UNS AND RANDOM GUESTS.

THIS IS BOOK THREE OF A SERIES THAT IS DEFINITELY GETTING WILDER AS WE GO.

YOU'LL HAVE TO DEAL WITH DESTROYING YOUR ONLINE ALGOS BY USING THE SEARCH FUNCTIONS.

CAVEAT: IF YOU CHOOSE TO KEEP READING, KNOW THAT AT NO TIME WILL I EXPLAIN TERMS, POSITIONS, THEMES, TROPES, OR ANY OTHER PART OF THIS NOVEL AT FAMILY EVENTS, IN GROUP CHATS, OR ON SOCIAL MEDIA.

DON'T ASK.

The D
The Firehou
The Cabal Quarter
The Por

The Homestead
Company HQ

The
Captain's Ship
The
Zoo
Widow's Peak
Coach
House
The
Ranch
The
Sanctum
The
Hallows
The
Wilds
The Tropics
The
Speedway
Star
Ship
Down
Under

The Maison
The Frat
Jaguars
The Pridelands
The Resistance Quarter

Dedication

To all the little girls who were told the arts
Weren't 'practical'

That they could never do anything
with those 'Hobbies'

Or that they needed to focus on
something 'profitable'

(Even if they hated every moment)

Your dreams aren't out of reach,
their perspective was outdated.

Start now. Try now. Be happy now.
You deserve it.

Narcissists don't pick losers. They target the best of the best—the strongest, the smartest, the most capable. They pick the ones that surpass their level so easily that it infuriates them.

Why?

Because the reality is, they need you to feed their delusion, not the other way around.

— ANONYMOUS

As with all good romances, this starts with a man and a woman—or rather, two men and a woman...

Centuries ago, humans believed in things beyond their comprehension more readily. Supernaturals and their non-magical counterparts co-existed by using fairy tales, myths, and folklore to create a world where they interacted on specific terms that protected everyone. But as all species do, both sides of the coin evolved and dissension within their ranks and with one another caused internal wars, famine, and other tragedies.

The supernaturals evolved more quickly than humans, so the ancient bloodlines gathered together to form a governing body for all the non-human species. For a long time, this group made sure to curate history in a way that did not dishonor the gods or destiny, but kept humans from interfering in their business.

The stories of conflict, triumph, and regret from human history were often supernatural, but the truth was concealed. Eventually, humans turned their efforts towards science rather than spiritu-

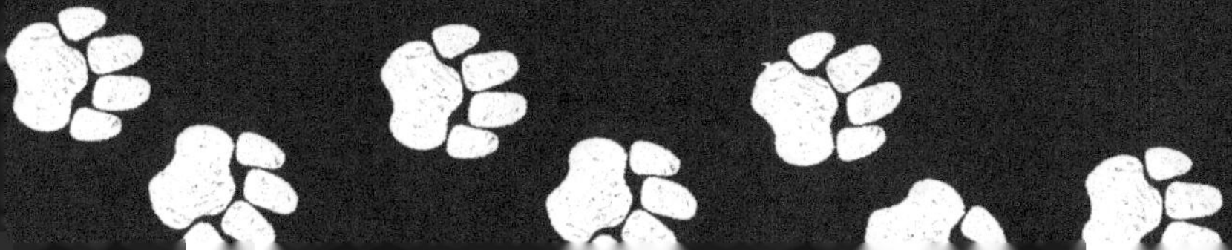

alism and the tales of things that go bump in the night became legend. This allowed the Society to focus solely on their own and as time went on, they expanded across the globe.

Our love story begins with an ancient woman who drew the attention of two supes in the Society. A warlock and a vampire, brothers in spirit if not blood, ascended to their council seats to become the last survivors of their names. Their families were decimated in various conflicts over the years and these two men grew resentful of the Society's leniency towards humans and lower tier supes alike. They were both in love with the ancient woman, though, and for a time after they mated with her, it settled their need for vengeance.

But evolution never ends and once humans advanced far enough to threaten supernaturals again, their thirst for revenge flared again. When they couldn't convince the Society council to conquer the non-magical beings, the brothers left their positions to work as undercover agents within a growing organization of humans dedicated to fomenting crime and strife. The warlock climbed the ranks of leadership over many decades and the vampire dove into the scientific program; together, they conspired to control the human population through their own weapons and technology.

When their true aims were discovered by the Society and their mate, they got exiled. By then, the warlock was in full control of the global criminal organization that operated under many names in many countries. He and his brother pleaded with their mate to join them, and when she refused to alter the course of Fate, he performed a forbidden ritual to unmate them from her.

The consequences of his reckless, selfish decision echoed through the world like wildfire. Wars broke out, treaties soured, crops died, and disease raged across the lands. Society members around the world confiscated all the tomes containing information on revoking a mate bond to prevent another ripple of magic that powerful from being released.

Unfortunately, the anguish of being cut off from their magically intended partner affected the vampire and the warlock as well. Their organization was thriving in the chaos the revocation caused, but they could barely stand to be in the same room as one another. The time came when they argued so often that it threatened their mission and they split the organization in half.

Each took the half they preferred—the warlock keeping the criminal wing and the vampire taking the technological sector. They vowed to share resources when required, but their empires would remain separated for good.

As technology continued to advance, The Company branched out into mercenary pursuits and the vampire blended magic and science so well that he created a pocket dimension to hide his labs, agents, and their secrets within. He named it The Rift in honor of the divide between him and his brother and once it was fully operational, he retreated into a world far away from the humans he despised.

That seclusion kept him from knowing his brother and their former lover were briefly reunited during the sparkling days of disco. Despite the cadre of new mates the Fates provided the ancient one, she relented one last time and from that tragic mistake, a child was born.

In order to protect her from her heritage, the child was left at one of the hybrid enclaves created by the Society and eventually adopted. She lived an inauspicious life as a 'lost one' until one day, the small amount of magic she could access sparked and she ran from her life, including the Guardian watching from the shadows.

Only the Fates could have conspired for this child to find her way to the portal to The Rift and settle there without knowing what she'd discover on the other side.

Delilah Lenore O'Hara was *never* meant to set foot in The Rift, but once she did, it started a cascade of events that cannot be prevented.

This time, the story begins with a a woman who has lots of men, but one who is changing her entire world.

The Writer's Plans Are Set In Motion

WILDE

"Our plans, my love, are complete," she declares softly, her fingers the last to leave the cool surface of the phone.

As the device is set aside, I take a slow, deliberate look around the room—a space filled with muted light and shadows that blend into the quiet anticipation of change. I wonder, almost reverently, how the environment will greet me upon my return. Will its corners seem resplendent with novelty, every detail shining freshly reborn, or will the familiar contours remain, only to contrast with the transformation within me? The uncertainty hangs palpable in the air as I offer a measured nod.

"Have you set in motion the pieces through which we will spread the word? And do you have the detailed timeline of the quests that will facilitate my return?" I ask, voice low and laced with both hope and trepidation.

I receive another nod in response. "Belle and Amanda are primed and ready to begin, and once Deli learns that there is a pathway to

repair, she will become as compliant as ever. Calista and Veruca have secured everything necessary from the other side," she explains with an air of quiet confidence.

Is it truly as straightforward as that?

I run my fingers thoughtfully over my chin, lost in contemplation. The intricacy of our meticulously orchestrated plan lies in the precise alignment of its moving parts. Without the correct pawns strategically positioned on the board, the entire game could stall before it ever begins.

Yet, when the plan finally reaches its full, vivid form, I know it will mend everything. I will be reborn, free from any lingering doubts about affections and allegiances. I hold on to the belief that, without a single harsh word, the chaos will be smoothed out.

I realize that those who have not yet been privy to our undertaking might initially be overwhelmed by a tide of raw emotion. But I trust that once my beloved steps forward and reveals this alternate path—a route forged by determination and hope—they will rally like a disciplined battalion, marching in unison until everything settles into a harmonious order.

Have they not always marched this way?

I admit, however, that Talia and Taurus have occasionally introduced a disruptive element, a wrench thrown into our otherwise methodical workings. Talia's candid confession just a few days ago spurred a moment of doubt, a whispered thought about whether we should delay our plans to observe the unfolding events.

No. The schedule must not be tampered with; the plan must remain steadfast.

In previous endeavors of this kind, my efforts had been thwarted by the anticipatory actions of those in the know, their foreknowledge altering outcomes with unpredictable behavior, leaving behind irreparable messes. I had never been afforded the chance to mend such a disaster before Talia and Taurus reentered our world—with calamitous results, as history has shown.

I wooed Talia partly out of a personal longing that I had nurtured for years, and partly to gain a strategic advantage concerning the dilemma of her mate. I had been certain that she would succumb to my affections—her heart always seemed to lean my way—and that her falling in love with me would grant me a measure of control over her tumultuous household as our plan progressed.

Now, with her heart securely in my grasp and her declarations of love echoing in the quiet, I find solace. I know I can rely on her to keep her headstrong companion from derailing my carefully plotted quest.

But why, you ask?

Because it is an absolute necessity. The realignment of power following the departure of our former allies has become more imperative now than ever before. Those vacated positions have been filled by new occupants—individuals who are far more combative and alarmingly resistant—and their presence is creating more complications than I ever anticipated.

I must return reborn and reclaim my rightful position in our family's intricate hierarchy, with my beloved by my side, each of us occupying the place where destiny has always intended us to be.

They will listen.

Mark my words: once our plan is set in motion, no conversation will stray from its reverberations for a long, long time.

The Blade And The Artist Meet Again

TALIA

He's sitting in his chair drawing when I walk in.

Disappointingly enough, he's wearing his ever-present track pants with an A-line tank, his hair streaming over his shoulders and down the back of the chair. I was hoping for something a little less clothed, but I'll take it. He looks comfortable and since my hackles have been up all morning for no reason I can determine, he might calm me down while he's riling me up.

"Evening, Blade." His grin is easy-going, and I wonder at the personality differences in the clones. They are so biologically similar, yet so different individually, particularly Rafe. His eyes slide over me, taking in the outfit I picked out for him—tummy baring, but all leather and lace.

"Nice shirt, though it seems like you're more covered than normal." I give him a saucy grin, but I am curious.

His brow furrows. "The relatives popped by while I was here with my girl—your bird is out of town and she hasn't heard about his harebrained idea to work for those loons—and I pulled it on. She pulled on something, too. Now that I say it out loud, it is rather odd." He scratches his head and looks puzzled, sitting his work aside.

"Should I be getting something from that?"

"Clothes aren't a big deal, not with family, but they came, and she pulled on pants—dumped me on the floor to do it, in fact—and I grabbed a shirt. I have no clue why." Shaking his head, he holds his hand out and I walk forward, unsure what he's trying to communicate with this story.

"I'd think she's hiding any signs of pregnancy, but that wouldn't explain your shirt grabbing. Plus, she's told all of them by now, right?" This is NOT helping my hackles being raised and I yank Precious out of her sheath, flipping and spinning without thinking about it.

"Yeah. It was awful defensive, I guess. Something is up, but I don't know what."

"Not a clue." I shrug, but it bothers me. I wonder if Deli told Taurus the same thing. We're all on edge, waiting for something to happen because people are — if nothing else—predictable, and we know that the gnome and her entourage can't be happy with Deli's announcement. That's what we fear, even with no one knowing about me and Rafe. He might not be sleeping with many people, but I bet a lot of them wish he were.

Smiling, he shrugs. "I'll ponder on it when I'm not busy ogling the delicious-looking bird in front of me."

Ah, there's the flirting I've been waiting for.

I pretend not to notice. "What, this old thing I'm wearing? I'm not all that." I wink, knowing I look good and his enjoyment only makes me feel better.

His look says he doesn't believe me, but keep in mind, he looked an absolute picture of grace and muscle when I arrived. He can't always look that good, right? "You look hot and you know it, woman. However, since I'm more interested in getting my hands on you than debating, come over here and plant one on me."

I walk towards him, my hips swaying as I make sure that he gets glimpses of tanned skin here and there. I kneel on the chair, straddling his lap, and wrap my arms around his neck. "I thought the whole expediency thing went right out the window." I drop my head and kiss him, surrounding myself with his scent with a sigh.

His growl echoes in my head as he kisses me back, his hands wandering over my bare skin. Warm palms make my skin feel hot and I rock against him, smiling against his mouth as his hand fists in my hair. I believe he likes my choice of seat. I'm not sure why I feel this hunger, this need, when he's around, but I damn sure refuse to ignore it. I lift my mouth from his and give him a stormy look, tugging his shirt off so I feel his skin against mine. "Damn. Now we're back to the want; that was fast."

"Mmm hmm," he replies, hands sliding to rest on my hip bones. "It's damned intense. It's especially intense when you wiggle like that."

"Like this?" I grin and roll my hips.

"Exactly like that, in fact."

"Do you think that's the intensity—physicality? I've been trying to figure that out." I nip his earlobe and murmur into it. "I want to figure out why I need you so much. It's hot—blood and sex and lust and everything else. But I don't know why it's so intense."

His eyes are golden when I pull back, and he tilts his head to allow me to nibble along the scars that are forming there. "Bloody hell, woman, now I *know* you're trying to get me riled up."

My laugh is husky and I grind against him again, tossing my hair and arching into his hands. "I thought you weren't great with the subtle."

"I have my moments." He pinches my rear, and I jump.

"Ow! That hurt!" I glare, looking put out.

"That was on purpose." His hands roam over me and I watch his eyes follow them.

"Is there a problem, dear? You sound worked up."

"That outfit's hot, but a bit of a puzzler. Where's the hidden spot, I wonder? I hate to ruin it with my usual rip and tear," he murmurs.

I grin. "There's the rub, I fear. You are a tummy man—so help me, I'll slice something off if you laugh at me for this—and I wanted to wear something special. This is the only thing I have that shows off this much stomach, so I wore it. It's not the easiest thing to maneuver."

"It's unbearably hot in here, pet. I adore the outfit, but it's a little too much clothing for my liking. Care to fill me in?" His grin stretches from cheek to cheek, and I can't help but wonder how many people have indulged him like this because he's thrilled by just an ensemble.

I return his smile, arching my back and reaching behind my head with both hands. Grasping the lycra at the nape of my neck, I stretch the fabric and pull it over my head, sliding my arms out of the thin straps. As I discard it, the material gathers around my waist, leaving me exposed from the waist up. "Better?"

"Definitely. I thought you might have hidden a tricky clasp or something." His hands wander over my body, fingertips brushing over a nipple as he lowers his lips to nip playfully at my shoulder. The sensation causes me to let out a low moan.

"No secrets here. Just a few bends and twists, and it's off. Keep caressing me, baby. Don't stop."

"I wouldn't dream of it, Blade."

My arousal intensifies as I feel his growing hardness pressing against me through our remaining clothing. Desperate for more intimate contact, I reach down to free him from the confines of his pants.

As I wrap my fingers around his cock, he slips his hand between my legs and finds my wetness. His fingers delve into me as I stroke him in rhythm with our kisses and moans.

"I want to be skin on skin with you, Rafe. I need you inside me."

"Sounds like a perfect plan to me." His hand continues to explore my pussy, brushing my aching clit over and over.

"Rafe, yes... don't stop," I moan, my voice heavy with desire. My heart races as the fingers of his other hand trail along my bare skin.

"I won't," he growls, kissing me deeply as he pulls me even closer. Our bodies press tightly together, every inch of our skin connecting in the most intense way possible.

His touch ignites a fire within me that spreads through my core and outward, making every nerve ending tingle with anticipation. His every move is met with a gasp or a moan as we move together in perfect harmony.

As his dick drives into me faster and harder, his lips find my neck, suckling and nipping at my delicate skin. Our hunger fills the room like a living thing, consuming us both in its intensity.

I don't know how much longer I can hold out.

Our climaxes approach, we are two souls united by desire and need. The primal sounds that escape our lips as we surrender to each other get louder as the shivers tickle my skin. Our kisses grow frenzied, each brush of his lips against mine leaving me yearning for more. We're two people dancing around an open flame, feeding off each other's heat and desire until we can contain it no longer.

With a loud cry that reverberates off the walls, our bodies collide in a climax so powerful it damn near shakes the furniture. Nothing exists in that moment but the fiery pull that drew us together repeatedly. While we come down from our high, we lay panting and sweaty but completely satisfied—something I haven't been in such a long time that I have no idea what to do about it.

I'm in such fucking trouble with this man.

The Cat Pines And The Bird Whines

DELILAH

The rhythmic patter of rain against the windowpane provides a soothing counterpoint to my focused efforts. Curled snugly in a blanket, I watch the liquid jewels race each other down the glass, as I wrestle with the yarn in my hands. Each stitch is a tiny battle, my fingers fumbling more often than not. The temptation to magically wave it all into perfection is there —a whisper at the back of my mind that feels like cheating—which is a shortcut I'm willing to take.

With every pull and loop, I wrinkle my nose, silently willing the yarn to cooperate. It stubbornly refuses to become the neat squares I envision, resembling instead a colorful tangle of good intentions. Crafting by hand appeared so simple when observed from a distance; in reality, however, it's proving to be quite the crafty adversary.

As the notes of Beethoven's *Moonlight Sonata* swirl through the room, mingling with the warm glow of candles, I feel him approach. My concentration breaks, and relief washes over me in a

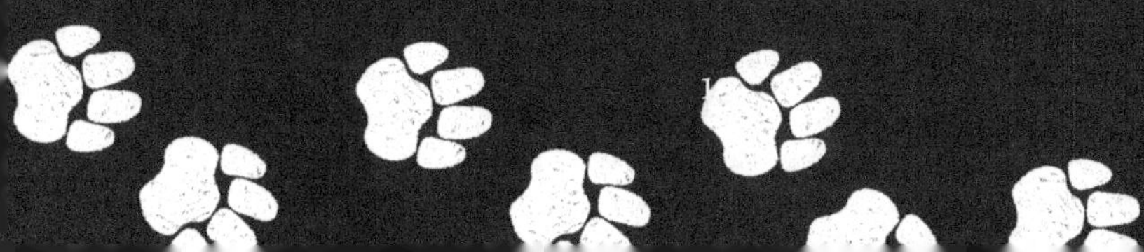

gentle wave. Setting aside the half-formed squares, I look up, my soft smile an involuntary response to his presence.

"Hi, baby. How was your trip?" My voice carries the warmth of welcome, even as I put aside my project, eager for him to bridge the distance between us. The serenity of our home wraps around me, the music and candlelight crafting a scene far removed from the dreariness outside.

Taurus' smile cuts through the room's tranquility, a sunbeam amidst the storm's grey. "Sod that. Nothing's as good as being here." With a fluid motion, he shrugs out of his duster and sends it arching across the distance to drape over the back of a nearby chair. Then, lowering himself with an effortless grace, he kneels before me, reverence in his gaze.

"Christ, you're the most beautiful thing I've ever seen."

His words, sincere and unguarded, stir something deep within me. I smile again, the familiarity of his adoration wrapping around me like the blanket I'm cocooned in. I lean forward, reaching down to let my lips brush his forehead, my touch a gentle benediction.

"You spoil me," I murmur. In this quiet moment, surrounded by the soft symphony of strings and flickering candlelight, his presence is the only embellishment I need.

The blanket falls away as I lean forward, my focus shifting from the window to Taurus. He gives me a casual shrug, a calm gesture that belies the tension etched in his expression. "It's part and parcel, my love."

There's something sheepish in his look, a crease of annoyance between his brows that softens as he meets my eyes. "That gnat Tamara texted me today, and she annoyed me so bloody much that I told her off." He pauses, scratching the back of his neck—a tell-tale sign of his discomfort. "I told her about being exclusive with you, but I couldn't quite remember the date you gave me the ring."

I blink, surprised by the question. The memory of sliding the band onto his finger feels as intimate as it is recent—so close I can still feel the warmth of his skin against mine. But the exact day? It slips through my thoughts like water. "I gave it to you a week ago now, but I don't know the date."

The numbers and days blurred into insignificance against the backdrop of our joined lives; time marked not by calendars, but by moments we shared. I watch him for a reaction, hoping he understands that some things—like the depth of our connection—transcend the need for specific dates.

Taurus's lower lip juts out in a playful pout, the corners of his mouth twitching as he tries to maintain an air of mock indignation. "Oh, fine. Take a husband and don't remember when." He crosses his arms, theatrically turning his head away. "When did we mate, then? If you don't know that, I'm out of here for the night."

I can't help but chuckle at his dramatics—the way he can shift from gravitas to childlike sulkiness never ceases to amuse me. "On a Wednesday," I reply, my voice a gentle sing-song, an anchor to draw him back from the brink of feigned exasperation.

Taurus huffs, his expression morphing from playful to genuinely curious. His hands find their way to his hips as he continues to pout. "What was the date, woman?" The question hangs in the air between us like a ten ton weight.

The needles in my hand pause mid-stitch, the soft clicking sound they made ceasing abruptly. My heart flutters like a trapped bird against my ribs as I feel the weight of his gaze, curious and expectant. I meet his eyes, a whirlpool of emotions swirling within me—embarrassment, frustration, affection—all tangled like the yarn at my feet.

Feeling blindsided by the sudden importance of a number, I give him a sheepish look. "I don't remember." My voice comes out softer than intended, carrying with it a silent plea. It isn't the date that holds significance for me, but the memory of our unity.

Rain patters against the window in a rhythm that seems to mock my lapse in memory. Taurus' eyes hold a playful twinkle, and with a dramatic flourish befitting a stage, he proclaims, "It's hard to forget, given it was on April Bloody Fool's Day!"

I can't help but snort, amusement bubbling up despite the tension. The irony of our poignant moment coinciding with a day of pranks isn't lost on me. "I thought we weren't telling anyone that," I say, the corners of my mouth twitching upwards into a reluctant smile.

Taurus' shoulders slump as he retreats to the couch, a silhouette of dejection against the flickering candlelight. His boots leave soft impressions on the carpet, carrying the weight of his mood with every step.

"Baby, I'm sorry," I murmur, pinching the bridge of my nose. Rising, I let the knitted squares slip from my lap like autumn leaves abandoning their branches, scattering across the hardwood floor in a silent testament to my carelessness.

Approaching him, I see his jaw set in a stubborn line, yet the warmth that usually radiates from him seems dimmer. "I really am," I add, seeking forgiveness for something I didn't know would matter so much to him.

But he will not let it go so easily, I think.

Kneeling before him, I reach out tentatively, my fingers trembling slightly as they brush against his cheek. His eyes close at the contact, lashes casting long shadows on his skin, a canvas of trust and vulnerability.

"It hurts, love," Taurus murmurs, his voice a soft echo in the candlelit room. His face leans into my touch, seeking solace in the warmth of my palm. "I shouldn't guilt you since I know you didn't mean to." Even with eyes closed, there is a sincerity in his expression that belies the casualness of his tone.

My heart clenches at the sight of him. This man who will face down killers, yet is wounded by an accidental oversight.

"I'm sorry, baby. I'll be better, I swear." My voice wavers, laden with the weight of promises and silent vows to never let such forgetfulness cause him pain again. Gently cupping his face, I press my forehead to his. We share a breath, a moment of connection to mend the tiny fracture of forgotten dates with the glue of our bond.

I hate knowing this small thing hurts someone I love so goddamn much.

Taurus' voice is a low, resonant balm to the tension in the room. "I'll heal."

I shake my head slowly, the motion stirring strands of hair across my face. A sense of self-reproach gnaws at me—an unpleasant companion that had lingered since an unexpected visit threw my day into disarray.

The candles flicker, their light dancing against the walls, as if to chase away the shadows that creep into my conscience. Beethoven's sonata ebbs and flows through the room, a soundtrack to my unease. The quiet melody is normally comforting, but it only serves to amplify the discord within me right now.

"You shouldn't have to," I murmur, my voice barely above the sound of the rain. "It's my fault."

The squares of knitting are abandoned behind me, colorful patches of intention that now seem trivial in the wake of our emotional exchange. With a sigh, I retreat further into the chair that feels more like a fortress of solitude than a nest of comfort. Its cushions embrace my form as I tuck my legs beneath me. Resting back, I close my eyes for a moment, searching for equilibrium in a world that is intent on keeping it just out of reach.

Nothing I do is ever right, even with him; I don't deserve the happiness I was feeling.

Taurus's gaze drifts to the scattered array of crafting supplies that invade the surrounding space. His curiosity pulls his attention from our earlier conversation, and he leans forward, peering at the needles and yarn as if they are artifacts from an alien world.

"It's what I do, love. What's with all the stuff you have here?" His voice is gentle, the timbre a soothing balm to my frazzled nerves. He's trying to change the subject, but that won't help me stave off the internal loathing in my soul.

I offer him a small, sheepish grin as I gather the knitting needles and hold up the jewel-toned squares for him to see. The colors capture the warmth of the room, reflecting the flickering candlelight in deep, comforting hues.

"It's an experiment. I've never done this before." The needles were awkward in my hands, a testament to my inexperience.. The squares, though imperfect, are a patchwork of my determination—a physical representation of stepping beyond my usual realm of abilities.

He reaches out, his fingers brushing over the soft yarn as he examines my handiwork. For a moment, the shared silence between us as Beethoven's notes filled the spaces words cannot reach. I'm not any good yet, but I'm determined to learn, even if it's just to spite the universe.

The former gifted kid in me simply refuses to let yarn and pointy sticks win.

Taurus's expression morphs into one of comic disbelief, his mouth opening and closing in rapid succession, a silent stammer as realization dawns in the depths of his warm eyes. He shakes his head, chastising himself with an exasperated chuckle that rumbles from deep within his chest.

"Oh, bloody buggering hell! You were pining and here I am whining about my hurt delicates." His voice is thick with mock horror, yet beneath it lays a genuine note of self-reproach.

A light laugh bubbles up from my throat—I'm always amused by his dramatics. Holding up one square, I shrug nonchalantly. "They're blanket pieces," I explain, hoping this minor revelation will help him connect the dots.

The colors of each square pop even more vividly against the backdrop of the dimly lit room, their purpose yet to be fully understood by the man kneeling before me. With a tilt of my head, I watch, waiting for the significance to register.

His brow furrows in concern as he scans the room, landing on the little squares of fabric scattered around me. "Did the furry princess lose that raggedy thing she carries, and I missed it?" His voice is tinged with urgency. "I'll send a sodding cleaner team everywhere she's been until they find it. I know how she loves that—"

I shake my head, cutting him off mid-sentence, and hold up one of the knitted squares between my fingertips. "No, no. Aradia did not lose her blanket. It's smaller. See?" The tiny stitches and the soft threads gleam under the flicker of candlelight.

He's normally not this dense, but the date thing shook his confidence, I know.

Taurus leans closer, squinting at the square, the gears visibly turning behind his puzzled gaze. A light of recognition finally ignites in his eyes, a slow grin spreading across his face. "Oh! That's for the wee one."

My heart swells and my lips curl into a broad smile. I let the needles clink softly together as I set them aside, the half-formed mess left waiting on the chair. Unfurling from my cozy nest, I push to my feet, the blanket pooling around my ankles.

"Exactly," I say, reaching out a hand to him. "Come here, you grumpy old man. I have a yen to be close to you. I've been itching all day."

He rises, the corners of his mouth twitching with a suppressed chuckle, any remnants of irritation melting away as he steps closer. The space between us closes as I melt into his embrace, the air charged with a current that only ever sparks when we're together. Taurus's hands settle on my waist, and I sigh softly.

This is what I've been missing since he left for his mission.

"I know how that is, heart of mine," he murmurs. "I've been feeling off and missing you like a hole in the chest for the past few days."

The raw honesty in his words stirs something deep within me. I lay my hands on his broad shoulders, the strength beneath them reassuring, and shut out everything else in the world for a moment.

"Stay close," I whisper. A soft breath escapes my lips as I visualize our destination, the familiar contours of our bed inviting and safe. The world shifts, a sensation of falling upwards enveloping us, and then it steadies.

My eyes flutter open at the sight of our bedroom from a different position in the room. We are now beside the bed, perfectly positioned as if we had always been there. A triumphant grin spreads across my face, mirroring the wonder in Taurus's eyes.

"Look at that. I did it!" I beam, the success igniting a spark of pride that dances in my chest.

Taurus's expression, a mix of shock and awe, is the kind of reaction that could fuel me for days. His lips part in disbelief, then curl into an approving smile, that spreads warmth through my veins like a sip of fine whiskey.

His praise makes some of the ugly goo inside me from earlier dissipate like mist.

"You did. Bloody hell, two people..." His voice trails off, tinged with admiration. "I'm so proud of you. You're getting better every day."

"I can get one person anywhere, I think. Aradia isn't small, but she's like another big person, and I can get her around with me." A playful smirk draws up the corners of my mouth, as I recall past attempts. The mishaps are now just humorous memories. "At least I didn't drop us on our asses midway there. It's happened a couple of times when I attempted both of us together."

The grin on Taurus's face matches mine, his pride in my progress a palpable thing that fills the room. Even the candles seem to flicker in time with our shared laughter, their light dancing across our faces as we revel in this simple yet magical moment. I settle astride his lap, looking down into his face proudly.

"Good form, love," he murmurs, his hands finding their way to my hips to steady me. "You could have gotten us naked, but points for the 'not dropping' thing." His eyes gleam with a respect for my burgeoning power. "I enjoy seeing you get stronger. It'll help when they send you on a test run."

"Test run?" The words slip from my lips before I catch them. "Holy hell, when? Why didn't I hear about it?"

I'm going to be a fucking super spy and he buried that lede?

His gaze holds mine amidst my sudden tempest of questions. The warmth of his lips lingers on my forehead as Taurus's chuckle diffuses the tension that momentarily gripped me. "Not for a while, heart of mine," he reassures. "I just found out myself, but we have a big class coming through. They'd like to get them settled before they bring in any wildcards."

A slow grin tugs at my lips at the thrilling prospect. With a playful motion, I kick off the silk boxers I slipped into earlier—the fabric fluttering to the floor in a whisper. My head tilts, challenging the notion of readiness with a daring sparkle in my eyes. "I'll be ready."

Taurus's eyes sparkle with an amused yet quizzical expression. "Those are the mysterious boxers," he says, the corners of his lips twitching with suppressed mirth. His gaze locks onto mine, and I feel the cogs turning behind those thoughtful eyes. "Talia mentioned you and Sampson had visitors earlier, and you both put on clothes." A pause hangs in the air as his forehead creases ever so slightly. "Is that something we should talk about?" The question hovers between us, tinged with a sense of unease. "It makes me itch when anything involves her and Rafe. Talia's..." He falters for a half heartbeat before shrugging off the words unsaid.

How do I answer this without making him worry about me and Talia simultaneously?

"You should see the huge ass stack of drawings Rafe's done," I offer, my voice laced with fondness. "I went in there today and it was like he'd been on an art bender. He got up early and got ready just in case she came over. It. Is. So. Weird."

My mate's gaze softens despite the fierce protective streak in him with those he cares for. Shadows danced across his face, illuminated by the flickering candlelight, as he ponders his next words. "I'm being prickish and protective," he admits with a reluctant sigh. "But I don't want her to get hurt." His fingers trace an idle pattern on my skin. "She likes him a lot—an unusual amount."

I feel the weight of his concern, knowing it mirrors my own. Leaning closer, I whisper, my voice barely more than a breath,. "I haven't seen him like this in forever. I don't know—maybe never. He's ador—"

The end of my sentence is cut short by a sudden jolt of surprise. "Ow." I yelp at the playful pinch from Rafe zapping through our bond. With a pout, I rub my bum where the phantom sensation still tingles. That was a way of reminding me that some things are better left unsaid by outsiders.

Jackass.

I shift on Taurus's lap, feeling the remnants of the pinch fade into a warm tingle. My new mate chuckles, a sound that is both comforting and conspiratorial in the quiet of our bedroom.

"She's in my head, too," he says, the corners of his eyes crinkling with mirth. "It's been more stereo since you and I drained."

"Let me just..." I mutter, rolling my eyes upward as if I can physically see the space where Rafe is. With a mental shove, I push against the familiar presence, trying to dislodge him from his perch. My brow furrows in concentration. "It's harder to kick him out for me now."

Taurus's grin widens, a devilish twinkle lighting his eyes. "They can watch along with the home game then, heart of mine," he teases, leaning closer, "because I feel like experimenting with the other things that came from our draining right now."

The prospect sparks a thrill in me, and my response is immediate. I let out a low chuckle. "Is that an invitation I hear?" The air between us crackles with the promise of discovery, and in that moment, I relish the closeness we share, a connection deepened by secrets only we can explore.

"Christ, neither of you are good with subtlety," he observes with mock exasperation.

The heat from our bodies creates an atmosphere of its own and my heart thrums in my chest like the wings of a bird eager for flight. I feel his heartbeat, strong and steady, against my chest. "Oh, I'm not so terrible at taking a hint." Winking at him, I push until he's reclining on the bed, my body draped over his like a silk scarf. "Despite what you think."

"Keep wiggling and I'll not be doing any thinking at all," Taurus murmurs, his voice a husky vibration against my skin. His hands move with purpose, tracing patterns of affection that send shivers down my spine.

"Bonus," I breathe, the word barely more than a sigh as I lean closer, allowing the magnetic pull between us to guide my actions.

I'll teach our nosy mates to peek in on our thoughts uninvited—Skinemax, here we come.

The Writer's Plan Comes To Fruition

WILDE

The inky sky stretched boundlessly above, stars punctuating the darkness like scattered diamonds. I stand still for a moment, inhaling the crisp air of the dead of the night. This is the hour when the world holds its breath, when the earth itself seems to pause and wait for something momentous to unfold.

And it most certainly will tonight.

I flex my muscles subtly, feeling the potent energy coursing through me—a silent testament to the strength and speed endemic to my kind. Night is our realm, the time when our powers find their true expression. With focused intent, I move, my form a whisper against the silence of the sleeping city. No one stirs; both humans and clones lay ensconced in dreams, blissfully unaware of the machinations set to unravel. It's just as well—there can be no interference tonight, no chance occurrence to thwart what needs to be done.

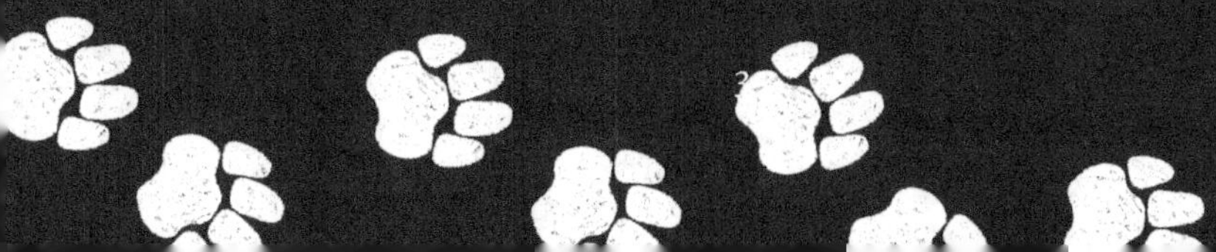

My destination is clear, her abode not far now. The message has to reach her in time—that is everything. I summon the swiftness granted by the gifts I was given after the War, my body a blur against the backdrop of shadowed alleys and moonlit pavements.

She will wake to the sound of the call, a carefully orchestrated communication designed to steer her actions. No one will suspect the truth—that it is I who bent the fabric of our reality to ensure the sequence plays out as needed.

She will be just in time to hear the worst and it will kick start my scheme perfectly.

As I near her dwelling, I slow, my senses heightened. My heart doesn't race; it is steady, metronomic, attuned to the gravity of the task at hand. The message will be received, and the timeline will unfurl with calculated precision.

Tonight, under the cover of darkness, I am the unseen harbinger of a new dawn.

Silent as the night itself, I drive past the final marker that separates the Resistance quarter from our home. My plan is a tapestry of action and consequence, each thread interwoven with meticulous care. The stillness of the night air seems to hold its breath as I approach the curve where I will meet the cold hands of Fate with determined glee.

The moon is a sentinel in the sky, casting long, silver shadows that dance with the whims of the whispering wind. I stand atop a hill overlooking the slumbering enclave she built, the weight of my decision grounding me to the earth. The stillness is a canvas, and I'm about to introduce a stroke so bold, it will rock their foundations.

"Sad that it comes to this," I murmur to myself, gazing at the luminous orb above. "It is such a beautiful night to be waxing dramatically under the moonlight." A wry smile curves my lips as I embrace the solitude. I appreciate the irony of my Bond villain style speeches of late, the grandiloquence that has crept into my soliloquies when no one but the stars bear witness.

I turn away from the lunar spectacle, the gravity of the moment settling in my chest. It is time to descend from my perch, time to step into the world that sleeps unaware of the tremors soon to ripple through their reality. My feet move with purpose, the weight of my decision to become a harbinger of change.

I don't have a choice; we've lost her and he will follow. It is unacceptable and I must fix it.

Leaves whisper secrets to the night as I stride through the underbrush, every step a silent vow. My mind spins with the intricacies of my plan, a web so vast and interconnected that the world's finest minds would reel to unravel it. This is not about mere shock, nor fleeting awe; this is the genesis of revolution.

"Big catalysts," I muse, my voice a low rumble against the rustling backdrop, "create the most undeniable changes." The darkness seems to lean in, eager to absorb the gravity of my words. In our little ribbon of reality, the impact will be profound—no corner will remain untouched by the tremors of my actions.

I pause, considering the scale of what I am about to unleash. The Big Bang itself was monumental because of its sheer magnitude; a smaller spark would have fizzled into obscurity. Mimicking the creation of worlds, my catalyst too will be titanic, an indisputable blast that would force adaptation upon all.

"Everyone will have to adapt," I declare, conviction hardening like steel within me. There are no half measures, no reticence in this plan. History demands boldness, and I am its chosen architect. With a final glance at the sleeping houses beneath the stars, I embrace the inevitable.

Death is only the beginning, after all.

The night air is cool, a gentle caress against my skin as each step brings me closer to my objective. I am almost to the road now, the threshold that marks the beginning of the end. Beyond the grassy area, my car awaits me like a blinking neon sign in the desert.

A breath catches in my throat, and for a moment, I allow myself the luxury of stillness, even in my mind. The enormity of what I am about to do settles upon my shoulders, a weight both exhilarating and suffocating.

Bravery has not always been my strong suit. There were times when doubt gnawed at my resolve like a persistent chill, memories of a winter past when hesitation cost me dearly. I can not afford to be that person again; the one who floundered in the face of adversity, whose actions—or lack thereof—left issues festering, unresolved.

I was the architect of this disaster and thus, I will be such for its resolution.

"Shore yourself up," I whisper to the darkness, willing strength into my limbs.

With a deep intake of breath, I step out from the cover of trees and onto the cold, solid certainty of the road. The soles of my boots meet the asphalt with quiet determination, the sound lost amidst the symphony of the night. Ahead, the beautiful vehicle seems to beckon, a silent accomplice to the history I am about to write.

There's no turning back, not anymore.

My heart hammers against my ribs, an echo of the urgency that propels me forward. "Tonight," I murmur, the word slicing through the silence, "history will remember the name Wilde."

The shadows dance at my periphery, but I pay them no mind. My focus is singular, honed sharp by the vision of what's to come. The thought of altering the very fabric of existence sends a thrill down my spine, electric and awakening. This is more than a mere message; this is the catalyst for a new era. The structures and norms they cling to will tremble at the revelation awaiting in the wings, ready to burst forth from the confines of my intent.

I let out a dry chuckle, a sound that seems too human for the monumental shift coming.

"Big catalysts," I whisper, the words a promise to the quiet world around me. "Undeniable changes."

With purpose etched into every cell of my being, I surge ahead, closing the gap between the present and the future. Getting into the car, I warm the engine up with a sigh as I prepare myself for what I'm about to do.

"Adapt," I say to the wind, "or be left behind. I, Wilde, will change the course of history in this world—starting tonight."

Now to race to glory and pain in order to regain my throne.

The Cat Roars Into The Night

TAURUS

The night was a cocoon of silence until her body convulsed, tearing through the stillness. A sharp cry pierces the air, wrenching me from sleep. My eyes snap open to find her already in motion, an abrupt blur of limbs and tangled sheets.

"Minx!" I call out, my voice rough with sudden wakefulness.

She's on the floor now, crouched low like a predator, her feline features contorted with alarm. Her tail lashes violently from side to side—an obvious barometer of her agitation. The room feels charged, a palpable current of energy prickling my skin with an otherworldly sensation. Is she harnessing some latent electrical force? That would be another twist in the ever-expanding enigma that is my wife's abilities.

"What is going on?" I press, my heart pounding a staccato rhythm against my ribs. "Minx, tell me what's going on."

But she offers no explanation, no reassurance. There's only the

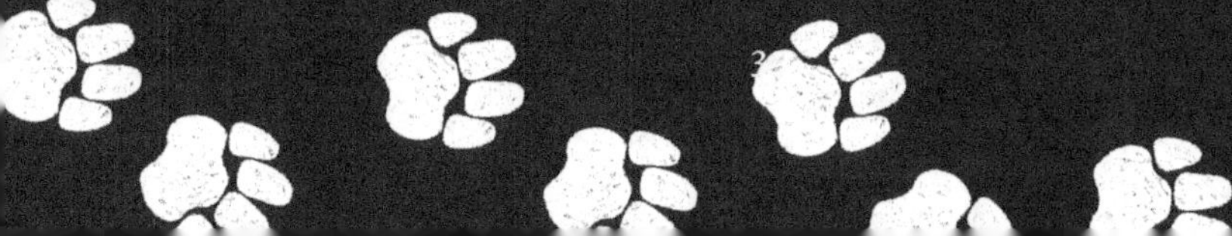

electric tension hanging thick in the air, the wild swish of her tail, and the unanswered questions swirling in the dark.

Whatever it is, it's bad.

A shrill sound splits the air, tearing through the charged atmosphere like a siren's call. It's coming from the phone on the dresser—a harbinger of bad news. The screen flashes ominously with the label "The Maison" in bold, urgent letters. I know without a doubt that it's an alert I shouldn't ignore. The droids from her house would rather send smoke signals than resort to a phone call. If they're actually calling, the situation has to be grave.

My minx's attention, however, remains fixated elsewhere. She's communicating in deep, guttural growls, a feral feline language known only to her and Aradia. The latter, now fully roused, mirrors Minx's movements, her own sleek tiger form prowling with the same manic energy. They move in tandem, two creatures bound by instinct; their conversation a series of snarls and hisses that my human ears can't decipher.

Feeling the sting of exclusion, I push myself off the bed. My feet hit the floor with determination as I head for the dresser. Someone has to answer the clarion call that beckons in the dead of night. With a resigned exhale, I pick up her phone, preparing myself to translate whatever impending chaos is lurking into terms I can grasp. Holding the vibrating phone with a hand steadier than I feel, I answer it with a flick of my thumb. The screen's ominous glow barely lights our darkened room where chaos reigns in fur and feral snarls, but the sound of panicked voices is immediate.

"Bloody hell, Nancy, you have to sodding pick up when we call! We're not ringing your bell for our health," The British accented voice is like a jackhammer to my eardrums, brash and unforgiving.

One of her droids patterned off of my template, I see.

I stifle the urge to hurl the device against the wall in irritation, focusing instead on my feral wife and whatever problem is causing her to shift. Her shadowy silhouette is crouched low, muscles coiled, the primal language she shares with Aradia an undercurrent to the cacophony erupting from the phone.

"This is Taurus, you nit," I respond, pressing the device harder against my ear as if that will bridge the gap between our worlds. "The cat's gone—well, catty, right now. She's not in a human speech place. What in the bloody fuck has you calling and her in feral mode at four sodding am?" My words are icy with a thread of concern, as I try desperately to subdue the tempest within me.

On the other end, there's a pause and in the silence, I heard my minx's tail swish across the hardwood floor, an ominous sound like the crackle before a storm.

The droid's voice, a guttering flamethrower of profanity, scorches through the phone's speaker. "Fucking hellfire, Taurus. When the shit hits the fan, you don't just stand there and bloody well paint with it. I'm calling because it's a sodding emergency."

I silently tip my hat to Victor's programming—his creations swear with an artistry I didn't expect.

"Are you done bitching?" I ask when the storm of continued curses ebbs. I watch my minx, her tail still thrashing in the dark like a live wire. Silence follows, heavy and thick, leaving me teetering on the edge of my patience. "Because we're wasting time, mate."

Just as I'm about to disconnect the call, another voice cuts through the static, the tone cool and collected as if ordering an evening cocktail rather than issuing an emergency summons. "Look, Clone in Black," the aristocratic tone commands, "you need to haul your fashionable ass here fast. We've got a 911 that will rock the foundations of this hellhole and we need you. Grab her furry fanny and pop over here before it hits the news. No time for explanations—the writer's been in an accident and it's bad. Now, mush!"

The shift in the atmosphere is immediate when I realize the gravity of what she just said. My hand clenches the phone so tightly I can feel the plastic threatening to give way under the strain. The voice on the other end, with its poised enunciation and slight hint of panic, painted an ominous picture. A cold sweat beads on my brow as I consider the impact of Wilde being injured on this community full of worshippers.

Not good. Not good at all, and not only because it will upset both of my women.

"Fuck," I murmur, the word barely escaping my lips as I struggle to get a hold of the thoughts whizzing through my mind. My glance darts back to my wife—suddenly understanding why her form is a blurred frenzy of feline instinct.

"Bring the emerald amulet, the moon-dusted blade, and don't forget the—"

"Enough!" I bark into the receiver as the Duchess's exhaustive list slices through my scattered thoughts like shrapnel. There's no time to entertain her manic inventory, but I know my wife will be upset if I ignore the droid's requests. Suddenly, an image of Talia and Rafe flicker in the back of my mind. They are at that house and their status is unknown—creating a gnawing concern that threatens to unravel me.

"Are they okay?" I mutter to myself, knowing full well the Duchess can't hear me over the noise in her background. Frantic scenarios play out in my head, each more dire than the last. If they're unaware of the catastrophe unfolding, it's on me to get these people to alert them—or worse, prepare for their reactions to the news. Since they're both involved with the git, they'll be just as upset as my minx.

This is a bloody fucking nightmare.

"Did you hear me, Taurus? Don't dick around—get over here now!"

"Got it," I lie, the contents of her ramble lost to the ether. My focus narrows on the impending storm outside and the tempest brewing within the walls of our home. With the determination of one facing the eye of a hurricane, I steel myself for what lies ahead. She continues babbling for another minute and I finally tire of it.

"*Philomena.*" The name erupts from my lips, cutting through her ceaseless chatter with the sharpness of a blade. Silence falls abruptly on the other end of the line, like a curtain dropping mid-scene. "Have you told Talia and Sampson yet? They're at your house."

The momentary quiet is shattered by a noise that booms through the receiver—a cacophony that can only spell disaster. There's an unmistakable sound of something heavy meeting an untimely demise, followed by a resonant bellow that reverberates in my chest.

Guess they know now, huh?

My pulse quickens as realization dawns on me; whatever force sent my minx spiraling into her primal state has struck the artist. Philomena's voice cuts through the chaos, issuing commands to her personal legion, before the line goes dead, leaving me clutching a silent phone.

"Damn it," I mutter, the device feeling like a brick in my hand. The darkness seems to close in around me, the weight of uncertainty a tangible presence in our room. Whatever we're hurtling toward, it's just claimed its next victim. The silence is deafening as I yank on clothes. "*Fuck.* What in the hell is going on?"

My gaze snaps to Aradia, her form a shadow against the pale moonlight filtering through the curtains. "Help me out here," I plead, my appeal a desperate entreaty that she seems to understand. With feline grace, she butts her head against Minx's crouching figure, the movement both comforting and urgent.

"Easy, girl. I just need my wife to be calm enough to transport us to your house," I murmur.

The tiger looks up at me, her eyes glowing embers in the dark. For a moment, I see the intelligence of the familiar and her devotion to my spouse. She's a mere breath away from being something wholly other, and it chills my blood. Until my wife, I'd never witnessed such a thing as a real 'shifter'—never even considered that even though I'm a vampiric clone, there might be other supernatural beings running around the planet.

It shouldn't surprise me that my witchy, furry woman's animals are truly connected to her, like the stories you see in the movies or on TV.

My heart hammers against my ribs, a frantic drumbeat as I wait for the beast to soothe my wife enough to leave. As the furry companion growls and grumbles with my woman, the tension in her recedes slowly, and she rises from the crouched position reminiscent of the feline she has inside. Her features and tail don't go away, but she's standing like a human, which has to be better. Right?

That notion is fleeting when our curtains suddenly flap wildly as a gust of wind forces its way into the room, carrying the scent of impending rain. I freeze for a moment, watching as dark clouds amass outside the window, suffocating the stars. The shadow play of the storm promises violence, and I honestly have no idea if that's because Deli is funneling her power from the shifter side to the witchy one.

With a sharp intake of breath, I spin around, looking around our bedroom. Clothes lay scattered on the floor, remnants of our play earlier in the evening. My gaze lands on the bag she left on the chair when she arrived home. I grab it, stuffing it with a change of clothes, her favorite boots, and the oddities Philomena insisted on.

Jar of newt eyes? Check. Vial of moon water? In it bloody goes.

"Okay, ladies. We're heading to your place to figure out how to handle the lot of you," I announce, trying to infuse my voice with more confidence than I feel. My hand touches Aradia's fur, then I find my wife's shoulder, grounding her jitters with my touch. The air is humming audibly, a testament to the magick that simmers beneath my woman's skin. I know she's doing her best to hold it back, but this is an awfully inconvenient time for her to unleash with more vigor than I've ever seen before.

"Time to sort this shit out," I whisper as I grip them both. I'm ready to face the tempest that awaits us beyond the walls of our home—or as ready as I can be.

Gritting my teeth, I prepare myself for the utter insanity that will be the house where over a dozen people are losing their shit simultaneously. A sigh escapes me, and I shut my eyes briefly, seeking a moment's respite in the darkness. If only the Company hadn't rewarded that floppy haired writer with transformation after the War, perhaps he and his mate wouldn't have been able to get such an iron grip on the members of both the Cabal and the Resistance. Maybe both of my mates wouldn't have ever gotten involved with him in ways that I'm certain have always been detrimental.

Maybe whatever happened tonight wouldn't be making people lose their goddamn shit at four a.m.

Opening my eyes, I glance at the feline duo before me, their agitated states painting a surreal picture amidst the mundane setting of our bedroom-turned-battleground. "This should be interesting," I say, a wry note of sarcasm threading through my words.

With one last look at our formerly serene home, I steel myself for whatever lies ahead. We're about to leap into chaos, and it's anyone's guess what awaits at The Maison.

Time to take a leap into the hurricane.

DISTRIBUTION: OPERATIONS DIRECTOR (MIKHAIL, 004); TRAINING DIRECTOR (TIBERIUS, 005); Oversight, ANALYSIS DEPARTMENT, INTEL DEPARTMENT, TEAM X1501, ALL Project Reality TEAMS
SUBJECT: DEMISE OF WILDE (056)

This is the clone that came into being after the conflict. X001 was heavily involved in that decision, though she is not aware of all aspects of our involvement in the solution.

This affects a multitude of subjects and rather than post updated profiles for all affected that will clutter team inboxes, we will update this information on profiles one by one as other events influence the need for a profile update.

002 is demanding an investigation of the crash and circumstances of it. He seems to suspect the incident, and having a mate romantically involved with 056 and a wife who mated to him has made him

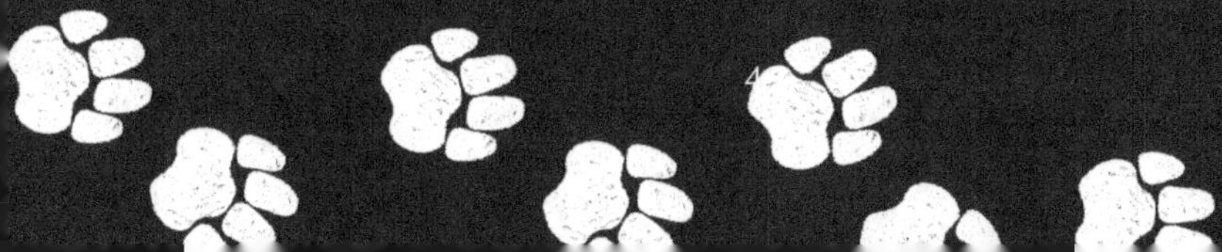

eager to resolve the question. His fear is that this was a pre-arranged plot used to harm x1501, her family and x001.

He believes it is possible that 056 is alive and being hidden—everything was staged. He believes that 056, x260, and others are using this to gain support for some plot to overthrow the Resistance leadership or undermine their relationships with his family.

Though it sounds like paranoid rantings, we have seen behavior that would support this theory, and 002 has displayed good instincts throughout his career when rooting out deep-seated plots in rebel groups.

We will send an investigative team across the portal to the hospital and mortuary. On this side, to the area of the crash (he was not in the Resistance Quarter). We will have all operatives in the Cabal Quarter keep their eyes and ears open for random chatter that could develop leads.

Intel department will work on the intelligence angle from the cyber perspective. We have assembled a task force to work on this, and that team will handle all inquiries and present their findings within three weeks' time.

The Cat Gives and Gives

DELILAH

I cradle the warm mug between my hands, the rich aroma of coffee mingling with the sharp scent of bourbon. The liquid's heat seeps into my weary bones as I take a slow, deliberate sip. "It was a lovely service," I murmur, more to myself than anyone else.

Roman stands across the room, his back to me, but I can feel the weight of his disapproval like a physical thing. When I'd asked for the alcohol, his eyes had narrowed into slits of judgment, that dirty look painting his face. But my reserves were scraping bottom, and I needed the burn of bourbon to make it through another minute. "Talk to Philomena," I'd said, deflecting his silent rebuke. She knew about the delicate balance of my magickal barriers, the intricate web I wove around my psyche to keep from unraveling. I wasn't inclined to offer Roman an explanation, or anything else, for that matter.

Considering how much I've done in this house since he died, jumping up my tail pipe about shit he couldn't possibly understand isn't a welcome occurrence.

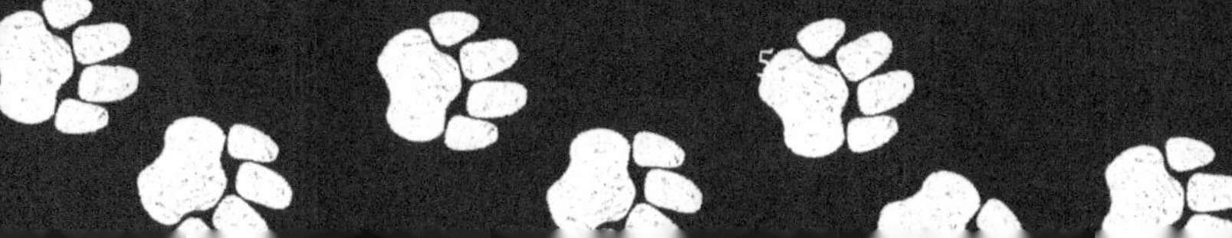

The past three days have been nothing but a kaleidoscope of chaos and despair, images and sounds swirling together in a maddening dance. Hospitals with their antiseptic smell and the mortuary's chilling silence have become my reluctant sanctuaries. My ears still ring with the echoes of crying, the guttural sounds of sorrow that no one should ever have to hear. I've witnessed Sari's grief manifest in screams that tore through the air, her tears mingling with snot as she clung to whatever scrap of reality she could find.

Sleep was an elusive specter, taunting me from the corners of couches and mocking me from stiff chairs. I've chased it desperately, but it dances just out of reach, leaving me to trudge through each day in a haze. And through it all, there's Sari, her soul fracturing before my eyes, relying on me to guide her through this treacherous terrain of loss.

So I sip my spiked coffee, letting the warmth and the sting anchor me to the moment, to the here and now where grief is a constant companion and rest is a luxury I can't afford.

I have to keep myself from collapsing under the weight of all the emotions I'm burying to support everyone else.

Setting the cup on the counter with a decisive click, my hands steady despite the weariness that clings to my bones. Rafe and I burnt out our anger in a spectacular display of unchecked emotion before this all began, leaving us hollow. Now, in the aftermath, we're spent forces circling the debris of our own turmoil.

"I think it's time for us to go," I announced after the first few hours at the hospital, my voice low but carrying. The room stilled, a collective intake of breath from the extended family showing their surprise.

"Are you sure?" Rafe asked, his brow furrowing, eyes still rimmed red.

"Quite sure," I replied firmly, not meeting his gaze. "We can't risk exposure. Not here." It wasn't just about the hospital's prying eyes —it was about containment, control, and the preservation of what little normalcy we could feign.

One by one, they filed out, murmurs of assent or dissent lost in the shuffle of feet and the quiet closing of doors. As the last of them disappeared around the corner, I sighed heavily. We needed to go home to work through our grief in private, not in front of this mass of people gathered helplessly in the hospital with Sari.

Turning back to the window, I watched as the hospital continued its relentless march of efficiency outside the room. White coats flashed by, gurneys rolled past. Life and death played out in sterile corridors, oblivious to the storm of grief raging in this small, secluded space.

I allowed myself a moment, just one, where the weight of self-neglect pressed against my chest. But the moment passed as quickly as it came, swallowed by the necessity of being the anchor in Sari's tempestuous sea of sorrow. She wailed and blubbered, insisting that I had to stay with her to help her work through the details, and though she'd pulled some awful things, the weight of our shared past forced me to concede.

My care would have to wait; there were no other options.

I could almost hear Taurus's thoughts clashing with mine when I decided on an unspoken battle of wills. He knew I was thoroughly wrecked and should go home, but my conscience wouldn't allow me to abandon someone grieving their mate.

This one day stretched to two, and so on, until now I've been here two days past the funeral. I'm so exhausted I can barely think, but each time I've tried to exit, Sari has fallen into a tempest of misery. She begged me to stay, and I caved... but my goodwill is waning with my ability to continue taxing my system.

And so, the couch became my bed, its cushions never quite yielding enough to let me forget where I was. Clothes arrived in nondescript bags, my toothbrush a stranger amongst the bristles of another's. Meals were whatever scraps I could scrounge up without leaving the house, as the simple act of going out to hunt was now a luxury beyond my reach.

That's why I'm going to try yet again, to gracefully take my leave so I can recharge and lean on the support of my family.

"Perhaps it would be best if I leave you to your family for a bit," I say, my voice barely above a whisper. Amanda catches my eye as she crosses the threshold; her grief feels manufactured, a caricature of the pain I can't express while I'm held in place at this house.

"Go? You think you can just go?" Sari's voice shatters the pretense of calm, her outburst reverberating off the walls. Her hands clutch at nothing, grasping for something I can't reject.

"This reaction is why this—" I motion to the steaming cup in my hand, "is necessary."

Sari wraps her arms around herself, her expression petulant as she struggles to find a reason I have to stay when everything has been taken care of.

"Maeve needs—"

"No!"

Trapped in this domestic limbo, unable to seek solace or strength, I watch in horror as Sari throws herself at me—acting as if I'm a lifeline amidst the wreckage of her world. Once I extricate myself from her clingy hold, I suck in a deep breath as I move out of range. This is out of hand, and I don't know how to make her understand I cannot remain here forever because he is gone. She will have to stand on her own, no matter how much it hurts.

I lean against the cool kitchen counter, my fingers tracing the edge as I work to ground my emotions. The texture is a poor substitute for the comfort I need, but it's all I have in the barren wasteland of empathy that surrounds me. Each person who enters this house since Wilde's passing sweeps in with their agenda—real or contrived—leaving my needs unacknowledged like specters in the room.

They've been sucking me dry slowly, and there isn't much left.

Sari is crying now, her face red and full of the fat crocodile tears she's been using to manipulate me into 'one more day' over and over. I turn away from it, looking into space as my mind tries to separate me from that spectacle.

Memories seep through the cracks of my composure. I can't shake the image of the small urn on the dais, stark and surreal. Wilde's essence was reduced to ashes, contained within a vessel far too plain for a soul as vibrant as he once was. The service was intimate, a collection of mere whispers in the grand tapestry of his life. Wordsworth's verses lingered in the air, mingling with the solemnity of Shakespeare's prose—each line a tribute to the man we'd lost.

Rafe stood by the urn, his eyes hollow as he unveiled the portrait he'd been coerced into providing. I knew the way his passion bled onto canvas, but this piece was different. Haunted by memories, it held a somber beauty that spoke of a joy long faded. I could almost feel the weight of expectation that had pressed him into using an old work—one from a brighter time when Wilde's laughter hadn't been tinged with evil.

Then there was me, my voice trembling as I sang 'Ava Maria,' each note a shard of glass in my throat. Singing sweetly for an audience of mourners, when all I wanted was to scream at the injustice of it all. By the time he died, Wilde had all but pushed Rafe and me into the roles of abused spouses, yet we had to celebrate his life as if he'd been wonderful. But I held it together, because that's what was expected of me, and I couldn't admit what we'd become.

"Beautiful rendition," people said. "It must have been hard for you," they mused. But the platitudes were devoid of concern for my well-being. They didn't see the effort it took to stand there, to pour my soul into a melody while every fiber of my being screamed in protest.

None of them asked if I was okay—not even once.

When I blink back to now, Sari is still sobbing, so I walk over to get my abandoned coffee. Setting the cup on the counter with a soft clink, I wait. It's clear as crystal—no one here gives a damn about what the ordeal is doing to me, emotionally or physically. They care even less for my wee mage, and their indifference is even more cutting. She needs a mama who is healthy and thriving—things I can barely guarantee, while under the crushing weight of shared sorrow and personal depletion.

Grief has turned this place into a vacuum, and I'm caught in its pull, unable to escape. I'm running on empty. Even so, I'm expected to be the rock for everyone else to cling to. Even rocks erode under the relentless tide of despair, and I'm no exception. I have to figure out how to get out of here before there's nothing left.

Clasping my hand with a grip born of desperation, Sari anchors herself to me. "I wouldn't have survived the funeral without you, Deli."

'I know that, but it doesn't mean I'm bound to stay here until your wound is healed' is what I want to say. But I can't, because she looks so incredibly pitiful and my heart is treacherous. It doesn't want me to ignore someone in need, although I believe it's slightly disingenuous.

If only I could slip away for a hunt—the night air on my face, the thrill of the chase restoring some semblance of life to my drained spirit—I'd be able to refresh myself. My body aches for the release, to tear through the forest and allow my primal nature to overtake the suffocating civility of these walls. I'd get to see my other mates, to share in their strength and solace, to intertwine our energies and find balance once again.

Sari's grasp is unyielding; she needs me here, tethered to her side. It pains me, this inability to step away, even for a moment, to tend to my own battered soul. I can hold my grief at bay, lock it away until the time comes for my private mourning within the sacred circle of stones that awaits me at home. But not for much longer, I fear. The energy drain is eating me alive.

"Please stay," she murmurs, a tremor in her voice pulling me back from the edge of my own dark thoughts.

"Okay," I reply, the word a promise I'm not sure I have the strength to keep. But for the bond that connected us all to Wilde, I'll try. I will stay, even as the vital essence within me cries out for respite, for the chance to grieve and heal in my time, in my way.

Why can't she see that she's hurting me? Or if she does, why doesn't she care?

Hours later, I jolt back to reality from the dream I was having. I don't remember getting to a place to lie down, nor falling asleep, but I suppose my body simply gave out. It was bound to happen, and as I look around, I remember the images from the dream as if they're still happening.

Taurus' aura crackles with a dark energy that could ignite the very air around him, his eyes smoldering embers of barely restrained fury. His towering frame looms in the room's corner, his presence like a thundercloud ready to burst. The tension stretches between us, a tangible force that seems to resonate with the silent cacophony of his thoughts—thoughts that scream for action, thoughts that whisper of the violence he is so close to unleashing.

"Did you hear me, Deli?" Sari's voice cuts through the charged atmosphere. "I was talking to you!"

I turn towards her slowly, the weight of her need heavy. Blinking rapidly, I fight to surface from the mire of my thoughts. The world around me is a blur of muted colors and soft sounds, all overshadowed by the weight of exhaustion that presses down on my shoulders. "Um, sorry. I didn't. What were we talking about?" My voice sounds distant, even to my own ears.

"I said that Amanda and Belle are coming back soon."

Her words break through the haze, and I cling to them, allowing their significance to keep me in the present. Amanda and Belle—names that evoked images of faces framed by fake sorrow and pretend pain whenever people were watching, but hatred at me when they were not. Their arrival will change the atmosphere, add new layers to the complex tapestry of emotions already hanging heavy in the air.

Bad ones—at least, for me.

I nod, acknowledging her statement with a small tilt of my head, even as my mind races to prepare for what their presence would entail. "Oh, that's nice. Will they be helping us sort out some stuff?" The question is rhetorical, a thin veil for the irritation that scratches at my insides like thorns. The two of them haven't lifted a finger once the entire time I've been here, and they aren't likely to now. This is theater for them, and they're using it to make themselves look good rather than actually help Sari do shit that will let me fucking leave.

Across the room, Sari clutches a pillow to her chest like a barricade against the world. Her eyes, red-rimmed and hollow, shift away from mine, avoiding the question. She knows they didn't do shit and that they both dislike me—Belle, more than Amanda—because of her coaching. But she wants me to be overjoyed that she's getting more 'support', so she's acting like it's a great thing.

I exhale slowly, watching her. I've been trying to steer her toward packing away Wilde's belongings for days. Books he'd read aloud to her, journals filled with his thoughts, scattered mementos—they're everywhere and it's a constant reminder of loss. They turn the house into a mausoleum instead of a place where life can someday resume.

Yet no one, not even her housemates, will stand up and agree with my very logical suggestion that we get it out of her sight.

"Maybe we can start with the living room? Just the books and..." My voice trails off as she tightens her grip on the pillow, her knuckles whitening. The refusal is clear, silent, but as solid as the surrounding walls. "I think it will help to make the house not feel... like it's missing something."

It frustrates me deeply, this self-inflicted stagnation. Every item she leaves untouched is another shackle holding her to a past that will not return. Comforting her has become a cycle of soothing words and supportive silences, but beneath it all simmers a growing anger —and anger at being trapped in a loop of sorrow that refuses to break.

"*Noooooo!*" Sari's voice cracks like thin ice beneath the weight of her words. "I'm not ready for that. I may never be ready for that."

A tightness constricts my chest, my breath caught in the vice of frustration and duty. The tick of the clock gets louder in the silence that follows, marking each second that drags us further away from the world outside this room. I feel the heat of my pent-up fury simmering just below the surface, a dangerous current threatening to break through my composure. The edges of my vision blur as I fight the urge to lash out against the invisible chains holding us both hostage to her sorrow. My feet shift beneath me, the carpet fibers twisting under my toes as if they too are complicit in this standstill.

I'm teetering on the brink, the precipice of my patience crumbling with each passing moment. I hear the echo of my heart beating, a drum of war against the siege of grief. The notion of escape is a siren call, tantalizing in its promise of freedom from this cycle of despair. The door, not ten paces away, is an exit from this purgatory of mourning, but it feels like it's miles away.

"Deep breath," I murmur to myself, a silent incantation to calm the storm within. But even as I draw air into my lungs, I know it's a hollow gesture. The resolve that fortified me is fracturing, fissures spreading through the stoic facade I maintained since the beginning of this ordeal.

Yet, I remain motionless as my desire for flight wars with the gravity that holds me steadfastly to Sari's side. Her pain is a tangible thing, and leaving her feels akin to abandoning a wounded ally on the battlefield. But I can't help but wonder how long before the caretaker crumbles under the weight she bears.

Her eyes are imploring, insistent, and I see the tremor in her hands as she clasps them together. The air in the room feels saturated with the unspoken words that hang between us. "It's important, this meeting. We all need to talk."

The finality in Sari's voice is a steel trap, snapping shut on any thoughts of escape. There's a resigned weight to my shoulders as I nod, the muscles tensing with a weariness that goes beyond physical exhaustion. With each passing moment, the walls of the house seem to inch closer, the space growing smaller, more suffocating.

"Okay. But if you don't mind, I might pop by my house so I can get a few—"

"No!" Her shriek pierces the air, her gaze locking onto mine with a desperation that roots me to the spot. "You can't leave. You can't." She is almost breathless, each word a plea, a command, a tether anchoring me to her side. "You're—you're the only tie left to him, and it makes me feel safe."

Of course, she said exactly the right thing to tie me down yet again.

A palpable silence ensues, its sound unbearably loud now in the aftermath of her outcry. Finally, I give in. "If it makes you feel better," I murmur, my voice barely above a whisper, betraying the inner turmoil that tugs at the frayed edges of my resolve, "I'll stay." The words feel like stones in my mouth, heavy with the weight of the sacrifice they represent.

I muster the strength to stand. "I need to go shower and clean up a little. May I borrow Callista's room for a bit?" My question hangs in the air like a fragile bridge between duty and the faintest hope of solitude.

Like magic, the droid appears, carrying a tray with more coffee. She smiles at me, but the warmth she's trying to give off doesn't make me feel any better. "You may. I am honored." Her voice, a melodic blend of artificiality and warmth, offered a comfort that felt strangely genuine despite its origins. "If you like, I can burn some herbs and oils to help soothe and relax you. The couch can't be comfortable."

"No, no. I'm very particular about my exposure to other people's magick." My words come out more brusque than intended, a defense mechanism against a world that seems intent on chipping away at my sanity. "Thank you for the offer," I add, softening the refusal with an effort to appear grateful.

Turning away from them, I navigate towards the promise of solitude offered by the shower. The water will wash away the grime of the day, but not the invisible stains that mar my spirit.

No matter what happens at this meeting, I have to go home today. There's simply no other option if I want to survive this mess.

The Socialite Plans An Exfiltration

PHILOMENA

The rhythmic tapping on the table syncs with my pounding heart. I watch Sandrine's fingers drum an urgent beat, each tap a silent echo of our collective resolve. Her eyes, usually so calm and calculating, burn with a fierceness that could ignite the very air we breathe.

"We have to pull her out," she declares, her voice slicing through the tension in the room. "We need to go over there for a visit and insist she come home when we leave."

I don't miss the subtle tremor in her hand, as it pauses momentarily above the polished wood. It's unlike Sandrine to show any hint of uncertainty, yet her concern is palpable. We all feel it—a visceral need to act, to protect one of our own from the suffocating grasp of emotional captivity.

I nod, silently reinforcing her words with my own unyielding determination. Sandrine's plan isn't just about confrontation; it's about liberation. And I can see in the eyes of those around me, we're ready to fight for it.

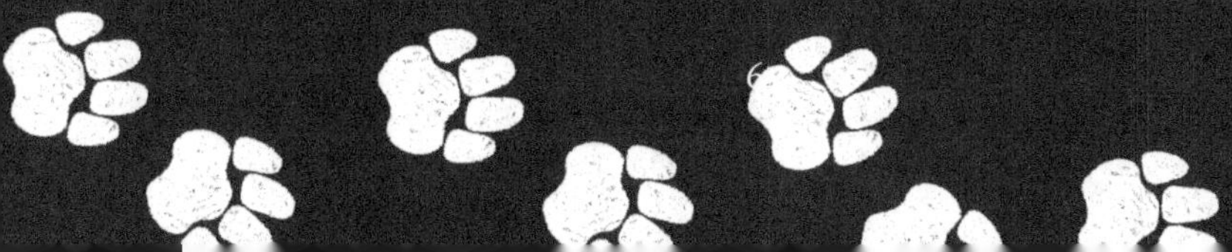

The cat is too kind for her own good and it's got to be harming her by now.

Leaning over the table, I squint at the intricate lines and scribbles that detail every nook and cranny of the Den. It's a blueprint for our audacious plan, but my gut twists with unease. Hex stands beside me, his gaze fixed on the diagram, as if he can will it to reveal the perfect strategy.

"We can say that we're there to pay our respects, yeah? Then we snatch her up." He nods, more to himself than anyone else, a look of conviction etched onto his face. His fingers trace a path through the hallways marked on paper, plotting a course as if it were that simple.

Across from us, the lounger shifts in his seat, a pensive silhouette against the dim light. The room is hushed, save for the soft creak of leather as he leans forward, his features shadowed. When he finally looks up, there's a weight in his eyes, a darkness that seems to pull at the very air around him.

"It won't work," he sighs, voice barely louder than a whisper, yet it cuts through the silence like a knife. "They'll make a stink and she'll refuse to leave. We'll have to force it."

His words hang between us, heavy and undeniable. The simplicity of Hex's suggestion crumbles with the complexity of reality. My throat tightens; I knew it wouldn't be easy, but the thought of forcing her leaves a bitter taste in my mouth. We're trapped in a game of chess where every move we contemplate feels like hurtling towards a checkmate—against us. And the cat has been forced to do enough, even by us, in the past few months.

I don't like it.

The tension in the room coils tighter, a serpent ready to strike. I run a hand through my hair, feeling the prickle of frustration rise like static electricity. It's there, at the edge of my thoughts, when Hex speaks up, his voice brimming with barely restrained aggression.

"I'm not opposed to a snatch and grab," Taurus grunts, the words slipping from him like they're coated in gravel.

Before anyone can respond, a presence asserts itself at the threshold of the dining area. We all turn, a collective swivel of heads, as two figures appear framed by the doorway. The bird and the fighter stand side by side, their postures rigid, anger radiating off them like heat from the pavement on a scorching day. Each is dressed with lethal precision, the kind that makes you take a step back even if you're already at a distance.

They look infuriated, and it's clear from their entrance that they've been listening—perhaps longer than we've realized—and have something dire to add to the pot already boiling over with opinions and schemes.

My nail file hovers mid-stroke as I glance up, locking eyes with the assassin. "Now, now. A forcible extraction will only exacerbate the problem. We don't want them applying more pressure," I caution, my voice as smooth as the emery board in my hand. The steeliness in my gaze belies the casualness of my manicure.

Talia's boots thud on the hardwood as she advances, a tempest in human form. The knife she's twirling—a blur of silver moments ago—slams down onto the table with a resounding crack, pinning the diagram at its center. "That knobby bitch is holding her hostage emotionally, and we all know it." Her words are a snarl, sharp and biting, echoing the dangerous edge of her blade.

The lounger's head lifts, a subtle shift from the map sprawled with potential strategies to the tension thickening the surrounding air. Talia is a shadow slipping through our ranks, a silent guardian whose presence is as calming as it is deadly. She reaches him, her hands finding his shoulders with an ease that speaks of countless moments like this one—moments of solace in our ongoing storm.

His body relaxes under her touch, the hard lines of resistance softening. I catch his eye for a split second and my nod bridges the distance between us. It's an unspoken acknowledgment of the care she provides, the bond they share. He's a fortress of self-reliance, yet within those walls, he battles grief—a tempest over the writer's death that rages in bursts of rage and waves of sorrow.

Taurus snarls, his frame rigid as a steel beam, and his voice cuts through the room like a siren call to arms. "No one—I mean, *no one*—holds my wife hostage. Got it?"

He's a keg of dynamite with a lit fuse, the kind where you know there's no prospect of snuffing out the flame. The man is a hair's breadth away from wreaking havoc, the separation from his wife and child drawing him ever closer to the point of no return. His fury is palpable, a tangible force that dares anyone to challenge his resolve.

We have to keep him on this side of sanity unless we want a slaughter.

I take a slow sip of my martini, the cool liquid a stark contrast to the heat of the room. The tension is a living thing, coiling around us as tightly as a python ready to strike. I set the glass down with a soft clink and clear my throat, pulling their attention to me.

"Calm down, assassin. We're not happy, either." My words are a balm, or at least I intend them to be. "It's bad enough this comes not very long after the departure of the fallen—the loafer was just getting back to normal." I lean back in my chair, my gaze drifting over each face. "We were ready to deal with baby madness, not community-wide depression."

Siren steps forward, her stance predatory yet poised, an elegant danger that commands silence before she even speaks. Her eyes lock onto Taurus, holding him in a grip more formidable than any physical restraint could manage.

"It's possible that she is trying to extricate herself on her own and has been unsuccessful because of emotional pressures." Siren's voice is smooth, calculated, like the stroke of a velvet glove over a fist of steel. "She does not enjoy being away from you."

Taurus's jaw clenches, the muscle ticking in a telltale sign of his barely contained wrath. He knows the truth in Siren's statement; it's etched into every line of worry marking his face.

"I fear it leaves us with very few tactical options, none of which are appealing." There's a certain respect in her tone, an acknowledgment of Taurus's expertise that doesn't go unnoticed. "You know that, knife thrower. It is your skill to assess such situations."

Taurus's hands curl into fists and then relax, the internal battle playing out right before our eyes. His love for her, his need for action—it's all there, written in the taut lines of his body, the hard set of his mouth. But he's listening, weighing her words, because if there's one thing Taurus respects, it's the cutthroat acumen of a fellow predator.

Talia's expression doesn't waver as she takes in Siren's analysis, her brow arching ever so slightly. The room holds its breath, waiting for her verdict. It's seldom that Talia concedes to a plan without some form of embellishment or dramatic flair. But this time, there's a gravity in her voice that matches the weight of our situation.

"Correct," she finally says, and I can see the gears turning behind those calculating eyes. "The only major options are: forcibly remove, grift our way in with condolences and convince her, or to allow her to find a way out on her own." She ticks off each option with a slender finger, dismissing them just as quickly. "Everything else—like a fake emergency, an appointment she forgot, a check-in call—will only arouse suspicion and they will double down on the pressure to keep her in place."

Her gaze sweeps across us, taking in the resigned nods and tightened jaws. "None of the three have more than a thirty percent chance of success given the variables."

A visceral growl emanates from Taurus's throat, the sound filling the room with his anguish and fury. He rises suddenly, his chair scraping back with an angry screech. *"I want my sodding wife back so she can grieve!!"* he bellows, fists clenched at his sides.

The intensity of his pain is palpable, and it ripples through the room, touching each of us with its raw power. He stalks toward the bar, movements brusque and filled with purpose. His hand wraps around a bottle of scotch, and with a swift, practiced motion, he pours a generous amount into a glass. Watching him, the liquid amber seems to glow with the same fire that's consuming him from within.

I can't help but feel a twinge of sympathy for Taurus. To be so close, yet so far from the one you love—it's a torment I wouldn't wish upon my worst enemy. His desperation is a mirror to our collective resolve; we will move heaven and earth to bring her back. It's not just about strategy anymore, it's personal.

And when things get personal, all bets are off.

The clink of the glass as Taurus sets it down punctuates his last word, and for a moment, there's nothing but silence and heavy breaths in the room. I watch Rafe, who's been quiet—a statue in this tempest of emotion—finally move. His gaze lifts from the shadows that seem to cling to him like an unwanted second skin, meeting Taurus's bloodshot eyes.

"She won't grieve until she's taken care of everyone else," he whispers, voice barely carrying over the tension that hangs thick between us. "Sari knows that. She hasn't once come looking for me, nor did she ask for me to sit with them during the service. The cat is her new lifeline." Rafe's fingers twitch at his side, betraying the calmness in his voice. "We need to get her home. We *have* to get her home."

The urgency in Rafe's whisper cuts through the fog of anger and helplessness, grounding us with its stark reality. It's not just a mission, it's a plea—one that resonates with all the unspoken fears we've been harboring since this nightmare began.

Talia and Taurus exchange a glance, charged with an electric current that seems to arc through the air. It's a silent communication, an understanding born of shared torment and the intimacy that only those who have faced darkness together can truly comprehend. Their eyes lock, speaking volumes in the briefest of moments —a confirmation of the unsaid suspicions that have been brewing beneath the surface.

The gravity of their shared knowledge weighs heavy, an invisible shroud that drapes over our gathering, binding us together in our collective resolve. We are a unit, fractured by circumstance and yet forged stronger in the fires of adversity. Whatever is happening between our two and those two, it's a catalyst, propelling us toward action with a renewed sense of determination.

I lean back in my chair, feeling the pieces of this twisted puzzle slotting into place with each passing second. The truth may be murky, the path fraught with peril, but one thing is crystal clear: we will bring her home or die trying. At that moment, there's no other option I can entertain.

Rafe's voice was an indistinct murmur, tinged with the raw edges of pain and determination. I can't help but watch him, noting the set of his jaw, the slight tremor in his hands as he tries to veil his turmoil. His words about Deli not grieving until everyone else is taken care of resonate with a profound truth that only someone deeply connected could understand. I see the fear in his eyes, a fear that the emotional vampire has sunk her teeth too deep into his mate, and it's a chilling thought.

"Unlike us," I muse silently, "they don't grasp the full extent of the danger. But who are we to shatter their hopes with our knowledge?" It's a secret burden, one we carry with the heaviness of shadows clinging to our souls. Still, Rafe seems oddly anchored, despite the chaos swirling around him. Perhaps it's because he's already walked through the darkest alleys of his mind and come out unscathed, but alive. Or maybe it's because Deli, the unexpected lifeline, is still within reach, providing a glimmer of light in an otherwise suffocating gloom.

I push back my chair; the sound scraping against the silence that has fallen like a curtain over the room. Standing, I let my gaze sweep across the faces of my companions—each one etched with lines of frustration and resolve.

"Okay," I declare, my voice slicing through the tension, "We all agree that no plan is perfect and none have a good chance of success." I pause, locking eyes with each person at the table. "But look at us—we're a storm of brainpower, experience, and raw, seething anger. That's got to be worth something."

I clench my fists, feeling the energy pulsing in the room, feeding off our collective fury. "I, for one, refuse to let that mangy mutt outsmart me." The challenge is obvious, thrown down like a gauntlet on the cold hard ground of our reality. "Who's with me?"

The question hangs in the air, thick with implication and the unspoken bond that ties us together. We're bound by more than just this mission—we're bound by a need to protect what's ours, to reclaim a piece of ourselves from the jaws of defeat.

"Me." The word is a whip crack, and we all startle as Talia's fist comes down hard on the table. The thud resonates, a sharp punctuation to the challenge I threw into the space between us.

Everyone's eyes swivel toward her, drawn by the sudden assertion of her presence. There's no mistaking the iron in her tone, the steel in her spine as she squares her shoulders. Talia is a force unto herself—her determination practically a palpable entity in the room. Taurus, standing rigid by the bar, his jaw clenched tight enough to grind stone to dust, hesitates for a heartbeat. It's as if he's measuring the weight of her words, gauging the fire behind them before he moves.

"Pull up a chair," she says again, and it's not a suggestion. Her command slices through any lingering doubts or second thoughts.

He obliges, dragging a chair with a scrape that echoes off the walls, its noise a minor testament to the storm brewing within him. As Taurus settles down, there's a collective tightening around the table —a silent acknowledgment of the task at hand.

We've got work to do, indeed.

I lean forward, elbows pressing into the scarred wood of the kitchen table. The room is a cocoon of hushed anticipation, the kind that comes before a storm or an earthquake—something life-altering and unpredictable.

"We will find all the things that we need," Sari declares with a conviction that is almost palpable, her fingers drumming against the tabletop. Her eyes, two pools of fierce determination, lock onto mine, and she delivers the promise of an ending—or a beginning—with a magician's flourish. "And once we do...poof!"

The word hangs in the air between us, a single syllable loaded with the weight of uncharted territory, echoing off the peeling wallpaper and the flickering bulb overhead. My heart skips a beat, and for a brief moment, I'm suspended in the gravity of what she suggests, feeling the pull of desperate hope against the anchor of hard reality.

She cannot be serious.

"*Poof?*" The word echoes in my mind like a gunshot in an empty hall, and it's all I can muster. My face contorts, the horror seeping

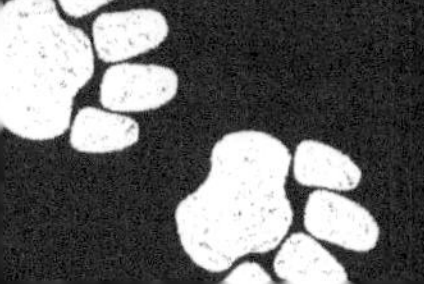

through the cracks of my worn-out facade. I've been running on fumes, each day bleeding into the next without reprieve. Comforting others, offering shoulders upon which they could unload their grief—it left me hollow.

Sari's nod is slow, deliberate, as if she's aware of the bombshell she's just dropped, but is too invested in her plan to back down now. The other two women, accomplices in this wild scheme, can't hide their excitement; their grins are like slashes of triumph across their faces.

"We've got it all worked out," Sari continues, her voice commanding. "I had Veruca use auto-scan to search records for every source available on the Internet, and Calista has been tracking down leads from practitioners on the other side." Her fingers dance through the air as if she's orchestrating the very elements. "We've got what we need to begin."

Their certainty chafes against my raw nerves.

How could they be so sure? So blasé about meddling with the thin veil between life and death?

"They will continue that work as we get further along, so we know where to go next," she says, leaning in, her gaze locking onto mine with an intensity that seeks to melt away my doubts. "But Deli, I've solved it. I can get him back."

The finality in her tone is meant to be comforting—to spark hope. Instead, it feels like a cold hand reaching inside my chest, squeezing around my already fragile heart. My throat tightens, and I can feel the pulse at my temples pounding with each erratic heartbeat. With a shaky hand, I push a lock of hair behind my ear and try to steady my gaze on Amanda and Belle. They're statuesque in their silence, offering no thread of sanity to cling to in the madness that Sari proposes. My eyes dart between them, desperate for an ally in this lunacy.

"Dead pets? Zombies? Hell, dinosaurs?" The words tumble out, haphazard and laced with incredulity. "It's bad fucking juju to bring things back from the dead, Sari." The images flash through my mind—scenes from horror flicks, cautionary tales whispered in the dark, all of them screaming that what lies beyond should stay beyond.

Sari's laugh is light, almost musical, as if we're discussing nothing more than a child's bedtime story. "Oh, come on, Deli! What about the elves and orcs? The lion? Hell, wizards come back from the brink of death. There are plenty of counter stories." Her hands sweep through the air, painting a picture of triumph over tragedy, of fantasy victories where the impossible becomes possible.

But her words, meant to soothe, only chafe against my raw, frayed edges. Fantasies. Stories. That's all they are. And here we stand on the precipice of reality, where actions have consequences, and playing god comes with a price too steep to pay. My fingers twitch at my sides, nails biting into my palms as Sari's ludicrous litany hangs in the air. The room closes in, a vivid swirl of misguided enthusiasm and dark promises.

I can't be a part of this—it is wrong and we will suffer the consequences of messing with the natural order.

"Yeah!" Amanda pipes up suddenly, her voice a sharp crack in the tense atmosphere. She leans forward, eyes alight with a fervor that chills me to the core. "Don't forget they do it in comic books all the time, too." Her hands animate her point, flipping imaginary pages of the countless graphic novels she's devoured, where death is but a temporary setback for heroes clad in spandex.

A twinge of betrayal knots my stomach at her words. Amanda does not have a *true* connection to magic or nature; she's just along for the ride.

Belle doesn't miss a beat, seizing the moment like prey. "It *is* how everyone's favorite vampire is still kicking it after one hundred and twenty years," she adds, the corners of her lips pulling upward into a smirk that suggests she relishes the scandalous edge of our conversation more than the gravity of its implications. Her dark humor feels like a lead weight in my gut—another person who doesn't comprehend the terrible possibilities of this mistake.

I stare at them both, the familiar faces twisted into cheerleaders for an act so outlandish, it seems ripped from the very pages of fiction they cite. Their eagerness dances before me, a mirage—or perhaps a mockery—of the stark, painful reality that looms just out of reach.

I clasp my hands together, knuckles white, as I funnel every chaotic emotion into an inner vault that's already strained at the seams. My chest rises and falls with a labored breath that feels like it might be my last before drowning in the tempest of my own making. The room blurs for a second as I wrestle control over myself, and when clarity returns, my face is an impassive mask.

"I won't do it." The words come out steady, despite my anxiety.. "It's not natural, and it goes against every law of the universe." I sweep my gaze across their eager faces, hoping to impart the gravity of my refusal. "Not only is even thinking about it unhealthy and insane, but the kinds of magick and the people you'd have to deal with working them, the bargains you might have to make, are unacceptable. I *can't* do it."

Silence settles like dust after a collapse. Amanda's eyes widen slightly, and her lips part as if she's about to argue, but no words come. She turns her head toward Belle, who mirrors the motion in a silent exchange that speaks volumes of unspoken thoughts and shared disbelief. Their synchronized movement is like a dance they've rehearsed in secret, and then both sets of eyes drift to Sari. The architect of this mad plan remains unfazed by my stance, her expression unreadable. There's a crackle of something unsaid in the air, a challenge left dangling from the precipice of choice. Amanda and Belle's silent exchange crystallizes into a cold, undeniable truth. The air thickens, my pulse hammers in my ears as I piece together the reality of the situation.

This was planned and they're all here to high-jack me into complying.

My chest tightens in betrayal. "Oh, fuck them all," I mutter under my breath, feeling the sting of deception sharper than any blade.

I scan their faces—one by one. Sari's serene composure, Amanda's expectant tilt of the head, Belle's barely contained excitement—they're not just complicit; they're invested. This was an ambush. A meticulously planned snare dressed up in the guise of concern and sisterly unity. They all knew what she was thinking about and signed on already. There's no ignorance here, no hesitancy to be seen in their eyes. They've already navigated the moral labyrinth and emerged ready to act, leaving me behind to grapple with the ethics of it all alone.

"Damn you all for this," I whisper, more to myself than to them. Their collective resolve is a wall I find myself unprepared to scale, especially now when every part of me screams to flee from the sheer insanity of their scheme.

Sari's head tilts, the motion as deliberate as a knife twist in my gut. "You didn't seem to have any problem coming back to life after you and that feathered jackass drained one another and that was a week ago."

My eyes narrow, lashes almost tangling with the viciousness of my glare. I feel it—the wave, the surge of raw emotion threatening to overwhelm the dam of my self-control. It's anger, it's hurt, it's betrayal—all roiling in a tempest within me. "That was different and you know it!"

My voice is a low growl, each word a stone thrown hard against her accusation. Heat creeps up my neck, a telltale sign of my boiling point approaching. Belle's lips curl into a sneer, her eyes glinting with mirth and malice. I can almost hear the crackle of her snark as she speaks, baiting me with every syllable.

"Oh, really? How?" The words slither out, coated in condescension, her smirk widening at the edge of her rouged lips.

The muscles in my jaw tighten, each tooth grinding against its counterpart like tectonic plates on the verge of an earthquake. I lean forward, my voice a venomous hiss slicing through the tension-thick air. "Let me count the ways."

The room falls silent, the others' breaths held in anticipation or maybe fear.

"One," I start, my fingers twitching with the urge to lash out, "it's none of your fucking business, Belle." My glare bores into her, daring her to interrupt. She doesn't, so I continue. "Two, we were out for thirty seconds, more like a blip in resuscitation in a hospital than actual death." The memory flashes, a short circuit of darkness and then light, but nothing like the finality they're proposing now. "Three," the word comes out as a growl, "no one cremated our fucking bodies and had the entire community sit through a funeral."

The image of grief-stricken faces and the smell of incense from that day claw at my senses, unwelcome and heavy. "Four," I say, the intensity in my gaze unyielding, "it was private, personal, short, and Sari wouldn't even know about it—much less you—if Talia hadn't spilled the beans to a whiny Wilde." The betrayal stings anew; trust shattered like thin ice beneath heavy boots. "Five," I finish, my voice dropping to a dangerous octave, "fuck you, I'm done with this shit."

Every word is a nail in the coffin of my patience, my tolerance for this absurd conversation. Each number hangs in the air like a verdict, my chest rising and falling with shallow, rapid breaths. I've laid it all out, stark and raw, the distinction between what happened to me and their ludicrous plan carved into stone.

I shoot up from my chair, a tempest swirling within me, feeling each muscle coil with the tension of a predator ready to pounce. The room seems to pulse with my fury, the air thickening like blood about to clot. My fists clench at my sides, nails digging into my palms as if trying to anchor me to some semblance of sanity. But even that feeble attempt cannot stave off the dark thoughts that beckon, whispering sweet violence to calm the chaos in my heart.

"If this is the way you thank me for supporting you from the moment I knew," I spit the words out like venom, each syllable dripping with the poison of betrayal, "for abandoning my mate who is dealing with his grief on his own, for not dealing with my grief, and how you honor your dead loved one, you can shove it where the sun doesn't shine and twist."

My breath comes out in ragged gasps, an echo of the exertion it takes not to act on the rage that's threatening to spew forth. I pivot, prepared to storm out, the floorboards creaking beneath my weight, a testament to the heaviness of my departure. That's when I sense him—my husband—the sudden drop in temperature, the faint shimmer in the air as he materializes.

Thank fuck.

He stands there, imposing, his eyes scanning the scene, confusion etched across his features like lines on a map that lead to nowhere. He's clearly walked into the eye of the storm uninvited, his presence an unexpected variable in their equation of madness. As I approach, his brow furrows deeper, reading the turmoil written all over me.

"Take me home. Now, please," I murmur, my voice cracking under the strain of suppressed sobs. His arms are my sanctuary as they encircle me, a shield against the madness that threatens to devour my resolve. He nods, understanding without needing any more words, and just like that, we're gone, leaving behind only the echo of our departure and the bitter taste of unfinished business.

His response is swift, a low growl of assent that vibrates through the tense air. "My pleasure, heart of mine." He casts a withering glare over my shoulder at the women who dared to push me to this precipice. In their silence, I can almost hear the cogs of regret grinding in their minds, but it's too late for second thoughts.

I feel his power coil around us, the world blurring at the edges as he prepares to whisk us away from this place of betrayal and reckless schemes. For an instant, the tempest inside me eases, making room for a sliver of solace. It's fleeting, this sense of peace, a mere wisp of tranquility in the storm that rages within, but I cling to it desperately. Because for now, it's enough.

It has to be.

The Coyote Bites The Hand That Feeds Her

SARI

I stand on the dampened doorstep, rain dripping from my jacket like a cascade of liquid silver. I raise my hand to knock again, but before my knuckles can rap against the wood, the door swings ajar. Lily's figure fills the gap, her eyebrows knitting together in surprise and concern.

"What on earth are you doing here?" Her voice, usually so composed, carries a note of incredulity that mirrors the arching of her brows.

Rainwater drips from my hair as I lock eyes with her, the droplets a chilling reminder of my desperation. "I need your help," I say, my voice barely above a whisper.

The sorrow must be etched deeply into my features because Lily's sharp gaze softens just a fraction. She's always had this uncanny ability to sift through turmoil and find clarity, a beacon in the storm that so often rages within me. If anyone can nudge the cat toward the path I need it to take, it's Lily.

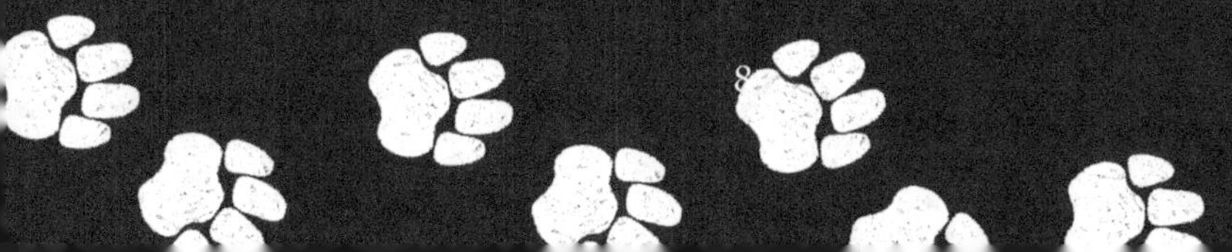

Squinting, she assesses my expression, her analytical mind working behind those calculating eyes. She steps back, granting me entrance, though her posture remains guarded. "Shouldn't you be at home with Deli and everyone else, working through the steps?" Her question is pointed, hinting at layers of unspoken conversation that we've yet to unravel.

But right now, her acknowledgment is a small victory—it's an opening, and I intend to step through it.

I shuffle past Lily, the warmth of her home chasing away the chill from my bones. She closes the door with a soft click, and I turn to her, my hands fidgeting with the hem of my soaked jacket. "I'm trying; I am. But I'm having trouble, and I need your help to figure out how to get people to understand what I need."

Lily doesn't miss a beat, her directness as reliable as ever. With a tilt of her head, she motions me further into the house. We navigate through a hallway that feels like a cozy burrow, lined with framed pictures and handmade tapestries that tell stories without words. She leads me into the living room, which is an explosion of life and color.

Every surface seems to hold a story or a memory—a collection of artifacts that speak of Lily and Mercury's shared existence. The floor is a labyrinth of pillow forts and stuffed animals, likely the remnants of their latest imaginative escapade. A cardboard pirate ship sits anchored near the window, its sails made from old curtains fluttering in the indoor breeze. Books are stacked haphazardly on shelves and tables, their spines exhibiting titles from philosophical treatises to vintage comic books.

I'm not surprised.

This ordered chaos is so them—so Lily with her ability to find peace in pandemonium, and so Mercury with his knack for bringing a touch of whimsy to the mundane. It's a living space that reflects minds unafraid to blend the fantastical with the logical, the dreamers with the doers.

Carefully stepping over a moat of blankets, I follow Lily to a couch that has miraculously escaped the siege of cushions. She gestures for me to take a seat amidst this delightful disarray, and I oblige, sinking into the cushions. Here, in the heart of their creative chaos, perhaps I can find the answers I seek—or at least the guidance to face the tempest outside. Lily settles into an armchair that's seen better days, its fabric telling tales of past conversations and spilled secrets.

"Sit down, Sari." Her voice is even, betraying nothing of her thoughts. She watches me with those knowing eyes that seem to peer straight through the façade I've been struggling to maintain. "I got your email earlier, but I hadn't responded because I hadn't planned a response yet." She pauses, tapping a finger against her lips, a sure sign she's pondering the weight of her next words. "I also haven't decided if I feel duty bound to share this with…"

"Deli. Yeah, I figured." I interrupt, a little too quickly perhaps. The idea of facing Deli's potential wrath makes my stomach clench. It seemed like a better idea to come and talk in person. Face-to-face, where you can see the sincerity in someone's eyes, or in my case, the desperation. Lily nods slowly, her gaze never leaving mine. She knows the stakes as well as I do, maybe better. And she understands Deli.

I shift uncomfortably on the cushion, feeling every errant feather poke at my thighs. The room is a collage of life's whimsy and chaos, but Lily's gaze cuts through it all with surgical precision. "Are you ready to talk now?"

She nods, her lips pressing into a thin line. "Do I need to have this conversation as a friend or as a leader of this community?" Her fingers drum on the armrest, a rhythm searching for clarity. "It's a different hat, see, and I need to know what viewpoint I'm answering from."

My hand lifts in a playful salute, an imaginary brim tipped in her direction. "We'll start with a leader. Does that work for you?" I coax a smile onto my lips, willing it to spread to hers—and it does.

She chuckles, and I can see the tension ease from her shoulders, if only just a sliver. "Okay."

I lean forward, elbows propped on knees, hands clasped as if in prayer. The weight of my words feels like boulders tumbling from my lips. "I'm struggling. I'm struggling a lot and the one constant in my world has disappeared." My voice catches, betraying the quiver I fought so hard to control.

Her eyes soften, yet she waits, patient as the moon.

"It's not my fault," I continue, pressing my palms into my eyes, trying to hold back the flood. "But my brain screams it's my fault. I have to deal with that." I drop my hands and look up at her, my plea laid bare. "But I know how to fix it and it's a good way and I need to do this. I *need* to do this quest, journey, whatever."

Lily leans back into her chair, the creak of the old wood a stark contrast to the silence that's settled between us. Her fingers drum on the tabletop, a staccato rhythm that seems to echo my racing heart. I don't know what she's going to say, but I'm worried just the same.

"I hear you need this, Sari," she says, her gaze piercing as she leans forward, forearms resting against the weathered surface. There's an intensity in her eyes, a focus that commands attention. "But you wouldn't be here if you hadn't faced some resistance. You may have found some people in your circle that want to walk this path— whether for you or to get him back—but you're mistaken if you think everyone will feel comfortable going with you."

My throat tightens around the words I need to say. It's true. The resistance has been more than just a few whispers of doubt; it's been an outright blockade. "You hit the nail on the head." My voice comes out stronger than I feel. "But I… she has to help. I need her to come with me, Lily. He needs her."

The earnestness of my plea hangs in the air, vibrating with the silent hope that Lily will understand the depth of my desperation. She sighs, a long exhalation that seems to carry the weight of all her unspoken thoughts. With a graceful motion, Lily sweeps her long hair off her shoulder, letting it cascade down her back like a silken waterfall. She shakes her head, her eyes not quite meeting mine, as if she's searching for the right words in the cluttered room around us.

"No, you want her to come with you." Her voice is gentle but firm, laced with an edge of disappointment that cuts through me sharper than any blade. "I think you're underestimating the number of people who will be uncomfortable with this resolution and what it will do to your relationships with people who have healed their wounds and finished their process to have them ripped back open with a resurrection." She pauses, her gaze finally locking onto mine, solemn and unwavering. "That doesn't even account for people's religious beliefs that might creep in and change their views of both you and Wilde."

As if anyone here has been worried about that shit before—they definitely have not.

My jaw sets, stubbornness flaring up like a fire within me. Heat prickles at the back of my neck; I can't let her words deter me. "Come on, Lily!" My retort is louder than I intend, and I see her eyebrows raise just slightly, a silent reprimand. I press on regardless. "These are the same people who've been cheering on the cat's magickal sleight-of-hand tricks for weeks. They're not that religious." I throw my hands up, frustration spilling over. "So what if it's on the dark side? Taurus kills people and no one's said a peep. He's swamped with sheep trying to jump into his knickers." I lean forward, my gaze challenging hers. "Morals aren't the problem."

Lily's brow arches, sharp as a scythe in the dim light of her living room. Her lips part, and from them escapes a hiss, each word a serpent coiling around my resolve. "Why are you here? If you don't care what will bother people, go on your journey, cleanse your soul, and get him back."

Her challenge strikes a chord within me, rousing a mixture of irritation and desperation that I struggle to keep caged behind my eyes. "You know why," I counter, voice firm despite the maelstrom churning inside me. "Why are you so against this?"

My hands clench into fists, knuckles whitening. It's rare to feel so cornered, so vulnerable. I lean forward, probing for an ally in her, seeking cracks in her composed facade. "You're not religious, you don't believe in hocus pocus, and I thought—" There's a tremor in my voice, betraying the depth of my plea. "—you seemed like the person who'd be the most supportive of me working through grief in the best way possible."

That's when the words hang between us, raw and unadorned, a plea for understanding—or perhaps permission.

Lily's fingers drum against the armrest of her worn-out sofa, a staccato rhythm that somehow reflects my racing heartbeat. She tilts her head, eyes searching mine for something I'm not sure I can give. "Can I switch to another role like a friend, perhaps?" Her tone is softer now, stripped of the leader's edge it carried moments before.

I shrug noncommittally. Annoyance nips at me, an unwelcome guest gnawing on my patience. Quirky—that's Lily, through and through. And yet, here I am, splayed out in vulnerability on her cluttered stage, seeking counsel when I only need a specific kind of support. "If you need to," I mutter, averting my gaze from her piercing stare.

All I require is for her to tell me how to sway Deli; no probing questions, no moral quandaries—just straightforward, unadorned guidance. But with Lily, even the simple becomes complex, every conversation a labyrinth where one wrong turn could leave me lost.

The shift in her demeanor is almost imperceptible, but I catch it— the way her shoulders drop just a fraction, the softening of her eyes. She leans forward, elbows resting on her knees, as if the space between us can be bridged by mere proximity. "I think you're doing this for another reason," she begins, her voice imbued with the kind of certainty that comes from long nights spent unraveling the threads of a friend's convoluted woes.

Her fingers trace an abstract pattern on the fabric of the couch—a nervous habit. "It's not just to get Wilde back, though I believe you want him back." The words hang there, yet they are merely the prelude to her deeper insight. "I believe this is more resolution to multiple issues, including your ex-mates, and you're using a nuke to drive a nail."

I blink, the unexpected penetration of her gaze making me feel exposed, like she's managed to peel back a layer I hadn't even realized I was wearing. "Well, that was insightful for someone who doesn't seem to pay attention too much," I say, my voice tinged with forced lightness, an attempt to deflect the weight of her observation.

"It's possible." I shrug, trying to appear nonchalant while a tumult of resentment stirs within me. "What makes me angry is that I take care of everyone and I help everyone. I give until I have nothing left." The words tumble out, raw and bitter, a confession of sorts. "The one time I need payback, people aren't willing to pay the piper."

My hands clench into fists at my side, the injustice of it all burning like acid in my veins. There's a momentary silence, a chasm that stretches out between understanding and acknowledgment, and in that quiet, I can almost hear the echo of my own frustration, bouncing off the walls of Lily's chaotic living room. I slump into the worn-out armchair Lily points to, my body language screaming defeat. The chaos of her living room somehow feels fitting, a mirror to the turmoil I can't seem to escape.

"Look at me," she says, her voice cutting through the fog in my head. "Not people. You have people. You mean Deli won't pay the piper."

"Exactly!" I explode, the frustration that's been bubbling inside of me finally finding a vent. "Yes, for fuck's sake. Tell me what I need to say to get her to understand." My plea is almost pathetic, but pride has no place in desperation.

The door creaks open, and Mercury's silhouette fills the frame. Lily's gaze shifts, and for a second, her eyes soften at whatever silent communication they share. But then she shakes her head, and Mercury retreats with a last glance thrown my way that chills me more than the words we've been spitting back and forth. I can't help but think of the tiny warriors he might unleash in my life as payback for this conversation.

"Sari, you can't," Lily says, turning back to me with resolve etched onto her features. "There is nothing *to* say. She will not do this. Her beliefs, her emotions, and her physical state," she continues. "She would never tell you 'no' if she could figure out how to reconcile it with herself."

A spark of defiance ignites within me, fuelled by necessity and raw emotion. "Then I have to do it myself," I declare, the words tasting bitter on my tongue. "I'll always love her, but if she doesn't care about Wilde or me..." My voice trails off. The thought of Deli with

Taurus twists my gut, the image too vivid against the backdrop of my desperation. "And if she's got her next ego feed set up with Taurus, she can flutter off into Rhea-land for all I care."

Before I know it, Lily is out of her chair and her hand lashes out, swift and unexpected—a sharp crack against my cheek. I fall back into the pillows of her makeshift fortress, the sting blooming hot across my face. My eyes widen in shock, heart pounding at the audacity, the sheer physicality of her rebuke.

"Where the *fuck* did that come from?" The words escape as a hiss between clenched teeth, a mix of pain and bewilderment clouding my voice. Lily stands over me, her chest heaving slightly, her eyes alight with an intensity I've rarely seen in her. It's a side of Lily I didn't anticipate—fierce protector, a guardian of boundaries—and yet it feels consistent with everything I know about her. Even as I nurse the red mark forming on my skin, I can't help but recognize the fire behind her action, the unspoken message that I've crossed a line.

Stunned silence hovers between us, a palpable entity in the chaotic sprawl of her living room. My hand lifts to my face, fingers brushing over the tender skin where her palm met my cheek, a reminder that words can ignite storms as surely as they can heal wounds.

"That's bullshit, and it's not fair to Deli," Lily's voice cuts through the tension, sharp and unyielding. "I don't know why you're using the loss of your mate to destroy your relationship with her, but you seem dead set on doing it as completely as possible." Her accusation rings with a clarity that slices into me, forcing me to look beyond the fog of my own grief and frustration.

Rubbing my face, I try to find refuge in anger or indignation, but all I manage is the slow shake of my head. "Coming here was a mistake. I see that now."

The words taste bitter, a confession dressed as defiance. In seeking allies for my cause, I've lost sight of the cost, the collateral damage inflicted upon those I claim to cherish. The echo of our confrontation hangs heavy, and I know that despite my bluster and bravado, there's truth in her rebuke—a truth I'm not ready to face. I stand motionless, the sting from Lily's slap still radiating across my face. Her gaze pins me, unyielding and stern.

Despite everything, a part of me yearns for her to retract her words, to offer a sliver of hope that doesn't feel like a knife twisting in my chest.

"No, Sari, it wasn't," she asserts, her tone softer now, but no less firm. "Coming here to get me to help you manipulate someone was a mistake. If you tried to work through your grief, it would have been beneficial." She pauses, eyes narrowing as if trying to peer into my soul. "As it is, I won't tell you not to do this and despite her strenuous protests, I don't believe Deli will try to stop you, either."

Her words are a lifeline thrown into the turbulent sea of my emotions, but they also serve as an anchor, dragging me down with the weight of their implication. I need Deli to understand, to be by my side, yet here stands Lily, telling me she won't obstruct—yet she won't assist either.

"However, before you leave, I'd be remiss if I did not point out you have tried quests like this before." She stops, her hand resting on the doorknob. "In December—this ended in disaster and likely set you on the path to this moment—and with Wilde going on those adventures with Amanda as she tried to find herself." Her eyes meet mine, steady and knowing. "I don't know what you and Wilde are missing inside, but consider that trying to find it by trampling everyone that loves you in a swath of rage, sorrow, and violence isn't working. It is the definition of insanity and all."

Her words hit me harder than her slap, echoing the uncertainty that has haunted me since Wilde's disappearance. A knot forms in my throat, and for a moment, I struggle to breathe around it. Lily sees through me, laying bare the desperation I've tried to cloak in righteous purpose. I clench my jaw and force a contemplative hum through my throat, nodding like I'm absorbing every bit of her sermon. My fingertips graze the cool metal of the doorknob as I step over a plush alligator, its glassy eyes mocking me with a silent, toothy grin. The pirate flags flutter slightly as the door closes behind me, their skulls and crossbones a stark contrast to the bubblegum pink walls.

"Take care, Lily," I offer, the words hollow against the weight of her judgment. Just outside her doorstep, a breeze skims across my cheeks, carrying away the stifling warmth of her cluttered sanctuary. I draw in a deep breath, trying to flush out the sting of her reprimand with the crisp spring air.

Lily follows me onto the porch, leaning against the doorway with a frown that creases her brow. "What are you going to do? I feel I need to be ready."

I hold her gaze for a heartbeat too long, searching for the flicker of solidarity that used to be there. Finding none, I turn away, letting the shadows from the overhanging willow tree dance across my face. "Don't worry about me, Lily. I've got it under control," I say, but the reassurance is for myself more than for her.

She doesn't move, doesn't speak, but I can feel her eyes boring into my back, heavy with unspoken warnings. I stride down the path, each step echoing the turmoil churning inside me. Lily's house, with its whimsical chaos and misplaced nostalgia, fades into the background, along with any hope of her understanding.

"I will ditch this," I call out to her, my voice firmer than I feel. The wind picks up, as if it carries away the last fragments of my resolve. "You're right, Lily. It's too much pain to dredge up. I'll find another way to figure out what I need."

A curtain flutters behind her, ghosting past her shoulder and for a moment, it looks like it might reach out and pull me back towards the chaos of her living room, towards reconsideration. But the fabric settles, and so does my decision.

Lily's stance softens, and the lines around her eyes seem less severe in the dim porch light. "What should I tell Deli?" Her voice is quieter now, tinged with something akin to concern, or maybe it's just the fatigue of dealing with my mess.

"Tell her... whatever you want, dear," I reply, not quite managing to keep the bite out of my tone. "I'm sure that scamp of yours has a recording. Share it with her." I don't bother to look back; I know Lily's eyes are probably narrowing in that analytical way of hers, dissecting my every word for deeper meaning.

My hand finds the handle of the car door, and I pull it open with more force than necessary. The interior light washes over me, casting long shadows across the driveway. I slide into the driver's seat, the leather cool against my skin, and shut the door with a thud that silences the world outside.

With that, I grin to myself, a private little victory dance inside my head.

That should do it.

The Bird Feels Helpless

TAURUS

" I tried, baby. I tried so fucking hard to help her get through this."

She leans into my shoulder and sobs as my heart breaks again. We're curled up in my wife's favorite place to shut the world out: the closet. After we arrived at our home, I convinced her to sleep for two hours because the dark circles under her eyes were making her look like I had made her up for a zombie movie.

When she woke, I had planned to take her to hunt so she could refill her stores, but her phone rang. I cursed myself for leaving it where she could see who was calling because she felt duty-bound to answer Lily.

I won't lie; I feel duty bound to kill the daisy and the fucking gnarly gnome.

Daisy thought she was doing the right thing by calling my wife. I know she felt as a leader that the minx had to know about things that affect the entire community. But as a friend, she should have known that my wife was in no place to deal with the full content of

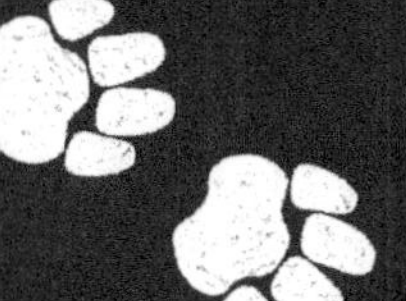

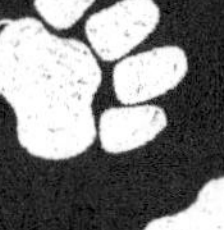

that conversation. So she repeated it all, and I could see the life drain out of my brave kitty's face as she listened. It was like all the color in the world faded. I guess the gloomy weather that's been hanging around since the writer kicked it doesn't help that feeling because it's been stormy, gray, and listless for days now.

My wife spoke with Lily for about thirty minutes and didn't give her even a hint of the emotions I could feel swirling around our home like a maelstrom, and hung up with the calm of a pro. Then she stood up, walked over to the closet, and shut the door without a sound. I followed her and she broke down in a crumpled heap of tears and pain, shaking as she described the conversation. She hasn't moved from that spot in five hours, nor has she stopped crying or repeating that blasted 'ego feed' line.

If there's something in this world I could murder an entire population for and not care if they locked me up for the rest of all time in the Company cells, *that* is one thing I'd do it for.

It devastated my poor wife. She's broken and hell knows they abused her before she came to me, but now she's lost three mates and maybe a fourth to this nightmare. I don't know how she's still functioning. I've seen what happens to clones that lose their mates in the field. Talia saved one for my brother.

Statistically, he's not a blip on the radar compared to the number of agents deactivated when they lost their marbles.

I did everything a dutiful husband *should* do. I let her stay alone and deal with the loss of her mate. I let her decide when she'd had enough on her terms—albeit, accidentally, but it counts, right? I sat here and let her snot the grief from her loss—now that she can even attempt to deal with her own loss—and her betrayal all over me without so much as a whimper. But whether or not she likes it, I want answers.

I should be clear—I want them from the stumpy little nit that hasn't told anyone *why* that knob was out in the rainy darkness. She also hasn't explained how he went off the road and couldn't get clear with clone reflexes and healing. No one has offered a reason we didn't send him to the nearby Company triage center where the docs deal with shit like this all time and clones come at the better end. They sent him across a portal and risked his life by losing precious time.

Why?

Only the gnome saw the body. They said it was mangled from the wreck and surgery. He was cremated immediately. No one saw the remains of the car. Now she wants to fucking resurrect him with magick or voodoo or some shit, and it makes me wonder if they pulled the old switcheroo because I don't know a legend in the Universe that resurrects beings from ashes. He's not a goddamned phoenix.

I think they kept the body because she had this in mind. Either that, or he was never dead. Maybe he's in hiding? I've put a Company team on it. Mikhail agreed that it's too dangerous to have rogue elements performing dangerous ceremonies that we do not know about. Luckily, the git knew better than to cough and mention my wife or I would have used his guts for violin strings. My wee princess might be a virtuoso.

A father's gotta plan, yeah?

I don't trust the whole thing, haven't from the beginning, and I'll be damned if I will let my wife get dragged through the muck over and over by that scheming little goblin and her minions. What I'm looking at now is heartbreaking, and while she should be sad, it shouldn't feel like the light in her soul is flickering to the nubs.

Closing my eyes, I contact Talia, knowing she's with the long hair again. The two of them have been tight as cuffs on a terrorist, and it makes me happy to see their love growing despite this sadness. She lets me know that he's doing better. She says he doesn't talk about it much, needs a comforting touch or things I need not know about, but the melancholy seems to have faded much faster than she expected. Something about the way he's handling it is tripping her wires—she thinks he was letting go long before the writer went splat, but he doesn't talk about them with her.

Leaning on her is the best thing for both of them.

My primary says the rest of the looky-loo mourners have stopped coming to the house to find my wife. That's good, because dragging her through their contrived grief until it rips off her Band-Aid is not part of my plan for the next few weeks. I would ask Lily to help her steer them away, but after today, I'll be lucky if I don't rip her head off. I'm not saying that she didn't do my wife a solid by smacking the living *shit* out of the gnome—Christ, do I envy her *that* joy—but she should have never shared the full details of that conversation.

Not now, never.

Sighing, I look down. Here she is, the mighty Queen of the Resistance, curled up in my lap. Tears streak her face and she's a mess of tangles and snotty clothes. Her heart is breaking and I feel it as if it's a visible object ripping into pieces in front of me.

"Why, love? Why would she hurt you like that?"

"I couldn't go on the journey with her. I told her it was bullshit and evil and bad and I wouldn't do it."

"Good on you, love. You know enough about this stuff to have an informed opinion and she should listen, not destroy you over it."

"She's been destroying me for days. I see that now. She's been breaking me down like a hostage. I couldn't sleep because I won't sleep in their room but only a lumpy couch; I couldn't hunt, so my energy intake was low; I couldn't grieve because she needed me to be strong. She wanted me physically, emotionally, and spiritually weak, so I'd agree to this madness."

I blink. I've not heard my wife talk about her mate in this way before, but she seems more familiar with the way someone would break down a detainee than I'm comfortable with. She hasn't taken a single Company class yet. How does she know this?

"If she didn't let you grieve, how did she get to your heart, my love?" I'm asking out of curiosity because I have to give Mikhail another briefing on her skill set if she knows how to Psy-Ops a subject in the field.

A shudder ripples through her and she doesn't lift her head, unable to look at me. ~*I wasn't there. He would have never been driving to the portal to go visit people on the other side if I'd been around for him to spend time with. My neglect put him on the road.* ~

I nearly explode. It takes everything in me to stay still and calm and harness my rage. This is horseshit. No one will admit he didn't *need* to see anyone at that hour or in that kind of weather. That snotty little midget is using her primary's death to torture my wife because of me. I'll rip her stubbly little limbs out of her sockets and pick my teeth with her bones. I'll—

"I think—I think it wouldn't matter if I helped her or not; she'd still be mad. I can't control rain or the roads or whatever. I don't know why, but nothing I do is ever enough and I know she hurts. I hurt, too, but I can't keep letting her beat me down and…"

My eyes find hers as I pull her chin up to look at me. "Minx, you need to slow down. You're not breathing and it's only making you cry harder. I don't know what you're talking about when you say that it wouldn't matter if you helped or not."

Drawing in a shuddering breath, she tries to calm and I feel the air around us get lighter. It's becoming obvious that her emotions affect her magick and while I think it's a suitable topic for later, now I need to know how to put Humpty back together again.

She was sad yet serene after dropping the bomb about Maeve on us. She helped us get to the hospital, and she stayed by the gnome's side during the surgeries. My wife knitted her blanket and rocked the little monster sitting in her lap like a child. She even went home with her and got bludgeoned with her grief for days before I showed up.

"Sari's messing with things she does not understand. She thinks she can bring him back and everything will be the same or better, I don't know." My wife chokes back a sob and puts her hand over her mouth, shaking her head. "You can't do it like that. It costs too much. It's not for us to make that decision. Even if we *could*, nothing ever comes back the same. There is a debt owed to the Universe that is so steep that it could change the course of the future."

I sigh and shake my head. If my magickal minx is this upset, she knows that it is not only a bad idea, but that it is possible to accomplish. She's not scoffing and pooh-poohing at the thought of doing so. My lovely wife knows it is possible to resurrect someone, and either knows how or knows people who know how.

That's terrifying.

~You can't do it like that. The costs are too high. She watches TV; she reads; no one does this unscathed. It's bad juju! ~

Now I'm certain that something is going on. Sari was a weeping, catatonic mess at the hospital. For days, she's been holding my wife emotionally captive using CIA style interrogation techniques. She's had time to plan a bloody complex magickal quest to gather items for a ceremony that maybe a handful of people on Earth know about?

She plotted the visit to Lily for maximum damage. *This is bullshit—my wife is a pawn in this scheme.* "I hate when you cry because it makes me want to kill things." I gather her into my arms. "Something is rotten, my love. You're not Rhea, and we both know it. I don't know what the gnome is planning, but I will find out."

Her eyes are red-rimmed as she looks at me. "You promise?"

"Without zombies, re-animated corpses, or killing anyone, I will find out what has happened here. I can't guarantee that I won't kill anyone after I find out, but I will stop them from hurting you."

Nodding, she buries her face in my shoulder and I hold her close, crooning and cooing into her mind.

I'm deadly serious. I will find out what the gnome's game is, and I will end it.

The Blade Slithers Her Way Into His Heart

TALIA

I stride in, looking around for him because I know he's here. He's been calm since the service. It's like he's getting over his mate, but making sure not to ask anyone for anything. I've done my best to comfort him when he seems the most upset, but he's never once talked about what he feels.

It worries the hell out of me.

There was something at odds about his relationship with the other mates. Rafe avoided seeing Sari—unlike Deli who got held hostage at her house. He complied with Sari's request for a drawing, but I watched him struggle for days before rooting through the only locked cabinet in his studio. He pulled out a beautiful watercolor of Wilde that he placed in a carrying sleeve, but he didn't look at it again, nor did he reply when Sari thanked him. He nodded and handed it over, staying quiet until we could leave.

Rafe is grieving, but he's conflicted, and it shows.

After Taurus told me about the cat, I'm not surprised. I've said it since the beginning and I'm saying it again now: something terrible

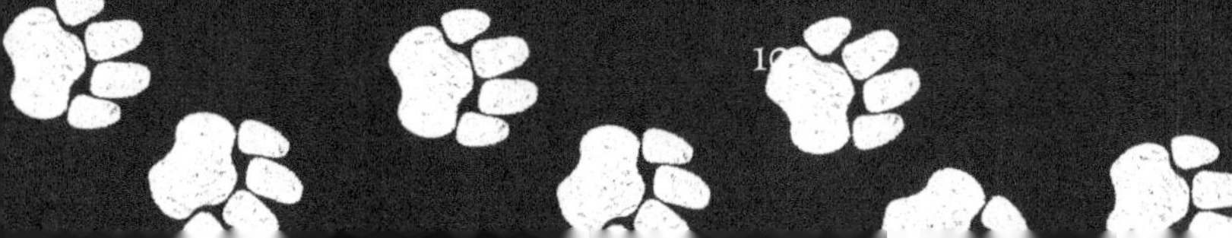

happened to these two and I realize now that Sari and her deceased clone were in the thick of it. Whatever they went through is awful enough that neither wants anyone—even us—to find out about it.

Rafe walks in with a pint of ice cream and a spoon in his hand. His eyes are dark and his hair is braided tightly down his back. He's been very austere since the cremation, and I miss his flamboyance. Giving me a smile, he drops onto the couch and sits the pint down on the table. "Oi, love."

He rubs his temples and I can tell he has a headache. It's from bottling everything up for so long. Taurus told me he's very concerned that something is hinky with this accident. He's got a team on it, but I feel cautious, especially with the information that he got from his wife. Resurrection?

Christ, I can only hope that the magickal kitty is keeping that from her primary. I don't want him to dig deeper.

I prefer to be ready if he needs me. The only time I've gotten unstrapped since the funeral is when we've been intimate; I've even been sleeping with Precious under the pillow. I don't trust Sari and her cadre of clowns for a second, and I'll be damned if waiting isn't making my fangs twitch. No use getting Rafe all upset, though. I'd rather him focus on healing, than worry about their bullshit.

So I pad over and ask him, "Did you bring two spoons or are you going to let me use yours?"

He smiles a bit, making room for me. "You can share. I'm not afraid of catching your cooties."

"That's good, because they'd be all over you by now." I scoot close, ducking under his arm. "Flavor?"

"Mint chocolate chip. Leo went to the place on the other side my girl loves this morning. There's nothing better."

I blink, shaking my head. "You're going to think I'm lying when I say that you brought my favorite flavor."

His lips curl briefly. "Nope. The more we get to know one another, the more we have in common. I'm sorry that stuff's making that less simple right now." He sucks ice cream off a sizable chunk of chocolate and I stare at his insofar 'non-sharing' spoon.

"You couldn't have known. None of us could."

Nodding, he offers a spoonful and I take it before he changes his mind. "True. The woman's upset. She says that the coyote is planning something she prefers no part of."

Shit. I was hoping she'd kept that to herself.

I regard him for a minute, but he doesn't seem as worried about it as she is. Sighing, I lick the last of the spoon and dip it back into the ice cream, holding it out for him. "Taurus is looking into the accident. He's wary, since that little conniver is talking about some hoodoo."

The quiet clone frowns. "It's bad if the woman said no. She's been to some dark places with magick. It takes a lot for her to say no."

Tucking it away to discuss with my mate later, I nod. Someone with that kind of power can only be on Earth. That means someone arranged this on the fly or long before the writer wrecked.

Interesting.

Grinning, I pretend not to worry. "Nothing to worry about, I'm sure. Just Sari spouting off about things she doesn't understand because of Beltane and sorrow. People grieve differently."

He nods, looking unconvinced.

"Besides, you have me and you're crazy about me. You just don't know it yet."

Arching a brow, he steals the spoon. "Who says I don't?"

He catches me by surprise again, and I drop a big dollop of ice cream. "Shit."

Leaning down, he licks it off, offering me a small grin. "Taken care of."

"Can't complain about that method. It beats the hell out of napkins. To answer you, no one said you were, either."

"Baby, I'm insane about you. I'm sharing my comfort ice cream, aren't I?"

Shaking my head, I mutter, "We are going to work on your communication skills, mister." I wait for him to finish his bite, then snatch the spoon again. "When one is crazy about someone, it's a good idea to tell them instead of hoping they have some kind of ESP and peep in your head."

"One would think you could feel it."

"I'm careful about shielding, thanks ever so. I'd be a basket case if I weren't. I'm not always successful with some, but there it is." I glance at my hands, knowing that my sorrow mixed with worry and frustration are scorching over my skin like tiny pinpricks and if he could see it, he'd realize how much I keep closed off. "I need the words just like every other girl. Not to mention, it'd be rude of me just to strip everything you feel and read it like the paper, now wouldn't it?"

He ponders. "Well, as you said before, the marks," he points to his neck, "come with some entitlement. But I'm not hiding anything, so I wouldn't get worried if you did."

"I'm here, aren't I? I read that much. When it's about me, I stay away. Sheesh. If you ever fall in love with me, will it be this hard to get it out of you?" My nose wrinkles because he's not only refusing to give me the answers I want, but he's using my own words against me.

Bastard.

"No, it shouldn't be difficult. I wonder if I'm having a little spillover from the woman. She's far more upset than me because of the assumption she'd be all in for some crazy necromancy or something." He reaches up and cups my face. "I'm "bloody crazy about you, pet. I'm falling harder every day."

"Thank you." I beam, smearing ice cream on his nose and then licking it off. I can't explain why I feel happy with him even when I should be sad, but I do.

"Ack! Tell a woman you like them and see what happens? Sticky, that's what."

I study him, words tumbling out before I stop them. "You know I'm falling in love with you, right? Because if that's a problem, I'd like to know now so I can prevent it from happening."

"We seem to be floating in the same boat, pet. It might be down the River Styx, but we're in it."

Laughing, I curl up next to him. "Can I tell you something?" I need to share this with him, because I never share this with anyone. But something makes me want to, so I'm going to try. If it distracts him from the whole Wilde mess, more the better.

"Of course."

"My fangs? They're not like yours."

"Neither are the cat's. She's got four."

"Mine are more serpentine."

"Huh. Curved and all?"

"Yeah. They're retractable like a snake's fangs, too. They come from the roof of my mouth."

He thinks for a minute, and I almost lose my courage. "Cool. Do you have two or four? Some snakes have four."

"Only two."

He studies me as if imagining and squints. "Are they long?"

"Longer than yours. Probably longer than your mate's, though hers are bigger than all of ours. Cats have some serious incisors." My eyes cut to his neck, finding the four holes and noting that I'm right. I've not looked at Taurus' marks from her, but I'm betting they're pretty large.

"Can I see or would that bother you?" he asks, looking curious.

"One or both? They're independently retractable," I reply, trying to make myself as brave as I was when I started this conversation. He's not making an issue about them, but this is not something I let people see. "Full set. I'm curious."

Swallowing hard, I blink my eyes once, twice, and my pupils contract to diamond slits. I hiss and stretch my neck and then turn to peer at him. Two and a half inches of sharp and wickedly curved fangs glisten wetly where my incisors used to be. I peer at him, scenting the air to taste his reaction.

His eyes rove over the fangs and meet my eyes before he reaches over to cup his palm along my face. "Very nice pet. Venom or no?"

Flushing, I meet his eyes and nod. "But like all poisonous snakes, I don't have to use the venom."

"Interesting. Fatal or ouch?"

"Very fatal. I can poison a cow."

"I could suggest a few."

I hiss, laughter not working well in the snake guise. "Um, mind if I put them away now? You're looking tastier than normal."

"Go ahead, if it's tempting you," he grins and leans back against the couch.

Slipping back into normalcy, my lips quirk. It worried me he'd be inconsolable with Wilde, like he was with the others. He's not. I still believe that there's something that was going on with them, but I will not ruin this moment by prying.

"Better now?"

"No, but at least I won't spear you."

"Wouldn't've minded unless it bothered you." He smiles, his handsome face making my entire body heat.

"My hunger for your blood keeps growing. I feed differently than you do, though I imagine you might have figured that out. I don't dislocate my jaw, nor is my tongue forked, but I've got better eyesight than an average chit. I'd break a fang if I fed like you guys do. I'm a 'strike and watch them bleed' type. If I get deep enough, I can hit more than one vein at a time. It's very bloody."

"Then what?"

He looks interested and hell, in for a penny, right?

Rafe's not running away in disgust and he's not playing some crazy 'mine is better than yours' game. *Why not?* "I drink. They die. I'm immune from my venom and it's an anticoagulant derivative. If I've got a dirty mark, I can kill first and sip later. It's not like a real snake."

"Obviously. But what are you?"

"This isn't genetic to me like it is to you. There's a long story about how this happened to me. I guess I don't know any other type of story but long. Serpentine is the best I can do to answer your question of what."

"You don't use the fangs because you can't do it without killing people, then?"

"No. I don't show my fangs because everyone has them and I wasn't in the mood to explain where mine came from, as if I was trying to rationalize being more special than everyone else." I shrug. "I have issues with lack of originality."

"Oh, well, that makes sense. Look at the woman—no sooner than her quest starts, other people pop up with special shit."

"I haven't killed with the fangs—hell, I haven't even used them in over a year." I pull out my arm blades and twirl them. "These are my weapons now."

He smiles and kisses my forehead. "Whatever makes you comfortable, pet."

I sigh. He is a good man, and he sure as hell doesn't get enough credit. "You realize that if he and I find out they've done this to mess with you—and I mean you and Deli—no one will stop me from using these, right?"

His eyes close, and he nods. "Hell will come knocking if his death is part of some grand scheme. That, my love, I did not need to be told."

Hell will come knocking. He's right about that.

The Coyote Strikes Again

DELILAH

"Love," I whisper to myself, tracing the letters with a fingertip that trembles ever so slightly.

The word hangs in the air, a lifeline thrown across the chasm of my solitude. I clutch Taurus's note like a talisman, the paper crinkling under the pressure of my grip. The inked words blur for a moment as I steady my breathing. I grip the edge of the note, feeling the rough texture of paper against my fingertips. It's a tangible reminder that despite everything, life keeps moving, keeps demanding.

"I got a summons from the Company today." My eyes dart across the lines, and I can almost hear his voice echoing each word in my head. His tone is always so matter-of-fact with business, but there's an undercurrent of excitement now that wasn't there before.

I love the way he switches back and forth.

"Both I and the golden goddess are being 'requested' to appear." I let out a breath I didn't realize I was holding. The 'golden goddess'—his primary mate who is now permanently bonded to *my* primary. A chuckle escapes me at the thought, a brief respite from the tension coiling within.

"My guess is the sods got her brief about what's been going on with us and are ready to grant my request about you helping with the shit I do." I blink, processing. I'm in this now, truly in it. No longer just a spectator to his world, but a participant. It's daunting, yet it ignites something fierce and eager in my core.

"I don't know what's going to go down, but I'll be back." There's a promise in those words, one that goes beyond the physical. He'll return to me, no matter what the Company throws at him—or us.

"I have to jet, pet." Just like that, I can picture him: leather duster, the slight crease between his brows as he steps through our door, determination etched into every line of his body.

"I love you always."

Though he isn't here to witness it, I whisper into the silence of the room, "I love you, too."

My voice doesn't tremble. It's strong, sure—a reflection of the new purpose blossoming inside me. I fold the note carefully, securing it with all the others, a paper testament to our strange, chaotic dance.

I trace the final signature with my thumb, the looping letters familiar and dear.

Taurus. His name is like a talisman, etched at the bottom of the hastily scribbled note. I trace the letters, finding a measure of comfort in their familiarity. With a deep inhale, I steel myself for what's ahead. For the Company, for him, and for me. The unknown may be vast, but together, we're a force to be reckoned with.

I'm ready.

The room is quiet around me; the stillness punctuated only by the occasional distant hum of traffic outside. It's a stark contrast to the chaos that usually swirls within these walls, the echoes of arguments and laughter now just ghosts in the silence. I'm alone—with his words, with the promise they hold.

I sit on the edge of our bed, the sheets cold and smooth beneath me. The scent of Taurus lingers—musky and warm—and I close my eyes for a moment, letting it envelop me. The spark he mentioned, it's there, flickering in the pit of my stomach, threatening to ignite something I thought was long extinguished.

A purpose, he says. A chance to be useful again, to not just exist, but to live.

A tiny spark of light flickers within me, an ember of hope that refuses to be snuffed out despite the accident's lingering shadow. The thought of working again, of having a purpose beyond the confines of these four walls, sends a thrill up my spine. Even if it means enduring arduous training or mind-numbing protocols, it's a chance to rebuild something lost—a chance to feel whole once more.

"Working would give me a purpose," I mumble, giving voice to the idea, testing how it tastes on my tongue. It's been too long since I've had anything meaningful to fill my days. The accident, that cruel thief, stole more than just my mobility—it took my sense of self. But this, this could be a way back to who I was, even if the path is littered with boring training sessions and company protocols.

The idea of accomplishment, of contributing to something larger than myself, chases away the cobwebs of inactivity that have shrouded my days. My fingers itch for action, for the tactile sensation of doing, moving, being part of the intricate dance Taurus navigates daily. The note in my hand is more than an invitation; it's a call to arms.

A smile tugs at the corners of my mouth—a rare visitor these days. To be with Taurus, to weave my life back into his beyond the confines of these walls and the whispers of pity from those who no longer know how to talk to me—that's a prize worth any obstacle.

My gaze drifts to the empty space beside me where he should be. Months have passed in a blur of avoidance and excuses, keeping everyone at bay. Shea's absence is a relief. Rhea and Alistair are mere memories, and Mercury—a comet passing through my orbit all too infrequently. Wilde and Sari, once fixtures, now repelled by an invisible force field of my own making. And Constantine... I can't deal with his drama, not when it's probably as fabricated as Amanda's near-death theatrics.

"Even if they make me go through a bunch of boring training," I murmur to the empty room, "I'd be able to have something to accomplish and feel good about." The words hang in the air, a mantra for the journey ahead. With each repetition, they grow stronger, carving a path through doubt and pain.

"I'm damned tired of everything being awful," I admit to the empty room. It's become my mantra, a loop that plays endlessly in my head, overshadowing moments of joy with its bleak refrain. Wilde's absence might sting less than I let on, and maybe, just maybe, I'm better off without the lot of them.

"Ouch," I say to no one, wincing at the bitterness that seeps into my thoughts unbidden. I stand, smoothing out the creases in Taurus's note before sliding it into the nightstand drawer with the care of a curator handling a priceless artifact. There it rests atop his other messages, each one a piece of the puzzle that is us.

Taurus—steadfast Taurus—believes in me enough to make this happen.

Pulling my hair back into a loose ponytail, I approach the window, gazing out into the darkened landscape. The night is still, almost expectant. I press a hand to the cool glass, feeling its solid reality beneath my palm.

"I need a purpose other than running the community," I reaffirm, watching my breath fog up the surface. Each word acts as a stepping stone, guiding me back to myself, to the life that awaits with open arms.

Taurus might be gone for now, but we're in this together. Every challenge, every victory—it's ours to share. I'm not just a bystander in his story; I'm a co-author, penning the next chapter with steady hands. When he returns, I'll be ready to stand by his side, no longer diminished but renewed.

"Let them try to train me," I say with a half-smile, drawing strength from the very thought. "I'll be ready for whatever comes next."

I shuffle through the clutter on my desk, searching for something that isn't there. The silence of the room is a stark contrast to the chaos I've kept at bay. It's been months since I've had to deal with Shea's insistent chatter or Rhea and Alistair's dramatics; their absence is like a balm to my overstimulated senses.

Rafe, bless his interference, has done well in shielding me from Wilde and Sari's incessant drama. My world feels smaller, quieter, and while it's not entirely empty, it's filled only with those I allow. With Taurus' return looming, a glimmer of anticipation cuts through the stillness of my self-imposed exile.

Leaning back in my chair, I consider the remaining thorn in my side—Constantine. His presence is like a persistent echo, a reminder of connections I'd rather sever. The news of Amanda's brush with death, or lack thereof, had given him an excuse to latch on, playing up his distress like a Shakespearean tragedy.

"Please," I mutter to myself as I toss aside another useless paper. "The drama of it all could fuel a soap opera."

I know I should be more sympathetic, but my patience wears thin. Sari's grandstanding about having 'powerful people' on her side makes me wary of anyone connected to her, especially Constantine.

Yet, I've let him hover on the fringes, his sad stories weaving around my better judgement.

"Enough," I say aloud, pushing away from the desk. Standing up, I stretch out the knots in my shoulders. It's time to reclaim my space, to prepare for the work ahead and the partnership with Taurus that promises to be my salvation.

"Let them gather their allies," I whisper defiantly to the four walls. "I'll be ready for that, too."

I open the drawer of the nightstand, the one where I keep the rest of his letters—the ones filled with promises and plans. This new one, with its potential for change, slips in with the others, a tangible piece of hope in a sea of messiness. Maybe working with Taurus will be the turning point I need, or maybe I'm just clinging to another dream destined to shatter.

"Either way, it's something," I murmur, closing the drawer with a soft click and letting my fingers linger on the polished wood.

For a moment, there's stillness. Then, with a deep breath, I square my shoulders and turn away from the nightstand, ready to face whatever comes next.

DETERMINATION SETS my shoulders straight as I face the closet. The big party looms on the horizon, a beacon of normalcy in a sea of grief and betrayal. I shuffle over to the closet, my hands trembling slightly as I reach for the leather-bound binders. They're heavy with possibilities—a collection of outfits meticulously organized by occasion and mood.

Wilde's death left a gaping hole in our tight-knit circle, a silence too loud to ignore. And Sari... her deceit stings like a slap, betrayal from within our ranks festering like a wound that refuses to heal.

My fingers wrap around the handle, ready to rifle through outfit binders for the perfect ensemble when my phone shatters the quiet, its shrill tone slicing through the room. For a heartbeat, hope flutters in my chest. It could be Taurus. I lunge for it, ready to melt into his words.

But no, it's her. Sari, with her impeccable timing for disruption. Why she chooses this moment to dredge up old wounds, I'll never understand. My hand hovers over the phone, indecision clawing at me.

"Fuck," I hiss between clenched teeth.

The timing is impeccable, uncanny even. Why she chooses now, when I'm adrift in a sea of hurt and scheming, to weasel her way back into my life is beyond me. But Sari always did have a knack for picking the worst moments to resurface.

With resignation clawing at my insides, I press the phone to my ear, bracing for her onslaught of excuses and manipulations. Her voice spills out in torrents, a deluge of half-hearted apologies and self-justifications that make my head spin.

"Okay. Okay," I cut in, the words tasting like ash on my tongue. "No, I'm not busy right this second."

A lie. I am busy—busy trying to piece together some semblance of control over my shattered reality.

The call ends, and the room echoes with a silence that feels like an accusation. In the reflection of the darkened screen, I catch a glimpse of myself—a puppet dancing on the strings of obligation. With a sigh, I stand, steeling myself for the confrontation ahead, each step a march toward a battlefield I never chose.

"Dammit," I mutter after hanging up, feeling the weight of the day pressing down on me. All I wanted was to indulge in the simple pleasure of choosing a dress, to lose myself in the fantasy of a party I don't even wish to attend.

Instead, fate conspires to drag me back into the mire.

The universe has a sick sense of humor, thrusting me into this farce when all I yearn for is a pause button on life's remote control. But no, the cosmos directs its twisted narrative with me as the reluctant star.

"Fine," I mutter to the empty room, echoing back at me like a judgment. I pluck a random outfit from the binder, not caring for its details or its promise. It's a placeholder, a uniform for duty rather than delight.

"The universe hates me," I conclude with a sigh, tossing the phone onto the bed as if it's the source of all my misfortune.

Why else would it conspire to keep me from the simple joys, to chain me to conversations I've already lived a thousand times in my head?

The Artist Frets and Fawns

RAFE

It's killing me.

I know that she's in pain, but she's trying to hide it. It's bad enough that it's seeping into me, so it's no joke. My primary is at Sari's house, letting our mate—if you can even call her that anymore—fill her head with Christ knows what. It's almost as if they are trying to send her over the deep end. Sari destroyed my primary the other day; now she's back for more.

When will it be enough?

Deli let me know she was going because Sari said she 'needed' to clear the air. Neither of them invited me, which leaves me alone, pacing in my studio as I wait for the other shoe to drop.

Wilde losing his marbles before the accident was bad enough; now the sod's fucking everything up from the grave. That's become so fucking on-brand for him that I don't even have to think about it to believe that this is all about the deceased blogger.

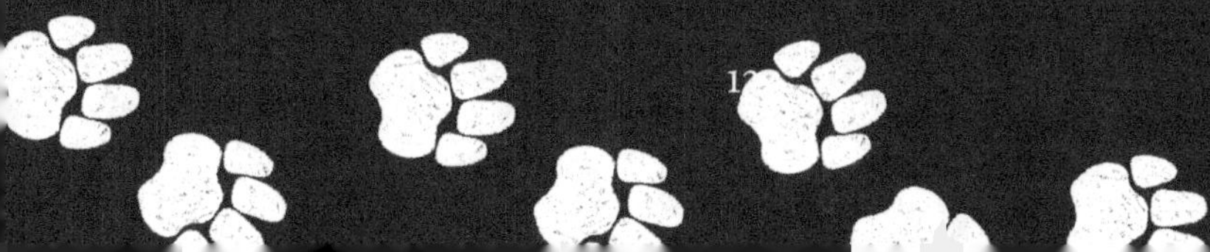

I sound awful—he was my mate. However, there's so much water under that bridge, and most of it is bloody. It's not surprising that I'm bitter or that my primary is swallowing her anger for the sake of old sentiment. She's being loyal and killing herself doing it.

The minute we put the urn in the ground, I was finished with that ball and chain. I knew I'd made the right decision, when the coyote announced her plan to resurrect him. I mourned in the days after his death and I'm not about to rehash it. Wilde passing meant I was not under any obligation to play their games. Sari is mated to Deli and I; I can't change that any more than I can the other ex-mates. However, I can choose not to take part in the emotional gladiator games anymore.

And I am.

There are still secrets, but they can rest now. If we told Taurus and Talia about the physical abuse, they might kill her. My primary is terrified that they will never want to touch either of us again. Fear and shame are life's great motivators, and it's keeping us silent about the goings-on at the Den, despite Wilde's death. We don't want anyone to know what awful things we let happen to us because we got spun in the silken webs of loyalty, love, and fear.

I pad to the bar and grab a glass, pouring a couple of fingers of bourbon,and toss it back.

It feels like that kind of day.

"Hello, love," Blade says, walking in with her blade, Precious, spinning in her palm.

Giving her a slight smile, I sigh. "There you are. The bird should know that the cat's not at home. She's prostrating, I assume."

She blinks. "Prostrating?" The knife spins faster and her brow knits in concern.

"She got called to the Den to 'work it through'. I can only assume they're raking her over the coals. She's keeping me out, but enough is coming through for me to know it's not good. That bloody git's torturing us from the grave, I fucking swear it." Her head turns slowly to look at me in surprise and I shrug, "I'm agitated today."

"I'll say." She stops talking to communicate with the bird mentally, and then she groans. "Taurus says he can feel her. She's upset, but she's keeping the specifics locked down. He only gets a general feeling of pain. It's making him angry, and it's pissing me off. I feel like taking a swipe at the stunted little bitch myself. If she thinks Taurus is bad—" The blade flies past my face and embeds in the door frame.

"Hex has to spackle the walls and shit every time you do that, woman. You're becoming high maintenance." I give her a reproachful look, then I sigh. "We have to stay calm and not let our anger feed hers. With Maeve, her emotions ride high, you know?"

"With every heart wrench, there's an apology from that twat—then vice that versa. When do the checks not cover the balance, I wonder? Words cannot be unsaid, and she said some horrible things to Deli at the last visit."

"I know. The cat will have to handle it, though, because she's not accepting any help from us."

Talia shakes her head. "Sari has some leeway because her mate died, but it only goes so far. Taurus will decimate her if she pushes too far with Deli."

I'm definitely aware of that.

I open my arms, hoping to distract her. "Come here. For now, I'd just like a hug. I need some contact; it keeps me grounded." Moving like wildfire, she's in my arms and squeezing me before I finish the sentence. I kick up a purr and she murmurs in happiness.

It's such a little thing that makes people so happy. "You flounced out this morning after saying something noteworthy, and I haven't heard from you since."

"I never flounce; I stride. I do an occasional sexy strut or a serpentine sway, but I never flounce."

"Uh-huh. Locomotion notwithstanding, the words were the big deal. It sounded like a profession."

"Be a little more specific? What kind of profession—doctor, lawyer, accountant?" she grins, teasing me.

"Not a career, but the other profession. As in, where you say something important."

"Ooh. I did that?" She bats her lashes at me and I chuckle.

"I think so." She doesn't answer and I frown. "Being difficult, I see. You don't care to reiterate it, huh?"

Her look is scathing. "Do I look witless to you? It occurred to me while I was at work that I've been the one doing all the spouting of declarations. I'm making all the decisions and taking all the risks. I'm scared, okay? I don't want to be out on that branch alone anymore."

Tweaking her nose, I wink. "I was only trying to get you to say it so I could say it back. If the flo—striding hadn't happened as you left, I would have earlier."

"Oh." She frowns and looks a little sheepish. "That was a whole stomach full of nerves all day for nothing."

"It was all your own doing, pet. You didn't give me a chance. It's the truth, though. I do."

Her smile is tender, happiness and relief showing in her dusky gray eyes. "How'd the melted ice cream issue go? You were sure we were in trouble for leaving it all night."

"Ugh. Bitch, bitch, bitch—that's what I got."

"Sorry. We were doing well eating it until we got distracted."

"It's okay. Besides, I enjoy making Hex grumpy. It's not a proper day if I don't piss everyone in the house off once."

Talia chuckles and tilts her head. "I think you should go first now."

"You do, huh?"

"I do it because I'm so shy and retiring." She makes an innocent face and I snort.

"Does anyone ever believe that rot?"

"No. It might be the pointies. What do you think?" Her blades spin on her palms and I grin.

"Your attitude might be a factor."

"I have a fine attitude."

"I like your attitude as well, or it'd be hard to love you so damned much."

Her smile creeps over her face like the dawn breaking. Her eyes glow. Launching herself at me, she knocks me to the lounge with a throaty laugh. "Ha!"

"Got me, huh?"

"Thank god. It took two days!" Her grin is wicked,and I roll my eyes. "Talk about a long chase. I love you too, long hair."

"Is that my nickname now?"

"I'm trying things as I go until I find one that fits. I like long hair, though. Taurus' Sampson crack was more intelligent than normal for him."

"I'm sure that he's more intelligent than that."

Her laugh is low and full of humor as she shushes me. "Shh! Sweet hell, if he hears that it's a whole puffy chested, swishy tail feather thing—and he's already impossible to live with because of all the compliments your mate dishes out to him."

"She has a problem with ego puffing. She can't help it. When she loves, she loves like today is the last day ever. It's how she's made."

"They're good for each other. He and I—he's a part of me, he always will be. But she completes him and he's happy. I thank her for that."

"I feel how happy he makes her. It's been a while since I felt that." I'm not lying to her; it's true.

I haven't seen her that happy since—well, since before the winter.

"You do not understand. Broody Taurus is never a good thing. Until her? Yeesh."

"I know what a moody kitty's like and trust me, the foundations rock."

"I'm familiar with the ground shaking. What can I say? We've got us a pair."

I scratch my chin. "Well, I do. If you do, I must have missed something."

She blinks and then bursts out laughing. "Shit, I am tired—that slid right past me on the first lap."

"I'm being a smartass."

"That's not the most intelligent area of your body."

Scowling, I growl. "I'm smart from toe-up, thank you very much. Sheesh, tell a bird you love her and she has a license to question your intelligence."

"I can attest to the smart mouth, but, baby, you're matching wits with a master now. You may as well toe up. As a consolation prize, though, I'll tell you I love you again."

"Ooh, I like that prize." I pull her down for a kiss.

Lifting her head, she grins. "I love you, but I'm going to need a nap. Today's taken the wind right out of me."

"You can do me up all improper later, love. Rest now."

"That sounds good, baby." She yawns and wraps around me as I carry her to the couch. I might have to think about a bloody bed in here.

Who would have thought?

The Cat Distracts Herself

DELILAH

I slump into the battered leather chair, a sigh escaping me as the door clicks shut behind Sari. The whole tête-à-tête was exhausting—the kind that leaves your soul feeling frayed at the edges. She had been all apologies at first, her words dripping with a sweetness that felt more like syrup laced with arsenic than genuine remorse.

But that didn't last—she didn't call me there for apologies.

The pandering followed, each sentence carefully constructed to remind me of old times, our friendship, the adventures we'd weathered side by side. But beneath those honeyed phrases lay veiled passive-aggressive jibes, tiny barbs meant to prick my conscience, to awaken some dormant sense of duty that would compel me to change my mind.

"Deli, I only said I wasn't going on the quest because of you," she had said, her voice quivering with a cocktail of anger and desperation. *"You know this is important to me, and now I'm going to resent you for holding me back."*

Her words hung in the air, heavy and suffocating. I could only stare at her, incredulous. Was she trying to paint me as the villain in her twisted narrative? The one who'd strap her down and keep her from her precious, ill-advised mission?

"I think you've gone off your rocker this time, Sari," I murmured, almost to myself, the fatigue from our argument settling deep in my bones. Her eyes had flashed, a storm brewing within them, but she simply turned on her heel and left without another word.

Now, alone with my thoughts, I can't help but wonder if there's any coming back from this. If the Sari I knew—the one who would laugh until tears streamed down her face, who would throw herself into danger to save a stray kitten—was still in there somewhere, or if obsession has truly consumed her.

Pacing the length of my living room, I feel like each step is a silent refusal of Sari's manipulations. The idea that she can push me into something so abhorrent is laughable, if it weren't so damn serious. I pause at the window, gazing out at nothing in particular, and murmur to myself, "To quote a rocker, I'll do a lot of shit for people I love, but I won't do that." My reflection in the glass doesn't waver.

I want *nothing* to do with this hare-brained plot—not one damn thing.

My hands ball into fists as I replay the accusations thrown at me again. In Sari's skewed vision, my steadfast refusal paints me as an awful friend. She claims my struggle to cope with Wilde's death and her mad quest to bring him back from the grave means I don't value our bond—or the love we supposedly share.

"Preventing her from being happy," I scoff, the words bitter on my tongue. As if happiness can be plucked from the depths of necromancy.

Congratulations on keeping up with Deli-ashians, babe.

Sarcasm drips from my thoughts as I consider how Sari and her deceased mate have been a cloud over my life for a year now. I stop abruptly, shaking my head. No more of this 'one answer, no gray area' bullshit. I refuse to let her dictate the terms of our friendship or my morality.

Not today. Not ever.

Unease coils tighter in my belly, the possibilities of what Sari might concoct sending shivers down my spine. She hasn't abandoned her dark designs; that much is clear. And those so-called friends of hers, the cackling crones who echo her madness—they're surely huddled together this very moment, concocting something vile.

I stop at the window, staring out into the darkening sky, the fading light mirroring the dimming of my peace of mind. What revenge is she plotting? What horrid scheme are they stitching together in the shadows?

A sigh escapes my lips as I turn away from the glass, the chill of the evening seeping through the pane. The thought of Sari's retribution hangs over me like a specter, invisible yet palpable. Whatever it is, I know one thing for certain—it's not cast off. It's brewing, bubbling under the surface, waiting for the right moment to erupt.

Walking to the fireplace, I pick up a frame that's face down on the mantel. I brush my fingers against the photo of Wilde and me, the memory stinging fresh like a wound that refuses to heal. Wilde's death was a tragedy, and we mourned.

Goddess, did we mourn.

Even after all the bad things that happened these past few months, his absence is a hollow ache that throbs with every beat of my heart.

A mate dying should hit you hard—I know it's supposed to—but reality isn't some cinematic arc where grief can just be neatly resolved or undone.

"Maybe we should cancel the party," I say to myself, my voice barely loud enough to carry over the silence that has settled around me. It hangs there, like a fragile bubble ready to burst.

That was something I said to Sari as well, but she simply snorted and brushed me off. Her opinion is that it won't be weird to have a huge BDSM party mere weeks after someone in the community died, and I wonder how it could *not* be weird. But there are larger concerns—our community could use something that will let them have fun, and our parties always lead to that.

But it's just so dour around town and I don't want to ruin Rafe's birthday because we didn't take him into account.

I don't see how in any universe everything would be better by the time the party happens. The thought itself feels like an insult to Wilde's memory, a mockery of the loss we're still nursing. Yet Sari seems hell-bent on this path, convinced that spending time with her mate amidst a crowd will somehow ease the pain.

That's when I tried to tell her how on guard everyone will be. Wilde's accident still seems unreal in this place where the amazing happens all day every day. I've noticed even the gear-heads have slowed down their antics since someone who shouldn't have been able to die was in a fatal car wreck.

Of course, clones and droids alike are watching their mates like hawks and neither I nor Rafe are exempt from that overprotectiveness.

Sari said it would be fine and we'd all hop from place to place, visiting and doing what people always do to prep for our parties.

Hide-and-seek, secret rendezvous, and all the typical prank war stuff would cheer people up, in her opinion.

"Seriously?" My eyebrows arch in disbelief. *"You think Taurus is going to let me out of his sight in that kind of chaos? And Talia—she's got her claws out for anyone who even glances at her new mate."* I shuddered at the thought of the potential bloodshed.

Her snarky replies are a distant echo as I picture the scenario unfold —a grotesque masquerade of forced merriment, while shadows lurk beneath our feet. I finally relented, knowing full well I'd rather face the wrath of a party gone sideways than the cold, creeping dread of what Sari might do in her desperation.

The thought of the upcoming social disaster doesn't sit well, but it's a risk I'll have to take.

Better the devil you can see, I suppose, than the one plotting your downfall behind closed doors.

My fingers tremble slightly as I fumble with the buttons on my blouse while I work to calm my frayed nerves. The fabric feels heavy, tainted by the weight of our conversation, and I'm desperate to shed it like a second skin. Clothes pool around my ankles, and I step out of the heap, feeling lighter, almost unburdened.

The cool air brushes against my bare skin, a welcome contrast to the stifling atmosphere that had clung to me since the meeting. I yank one of Taurus's shirts from the hook behind the door, the familiar scent of him—a mix of pine and something indefinably wild—wrapping around me like an embrace. I slip into it, finding comfort in the way it hangs loose and long on my frame.

I can't let her consume every moment, every thought.

My resolve hardens; I need something, anything, to divert this torrent of frustration before it consumes me entirely. The last thing

I want is for Taurus to come home to this storm cloud hanging over us.

Glass clinks as I pour myself a drink, the amber liquid promising a temporary reprieve. Drink in hand, I summon the binder with a flick of my wrist, the magic pulling it through the space between where it lays in my closet at the Maison to here, now, landing with a soft thud on the bed.

The binder opens with a whisper, and I flip through the pages, each one a meticulously organized parade of outfits. Skimming past corsets, masks, and feathers, I search for inspiration, for some spark that might ignite a sense of anticipation for the party rather than dread.

At least this won't make me want to stab myself in the eye balls.

Outfits blur together, sequins and silk vying for attention, but it's all just background noise to the cacophony in my head. Still, I force myself to focus on the task, to drown out the echoes of Sari's words with the quiet rustle of pages turning under my fingertips.

It's a small victory, but it's mine.

Flipping through the binder, I can't help but let out a sigh. It couldn't hurt to lose myself in this mini-universe of fabric and fantasy, even if just for an hour or two. The pages fan out before me, each tab a gateway to memories of wild nights and the warm buzz of laughter.

I linger on a page, fingertips grazing over the glossy photo of a crimson corset paired with a raven-feathered mask. Rafe really outdid himself with this system. After a few parties where we'd dug through piles of costumes like scavengers at a feast, he came up with a brilliant plan. We would sort, catalog, and store our entire myriad of costumes and accessories in tabbed binders.

Hex built the basement vault. Then he and Rafe spent six weeks making the seven binders full of items. They annotated outfits with accessories, locations, hair accessories, and shoes. Everything is cross-referenced and organized down to the last sequin.

Our house is an icon of well-oiled cooperation and support.

As my fingers trace the edge of another costume's page—a latex ensemble that could make a succubus blush—I hear the familiar sound of Taurus's presence. I don't need to look up to know he's here; there's an energy shift in the room that heralds his arrival every time.

But I turn my head anyway, catching him as he walks out of our closet, his movements silent yet commanding. The tiny bird tattooed on his chest catches the light from the chandelier, its metallic sheen alive against his skin, feathers practically rustling as if caught in an imperceptible breeze.

For a moment, I'm lost in the sight of him, the chaos of my earlier confrontation with Sari fading into the background. It's just Taurus and me, and the promise of distraction within these pages.

He crosses the room, each step a silent assertion of his presence that commands my undivided attention. The sight of him—so familiar yet so capable of leaving me momentarily breathless—sometimes makes me stop in place, even now.

The small, inked bird seems to take flight across the expanse of his chest, its wings subtly shifting with the play of light and shadow as he moves closer. Taurus's tattoo is not just a mark on his skin; it's a part of him, an emblem of something both wild and intimate that we share.

"What's in the binder, baby?" His voice is low, the words rolling out like smooth pebbles in a velvet drawl. The tattoo turns its head towards me, as if curious about my answer, and I smile, finding myself drawn into the comforting orbit of his aura.

The pages of the binder flutter under my fingertips as I flip through the catalog of memories and materials, each costume a story in itself. "I'm looking for clothes for the party," I say, my voice trailing off. The enormity of my collection is a reminder of past revelries, a treasure trove hidden away and seldom acknowledged for its vastness.

As Taurus prowls closer, a living embodiment of strength and assurance, my focus falters. The book, once an escape, now pales compared to the allure of his approach. His presence is magnetic, pulling my attention away from the task at hand.

"Party's still on? Good for him." His voice ripples through the room, a low rumble that seems to vibrate along my skin. As he speaks, his scent, wild and familiar, envelops me, filling the space between us with an intoxicating warmth. He climbs up on the bed, his movements deliberate and fluid—a predator in his element, graceful even in the confines of our shared sanctuary.

I nod, the motion an involuntary response to his question rather than a conscious decision. My tongue darts out, tracing the curve of my lips in anticipation, as if preparing for some wordless conversation we're about to engage in. The binder, thick with the weight of fabric and fantasy, slips from my grasp like it's been waiting for permission to abandon its post. It thuds against the carpeted floor, pages splayed open to endless possibilities now ignored.

He grins wickedly, the expression dancing across his features as if he's privy to an inside joke only he understands. But I'm quickly learning the punchline is shared between us, unspoken yet mutually comprehended. This man, Taurus, with his predatory grace and tattoo that seems alive under the play of light, doesn't need words to articulate his intentions.

Okay, this kind of distraction I can deal with.

The chaos of earlier, the tug-of-war with Sari, all of it fades into the background. Right here, right now, there's no guilt, no quests, no resentment—just the two of us, and the promise of what's to come.

The Blade and The Artist Contemplate The Party

RAFE

I lie back and let her pace, drinking in the sight of her like it's my last meal, and she's the feast. She's completely naked, spinning a blade in one hand like it's an extension of her mood—beautiful, dangerous, and impossible to ignore. Every step she takes radiates heat and tension, both of which I soak up like the warm summer sun. Talia is so full of vibrant, violent emotions when we're alone; it's hard to reconcile with the cool, intelligent predator she portrays in public sometimes.

But this is one of the moments I live for: her, raw and real, stalking the room like a restless predator, while I sketch her with the lazy precision of someone who knows he'll never quite capture the lightning he loves.

She's trying to figure out what claiming me means, and what it looks like walking into a party knowing you might be on the menu if it comes out. No one else knows besides our families—it's not public, not official. The truth is just between us, and that gnaws at her because it creates a weak spot.

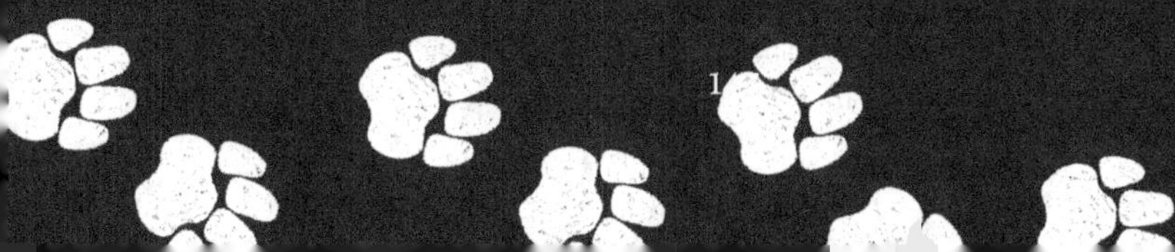

1

"We claimed one another, but no one knows," she mutters, and I feel the ache in it. The way it lands like a weight between us. "I'd prefer they did so it won't be a *thing*, but I also know why we can't tell them yet."

"I know, pet," I reply, voice low and steady. "And I appreciate you allowing that time after the blogger's death for things to settle down in the community."

Flicking my wrist, I let the pencil do its thing. She comes to life on the page: the precise angle of her spine as she twists, the controlled chaos of her hair, the flicker of metal as she spins that blade with practiced ease. She's fury incarnate in bare skin and muscle and grit.

"The party is for me and we can't cancel it," I say, as if that explains anything. "Bad timing all around, but no one else seems to care about that. You're invited," I add around the second pencil I've stuck between my teeth. I say it like it's a joke, but it's not.

It's a social powder keg, and apparently, I'm the only one holding a match and shouting 'don't'.

"Taurus will go with Deli. I'll look stupid."

A blade whistles through the air and embeds into the bedpost, not an inch from my ear. The old me would've flinched. Hell, the old me might've screamed. But that was before her. Now, it barely earns a raised eyebrow.

"I doubt that," I murmur, still sketching. "You can hang out with me; I might need a bodyguard."

She snorts. "I have a small socialization problem."

I pause, lift my head just enough to catch her eye, and deadpan, "I can't imagine why you think so."

She eyes the embedded blade, then starts twirling another, almost absentmindedly. Nervous energy coils around her like a storm cloud. I love that about her—the way she funnels discomfort into movement, the way her fingers speak even when her mouth doesn't. "Don't be an ass."

A new image blooms in my mind, vivid and ridiculous: me, lounging like a well-fed cat in velvet; her, in full death gear, glaring down anyone who so much as looks our way. The contrast is delicious. I send it to her without a word.

Her lips twitch. "So you want me to hang out with you? I don't want to assume. I mean, I don't look like the others at this damn thing in that pic."

The honesty in her voice pulls me upright. I set the pad down, my fingers smudged in charcoal, and meet her gaze. "You're a perfect contrast to me, love. Nothing wrong with that picture, except maybe you're standing way too far away from me."

She smiles—just a little, but it's the kind of smile that makes me feel like I've won something rare. She sends the second blade flying —it hits the first with a musical ring, like twin tuning forks vibrating with tension. "If you want me to, I'll go."

My mind snaps back to the vision, only now she's sprawled across my lap, the same glare in her eyes, but possessive, defiant, even. It shows that I'm hers. I push it towards her and grin. "That's much better," I say, reaching for a fresh sheet. "I'll let you help paint me into the latex."

She makes a face. "Is that what I'm supposed to wear? Hell, I don't even know what one wears to that kind of party."

"Leather, feathers, latex, fishnet—anything can be a fetish, baby."

"Since that covers most of my daily wardrobe, I think I'm good."

I grin. "The cat's wearing the better part of two jars of liquid latex, some leather, and not much else, I think."

She groans. "Christ, the bird will have his feathers *all* over her."

I shrug because that doesn't bother me. "I've seen the picture. We won't see them much, I think."

Her gaze darkens, and she saunters closer, all sin and shadows, flashing a grin that promises danger and delight. "Baby, if I do it right, you wouldn't notice them if they were sitting on your lap."

Gods, I love her.

"I like the sound of that."

"I'll think of something, and it won't be subtle. You have trouble with that. Maybe blood body paint?"

I make a show of looking scandalized. "That would only draw drooling hordes and cramp your body guarding gig."

"Hordes?" She arches an eyebrow, intrigued for half a second, then shrugs. "Eh. Not if it interferes with my job, alas."

"Hell, yes, hordes. I would get lost in a sea of chits trying to remove my pants with their sodding teeth."

Okay, so maybe a dramatic exaggeration. But the way her eyes slit and her smile curves—yeah, she's picturing it. She sends the image right back: blood-drenched females, rabid-eyed, crawling toward me like I'm dessert. I bark out a laugh. Only Talia would think that's the appropriate reaction at a social event.

"That's not the besssst idea for their health."

"There are two chits I want to keep a distance from, so it's good you're going to be there," I add, serious now.

She stops, narrowing her eyes. "Who? I need them on my list."

"Heather. Tamara. Amanda. All of them hit on every clone and droid that moves, and my girl kept me away from them in groups. But Amanda's the worst, given her connection to Constantine."

She slides into my space, her skin brushing mine, warmth grounding me. "Deli hooking up with him puts you in Amanda's sights?"

"Think so. Amanda was kind of... involved with Alistair too, maybe. She got hurt—not like us, but still. I think she's trying to fill a void."

"And now she sees you as a replacement for something she lost." Her voice is steel under silk.

I nod. "Probably. But what I told you before was true—I never move fast. I'm not in the market to be anyone's emotional bandage."

Her legs straddle mine now, her hands on my shoulders, grounding both of us. "Why me?" she asks, voice low and thoughtful. "Why did you move fast with me?"

I stare up at her, and everything that ever made sense slips into place. "Because I trusted you," I say simply. "You weren't looking to use me to patch a hole. You didn't want a distraction. You wanted me. For me. That's... never happened before—not really."

She's quiet for a moment, processing. I love this about her—how she doesn't rush the answer, doesn't pretend she already knows everything. She listens. She thinks. "I'm not large on conquests or headboard notches, no," she finally murmurs.

"That's why you intrigued me. Strong chits always do. But you—there's fire under your scars. You know your own sharp edges and don't apologize for them."

Her eyes glint. "I love you, and I'll keep you away from uncomfortable situations, even if it ends bloody. Not just at this shindig, either."

That nearly undoes me.

"That, my love, is bloody perfect."

She leans forward, kissing me like she means it—like she's sealing a vow with her mouth. Her warmth floods into me, and for a second, the world disappears. Just her lips, her breath, her skin, and me, anchoring in it.

Eventually, I grin against her mouth. "How about we get some clothes on and find something to eat? I think the outfit picking is going to take it out of us. I have these binders, you see..."

She laughs, a real, full laugh, and it vibrates through me.

This is what home feels like, I think. Not a place, but a person. A blade-spinning, chaos-making, kiss-stealing person who owns me without trying.

The pencils roll from my lap and clatter to the floor. I don't reach for them. Not yet.

She kisses me again, deeper this time, and I let myself fall forward into her heat, her chaos, her gravity. The storm is already here, and I'm not trying to outrun it. I've already found the eye.

It's her.

And gods help anyone who tries to pull me out of it.

The Cat Talks Clothing

DELILAH

"That was one hell of a 'welcome home' present," I murmur as my tail coils delicately around him, our bodies entwined in the quiet intimacy of the moment. The Beast, sated and tender, relaxes against me while my form melts unwaveringly into his strong embrace.

A low, rumbling chuckle escapes him as he murmurs, "No more so than the wee one reaching out and touching us. She's a powerful mite. She's going to be like her mum." His voice carries equal parts amusement and awe.

I return his smile with a soft, affectionate rub of my cheek against the warmth of his chest. "Sure is."

For a moment the air thickens as he hesitates, his gaze searching mine for understanding. "I know it didn't go well today at the gnome's house. You blocked everyone from the details. You kept quiet about the specifics. Talia said it worried Rafe."

A long sigh escapes me, the memory of fleeting bliss overshadowed

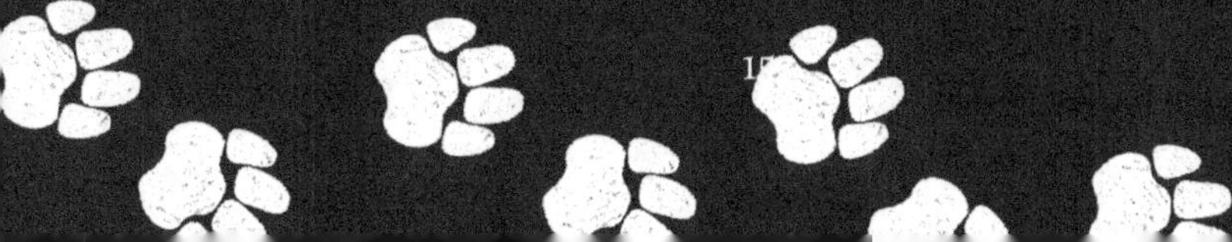

by the inevitable spill of darker moments. "It did not," I confess, my tone heavy with the residue of heartache.

"Tell me," he implores, his voice a blend of concern and gentle insistence.

Closing my eyes to steady the torrent of memories, I try to compress three agonizing hours into a few simple words. "Sari spent the entire time explaining why she needs this, why she wants to do it, and why I'm awful for not helping. Every word tumbled out, steeped in her own insecurities, yet I'm painted as the villain for choosing to sit this one out. I've made my peace as best as I can, but I still cradle my pain like anyone who's lost someone dearly. I simply cannot allow her to tear open my raw, healing wound and douse it in gasoline. That makes me seem selfish, self-centered—just another accusation."

His muscles visibly tighten as he fights the swell of anger that threatens to burst forth. "I see." His voice softens further, "Can I ask you something somewhat related?"

"Why not?" I reply, a spark of intrigue mingling with my concern.

He continues, "The other day when she lashed out at you, you told her that Wilde was never really yours, that Victor was never truly yours, and even that Rafe wasn't entirely yours—at least, not all yours, right?"

I offer a relaxed shrug, embracing the truth in his words. "It's true. I've always shared people. It's not meant to demean anyone—I just can't claim every part of who they are. I don't love Rafe any less, nor Victor."

His eyes narrow as he pauses, then adds, "What about me?" He stops, tilting his head as confusion mingles with tenderness. "Wait —instead of answering, let me explain something: I AM yours. Talia and I, we're the best of friends, lovers, entwined in every possible way—but it's never been like what we share. That doesn't take anything away from her; it's simply different. I needed you to know that."

A soft smile spreads across my face as I gently stroke his rugged features. "It always felt as if, in some subtle way, even a little, you were mine. I would never dare to ask you for more."

"Since the gnome seems intent on making you feel like every fragment of you is flawed, I wanted to remind you of something that's true." His sincerity radiates, grounding us in this tender interlude.

I pull him even closer, arms wrapping around his strong frame with a fierce protectiveness mingled with adoration. My heart aches with both love and an impending need to untangle the lingering bonds of my past so I can offer him something no one else ever has —complete, unreserved unity. With Wilde's death, we've grown closer, edging out the chaos of conflict... or at least, that's how it felt once upon a time.

Then he shifts the conversation, his tone lightening again. "Now, love, what's all this about an outfit for that damn fetish thing you're still madly obsessed with?"

A laughing warmth fills me as I rip a glance his way. "I think I've already picked out my outfit. You want to see?"

"Probably best—so I can figure out how to drag you out of it every couple of hours."

I snort playfully and raise my hand; from the scattered clutter on the floor, a well-worn binder ascends to my palm. Its pages flutter until settling on the right picture. "Here we go."

He blinks in surprise, his mouth momentarily caught in the wonder of it, before finding his voice to cough. "You wear that, and you won't emerge from your room to meet and greet anyone, got it?"

My smile turns wicked with mischief. "No need to worry about extracting me from it, though."

Darkness pools in his eyes as he shifts to another matter. "Is the goddess invited to this? What about Damien and Theodora?"

"The invitation was community-wide—everyone is welcome."

"That might be a kicker. They don't come out as often as we'd like."

I grin broadly. "Damien in fetish gear—now that's a picture worth a thousand laughs."

His tone turns teasing as he muses, "Hell, I don't know. For all I know, he might even consider a suit and tie to be his version of fetish gear." With a contemplative frown, he asks, "What's Sampson going as?"

Flipping the binder open, I reveal his chosen attire with a flourish. "He's gearing up with leather on the bottom, fishnet on the top to highlight his piercings, his hair wild and tangled with leather thongs, and of course, a collar—although I need to sift through the box for the perfect one. We tossed out a whole bunch last month."

"That sounds incredibly hot," he remarks, his frown softening into a giggle before he clears his throat. "You really threw out a lot after they...?"

"Yep," I nod succinctly. "Every single thing they touched was banished—I didn't want any reminders cluttering the house."

"I suppose that'll delight the gnome. And who knows, maybe even that bloody writer if she's finally done with her nonsense."

My breath catches as I fix my gaze on the open page, trying to hold in the cyclone of emotions stirring inside me. He's gone—truly gone. There's no need to fret over collars at this party because his memory is etched in our silence. And *Jesus Christ*, shouldn't she know that's precisely why you shouldn't attempt to *resurrect* him?! Okay—deep breath—I remind myself to laugh it off, to make light of this macabre theme and let it dissolve into the humor of a deli. Why let this grim motif linger? Ah yes, because sometimes I'm an absolute fucking idiot.

After a moment's attempt to regain control, I shake my head. "I find it doubtful on all counts. First, she won't even bother with him because she'll be too busy cackling with her cronies or pouting in the corner. Second, even if he were back, Wilde never really wanted Rafe unless jealousy was simmering. And third—this one's the kicker—after this brush with death, I don't think either of us will ever look kindly on that tree branch again, if ever. So, why are you worrying?"

His sigh is soft, the weight of his care evident. "I'm thinking about Talia. I must be sure she likes that getup, and while I'm watching you, no one else will be paying attention to her. If Sampson struts out looking like that? He'll be swarmed all damn evening."

"I'm sure he'll stay glued to her," I assure him with a playful shrug. "You don't know him as well as you think. Yes, he flirts and exchanges polite pleasantries, but he's not nearly as outgoing as he used to be. And besides, you haven't been to these big parties before—people tend to huddle into little groups, and it won't be an issue."

"The things I do for you," he sighs, his tone a blend of exasperation and fond affection.

"You big blowhard. You'll have your fun even if disaster strikes, and at worst, you can lounge and growl around me wearing nothing but that dazzling mark emblazoned across your chest."

His eyes light up mischievously as the idea takes hold. "Only those bloody stripes of latex and leather—and that enormous feather! Now I must decide what I'll be wearing."

"You'll look hot no matter what, especially if you're draped in me," I tease with a sultry smile.

He ponders for a moment before half-jokingly suggesting, "Maybe I'll just go naked—save an earring and an irritating little bird as a statement."

I narrow my eyes, playfully stern. "Nuh-uh, buster. I'm not letting those drooling simpletons get a peep at you or your idiot self. Mine's already covered, so yours will be too. I'd end up wreaking havoc before the night's over and then have to punish myself—and I do plenty without you."

He chuckles, preening slightly as his pride swells. Then, with a playful growl, he exclaims, "Oh, great! Now you've crowned that pernicious little git, and he'll never let me forget it."

"Hmmmph. They need not have their eyes on us anyway," I murmur lowly as I run my fingers over the delicate feathers of the bird, which preens and coos as if caught up in our private moment

A tender teasing note colors his voice as he says, "I'm feeling all kinds of kindly because you're promising to eviscerate chits for me. It's so bloody cute." He tweaks his nose affectionately and pulls me in closer, prompting a mock glare in return.

"I'm not cute. I'm mean, snarly, and downright shred-y," I snap back, a playful fire in my tone.

"Hell, yes—you are to the sheep of the world. But to me, you're as soft and tender as it gets. It's exactly the same for me," he counters warmly.

I lean in and kiss him deeply. "I love the lion and the lamb in you."

He grumbles a bit but returns the kiss with equal passion. "Only you get away with saying that. Anyone else would... well, they'd be history."

"Even Rafe? He'd look all hot and bothered." I tease.

His eyes narrow mischievously. "To sleep with you, woman—no one else matters. I was speaking for the goddess. It's been a good night despite a shitty day, and we've got plans to shape tomorrow."

A soft yawn escapes me as I curl up contentedly against him. "Okay, baby." My sigh mingles with sleep, the moment wrapping us in calm intimacy.

"Sleep, my love," he whispers gently, his voice like a promise. "Everything will look better in the morning."

I smirk defiantly as I murmur, "Now you jinxed it."

The Cat Takes A Walk

Minx-

I hate to—no. Bloody hell.

Talia forgot we booked a gig. I'm not happy. Bonus is, neither is she. She's right fond of being with your mate. We can't wiggle out of this bloody job, and it makes me need to murder someone.

Luckily for me, that is my job.

We'll be back to you both late this evening, so if you let Sampson know, Talia would be much obliged.

Gotta get moving on this if we ever want to get home.
~Taurus (aka the Hunka of Burning Clone)

I wrinkle my nose, grumpy beyond words that he won't be home until late.

Dammit.

The room around me feels suddenly too quiet, the dim lighting casting long shadows across the furniture. It's one of those silences that creeps into the bones, making you feel as though the world itself has paused, holding its breath. My sigh echoes softly as I turn to Aradia, her eyes glinting with curiosity and a hint of mischief. "Well, love, it looks like we're on our own for the evening. Should we go home and check on the party prep since it's coming in the next week, or should we go find the lazy bones or..."

A shrill tone breaks the silence, and I glance at the Caller ID on the phone. *Fucking Sari.*

I am not going over there to get lambasted again and I am not taking part in this harebrained horseshit they have planned. The thought fills me with resentment, and I stalk into the closet, my peaceful mood shattered. The closet is cramped and filled with the scent of leather and old wood, a sanctuary now tainted by frustration. I've been following her blog, where despite her protests, she seems to go on half-baked quests from a Tolkien novel to be worthy and blah-blah-blah with her coven of cu-next-Tuesdays.

In this moment of frustration, I remember the times when Sari's antics were amusing, even entertaining. Those were the days when her impulsive nature led us on adventures that often ended in laughter and the sharing of stories over cups of warm tea. But now, it seems, she has taken a turn for the erratic, her quests becoming more like follies, dragging others into her whirlpool of absurdity. It makes me want to heave and kill things and then heave again.

Being preggo sucks, if you weren't clear on that.

The hormones swirl within me, a storm of emotions that I'm not quite used to navigating. My mind flickers back to a time when I could handle such annoyances with grace, but now, everything feels magnified, intensified.

Aradia rumbles a deep, resonant growl, feeling my anger through our bond, and I nod at her. "Alright, sugar, let's go find some bad people and make them wish they weren't. I'm getting hungry." There's a comfort in knowing she understands, a shared consciousness that allows us to move as one, our intentions aligned.

As we prepare to leave, the memories of past escapades with Taurus and Talia flood my mind. Nights spent under the stars, sharing stories, and planning futures that seemed so certain. Now, with Taurus away on business, the world feels a shade darker. But there's something freeing about the night, a promise of adventure and the unknown. Laying my hand on her head, I close my eyes, feeling the familiar warmth of our connection as we disapparate, searching for trouble in all the right places. The world blurs around us, the air crackling with energy as we slip into the shadows, ready to embrace the night.

Here we go...

THE CITY UNFOLDS beneath us like a tapestry of lights and whispers, a place teeming with secrets and stories waiting to be uncovered. We wander through the alleys and hidden corners, each step guided by an unspoken understanding. The streets are alive with the hum of night, the distant laughter of revelers mingling with the soft rustle of leaves in the breeze. It's a world that never truly sleeps, and tonight, it feels like our playground.

Leaving The Rift for a little while probably isn't the worst thing in the world for me—perspective is good.

Our first stop is a small, dimly lit bar tucked away in a forgotten corner of the city. The kind of place where time seems to stand still, where the ghosts of stories of the past linger in the air. As we step inside, the air is thick with the scent of smoke and old whiskey, a comforting embrace that wraps around us like an old friend. The patrons glance up, their faces reflecting a mix of curiosity and wariness, but Aradia isn't visible to them, so they don't freak out. I nod to the bartender, a grizzled old man with a twinkle in his eye, and settle into a corner booth.

It's probably not a great plan to come to a location so close to my actual home town, but occasionally, I feel the need to return to my roots. As long as I stay far away from the Hollow, it shouldn't be a problem. Clea won't find me simply because I show up in my former state, right?

The conversations around us ebb and flow, a symphony of voices that create a tapestry of human experience. We listen, picking up threads of stories, tales of heartbreak and hope, of dreams lost and found. It's in these moments that I find a sense of peace, a reminder that we're all just trying to find our way in this chaotic world. The bartender slides a drink my way—a concoction of ginger and lime that smells good—and I sip it slowly, savoring the sharp tang on my tongue.

I'm not sure how he knew, but I'd peg him for someone with some kind of special ability.

Aradia nudges me, her eyes fixed on a group of men gathered at the far end of the bar. They're loud and boisterous, their laughter echoing off the walls, but there's an undercurrent of something darker. I can feel the tension in the air, the way their words drip with malice and intent. It's the kind of trouble we were looking for, and I can feel my pulse quicken in anticipation.

We rise, making our way over to them, our presence casting a shadow over their mirth. They glance up, surprise flickering in their eyes as they take in the sight of me. "Evening, gentlemen," I say, my voice smooth and calm, a stark contrast to the storm brewing inside me. "Mind if I join you?"

There's a beat of silence, and then one of them, a burly man with a tattoo snaking up his neck, gestures to the empty seats. "Suit yourselves," he mutters, his eyes narrowing as he studies us. Aradia settles beside me, her presence a silent threat, and I lean back, taking in the scene before us.

The conversation resumes, a disjointed mix of bravado and bravura, but I listen closely, picking up on the threads that connect them. It doesn't take long to piece together their story—a plan to rob a local business, a place owned by a family barely scraping by. The injustice of it stirs something within me, a fire that burns bright and fierce.

Putting a stop to people who need to be punished is more than I ever knew before meeting Taurus.

I exchange a glance with Aradia, and she nods her big furry head, understanding my intent without the need for words. We've done this dance before, played the roles of justice and retribution in a world that often turns a blind eye. With a graceful motion, I lean forward, capturing their attention with a single look. "You know," I begin, my voice as smooth as silk, "there are better ways to make a living than what you've chosen."

The man with the tattoo sneers, his bravado masking the flicker of uncertainty in his eyes. "What's it to you?" he challenges, but I can sense the wavering resolve beneath his words.

"It's everything to me," I reply, my gaze steady and unyielding. "People like you give people like me a reason to exist." The tension in the air is palpable, a tangible force that binds us together in this moment. I can feel the weight of their decisions, the way their paths have led them to this point, and I find myself wanting more than just justice.

I want change, a shift in the way men like them see the world and their place in it.

Aradia growls softly, her eyes fixed on the man with the tattoo, and I know she senses the shift as well. "Perhaps," I suggest, my tone softening, "we could offer you an alternative. A chance to walk away from this and start anew."

There's a moment of hesitation, a flicker of something akin to hope in their eyes, and I seize the opportunity, leaning forward with an intensity that brooks no argument. "Consider it, gentlemen. The world is full of choices, and tonight, you have the power to make the right one."

Silence stretches between us, a fragile thread that holds the potential for transformation. I can feel the weight of their decision hanging in the air, a delicate balance that could tip either way. And then, slowly, the man with the tattoo nods, his gaze dropping to the table as if in surrender. "Alright," he mutters, his voice barely audible, "we'll think about it."

Relief washes over me like a gentle wave, unraveling the knots of tension within. I nod, acknowledging their tentative commitment to change—a small victory that feels monumental in this world where such moments are scarce.

Of course, now I have to come back and follow up on his words, but we shall see.

Aradia and I rise together, leaving them behind to contemplate their choices. As we step into the cool embrace of the night air, hope swells within me, reminiscent of pockets of light we create amidst shadows. The breeze whispers through the desolate alleyways, carrying the faint scent of jasmine from a nearby garden—a fragrant reminder that beauty endures even in unlikely places.

As we walk, I turn to my familiar, an old friend whose presence is as familiar as my own shadow. "It's weird to think about how much I've changed over this past year." I say, breaking the comfortable silence. She looks at me expectantly and I chuckle. "Yeah, I know it's inevitable that people change."

I recall those youthful days when the world felt like an unexplored map, each corner a mystery waiting to be unraveled. "Back then, I was restless," I muse. "Eager to grow up, to get out of the Hollow, and leave my mark on the world. Now that feels childish and naive. The world—or more accurately people in it, have left their mark on me."

We pause at a familiar intersection, where the cobblestone street meets the edge of a small park. The silhouettes of ancient trees stand like sentinels, their branches swaying gently in the night air. "I feel old, even for my thirties, when I say it used to be safer to walk around like this when you weren't a witch and a giant tiger. But it's true... even in the smaller cities and towns."

Aradia gives me a look that I think is the tiger version of an eye roll and I hold up my hands in defeat. "Okay, okay. I'm being weirdly nostalgic and shit. I get it. I just... I thought moving to The Rift would solve all my stupid problems, not make it so much worse."

As we resume our walk, I reflect on the truth of my words. As adults, we find ourselves writing new chapters in life, our narratives shaped by experiences both bitter and sweet. It's hard to reconcile how your outlook changes with time.

The streets are empty, a silent witness to the passage of time. Street-lights cast elongated shadows, creating a patchwork of light and dark that mirrors the duality of change itself. I think of the people I've met along the way, each encounter leaving an indelible mark on our souls.

"Sometimes, I wonder how many other people have the kind of gifts I do. I even wonder if people have the gifts the clones do. How many of them are living on this side of our portal, do you think?" I ask, my voice tinged with curiosity.

My tiger doesn't answer even though she sort of can, so I let my question float through the air. If I'm possible, and the others are possible... so are a lot more things than just what I've seen in The Rift. It has to be bigger, and I'm very curious about how I can go about finding out.

Maybe that's something I can use the assholes at the Company for without their knowledge?

We turn down a side street, the pavement glistening under the soft light of the moon. Here, the houses stand in silent rows, their windows like eyes gazing out at the ever-changing world. I wonder about the lives unfolding behind those walls, each one a unique story in the tapestry of existence.

"Do you think any of these people know what's *really* out there?" I ask, my voice barely above a whisper. "I mean, besides magic or shifting or clones... just the dangers that lurk in shadows they don't even think to check for? I guess that's why superheroes are such a big draw—someone who will save us makes life a little easier to bear."

Aradia snorts, tossing her big head and I know it means she thinks I'm being ridiculous. I might be; pregnancy changes everyone because of the hormones, I've read. I'm certainly being flooded with them and maybe it's making me murderous *and* maudlin.

The night deepens, the sky a canvas painted with stars, and I find solace in the rhythm of our footsteps. They echo the passage of time, a reminder that while change may be constant, it is not something to be feared. Instead, it is an opportunity—a chance to redefine ourselves, to forge new paths, and to embrace the unknown with open hearts.

Eventually, we find ourselves back where we began, standing at the edge of the park. The air is still, the world bathed in a serene tranquility that belies the chaos of the day. I take a deep breath, savoring the coolness, the sense of continuity that this place offers.

"Well," I say, turning to my friend with a smile, "we didn't kill anyone, but it's probably time to get back and see if the bird is home. He'll freak out that we're still gone. He wouldn't know how late we slept today so we had a late start."

And then I can talk to someone who isn't a damn tiger people can't see—I won't look nearly as crazy.

The Blade Is A Stubborn Woman

TALIA

I stagger, trying to breathe, through the long, dusky hallway. Every step sends a white-hot spike of pain through me, jarring my bruised ribs. Agony gnaws at my side, a rabid dog refusing to release its hold. Each tortured breath smashes against my lungs. I can't stop muttering curses—at my frailty, at my wounded pride, at every calamity the night dumped in my lap. My left hand clutches the torn flesh as if I could hold it closed through sheer force of will. My right drags a weather-beaten suitcase behind me, its wheels stuttering and protesting across the marble floor.

I could have left it for the morning, but it's a promise in physical form—symbols matter, damn them.

Outside, Taurus' low, exasperated roar still thunders in my ears. He'd offered help when I rolled that case to his sleek black car parked under the sickly amber glow of the lamppost. I'd made him regret the offer, snapping at him before flicking the blade his way, sending him off with vivid bruises blooming across his knuckles— bruises Deli's whispered coos will erase by dawn.

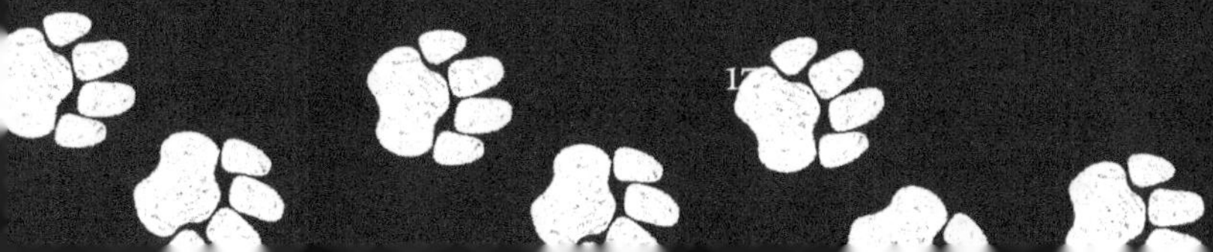

Because the moment I break, Taurus will storm in with his conjured cat at heel, swearing to protect me—just like he always swore he would when he met her. I refuse that fate. My knees quiver like saplings in high wind as I steer the suitcase toward the private patio entrance. My breath comes in shallow, jagged gulps. I'm fine.

Christ, this fucking ache. It's my fault, my mess to clean up. If I don't cry or black out, no one will ever need to know.

It's not that bad. Just because my knees are weak doesn't mean I need someone to coddle me. I'm a little pale and it's making me out of breath to roll this damned thing to the patio entrance to his room.

I'm fine.

At the wrought-iron French doors, I peer inside—no sign of the prone Picasso lounging in the shadows. Encouraged, I ease them open, sliding around the side so the rest of the house won't hear. If rumor of my injury reaches Queen Kitty's inner circle, they'd trade me for a barely chilled scotch without a blink. Loyalty here is currency, and I'm bankrupt. Better Rafe stay engrossed in the kitchen games with his family; I need solitude to pull myself upright.

The hidden closet awaits like a secret chapel. I yank it open—rows of hanging coats, stacks of shoes, and at the top, that brand-new bed he'd built for me days ago: carved dark wood, cushioned mattress piled high with pillows. My chest tightens; longing cuts sharper than any blade. There are miles to go before I sleep. Abandoning the hopeless thought of unpacking, I pivot toward salvation: the bathroom.

Shit. I can't lift this bastard onto a shelf or any perch so I can empty it, which meansI can't put the damn clothes away.

Abandoning the hopeless thought of unpacking, I pivot toward salvation: the bathroom. Each tentative step towards those other hidden doors makes my world reel. I fling the door open and warm circulated air greets me. With a mute hiss, I tear off my blood-soaked shirt. A brutal slash yawns from breast to waist, rims slick with darkening blood. Later, the lab-coats will regenerate my flesh.

For now, I gotta stop the bleeding.

I close the door behind me. There are too many predator ears in this house to do anything but tiptoe quietly. Stripping off the bloody shirt, I look at the long, vicious-looking gash running from my breasts to my abdomen.

Christ. I'll have to let the lab coats regenerate my flesh again. That hurts like a bitch if you're wondering.

Stepping into the shower's gentle spray, I let the scalding water and soap sting as they wash across the wound; my teeth grind together. When I reach for the towel, my fingers brush a black cotton hug faintly scented with jasmine and something earthy—Deli's signature 'Night Bloom' detergent, I realize, a private fragrance from the bots she loves.

Even here, the little miracles of this house overwhelm me: cabinets labeled with names, a fridge sectioned like a chemistry lab, laundry washed in bespoke potions, Taurus' single-malt beckoning from the dining-room bar, soft baroque music whispering from hidden speakers.

Theodora keeps an immaculate house for us , but this place runs like I'd imagine Buckingham Palace does.

My legs quake so hard I reach for the towel rack to steady myself. Vertigo spins the world into a funhouse blur. I blink and find my gaze trapped on a silk robe hanging beside the cabinet: jet-black with blood-red trim, my nickname emblazoned across the back in a jagged, punk-rock script, and a snarling scimitar arching beneath.

Buckingham fucking Palace, I goddamn swear.

It takes everything in me to stay upright and conscious, but I open the medicine cabinet, hoping to see first aid items in there. There's an actual small field medical kit in it, along with every toiletry a male or female could need. I shake my head in amazement and it gives me a head rush, so I put my hand on the towel rack. The world spins for a second again, but I keep it together.

The door crashes open. Rafe fills the frame, eyes wide. "I felt you trip the sensors," he exclaims, voice thick with worry, "but I had to scrub the kitchen so Leo wouldn't skin me alive. It was weird you didn't come in the front door." He strides forward, concern sharpening his features. "Something's off. What the sodding hell happened?"

Goddamn cat-sensors on the driveway—they know every arrival. Magickal perimeter or not, he knows it's me.

He drops to his knees and inspects the gash as though he graduated *summa cum laude* from med school. "You need a doctor. Why aren't you lying down? How did you even get here?"

I clamp my jaw against a scream. "Damn mating senses. I'm fine. It's a scratch. I don't need a doctor."

"No glossing over this with me. You need a bloody doctor."

I fling myself at him, defiance burning in my veins—then the edges of my vision fray. My knees give out. I reach for him, and everything goes black.

This isn't going to end well...

The Cat and the Bird Pet Interrupted

DELILAH

The front door creaks open, and the sound of his boots on the hardwood echoes down the hallway like war drums. Measured. Heavy. Deliberate. The kind of gait that says he's had a day—one of those endless ones that grind you down to the bone and still ask for more.

I look up from my perch on the edge of the bed, the covers half-pulled back, the room bathed in golden lamplight that flickers faintly like candlelight in a storm. He steps into the doorway like some weary titan returning from battle, clutching a bouquet of flowers so vibrant they look unreal, like something conjured by a magician. The scent hits me instantly—roses, freesia, something citrusy and sharp—and wraps around me, warm and dizzying.

In his other hand, he carries a bottle of aged scotch, the kind that costs more than my first car and smells like bonfires and bad decisions. I don't even need to ask how his day went. It's etched into the tight line of his jaw, the furrow of his brow, and the faint twitch at the corner of his mouth that he thinks I don't notice. But there's

"

something else under all that—contentment, maybe. Or relief. Like he's stepped across the threshold of safety. Like I'm the destination.

He doesn't say anything at first. Just sets the scotch gently on the nightstand and the flowers on the dresser like they're offerings to some domestic goddess, and then turns to me. His eyes roam over me, cataloging everything—my expression, the slump of my shoulders, the tension I'm doing a piss-poor job of hiding.

He sighs, and that deep, rumbling voice that I swear lives somewhere in my spine says, "Oi, my minx. Did you have a good evening?"

It should be a simple question. Polite, even. But it slices through me like a dull knife. I swallow hard and shake my head, pressing the heel of my palm into one eye, like maybe I can erase the whole night with pressure. "No," I say quietly. "But I don't want to dwell on that stunted little beast and her nonsense right now. I'd much rather be here. With you."

His eyebrows lift in surprise, just for a heartbeat. He's so rarely caught off guard, it stuns me every time it happens. That flicker of unguarded emotion across his features—it's like catching a glimpse of the stars through a stormcloud. Then he recovers, smoothing his expression like he's pulling a curtain over a window.

I exhale, long and slow, my body still humming with residual irritation and acid reflux. "I had Italians tonight. Spices are still kicking around in my gut like they're trying to throw a rave."

He chuckles, but it's laced with that knowing edge. "Italians? Again?" He crosses the room in a few strides and sinks down beside me, the bed creaking under his weight. His arms loop around my waist, anchoring me, and I melt into him instinctively. "I told you, pet. You've got to ease into international cuisine. Not everything agrees with you."

"They must've been Sicilian," I mutter into his chest, my voice muffled by the soft cotton of his shirt. "Angry ones. Spiteful little peppers with vendettas."

His laughter rolls through his chest, a warm vibration against my cheek. "Christ, I missed you."

I tip my head back and grin up at him, the tension starting to melt from my shoulders. "You did. And I was a bad girl who didn't listen."

"Mmm." He smirks with that cocky curve of his lips that always gets me into trouble. "I like it when you admit it."

I roll my eyes and nip playfully at his chin, catching the rough edge of his stubble between my teeth. He growls low in his throat, the sound curling around my spine like a caress. I feel his hand slide along my waist, fingers grazing the sliver of skin between my pajama top and the waistband of my shorts.

His eyes darken, heat flaring in them like banked embers suddenly fed oxygen. "You've got that look," he murmurs. "Like you're about to get yourself into mischief."

I shiver, the anticipation crackling under my skin. "You think you can handle me tonight?" I challenge, my voice soft but dangerous, laced with the same teasing edge that always drives him wild.

He doesn't answer with words. Just presses in closer, his body all heat and promise, his arousal a bold, insistent pressure against my lower back. His hand slides down my side, lingering at the curve of my hip before delivering a playful smack that makes me gasp.

"Oh, I can more than handle you," he growls, voice dropping low and rough. "But maybe we take our time tonight. Get you out of those clothes slowly. Proper and all."

The hunger between us is familiar and electric, a current that's run between us since the moment we met. But tonight, there's something else in the air. Something strange. A shift in pressure, like the static before a storm.

I lean into him, my breath hitching as he nuzzles the curve of my neck, his lips brushing over the pulse point there. "We've got all night," I whisper.

But the second the words leave my lips, something slams into my mind like a battering ram.

A rush of sensation—cold, frantic, metallic—surges through me. Not emotion. Not thought. Presence. Something wild and desperate, clawing at the edge of my consciousness, demanding entry. A psychic knock that rattles the hinges of my mental doors.

I jerk back, gasping, the blood draining from my face. My hands brace against his chest, pushing him back. "We have to go."

He stills. One heartbeat. Two. Then he curses, low and vicious. "Oh, for fuck's sake." But he's already moving, already on his feet. His expression hardens into something ruthless and focused, a general before a battle.

I'm still trying to catch my breath. Whatever just brushed up against my mind left behind icy fingers, wrapping around my ribs and squeezing. "It's bad," I whisper. "Worse than usual. It felt... torn. Ripped open. Like something bled through."

He pulls open the wardrobe, grabs the go-bag without even needing to check its contents. We've done this before. Too many times. We live in this balance between tenderness and chaos, between stolen nights and inevitable calls to arms.

I yank on jeans over my pajama shorts, fingers trembling. My mind's still reeling, echoes of that mental intrusion making my thoughts feel like a scrambled broadcast. "It wasn't a cry for help," I murmur. "It was a warning."

He's beside me again, his big, calloused hand closing over mine. "You're shaking."

"I'm fine." I lie with a smile that I hope sells it.

His eyes search mine. He doesn't believe me. Of course he doesn't. But he lets it slide for now. We both know the dance.

"I've got you," he says, and it's a promise. "No matter what we're walking into."

I nod, swallowing hard. I don't know what we're walking into. I don't even realize I'm this tense until my chest starts to burn. It's Rafe. The psychic echo settling behind my eyes is unmistakable.

His mind doesn't touch mine gently. It barrels in—wild, raw, splintered at the edges. Not like him at all. Rafe is meticulous with his magic, usually reserved to the point of annoyance. He doesn't call unless it's urgent.

And this? This isn't just urgent. It's desperate.

"It's Rafe," I whisper. "He's in trouble."

My husband freezes mid-motion, his hand still hovering near the bottle of scotch. "Are you sure?"

"I'm sure," I say, grabbing the charm-laced ring from my bedside and twisting it onto my finger. The metal warms immediately against my skin, responding to the rising tide of my magic. "He's calling me—psychically. Not subtle. He's practically screaming inside my skull."

"Where is he?"

"I don't know," I admit. "But he's not shielding, and he's not alone. It's... scattered. Something's wrong."

His lips flatten into a grim line. He's already crossing the room, heading for the wardrobe where we keep our gear. Not because we expect a fight—but because when Rafe's voice is ragged in my head like this, something usually follows.

I close my eyes and focus. Try to push past the static and agony to get a clearer lock on him. My fingers twitch against the familiar coolness of the ring, trying to ground myself in the present as I listen to the pull in my bones.

"Sunlight," I murmur. "Glass. Paint. He's at my house. In the sunroom. Rafe's studio."

"Why would he be at your place and not his?" my husband asks, already tugging on his jacket.

I shake my head. "I don't know. I just know we need to be there *now*."

He doesn't question it again. Just moves to me, one arm sliding firmly around my waist, the other hand closing around mine.

I take a breath and reach for the tether between worlds. It's second nature now—like slipping your fingers into a familiar glove. The sensation rises in my gut first, a crackling tug of static and magic, then lifts behind my sternum like wind catching a sail.

And then, with a whoosh of displaced air and a shimmer that bends the edges of reality, we disappear.

The Artist Uses The Cat-Signal

RAFE

oly hell in a handbasket, she's sodding out.

H Her body is limp in my arms like a marionette whose strings have been sharply clipped. The room is deathly silent, every shadow inching closer as if waiting to swallow us both. I can feel the slick of sweat and congealed blood on her uniform sleeve, warm and sticky against my skin. My heartbeat slams against my ribs like a war drum; my lungs scream for air while I carry her across the creaking floorboards. Every step echoes, a reminder that time is slipping away.

Thank Christ I hauled that bed inside yesterday—otherwise I'd be on my knees on this scratched hardwood, praying she doesn't slip through my fingers. I clear a path through the clutter of suitcases, discarded magazines, and half-empty takeout boxes. My eyes flick to the window where moonlight struggles through dusty glass, streaking the room with pale blue beams that land on her flushed cheek. Just another reminder of how quickly things can turn icy-cold when the blood stops moving.

I lower her gently onto the rumpled sheets, gingerly tucking a stray lock of her blond curls away from her face. The mattress dips beneath her weight, springs groaning in protest. Bile rises in my throat—memories of past failures and empty promises crash in— but I clamp my jaw shut and swallow it down.

I need to focus.

Leaning back, I gather my strength and close my eyes. In the hush of my mind I murmur, *~Night Bloom... I'm sorry to bother you, but the bird will riot if his mate dies. You understand, yes? ~*

My heart hammers as I wait, listening for that familiar pull at the edges of my consciousness, a flicker of emerald light brushing across my thoughts. The reply snaps into my skull like static, urgent and clipped.

~Don't faff about, woman. She's critical. ~

I blink and glance across the bed at Blade. She lies still, her dark curls matted with sweat, her shirt torn aside to reveal pale skin pooling bright drops of red. Anxiety carves deep creases into my brow. She stirs, forcing out a soft, ragged groan; her eyelashes flutter like wounded birds. It's the only thing that keeps me from falling apart.

"I'm fine," she whispers, voice cracked and distant. "Don't—don't freak out."

I grit my teeth. *Fine?* She's halfway to the underworld. I refuse to dignify that protest with an answer. Instead, I tap my foot against the floorboards, each thud a plea for my primary to show. My breathing moves in tandem with my racing pulse, building like a wave about to crash.

And then she's here—flickering into existence at the foot of the bed, a living embodiment of raw power. One moment the corner of the room is empty; the next, a reheaded figure stands draped in shadow until she steps forward to get a better look at the room. Her eyes burn with emerald fire, and concern knits her brow.

I don't wait for her to size up the situation; I seize her arm and yank her to the bedside. "She passed out cold," I blurt before she can ask. "I have no clue what happened—must've been during the fracas in the bathroom. But look at this wound." I tug open Blade's shirt further, revealing a jagged slash at her ribs, blood caked around the edges and seeping between her fingers. "It's... deep."

Behind me, I hear the faint whisper of her summoning spell; when I turn, her long red hair is alight with her magick. She blinks at the wound, expression unreadable, then lets her hair slip from her face. "You never shout unless someone's hurt, so I knew it was bad," Deli says flatly. In her hand, she conjures a battered leather travel bag—it appears out of thin air, landing on the old window seat with a soft thump.

The bag gapes open, revealing vials of iridescent liquids, cloth wrappings, a small carved mortar, and a dozen ungainly bone tools. She arranges everything with crisp precision, snapping lids and laying out items in neat rows. Three cinnamon–scented candles flicker to life beneath her fingertips; she strikes a match for a stick of jasmine incense and places it in a simple clay dish. The smoke curls skyward, sweet at first, then carrying an undertone of something bracing and bitter.

My primary hums under her breath, the sound low and steady, grinding roots and petals into a fine gray powder that drifts like powdered iron in the candlelight. I can't tear my eyes away from her movements.

Talia's head tilts to one side as she finally realizes what's going on. "Oh, shit. Deli." She squints, as if reading invisible runes shimmering in the air. "He's not...?"

My woman offers my new mate a knowing smile—sharp, half-mocking. "He'll be along. I told him to go stew a bit with the others before he came in so his energy wasn't as disruptive." She slides the small bowl she's filled with powder onto the bedside table, the porcelain clinking against chipped wood.

"You should've come to me first, or let Taurus get me," the kitty chides Talia, her voice low. "This one's bad—you knew it."

Blade's gaze softens fractionally. "Deli, block him out. Please. I don't want him to know."

My primary's emerald eyes flare as she turns her glare on me, silent thunder crackling in the air between us. Talia's gaze flicks between us, but I know she sees the reproach in every line of Deli's face. "I'll try," she sighs, voice suddenly tender as silk, "but I need to focus, and he'll feel it anyway. Now I must... touch the wound. It will hurt."

Tension crackles between the three of us like lightning, and I flex my fists. "Taurus will be pissed, I'm sure," Talia warns in a hoarse tone. "The drugs—I got shot up in the bathroom. Some bint associated with our mark, I think?"

My heart pounds in my throat; Blade's breathing is ragged and shallow. I lean closer to her. "Help her, love. She's hurting," I plead softly under my breath.

Blade snaps her head toward me. "Stop—stop saying that! I'm..." Her face flushes white with fury, and then, after a breath, she seems to settle into an uneasy truce. "...fine."

"He won't be pissed. She's skewered—he'll be furious that she hid it." Deli doesn't wait for our reply; instead, she lays her hands lightly on Blade's abdomen—her fingertips ghosting over the wound. The dull ache of her touch makes my prone mate wince. A ripple of quiet power moves through the room, the air humming like a plucked string.

I swallow. I need my primary to fix Talia. I can't lose her because of stubbornness when I just found her.

The magical kitty mutters under her breath, reciting syllables older than human speech. "Torn ligaments, nicked organs, a broken rib... damn." Her voice turns clinical as she pauses, looking at me. "Gut wounds bleed but rarely kill. Talia, was that all you remember from when you get shot up? Do you know what they used by any chance?"

Blade groans, bracing a hand above the damp patch at her side. Her lips tremble. "I... I felt... euphoria. Colors... everywhere... couldn't fight."

Deli's gaze sharpens, slicing through the haze of incense. "Immediate or delayed onset?"

Blade presses a shaky hand to her neck, as though seeking to reassure herself she's still alive. "Immediate. A needle behind my ear." Her voice cracks and tears slip down her cheeks.

My primary straightens, tension pulling at her shoulders. "Could be scopolamine, flakka, Seconal... lots of nasty options. I have to flush it out first or she'll be damaged beyond my ability to mend." She looks at me, eyes fierce. "Rafe, bring a bucket—she's going to vomit and we don't want it on the floor."

I bolt from the room as if struck by a bolt of lightning. My boots thump the hallway floor as I head for the laundry room. It takes me a minute to remember how Leo organizes his supplies. Once I do, I yank a plastic mop bucket from under the sink, heart pounding so hard I fear my ribs will crack. Something sticky makes my hand skid on the rim—old toothpaste? Dried blood? Doesn't matter. I haul it back into the bedroom, trying not to stumble over discarded shoes in the hallway.

The kitty's altar of scattered herbs, glowing bottles, and chalk sigils radiates energy, pulsing in time with the candle flames. The incense smoke coils around her, thickening the air until it tastes of rain and metal.

And then it happens—Taurus arrives in an infuriated burst of feral energy. The clone steps inside the door, fangs bared as he glares at the room. He fills the doorway with an exasperated growl. "What happened?" His voice is a quiet thunderclap.

To her credit, Deli doesn't look up; she keeps her eyes on Blade's wound. "She was drugged and stabbed in the bathroom. That's all we know."

His gaze snaps to mine, gold eyes flickering with betrayal. "Why didn't I know?"

I hesitate, words knotted in my throat. "She blocked you, mate. When I carried her in, I felt her blackout lock you out."

Deli's shoulders stiffen; he advances, forehead ridged with anger. "She *can't* block me—"

Blade moans, her voice hoarse but insistent. "Stop, damn it." She tries to lift herself, pain etching a scar across her features, but I press a hand to her shoulder, urging her to lie still.

"Lie back. I only sensed she was off. Nothing more." I try to reassure my new mate's primary, so he doesn't crash out and make everything harder.

He exhales, the cool press of his palm settling on her leg. "Alright." His tone is curt, but something softens behind the anger. "But I'm going to murder someone if this isn't fixed *now*."

The room seems to shrink, the candle flames flaring as Deli lifts her chin. "Both of you—*calm down* or I will remove you. I'm not joking."

She's definitely serious and I'm not going to mess with a pregnant magical shifter who is here to save my mate's life—that'd be stupid.

The Cat Makes A Mistake

DELILAH

~Can you help her, baby?~

~ My husband speaks into my mind, deciding to take the wiser route of listening to me rather than blustering. I nod, giving him a serious look as I sit back down. I float the poultices and tinctures close enough to reach. "You're going to want to move back from her while I pull out the drugs. I need some space." I murmur into his mind, not wanting the others to hear. *~I can do this; you have to trust me. ~*

~With everything I have, minx. ~ His heart touches mine and I sigh, feeling much better now that I know he has faith in me.

"Talia, I need you to drink this. It tastes like ass—sorry. Brace yourself for it to burn. I mean, it will burn like your veins are on fire."

Talia pushes up on her elbows, taking sips from the vial I'm offering her. She makes a disgusted face and I give her an apologetic smile. I wasn't kidding about how bad it tastes. She does *not* want to know what's in it, that's for damned sure. The screaming starts and I watch her arch and writhe. I hold a hand up at the mates who

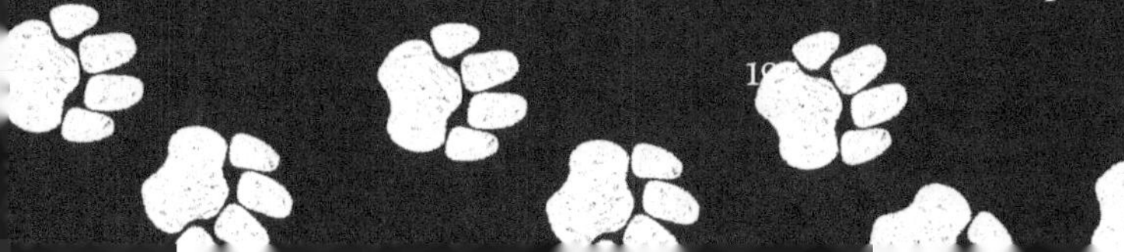

are champing at the bit to move closer. They can't help and I need them to stay back. This is way more dangerous than I've let on and I need to concentrate or I'll fuck it up.

Ever so slowly, I feel the trickle of ooze coming out of Talia's pores, invisible to them as it snakes its way into the air. I keep my eyes on it, bidding it to gather in a ball so that I can cordon it off. I have to keep it from escaping into someone else in the room. This is the most dangerous part of the procedure. It could fail and we're all fucked. I don't know how long I can hold it, which is why the last part being quicker is optimal. "Your gaze should clear up soon. You're doing great—only a little more to go."

Taurus is staring at me, and I know he's trying not to connect to me. He wants to see what I'm doing and to stop her screaming pain. It's good that he's resisting because he would break my flow —which would cause a major problem. Rafe watches me and then Taurus; he nods in understanding at the helplessness I know they both feel right now. The power emanating from me nips at their skin like fleas, trying to get in, trying to soak up their energy. If they stay back, they'll be fine.

When I feel the last remnants of the drugs leave her system, I smile in relief and reach out for the tiny ball of cordoned energy. I will it to stay that way until I remove it again to dispose of it. Since I haven't done this before—only read about it—I'm hoping that works. I tuck the ball in the robe's pocket I threw on before I came and look at Talia. "You okay down there?"

She's sweating, but she looks more in control. Her face is a mask of pain and discomfort, but I see nothing else that worries me. A brief nod makes me sigh in relief. "Yeah, I think so. If the choice were to go through that again or die, though, let me die."

Taurus falls to his knees, and I can only guess that the removal of drugs lifted the bond blockage between them. Talia's pain must have slammed into him like a freight train. "Christ. The drugs were causing the block. I feel her; I feel all of it now."

Rafe's teeth grit, but you wouldn't know that it hurts if you looked at him. I give him a sad smile. The knowledge of our high pain tolerance and where it came from passes back and forth for a second. I'd take it, but I can't do that and focus on his mate. His jaw clenches, but he looks calm.

"You're a bigger girl than that and we both know it. You can handle it. We're at the tough part now because, um, I don't know what—okay. The wound is severe. First, I'm going to put this stinky stuff on it, which won't hurt, but to um, activate it, I have to—well, I mean. I don't know what you want me to do." Turning to Talia, I prepare for a struggle of my own. I know what I have to do and she won't like it. She's strong and smart and dangerous and beautiful and *not damaged* like me. She doesn't have the taint of the others like I do. How can I tell her she's going to have to...?

I have magick, but this isn't all magick. My mutant shit is part of how I do this, and I can't activate this poultice without my blood. They have a blood thing, and the amount of me in Taurus or Rafe will not knit organs. She's too weak to even try it. Okay, Deli, calm down and say it. Stop being a pansy. Fuck. They're all going to kill me. Stop being a pansy.

"Spit it out, minx," Taurus growls and I glare at him.

"Don't be a bully! To heal, it's not wavy, sparkly magick. It's me. You know that, baby. I have to mix it in the stuff or it won't work!"

His eyes widen and I know he gets why I'm stuttering like an incompetent. "Your blood."

"Yes!" I turn to Talia, looking embarrassed. "So, um, do you have a problem—I mean."

She blinks at me and then looks at Taurus and then at Rafe and then at me again. Rafe is giving me a frustrated look, and I'm feeling self-conscious and stupid. I hate that I'm the village bike to them. Hell, it's so bad that you'd rather die, right? "Look, I want to help, but I don't want to do something that you'll get pissed about later."

"The way I figure it; we've already shared blood, albeit round-about. Do what you have to do." She grins a little. "But don't give me a tail and we'll be good."

"*One time*. It happened *one time*," I grumble. "A *goddess* did it, and how's that *my* fault?" I flick out a claw, trying to get myself into focus because I have more to do. "Do you want to stay comfy and do this the messy way, or should I make it cleaner but harder on you? Either is fine."

Talia blinks, looking at me for a moment, and then grabs my hand. "You don't have to do this—none of it."

"Duh," I say, waiting to see if she's going to pass because of the Deli-cooties.

"I'll heal on my own if you don't want to do this."

"I came here on request, not by command, Talia. Free will— woohoo! If I do it, you'll heal faster and without major interven-tion. It won't hurt, and it won't take days or weeks. I promised I would, and even if I hadn't, I'd do it because you're important to them. Plus, I'm a bleeding heart milk dud with no ability to not take in strays—everyone knows that."

She keeps looking at me and I get more nervous, more flustered, wondering if she's worried what else she'll get from me. It's my self-conscious bullshit, but even broken and bleeding, she's strong and feminine and ethical and intelligent. I'm many things, but some-how, she's making me feel like a tiny speck in the universe's eye. It's not on purpose. But I'm sitting here in my robe and Taurus' shirt, trying to finish healing a warrior who's looking at me funny despite being ripped open and half naked. I feel ridiculously small. "I don't —I don't have to."

She nods and lets go of my hand, her eyes closing. "Do it anyway; it doesn't matter."

I nod, doing my best to keep my expression as blank as possible. The hanging moments of her indecision tell me all I need to know about who I will be in everyone's eyes forever. My voice is soft and my eyes stay on my extended claw as I force myself to ask again.

"What I need to know is—shall I cut or do you want to take a bite and go from there? It's more for your comfort because either way, it'll work. Either way is fine with me." I don't look up, but I'm sure the looks are passing between them and I close my eyes, trying to stave off the sensation of unworthiness. It happened with Taurus, too, but for a different reason. I'm paranoid and I don't know why. Talia's said nothing bad about me that I know of. She's never shown that she thinks I'm less than, but that's what I'm feeling and it's getting worse by the minute.

"Whatever you need, baby," Rafe whispers.

The discomfort of the situation is eating at me and I can't take it anymore. "No, no. It's my bad. I didn't think. Here, let me do this." I pull my arm away and slice it from wrist to elbow, not even batting a lash at the sting.

My poker face for pain matches my primary's—skills we honed at the feet of the dearly departed. No one can see you flinch; no one can know you cry. Keep it all inside and you survive another day. The pain distracts me, makes me focus on that rather than the emotions making my heart hurt. I squeeze it hard, dripping it over the wound and the poultice, keeping the pressure so it gets every-where it needs to be.

I murmur under my breath, mixing the paste and the blood, feeling the power flow from my fingertips. Feeling the muscle and tissue knit, I watch inside as nicks, muscles, and organs heal. I make sure every tiny injury—layer by layer, inside to outside—is healing. Mending all the bones and flesh, I reach the outer part of the wound and then let my cut heal. The energy I'm using keeps the pressure, so it gets everywhere it needs to be.

They're both trying to see into my mind while I do it, I know, as neither of my mates has ever seen me do this in person. But they can't and I'm sure it's frustrating them. I'm only able to focus on what I'm doing right now. I feel everyone's eyes on me, watching me, watching her wound.

Sensing the closing of the gash and the smoothing out of her skin, I hear the pop it makes when the skin seals and let out a breath. It's fucking draining, and I let go of the tight hold I have on my powers, trying to shake off the tired and the feeling of ick I got from my earlier paranoia.

It hits me like a ton of bricks right in the face. I don't even have time to speak before I feel myself blink out of the room, falling onto the satin comforter—somewhere—in a heap of arms and legs with a flop.

Jesus Fucking Christ, where am I?

The Bird Has A Rough Night

TAURUS

Everything happened so bloody fast that I barely had time to steady myself before the world lurched beneath my feet. Stone walls quivered with a dull roar, as if the very foundation of the chamber had been shaken loose from its moorings. Somewhere beyond the fraying edges of my senses, my heart hammered so fiercely I thought it might burst. It was only by sheer force of will that I managed to stay on my feet, though my legs felt like jelly and my vision swam at the edges.

My primary is alive and well... but my wife is missing.

Sampson's feet slap on the wood floor, each step echoing off the floorboards. He wrenches himself around, blond hair whipping unsheathed across his forehead, eyes wide with panic. The sheen of sweat on his brow tells me that he, too, is panicking. "Where the hell did she go? What happened?!" His voice cracks on the last word, a raw edge that betrays his confidence, and for the briefest heartbeat I wonder if this is my fault.

Did my pleas to save Talia encourage her to overdo it with weaving her magic, making her fuck something up she wouldn't have otherwise?

My goddess, the one whose body my wife just labored to heal—lays on the thick, plush rug in the center of the artist's room. Her chest rises and falls in slow, even breaths, a stark contrast to the chaos ringing in my ears. Every inhalation is calm; every exhale a gentle sigh of ease. With an almost languid grace, she pushes herself up on trembling arms, brushing damp strands of hair from her forehead, and draws a deep, untroubled breath as if nothing at all has gone wrong.

Relief should be washing over me in a flood, but instead there's only guilt—gnawing, insistent, and gut-twisting. She's safe, whole, and unbroken once more, but someone else has vanished in her place.

Someone I cannot live without.

"I can't find her," Sampson mutters, his voice low but fierce. He pivots, gaze flicking to me as though I alone hold the missing puzzle piece. Concern flits across his unreadable features, as if he's searching for an answer in the hard lines of my face. My stomach twists with shame—confusion mingled with need as I realize how desperately I crave that flicker of vulnerability I know I shouldn't take comfort in.

At the foot of the bed, Talia hovers nervously, her blond hair catching the lamp's soft glow like molten gold. She frowns, her bronze hand slicing through the empty air where my wife was a moment ago. "Is she...?" Her question tapers off, swallowed by the sudden hush. The only response is the echo of her uncertainty bouncing off the walls.

Hell if I know, but I'm doing my best not to lose my shit.

Panic slithers tighter around my ribs, constricting breath and bone alike. I force my eyes shut, trying to still the chaos of my thoughts and reach out through the bond I share with my minx. Lines of energy from our bond—faint, trembling filaments of light and color—snake from my mind toward where Deli should be. I send them out further, tentative and desperate, seeking even the faintest spark of recognition. "Minx? Where are you?" I whisper, the voice in my mind so quiet it feels like a secret.

No answer comes, only empty echoes of my own words. Every comforting vibration in that psychic link—the small flutter of her heartbeat against mine, the sound of her thoughts whispered through memory—has been snuffed out. I feel as if I've stepped off a precipice and hit rock bottom in the dark.

I can always feel her since we mated, but now there's nothing.

Sampson grinds his teeth. The low growl he lets out reverberates across the room. "I can't even *feel* her," he says. His lithe shoulders tense as he flexes his arms, as though trying to will her presence back into being. I want to scream—at fate, at magic, at whatever unknown force has spirited her away, and most of all at myself for letting this happen.

Talia draws in a trembling breath and closes her eyes. Her hands lift, obviously looking for her blade as she sifts through the web of emotions that must be swamping her. There's no tremor of her energy, no hint of her laughter, no echo of the gentle warmth my new mate always brings to my mind. After what seems like an eternity, Talia growls softly. The blue of her eyes is cold and hard as hunted game. She stalks over to the nightstand where her blade is resting to grab it so she can spin it maniacally. "There's nothing," she says. "No trace of her as far as I can tell."

Sampson stalks to the cluttered surface against the south wall—its surface a riot of charcoals, erasers, markers, and half-finished sketches splayed out like broken promises. With a brutal motion he shoves aside a pile of art pencils. They tumble to the floor, but luckily, don't break. "She'd never leave without warning," he mutters, staring at the mess as though it alone holds the solution. "She always—" His voice falters. "She's never disappeared after finishing spellwork; she doesn't like leaving her tools everywhere for amateurs to pick up."

A coil of dread tightens in my gut, and my hands clench in fists at my side. I shove past them both, pounding my fist against the desk's dark wood. "Bloody buggering *hell*—how much more am I supposed to take tonight?" The words are a jagged scream. They hang heavy in the air, and for a moment I hate myself for blurting them out and making it all about me.

But almost losing my primary because of her stubbornness and now facing a missing wife is pushing my limits.

Then, as though summoned by sheer will alone, my primary's voice rings out to bring me back to earth.. "Taurus," she teases, "I doubt this is your fault, you self-absorbed frill-hound—so pipe down."

Relief surges through me like wildfire, scorching away the last flickers of panic. Talia is safe and laughing at me. I don't have to worry about her, thanks to Deli. But the relief tastes bitter, for that's also why we have one person unaccounted for. It's a Catch-22, and I'm not a clone who enjoys ambiguity. We have to find her now, or I'm definitely not going to be able to keep myself from going on a Rift-wide rampage.

Sampson's footsteps echo as he paces back and forth. He's muttering, and I pause to listen to his ramblings. "No ward, no barrier," he mutters around clenched teeth. "The house magic is unchanged. That means it's tapping into mate shit, and I don't have a clue what to do with that. This isn't something we've done together, and her book of shadows won't let me read things we haven't done. For safety, she said, but this doesn't feel very fucking safe..."

Talia shoots him a sharp look, full of impatience. "What do you know about her powers that we don't? Where might she vanish to?" Her voice is level, controlled, but the tension in her shoulders betrays her eagerness for answers. She turns bright eyes on me, searching as though I might conjure a solution from thin air.

Sorry, the witchy woo shit isn't my forte and the lounger is much more likely to know about it.

I stumble forward, throat tight as my heart thunders like a war drum. I steady myself against the edge of a cabinet block inches from my primary as I look at her earnestly. "Love, I'm grateful you're healed—but I can't stay here. The minx could be anywhere —hurt, frightened, caught in some net of wild sorcery. I have to check every hidden corner of this fucking place to find her."

My goddess props herself on one elbow, the silk of the robe she slipped on flowing like water over her skin. With a single perfect brow arched in that look of hers—equal parts soothing and mocking—she gives me her unstoppable smile. "If you're as riled as you sound—then go. Find her."

Thank fuck.

Beneath the teasing lilt was unwavering trust. Her faith in me cuts deeper than any of her blades, and I can't fathom not having it. I press my lips briefly to hers, swift and fervent. "Thank the gods," I whisper, voice choked. "I love her too much not to go, but my alliance will always be to you, too."

Turning to Sampson, I bark, "Stay sharp. I'll call if I find anything." Then, without another word, I let the world around me dissolve. The hum of disapperation tugs at my bones—the warp and weft of space and time unraveling and knitting back together in an instant. It's usually unremarkable to me because I'm used to it, but tonight, I feel every bit.

A heartbeat later, I stand in the familiar foyer of the new home I'm building for my family, drenched in the warm golden glow of fancy lamps. My hand lingers on the carved wooden banister, its smooth surface a comfort beneath trembling fingers. Behind me, the massive front door is still shut, so I know no one has entered our private space. If she came here, for whatever reason, she'll be in our room—that's the only place she knows yet.

When I find her, I'm going to request that every entrance, every corridor, and every door get decorated with wards and runes just in case. I stomp up the steps until I reach the door to our bedroom, knowing that this is the place where I'll find her if she's here.

"Minx?" I whisper as I sweep my hands in wide arcs, checking behind the furniture and bed. I don't see her, so I slap the panel to open the bathroom door, not finding her there, either. Opening the closet, I rifle through everything, making sure she's not curled up amongst the things on the floor, but nothing.

Where the fuck. Is. My. Goddamn. Mate!

Tears burn beneath my lids. I press a hand to my forehead, wincing as if I could palm away the ache. How did I fail her? I replay her ritual in my mind—the precise incantations, the shimmering paths of energy she guided around my primary's frail shell. I don't think I could have done anything more to help, nor could Rafe, but I still feel like this is my fault. Her disappearance has to be tied to over-taxing the new powers she's not totally comfortable with—something I begged her to do.

Yet the world does not pause for my guilt. Somewhere, she might be scared and alone. I can hear the steady rhythm of my primary's voice at the back of my mind, urging me to stop feeling sorry for myself and find Deli. The colors and emotions flowing through our mate bond are Talia's hallmark because she cannot mind speak, but unlike normal, they aren't helping me calm down. She's doing what she can; I know. It's just not enough as the terror sets in.

I catch my reflection in the glass of the mirror on the back of the closet door. My eyes are rimmed red. My hair, typically perfect, is in utter disarray. The silk of my bespoke shirt is rumpled. I'm a mess, and my pride isn't even rearing up to make me adjust myself. That tells you just how fucking worried I am right now.

Skirting the edge of the room, I pause before the top of the back stairs. I know she hasn't explored the additions I'm making, so she won't have gone down to the kitchen or outside of her own volition. But that doesn't mean she didn't *appear* in one of those places, right? She could have zapped to a wrong location... I think?

Taking the steps two at a time, I walk through the kitchen, then I see a faint shimmer out the back door. The yard is in flux as I imagine what I want the space to look like, but there are large flat stones at the edge of the cliffs. That's where the sparkles are coming from, and it might be where I need to go.

I exhale. If she's there, why hasn't she answered and why can't Sampson or I feel her? I don't have a clue, but I have to find out. I can't stand here like a fool and wait.

Summoning strength, I head out towards the rocks with purpose. My heart pounds in my ears, but I'm guided by the fragile thread of hope and terror that is fueling me. I have to know if my minx is okay, and then I can worry about everything else... including the answers to all my questions.

Hopefully, she'll be able to give them to me.

The Cat Sees Rainbows and Sparkles

DELILAH

y head is swimming. I can't hold it up.

It feels like my body is whirling inside and I'm trying to figure out what the hell happened. Everything was going fine! The only time I've healed someone besides me was that time with Taurus, but he drank and that was much easier. This was different and hell if I'm going to admit that I was making it up as I went along.

"How did I...?"

Oh, fuck, I'm an idiot.

I close my eyes to make the room stop spinning before I hurl. I can't feel anyone or anything, but the roller coaster my senses are on. Breathing as I try to get myself under control, I lay still. People have to be wondering where I am, but I can't tell them. My body's not responding well, either, or that *might* become a problem in not too long, considering I drank a pint of juice like an hour ago.

Something about this feels familiar, but I can't put my finger on why or what.

Suddenly, Taurus pops into the room right next to the bed where I've landed, looking at me like a crazed fan. He smells like our garden and fear, as he looks down at me. "Baby?"

"Mmm?" I reply, burying my experience in the pillow I'm holding onto as the world does merry-go-round things. I feel like I'm made of clouds and it takes everything in me to crack my eye open again to look at him.

Super speed has him at my side before I blink, and his hands stroke down my back. "You alright, love? I didn't know—what's going on? You left without saying a word."

"I don't know," I say, flopping over to look up at him. I have kitty eyes; I feel the emotions swirling in them. It makes me grin when I think about how silly I look. "I went *pop*! How d'you find me? I couldn't find anyone."

He shrugs, blushing. "I didn't know—not really. Didn't have a clue where you went, but I hoped you'd come home if something was going on. It seemed smart to check here before the real search began."

I giggle. "I didn't mean to go anywhere. Then it was all 'wheeeeeee'. I hit the bed. And I'm all grrr-y."

Not looking a bit amused, he tilts his head. "I don't know, baby."

My tail twitches, I feel it, and I scrunch up my face in frustration. "All I did was let go a bit and now I'm all fluffy." I blink, stopping for a moment to get my brain working.

"What do you mean, you let go for a moment?"

I frown again, not liking his tone. It's not nice. "I quit focusing because I didn't have to hold everything in place. The healing was almost done. I let my arm heal and all."

"So, you 'let go' and you popped up here?" He asks me, his fingers brushing the hair off my face.

"No. I let go and something weird happened. Then boom! I was here and I'm all fuzzy and stuff."

He speaks, his voice not rising at all. "Okay, baby. I'm trying not to lose control, but I can't feel you."

I nod. "Yup. I can't feel you, either. I know you're here, but it's like you're not."

His face flickers with emotions as if he's trying hard not to let them show. "Okay. What could strip away the bonds from your two closest mates? Sampson said he couldn't feel you either."

Shrugging, I flop onto my back again. "Not a clue. My head's all 'wooooooo'." I twirl my finger around as I say that, watching it move in fascination.

"Deli! Concentrate. Stop watching your sodding fingers move! The babe—is she…?" His eyes narrow, and he is scowling, which I can't understand.

I saved her, right? Talia's okay? I did a good job, right?

"Is she alright? I can't feel Maeve, and I always feel her a little."

Looking inside, I search through the muddled haze in my head to locate the little one. "I felt nothing wrong inside, but everything is muzzy. It's hard to focus." I look up at him, watching his features, and sigh. "Have I ever told you how pretty you are?"

He flinches, looking at me like I smacked him in the nose. "I'm pretty?! Christ, woman, are you drunk?"

That was mean, and there's no need for him to be mean. I don't like it.

I sniff, not wanting to cry in front of him, and turn on my side, putting my back to him. See if I ever say something nice to him again. "I told you I don't know what's wrong!"

I bury my experience in the pillow, determined to keep the tears on my cheeks hidden. *Why does everyone hurt me?* I squeeze my eyes shut, and colors explode behind my lids. *Why am I trying to think?* He doesn't care. "I'm gonna sleep now." Feeling his eyes on me, I wish he'd just go away. I've had enough of mean, hateful people.

"I don't like not feeling you in my heart," he whispers.

"I'm not doing it on purpose, so I can't fix it. I let my focus drop for a minute to rest, and suddenly, I'm flying. Did I forget anything? What did I do wrong?" I'm asking myself more than him and I push my hair off my face. "I'm hot."

"Hot? Hot?" He touches my cheek. "Christ. You are hot."

"Yup," I smile. "Help me get the robe off and stuff?"

He gives me a weird look and picks me up, making my world spin as he carries me somewhere. "What robe, baby?"

I look down at myself. "Where the bloody hell did it go? I was wearing it in the other house because it was in my pocket..." I try to remember, pushing myself hard to focus and find real thoughts.

"I'm drawing you a cool bath. That temperature worries me." He sits me down and dribbles cool water over me. It feels fantastic. "What about the other house?"

"When I was fixing her, I had it on. I can't seem to figure out where I went wrong or why I can't get rid of the 'grr'."

His eyes widen as he looks at me. There's panic all over his face, and I do not understand what he's thinking. "What? What's going on?"

"Oh, Christ, Deli. The drugs. You had the ball with the drugs in it in your sodding pocket!"

"Ooh," I coo, everything falling into place. I smack my head, making everything spin again and fall back against the tub. "No *wonder* I feel like I'm in the electric light parade. Fuck me sideways."

Before I get my fuzzy head around that, he shakes my shoulders. "Tell me what to do. This could kill the baby! Think."

"You can, uh—I don't think you can take them out. You're not powerful enough. I'm too weak from healing to help you. Maybe..."

"*Deli! Maybe what?!*" he roars, seeming to lose it all at once.

That is not helping because I'm going to cry again if he doesn't quit yelling. I can't help it; I'm scared, too. "Dry me off and we can lie on the bed. Maybe if you drink, you can feel the baby and see if she's okay." I blink, mind feeling more fractured and emotional, making it harder than ever to concentrate. "Take a little. Only go deep enough to see her."

Without a word, he scoops me up and grabs a towel, then has me in the bed within seconds. Sitting me down, he uses the towel and then wraps me in the blankets. Lying down next to me, he growls, "Where?!"

"Quit bloody yelling," I mutter, feeling a little peeved. I'm trying; can't he tell I'm trying? "I can't make my brain work. It's making me more nervous when you yell, and it's making it harder to focus because I cry. You can bite anywhere."

"You think it's nervous over there? Try my seat, woman." With that, he lowers his fangs and bites my wrist.

"You won't cry, though," I grunt, the sensation always making me react. Sparks and showers of color burst behind my eyes when his fangs sink in and I wriggle. The drugs in my system tickle all my senses and when he bites, I feel stirring, hunger and need. I push it away, determined to focus on Maeve and him. "Did you find her yet?"

He doesn't respond, trying to sift through my drug-laced blood and muddled mind to find the wee one through our connection.

I reach inside, trying to locate one or both myself. If only I could feel something—anything. I'm so alone and he's so mad at me and I don't know what to do. I feel the tears again and I struggle inside, hoping to make contact. Nothing comes through and I sniffle, waiting for him to tell me.

Pulling back, he lets go of my wrist and looks at me. "You're fine. The wee one is safe. In fact, it seems like she's not affected at all by anything."

"Good," I whisper, closing my eyes as relieved tears cascade down my face. I've cried more in the past twenty minutes than I ever have in front of him. "She's strong that way."

He glances at me and bares his neck. "Maybe if you feed, it will dilute the poison in you. Maybe you can find us all again," he chokes a little and I realize that his yelling was coming from fear.

"You think?" I try not to hope, licking my lips.

"You're drained, you're drugged, and you're feral. I don't have any other ideas. It's the best I've got."

"Then come here," I whisper, reaching up to him. Stretching out along my length, he bends and kisses my lips. He offers his neck again. Pushing up as much as I can, I drag him down with me as I settle. I kiss his mark, murmuring low, "I miss you. I've been so scared." Sliding my fangs into his skin, I feel my head reeling as I drink.

He turns his head and strikes, biting into my mark, and I gasp. I didn't expect it, but I drink him in as he drinks me in, wiggling close enough to feel sheltered in his arms. I need the touch and I need it to help me shore up our connection. I feel a small brush on our connection, just a wisp, and he gathers me under him, covering me with his body and drinking as deeply as he can. He lifts a little, disapparating the rest of our clothing so our skin is touching and I sigh, the sensation and his warmth helping.

If only this works.

Our bodies move together, and without even a thought, we're one. Moving together as we drink, I feel the first brushes of our connection coming back. There's a sound and I realize that it's getting louder and I hear it. Straining, I wade through all the spider webs in my mind.

~Baby, please, love. Come back to me. I love you so much, my mate, and my only.~

~Please come back to me. I love you so much, my mate, and my only. I can't survive without you, love. I won't. I need you. Please, baby.~

I hear him and it's like fucking angels are singing because, for the first time in almost an hour, I *hear* him. *~Baby, please hear me. Oh god, please, I need you. ~*

~Deli? Damn it, woman, fight! Fight for us like you promised you would, baby. I don't want anyone but you. I don't work with anyone but you. Hear me, baby. Hear me and fight for that. Follow my voice back. You can't leave me here, baby. It's too cold, too lonely without you. Speak to me, baby. Can you speak to me again? ~

I push harder, fighting the haze and the fractured pieces inside, struggling to get to him.

~I'm trying so hard because I want you back. I need you; I love you. I can't be without you inside me; it feels like I'm dying. Please hear me. ~

My eyes pop open, and I have to fight pulling away from him when I answer. *~Baby? Did I—are you there? ~* I'm scared that I imagined it because I can't do anything else.

~God, yes, love of my heart, I'm here. I'm here, baby. I'm not leaving this place without you. Christ, I love you, woman! Do you hear that? I love you! ~

I feel him a bit and I know he has to be sending every emotion and thought he has, so I reach out, putting every bit of what little focus I can muster into finding it. *~I love you, baby, so much. I'm trying. ~*

His hands grip my arms as we reach each other for the first time in hours, and though it's small, he keeps murmuring into my mind. *~I love you like no other, so help me. ~*

~I thought I lost you. ~ Now that I've found him, I sink into our connection, immersing myself in us. I've never had something so deep, even for a short time, that being apart like this feels like dying. I don't know what I'd do without him. It's wonderful and scary simultaneously. Our souls re-bond inside and everything comes back: bodies, hearts, and minds joined as one.

~I was scared as fuck. I can't get along without you. ~

Tears leak down my cheeks and I hold on to him like I'm never letting go. *~Me neither. I need you; I crave you. I felt like I was dying and I didn't care with you gone. ~*

~Mine, baby. You're mine. Only mine, sod it all. I want you, and no one else will ever get me. ~

He twines our fingers, squeezing my hand, and I feel the cold metal of his ring against my palm. I rub my finger over it, pushing any small nuggets of doubt over that situation out of my mind, finding joy in having him back with me as he belongs.

"I'm kind of tired, baby. This has all taken it out of me. Can we sleep, do you think?"

His brow furrows. "Are you sure you're okay? I'm still feeling—it was a rough night."

"I'm sure. Want nothing more than to be with you."

"You got it, baby." He kisses my forehead and snuggles me close. "Love you, my wife, my everything."

"Love you, too. Forever." With that, I close my eyes, emotions so huge that I can't even fathom them until I get some rest.

Until then, everything else can wait.

The Cat Gets Good News

DELILAH

The shopping trip I planned for today was to places that would make Taurus want to kill everyone in sight.

Luckily, he got called into work *after* our intense 're-acquaintance session'. That ended in a tumble of sheets and snarls, as well as my promise not to be as careless in the future. Taurus doesn't know how unlikely that scenario is because I didn't mention it, but I was comfortable making a vow for caution.

I can't really talk about why I lost focus and control—it's humiliating and I'm keeping it to myself.

After popping to my house to check in with Rafe, I set out on my retail adventure. I need ingredients for stupid magick rooms and a couple of costume pieces to get this bloody party ready. Life has been distracting, and the date is looming ever closer; I don't want to be ill-prepared, even if Leo and the gang are handling a lot of the details.

Parties at the Maison are known for being the best—this isn't the time to challenge that reputation.

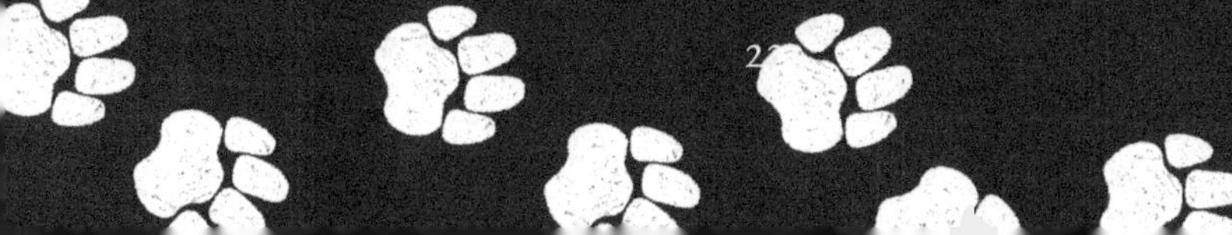

I DROP my bags on the floor of our room when I return. I left the magickal things at the Maison for the boys to take to my sacred space, but I want the pieces of my outfit here to keep it secret. Taurus is *not* ready to see what it looks like when my entire family is getting ready for a large party—the master bedroom there is enormous for a reason. He and Talia aren't the type to hang about a Vegas backstage-style experience as we all help one another dress, so I assume they will do their thing at their own house.

Dressing for events is a very efficient and thorough process at the Maison. Rafe does faces and my hair. I style everyone else's hair, and our clothes get passed from Hex's expert treatment to Sandrine. She helps people get buckled, zipped, or whatever, so their outfits fit perfectly. Philomena critiques, criticizes, and keeps everyone with a drink in hand. Vic keeps mood music going and Caesar handles any last-minute runs to the store. Leo keeps everyone fed, and together, we're a well-oiled machine.

It's—well, it's chaos that would make him and Talia want to retreat for two years.

They should come to the house once they're ready to be attendees, not to take part in the day-long getting ready event. Our family's comfort level with one another is not something I think they're ready to witness.

The clone in question pads in from the bathroom, drying his hair. He must have come home and gone for a swim, because he smells like the ocean. "How's your day been, love?"

I smile, watching him with soft eyes. He looks unscathed given our rather fierce re-mating this morning. It must be my blood in him, pumping him full of healing and regeneration. "Not bad. You're looking unblemished and tanned."

Chuckling, he shrugs. "You know, when I asked if you'd fight for me way back when I didn't imagine it'd be fighting *me*. You and that lovely beast inside didn't want to take no for an answer this morning."

My lips curl. "I have no interest in our connection being less than it should. I had to fix whatever those drugs screwed up. She agreed with me, for once."

"So, I'm not crazy, then? Your lovely and my demon mated—which is why I feel that bugger more than I have... ever."

I pad over, nipping his chin. "I believe so, my darling. You're entwined with every part of me now. Dark and light, though lately...?"

"It's more dark than light and trust me, not a complaint from me, my little blood warrior." He grins and tugs me over to the bed. "What did you buy and how bad is my wallet screaming?"

Sniffing, I give him a look. "I bought outfit stuff for the party. You'll have to wait to see it all. Trust me; you will *not* want to be at the house until a little before it starts. Our family getting ready is more than you'd want to experience just yet."

Taurus looks wounded, pouting. "Do you think I'm too much of a prude to handle it?"

My lips quirk up. "Yes. If Damien is dressing you guys, you're getting ready won't last as long as we all take. Trust me on this, my love."

"Okay, okay. The goddess and I will have to live without the two of you for a couple of hours." He stops and murmurs, "He loves her, right?"

I blink, taken aback. "Very much—I don't even have to poke around to figure that out."

"It's—she's not like me. She avoided relationships for much longer than me, even friendly ones. I worry about her."

"I don't blame you, but he's—well, he's always been more selective than me and after all the shit with the exes, I didn't think he'd ever venture out again."

"We walked on the beach today and she'll kill me for telling you, but I think the magnitude of everything hit her last night. Especially since that rotter you're mated told her he wants to make her as happy as I do you. It's a tall order and even wanting to try is big. It made her girly and happy, then terrified."

That makes me a little nervous, especially with Talia having a problem with it, but I need to let them find their own groove.

I arch a brow. "Did he? Good for him."

"She's afraid she doesn't have it in her to give him what you give me. She thinks she's forgotten how to trust that much. It's some shit with the departed and his gnome making her stumble."

Sighing, I nod. "That I am familiar with. Last I heard, the lunatic fringe says they're halfway through their 'quests'. Lily says they're blogging about it, but I refuse to even look. I swore I wouldn't get sucked into it and I won't. Goddess only knows what they're saying about me."

His eyes narrow and he snarls, "About any of us, really. It's best I leave that alone—you can't have a party if I kill a lot of guests."

"Rafe's crazy about her. He's not even been around much of anyone else, and with Wilde not being here, that's been easy. I knew the minute he gave up a chance to prod at me in favor of flirting with her the night we drained."

"I know you said it went fast with them. I hate to pick at a scab that I'll wish I hadn't, but can you clarify?"

"My primary started up with Sari in August that year, and they didn't claim until November. Rhea and he were about two months. My experience was maybe a tad quicker, but it should be even."

Sitting back in his chair, he runs his hands through his hair. "Holy fuck, woman. I didn't know it was that much faster."

"When you know, you know," I shrug, leaning in to nip his jaw. "I knew."

Taurus studies me for a moment and says, "I'm withdrawn, aren't I?"

"Yeah. You get that way sometimes when you're broody."

"I do not brood!" Huffing and looking affronted, he yanks me closer. "Baby, being with you, having you curl up on me makes everything better inside of me. I realized a long time ago that the only place I'm calm, the *only* place I feel right, is where you are. Not just the sex—which defies description in the best of ways— but you. Your heart, your mind, and your soul put me at peace. You said it right this morning; I can't breathe when you're not the air."

My arms tighten around him, and I kiss all over his neck and shoulders. "You are my safety, baby. I can hide with you; I can be me without it being filtered into someone that other people want me to be. I trust you. You make me feel safe and warm and loved even in the hard spots, because I know you still love me."

"In the tough spots, I love you even more. I'm so bloody proud of you." He palms the back of my neck, rubbing the muscles there. "Even when you've gotten hurt, you let me in, and it humbles me.

There isn't one aspect of your personality that I'm not ass over brains for, baby."

"Sometimes, I need to do stuff myself, but I've been trying to be honest and open and trust you. I want to give you as much as you've given me. Even when you want to rip and tear and slay my dragons, you let me do what I can to handle things myself. It means a lot to me that you respect that need, even when you're livid."

His brows furrow and he frowns. "Is it tough to be straightforward with me, love? Is it hard to trust me? I know you don't enjoy seeing me hurting, and I figure that honesty might weigh on you when you're sure it's going to set me off. I'd hoped I've acted in ways that prove to you that while I get angry and hurt, I'd rather know the truth, even if it's painful. Otherwise, we're living under the pall of a lie."

We're treading in some deep, dangerous water here with the secrets of the past. I'm still not ready to relive that through the telling of it, and I'm hesitant to drag myself and my primary through the mud with them by giving up the truth in its entirety.

"It's hard to be totally honest with anyone. As you know, I've learned being honest gets you punished. Trusting *you* isn't hard. I have knee-jerk reactions—moments where I'm sure I'm going to lose you over something that I can't control. I still get scared. Then I get mad at myself for it because you have done nothing to warrant my reaction."

This is as close to real vulnerability about the past as I can be at the moment, and I hope he understands. Even with Wilde dead, the fear hasn't faded yet.

"You will not lose me over something you've no control over. I'll keep reassuring you every day until that demon is exorcised. You have my word that I won't punish you if there are truths you've got to spill. They may hurt me a bit, and I may need to be by myself for a time, but that's not a punishment. It's survival for me."

"I work hard to remember that and not panic." My expression is rueful as I sigh. "I have my own insecurities because I love you so much. You've become my haven, my refuge."

"I'll be whatever you need me to be, wife. Depend on me, for I depend on you; love me, as I do you; cherish me, as I do you; respect me, as I do you. The rest will either sod off or shrivel up and go away."

I kiss him again, smiling. "You have a way with words, buddy. You always say the perfect thing."

"When the feelings are there, the belief in something so strong — the words set themselves up right. I've nothing to do with it. But I promise you, we're going to have one hell of a good time working together."

I blink. "*What*?!"

His entire face lights up as if he's been waiting to tell me this for hours, maybe even days. "I heard this morning. Talia and I were at a meeting and found out, and then we took the walk on our way home. You're a newly minted contract agent at the Company. Meet with Mikhail and let him see your skills in training. There's some paperwork to do, but you're my partner."

Throwing myself into his arms, I beam. I sort of have a job being a leader here. That takes up some time, but I need something more. I need a purpose, an outlet, a place that isn't where everyone owns me and I can be who I've become.

Everyone here remembers the old Deli, but this extra dimension doesn't fit into their picture of me and no one will adjust their view. They just keep putting me back in that box and are so disappointed when I don't fit into it anymore. Wilde and Sari were the worst about it, but it's not an uncommon problem of late.

I need this.

"I can go on missions and be a super spy now? That's awesome."

Narrowing his eyes, he gives me a look. "Partner. That means you're going with me, woman."

Sniffing, I grumble, "I can pop in and out. You know I can take care of myself."

I feel the long-suffering sigh as he shakes his head. "You know, I hate when she's right. Talia bet me a bloody Wright print that you'd be off on your own before I could bat a lash. You haven't even signed the papers yet! Women are going to be the death of me, I bloody swear."

"She's a smart cookie, that one." I nod. "When can we go? Can we go now? I want to go now."

Taurus sighs again. "There goes my plan, up to and including naked gymnastics for the night. Alright, love. Throw on some clothes and let's go see the uptight nit that runs the agents."

It started out rough, but this is shaping up to be the best day ever.

The Bird Loses His Temper

TAURUS

*R**age. All I feel is blinding, scorching rage.*

Which is really unfair, because today was good. I was good. The sky was clear. The blood bag was hot, just how I like it. Deli actually smiled at me this morning—really smiled, like the scare from the drugging hadn't eaten her alive. She made one of her sarcastic little comments about my blood bags tasting like warmed-over regret. I almost choked on it from laughing.

She seemed like herself again. So I let myself hope. I let myself breathe. I went to work humming like some idiot in love. And I was. I am. I thought maybe—*maybe* we could start to move forward.

Then that gnobbly little troll reached out.

Of course it was Sari. Her name alone makes my molars grind. My minx's *other* mate family and self-appointed moral tornado. The woman looks like she collects haunted dolls and bad intentions, and somehow still acts like she's got the ethical high ground. She's been circling Minx like a buzzard since the blogger died, clinging to

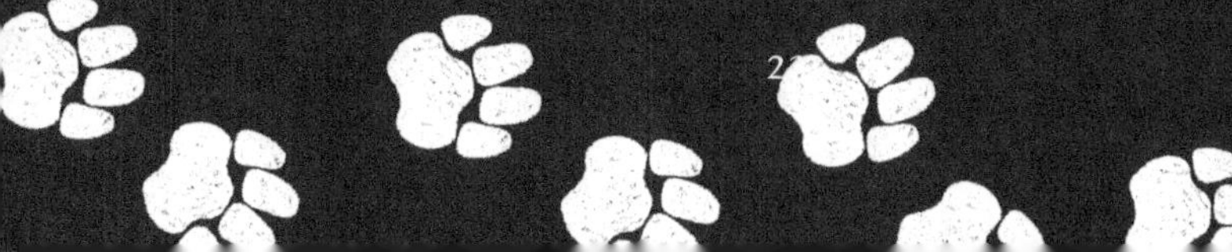

the past, playing on her grief. Wilde and Sari were her mates first—Sari never let go of that, not even after death took him.. She's been trying to twist Minx's pain into something useful ever since.

She's still on this stupid resurrection kick, and I need her to fuck off and leave my minx alone. So when she wanted to talk, said she had questions about grief? I figured I could use this opportunity to get her to back off. If she needs my input on a theory, then she's going to listen to me when I tell her why she can go straight to hell.

I should've said no.

Instead, I told myself I could shut it down. That I could go in there, look her in her raccoon-eye-shadowed face, and tell her to back off from my wife, once and for all. But I didn't shut it down. She opened the door looking smug and unbothered, as if she hadn't spent the last month trying to coax Minx into some twisted spell that would bring Wilde back from the dead. Her tone was syrupy sweet. Her house smelled like dried blood and lavender.

"You're here to try and stop me," she said, already pouring tea like we were girlfriends catching up after brunch.

"Damn right I am."

"Too late," she said, smiling like a snake. "The theory's sound. The spells are aligning. I just need a little more. A final ingredient. A final *push*."

"You're not dragging Minx into this."

She waved a hand. "Deli already said no. Refused flat-out. Said it was wrong—said bringing Wilde back would break the universe, that some laws aren't meant to be rewritten. She's been avoiding me ever since you lot dragged her out of that ruin. Typical. She thinks staying away is the same as staying uninvolved."

For a second, pride swelled in my chest. That's my Minx.

But then Sari leaned back and said: "You know Wilde asked her to marry him, right? Long before you ever did. Gave her a ring and everything."

My world stopped. "What the fuck did you just say?"

"Oh, she didn't tell you that part?" Sari asked, tilting her head with mock concern. "How awkward. You gave her your heart, and she just forgot to mention she already had someone else's ring once upon a time."

My fists curled into themselves. "You're lying."

"Ask her," she said lightly, sipping her tea like it was gossip and not a live grenade. "I'm sure she'll come clean. Eventually."

I left. I don't remember how I got out. I don't remember the drive. Just the pounding in my temples and the sharp taste of betrayal clawing up my throat like bile.

My mate lied—again.

She didn't tell me when she was hurting after Wilde died. She didn't tell me she went to Sari first. She didn't tell me about the ring. And now I'm supposed to sit here and pretend it doesn't mean anything? What else is she hiding? What other pieces of her past is she keeping quiet because she thinks I'll get mad? Is that what I've become to her? Some temper she has to tiptoe around?

I've never asked her to be perfect. I've only ever asked her to be honest. And still, she didn't come to me with this either. So now I'm here, back in our home. My shirt is half-ripped from yanking it off. My boots are scattered somewhere down the hall. I smell like sweat and bourbon and betrayal.

I storm into the gym room, lock the door, and crank the music to near-illegal levels. Sound pours through the speakers like thunder, loud enough to shake the rage loose from my bones.

And then I start to *destroy*.

I HIT the bag so hard it swings like a pendulum, slamming against its chains, creaking like it might rip free. Good. Let it. Let everything break. Let it all come down.

My fists ache. My wrists protest. I don't care. I can't care.

Because now I can't stop picturing Minx, sliding that ring on her finger, accepting it, holding onto it, never once thinking that maybe I should *know*. What did she do with it? Does she still have it? Did she keep it somewhere—quietly, privately—like a memory she couldn't let go of? Like a secret she didn't trust me to handle?

I slam the bag again, this time with both fists, palms open. The impact rattles my elbows. Why didn't she tell me? I would've understood. I would've listened. Even if it stung, even if it tore something open—I would've rather had the truth. But now it feels like she let me give her my everything when she hadn't let go of his.

The mirror across the room shows me my face twisted in fury. My hands shake. My breath comes in short, harsh bursts. I can see the blood where my knuckles split open, dripping down into the padding. Good. Maybe I deserve to bleed.

Sari meant for this to hurt. That's what really twists the knife. She *wanted* this wedge. She planted it with precision. But the soil she used—Minx's silence—that's what let it grow. The bag bursts, and sand spills out like guts, spraying across the floor.

It's still not enough.

I grab the dumbbells, start curling them not for form, but for fury. My arms scream. My jaw aches from clenching. I think about her in that hospital bed. About the way she trembled when she woke up. About how she reached for *me*. The thought is acid behind my eyes. My whole chest tightens, like my ribs can't hold the anger anymore.

The bag's gone. The weights are dented. The floor is cracked beneath one of the plates I hurled.

And still I want to scream.

So I do. I roar into the silence between songs. A sound that rips something open in my chest. A sound I didn't even know I was capable of. It doesn't make it better. I sink to my knees in the mess. Breathing like I just ran a marathon. My hands are shaking. My vision swims.

She's my wife. My mate. My Minx. And she didn't trust me with this. Again.

I bury my face in my hands, blood smearing across my cheek. I love her so much it hurts. And right now, that love feels like a cage. Because what if I *am* the reason she hides things? What if she really thought I'd lose it? Am I proving her right? I want to believe I'm better than that. I *have* to be better than that. But I didn't give her the safety to tell me. Not really.

So I kneel there, in my own wreckage. Punishing myself the only way I know how. I don't know how to forgive someone who didn't trust me. And I don't know how to stop loving her, even when I'm shattered by her silence. I dig my nails into my thighs as I sit in the wreckage, surrounded by torn equipment, spilled sand, and the smell of my own blood.

This isn't just rage anymore. This is despair with claws.

If she doesn't trust me now—after everything we've been through —*will she ever?* I wrap my arms around my knees and lean back against the shattered punching bag stand, bones aching, muscles twitching from overuse. Every breath feels too sharp, like I'm swallowing broken glass. The silence between songs stretches out, but I don't move to restart the music. I want to scream again. I want to punch a hole through the floor. But none of that will change the fact that she made a choice—not once, but *over and over*—to shield me from her truth.

The worst part? I understand why.

I *am* the clone who once ripped a man in half for looking at Talia wrong. I *am* the brute with fists like wrecking balls and a mouth that forgets gentleness when I'm hurt. I've tried so hard to be better. I've fought every day to make this life with her something *safe*—something she doesn't have to survive. But what if she still sees me as a threat? What if she still thinks my love is conditional, that if she says the wrong thing, I'll walk?

Or worse—that I'll stay, but not the same.

I grind the heels of my hands into my eyes, like I can force the storm to stop. I feel like I'm unraveling. Not just from the betrayal, but from the fear that I'm not what she needs. That I never was.

My Minx has every right to her past. Every right to love, to mourn, to make impossible decisions and regret them. Wilde was her mate. She lost him. And maybe in some corner of her heart, she still holds a piece of him so tightly she can't bear to share it.

But I need her to let *me* be the one she shares it *with*. And if she never does? I don't know how long I can be the second heart in a bond built on silence. I don't know how long I can watch her choose quiet instead of truth. Because it's not about Wilde. It's not about some ring hidden in a drawer.

It's about me standing here in the wreckage—alone—again.

I thought we were past this. I thought we were building something stronger. Realer. Something rooted in honesty and fire and mutual ruin. But she didn't give me that. She gave me what she thought I could handle, and now I have to decide if that's enough. If she can't bring herself to let me see her whole—flawed, grieving, messy, raw—then what the fuck are we doing?

Am I her husband, or just the consolation prize that came after the tragedy?

My hands tremble. I flex my fingers, watching the dried blood crack along my knuckles. If I lose her again—if this becomes one more fracture we try to plaster over—I don't know if I'll come back from it. Not this time. She's my wife. My mate. My *Minx*. And I love her with every monstrous inch of myself.

But I can't be the only one willing to burn for this.

The Cat Corrects A Wrong

DELILAH

I pop in from the long-assed orientation that Taurus *swore* I wouldn't have to go to and look around. His duster is on the couch, silk shirt on the floor—this is strange. I hear the muted bass in the workout room despite the sound proofing and I take a deep breath.

Something is very wrong.

Trying the door, I find it locked. I close my eyes and apparate into a corner, hoping that if anything is flying, it's not coming straight at me. I'm coming in blindly, after all. "Baby?"

He whirls to look at me, eyes golden and fierce, with a ridged forehead and fangs. Bleeding from his hands, his chest, everywhere—I can see where his destruction cut him, sliced him, and wounded him. He growls low in his throat and stands, chest heaving as he stares at me. I lick my lips and look at him, trying to ignore all the gore as I murmur, "What's wrong?"

"I. Locked. The. Door."

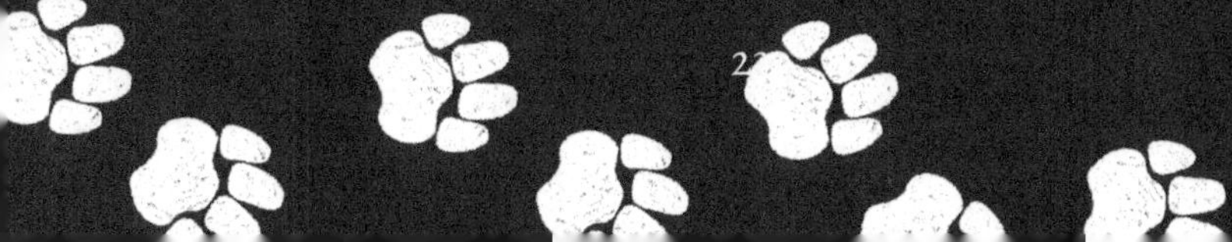

"The last time I locked the door, you threatened to break it down. I was subtler," I tilt my head, studying him.

Taurus snarls and turns his back on me, ripping at the punching bag and tearing it apart. Sand flies out and dust chokes him as he continues to beat on it. Sensing his unwillingness to talk, I sink to the floor, curling in the corner. Watching, I just tuck up small and wait.

I can be patient if this is what it takes; it's not my first male tantrum.

My mate strides over to the stereo, cranking the music louder. He grabs a sword off the weapons wall and advances on the training dummy. Hacking and slashing, a shard of the blade breaks off and imbeds in his chest, debris nicking and cutting him as he just keeps going, intent on more self-harm than practice.

I have lots of experience with clones flying off the deep. If he doesn't aim it at me, it shouldn't trigger my issues. Hell, I've been this person. "Just let me know when you want to tell me what happened."

He spins again and snarls, "Your *other* mate called me and asked to visit the house while you were at work."

Rising, I stride over to him with my arms crossed over my chest. "How did this make a problem for us? Is her stupid bullshit going to tear us apart? I don't even know what she said to push your buttons."

"I didn't ask you to fix me."

"You know what? I don't care. You're going to hear this whether or not you want to. Rafe filled me in on his first run-in with her since the funeral this afternoon." He gives me a surprised look and I stand my ground. "Based on his conversation with her, I realize what she said to you. I know what she did."

Taurus says nothing, but I see him flinch when I tell him that Rafe saw her, too. He's worried about Talia, but he doesn't need to be. What he needs to worry about is what he's letting that stunted little witch do to us.

I'm the one being vilified unfairly here, and I'm doing my best not to flash over to worse situations—but it's difficult.

"I am not, nor have I ever, been called or asked to be, Wilde's wife. She's baiting you. He never gave me a ring—someone else did, but I stopped wearing it months ago."

He blinks at me, his expression still enraged.

"If you now doubt how much you mean to me in comparison, I'll tell you something I've not told them or you yet. I let you bite in a place that's almost over his mating mark from day one. I don't know if it was subconscious at first, but after a while, I allowed it. He didn't bite me there after we mated. He, uh, he bit other places for, uh, other reasons." I swallow hard for a moment and press on, hoping to cut off that memory montage. "Speaking of marks, I've been healing all the ones that belonged to your brother until I erased them. Maeve healed the tattoo during the draining, but I think she knew I was ready for that. On Rafe, too, if you're wondering where he is in all of this."

Maybe that got through to him because he stops glaring at me, expression surprised.

"Last, I've never allowed anyone to drink as much from me as you have. We mixed our blood like our souls are. It's why you've been able to access a little of my healing and some of my power. You didn't notice because you're a clone and assumed it was part and parcel of that. I'd drain again with you, even if I couldn't come back. When I came back, I was yours in a brand new way. I'd never have considered doing that or having a child with Wilde, even if he asked."

My claim is one hundred percent true, and I wish I could get him to believe that without giving up so much trauma. I could lift the burden if I could accept that I was so beaten down before that I let a serial abuser keep me emotionally—and physically—hostage for months until I met with Taurus. Rafe and I could face it and heal, but it is not time yet.

I'll know when it is—it's just not now.

I take a breath and let it out, voice softening. "I love you more than I thought was possible."

His golden eyes blink, and his chest is heaving. He's still snarling, but the ridges on his forehead melt away and his body unclenches. I might get through to him.

So I push the long, curly tresses out of my face, shrugging. "That's all, I guess. I kind of flew off half-cocked and ran out of steam."

A shudder ripples through him and he crumples to his knees, his head bowed on the ground. I watch, not sure what to do or say, except that I feel like I have to keep my distance. He doesn't want me nearby; I feel that. I chew on a fingernail as I watch him, not knowing what else I can do or say but wait. Sucking in a breath, I reach out, not quite touching him.

He shrinks back and I flinch, trying to stave off the pain that causes me, so I focus on him. His voice is raw and weak as he speaks in my mind.

~What I know isn't what she knows. She was in my home and she thought—she thinks... ~ His shudders intensify and his teeth chatter from draining adrenaline. *~I can't tell her. I have to say nothing; I took it. ~*

My heart breaks in my chest at his words, and I close my eyes. I need to control my reactions because I don't deserve comfort; this is my fault. I've made him feel this way because he's trying to be respectful of others. My inability to cut these last few ties has made him *vulnerable;* it's made him hurt.

I scoot back, letting my hair curtain over my face so it hides my face. *~What can I do? ~*

His dry chuckle is a mockery—echoing a soul laid bare.

~I can't ask. I won't ask. I wonder sometimes, though. Why is hurting them by telling them how it is with us a more grievous sin than hurting me by not telling them? I wonder. I bleed inside with it. ~

Dropping my head more—this time in shame—I suck in a breath.

~Maybe it's not. Hurting anyone is a sin, baby. But hurting you like this is making me ill. I suppose I've always thought of you as stronger. I thought you were secure in how much you meant to me and it didn't matter what anyone else knew, didn't know, or poked their nose into. I don't know. Sari knows about the ring; she used that to hurt you; I think. I should have a talk with her once she sobers up; you're right. I can't promise that I can change her mind about how she views us. I've never been able to change her views on me, not once the whole time I've known her. ~

~I don't care what the lemmings know or don't know, but she came into my house. My family's home and I wanted to tear that smug superiority off her face, but I didn't. I didn't. ~ He keens low and deep, the pain and pride warring in him. *~The skilled manipulator strung me up in my home and I let her. I'm ashamed of myself. ~*

I blanch, feeling even more ashamed, even dirtier inside. If I've questioned myself about why I haven't revealed the whole of my past with Sari and Wilde, this is why. This kind of shame is unbearable. I've kept it so long that I can't even speak of it, and this is not helping me get closer to doing so.

Swallowing my pride, I reach out with my heart instead of my hand. "Baby, don't get upset. Sari has been playing this game for a long time. She was looking for things to hurt you because she's hurting over Wilde. Last time we talked, she compared me to Tamara and Rhea—traitorous emotional vampires. She struck out with the most painful accusation she could, and she knew it. She did the same thing to you today. Instead of bringing up a million other things, she brought up me. She knows I'm your weak spot and the more we protest it, the more she knows it's true."

Taurus doesn't answer, so I keep going. "She does it when she's lashing out and I'm pissed. She's at her house, lolling about drunk, watching cartoons and giggling like an idiot, knowing she's caused you pain. I'm so royally pissed right now!"

Sucking in a huge lungful of air, he raises his head. He looks around the room with no expression on his face, taking in the devastation with cool detachment. "Maybe cartoons are the sodding way to go. I should have thought of that when my heart was being ripped out of my bloody chest."

"I'm concerned about you. I'd lay myself down and let you grind your heel on my heart if it helped." My voice breaks and I let my head fall again, wanting my face hidden so he can't see the pain and regret written on it. "I don't deserve you. I live with that knowledge. My choices mean I live with knowing I hurt you because I'm not strong enough. I hurt others because I'm not strong enough. I can't lose you, so whatever I need to do to help you, I'll do it. You are my mate, my match, the missing piece from my soul, and I love you with every corner of my rotten little heart."

Pain arcs across his face. "Set me free. Release me from the bonds that kept me silent today. Allow me to be me—to not care, to stand up for what's true. I didn't do that today. I let your affection for a cancer in our relationship seep into me, sicken and weaken me. I can't and won't do that any longer."

This will splash back on me, but I owe it to him to let him be who he is, even if it's going to make my situation worse.

I nod, still hidden in the long waves around me. "I won't hold you back anymore."

It takes everything in me not to sob when he speaks. "I never doubted, not once, what I mean to you. That wasn't where my pain was. I've gotten neutered by your affection for Sari and her ilk; I can't live like that. She treats me with no respect and she seeks to destroy. I have nothing but contempt for her, her posse, or the departed mate. I let them do this to me."

Looking down at himself, he yanks the shard of the sword out of his chest, looking around the room. "I'm doing this while they watch cartoons and pick at semantics and other lunacy. No more." His expression is fierce as he spears me with his gaze. "I. Am. Not. What. They. Would. Have. Me. Be."

"I won't ask you to hold back anymore. I shouldn't have," I murmur. I curl tighter into myself, trying not to shake as the emotions rocket through me. "Frankly, I don't even care if you kill her."

I'm surprised to find that I mean that.

His brow furrows, and he feels like he's focusing hard, sweating. I feel him trying to heal the wounds through our bonds. I'm proud of that, proud of him for learning, and for being such a part of me that he can. His breath is raspy when he finishes, and I know that it's because that's not an easy feat when you first learn how. It drains you until you learn control.

"You are mine. Wife. Lover. Mate. Everything. You're mine. I'm not playing by any rules anymore unless they are my own. No more weapons to the enemy. They have enough and are well skilled at using them. They are all enemies."

My eyes are empty as I push to my feet, warring with myself inside. I can't stand him looking at me right now. I'm so filled with black, oozing self-hatred and loathing that it's like it's seeping from my pores like a disease. I smile, nod at him, and then I disapparate to the bathroom.

~I know. ~

Popping into the room, he growls. "What is that look for?" I feel him reaching for me inside and I'm not ready to let him in, so I ignore it. "Please talk to me? You can hit me if you'd like. You could use something sharp and pointy, maybe?"

"It's not about you." I drape my body over the toilet, having lost the lunch I'd eaten at the orientation. My face is red and swollen from tears. I lean my head on the cool ceramic fixture. "I'm frustrated with myself. Things from my past, my life, keep coming back to bite you. I've been too passive about it, and I'm angry at myself. I couldn't hit you if I tried."

What I need is space. He had his time to do what he needed. I need self-flagellation time, too. I don't need him to make it better. I want to burn.

"You'd think not, but I felt like I'd been pole-axed when you popped out on me. Can you not do that? The last time you did, you got drugged, and I thought I'd lost you forever and that's still a little fresh."

Wiping my mouth on my sleeve, I close my eyes. "I'm not in the best shape. I had to get to the bathroom before I barfed in the gym."

"You're—the—are you alright? What's wrong?" His face is full of panic and I feel terrible.

I don't want him to worry about Maeve; I simply need some time to deal with my self-destruction. "I'm fine. I'm a little queasy. I've been like that all day and covered it up so none of those jackasses looking at me like a ninety-pound weakling would haze me. The emotional stuff didn't help. It makes me sicker."

"This is baby stuff?" Almost like he just realized it, he stops. "I'll kill the entire sodding class if they so much as lay an eyeball on you to haze."

Sitting back on my knees, I shake my head. "No, no. I have to take my lumps like every newbie or no one will ever respect me. It's bad enough that they know who I am and assume I'm skating on your coattails. I have to stick up for myself. I'm not even supposed to show them what I can really do past some minute mutations until much later. I had some morning sickness. I siphoned a bit of my emotions off to Rafe to help control it now, so he's probably a little shaken, but nothing major. I'm okay now."

He drops to the floor and sits next to me, tilting his head. "I still plan on killing them."

I watch, hoping he keeps his distance—I crave the balance of being touched, but I don't deserve it. I need to feel this ache. *Yeah, I'm broken in terrible ways; I'm aware.* "That's unnecessary, I promise. I'm angry that as soon as I left, she hit up Rafe and then you. Rafe said she acted like everything was fine. She made him play the 'hard question' game—poking about you and about Talia. She seemed normal when she left. He didn't know the two of you had a fight."

"I'm through with her, baby, and through with the dearly departed sod of hers. She's cancer."

"Sari tried to make him paranoid about the both of you. She failed, but she pushed the right button to try. She said she was nervous because Talia had told Wilde she loved him, but hadn't been around since he left. She said Talia hasn't been upset, but she realizes now that it's because she'd replaced him with Rafe. She said it was convenient for Talia to step right in as Rhea left, falling for

Wilde, and you becoming my mate as she'd aimed for her spot in our family."

I know this because of Rafe, who quietly handled his own panic over this shit.

"That's sodding funny. I mean, come on. That's funny." He chuckles, shaking his head.

I arch a brow, not finding it funny at all. I find it appalling. "How in the hell is it funny?"

He laughs like a loon. "Talia's set herself in *our* family. Oh, come on! That's a bloody riot! Man, that 'our circle' shit *kills* me."

"I think the drugs fried me because I don't get it. Speaking of those, remind me later that I want to talk about those. I have some thoughts."

"Christ, woman, you've *really* got to stop yammering at that bint about us." He brushes my cheek with his fingers.

"If I don't talk to her at all, she thinks I'm holding stuff back from her. She's not perfect, but she lost her mate. I'm trying not to abandon her—because that's what she implied with the resurrection stuff—so I text her back and drop by sometimes. If she stays *off* the Wilde thing with me, I figure it's better for the entire community if she's not on a rampage. I try to keep some stuff private because I don't feel she needs to know."

Plus, I need her to stay away from Rafe so he can heal. It's my turn to take some lumps.

"From what she did, I see little that you haven't told her. You gave her all the weapons, love. Honestly, until my sweeper team confirms her story about the writer, I'm not buying all this mumbo jumbo about a quest and bringing him back. I'm not convinced, and neither is Talia."

"I'm trying to be a good friend and avoid causing a problem with us because she's off the rails. I can't even think about the possibilities of her 'quest' because I think he's dead and I think she's trying to bring him back. Everything about what I hear about these journeys is troubling to a real practitioner like me. She's doing the work, but not the soul stuff." I sigh and rub my temples.

I should have never, ever let inexperienced people work Beltane with me. It opened up far too many dangerous doors.

"From where I'm sitting, you've given her plenty of firepower through idle chatter. You left out how it'd affect you if she used it. Meaning, she knows almost as much about our relationship as we do except how different and important it is from anything else in your life. I can't rightly figure why it matters if she thinks you're holding back on her, but that's your gig, not mine. It explains why today was such a bloody good time, though." He leans back, stacking his hands under his head and pausing as if to think.

"I've been trying to get her to be—I don't know. It felt hypocritical not to share if I'm asking her not to conspire in the background like a secret agent. If I ask her not to do things like the bar again without at least talking to me, but don't reciprocate, then I'm no better than her. She's so very unstable right now; I'm worried about the quests and those bints whispering in her ear. I'm worried about the community."

Sari is a seductive, manipulative bitch. Without my physical relationships holding some of these looney tunes close, I don't know that I will keep them from joining her side on anything important. That goes double for Belle, who I believe whores her family out to help keep people on their side.

"The irony in all this is that I made sure it was only me at the house today so Talia wouldn't get a 'woe is me' about Wilde and get forced to admit her connection with Rafe." He shakes his head, still sitting a few feet away from me. "Here's the deal. From now on, remember that while she may be your friend, she's not mine, and she's not Talia's. We're enemies. Please don't give her anything else she can use against me. Not that it matters because next time I see her, I'm setting a few truths on her doorstep."

"I will be much more careful about what I share with her," I murmur.

I don't tell him I believe that this moment has put the shreds of what was left of my friendship with Sari on a slab. We no longer have Wilde to bond over. She never cared for me as a mate, and now I can't even have a casual, girly conversation with her. She's done nothing but seek to destroy everything I am or have for months. I have to figure out how to do this without her leading a fucking mutiny.

"I love you, baby. Come hunt with me. I'd like to make some things bleed now." He stands, holding his hand out and giving me a grin.

Nodding, I stand and take his hand, still feeling the need to earn forgiveness. It's not him asking, but I'm not ready to let my transgression go yet. However, I can get behind taking my frustrations out on others. I clear my throat and force a small smile. "Let's go make some people scream. Then maybe I'll make you scream, too."

"I like the sound of that."

With that, I head off to take my vengeance on everyone but the person who deserves it—and I forget to mention my thoughts on the drugs that almost killed us.

The Artist and The Blade Make A Promise

RAFE

Blade and I are watching the stars in the backyard. She's been quiet, but I understand that. We've been suffering through the vast waves of emotion being siphoned off to us by our mates as they battle over the coyote's experiment in emotional manipulation.

It's put a big ass crimp in my day and I'm pissed as hell about it.

Sari visited me earlier, and while in rare form, she wasn't behaving as badly as she did with Taurus. I mistakenly thought everything was on an even keel. Whatever quests she was doing kept her busy, and she left me alone. I thought maybe things would settle down. It's the only bloody reason I even let her in.

I should have known better.

"She told Taurus she had something that Wilde had meant to give you before the accident. She called it a John Thomas something or other," she says.

I pinch the bridge of my nose. For Christ's sake, this is the same shit she pulled with Taurus. Sari tried to use Wilde as a weapon to divide them. Taurus didn't know the terminology well enough to catch what the coyote was saying. She was also trying to drive a wedge between Blade and me.

"I'll bet she did. She didn't mention it to me on her brief visit. My guess is that she didn't realize that neither of you knows what she means," I growl, looking out into the sky. Frustration is zinging over my skin because I know this is a lie. Sari made this whole thing up to discredit us with our mates. "She means a ring for—"

"Oh!" She drops her head, looking defeated again.

I lift her chin, looking into her eyes. "It's a flat-out lie, pet. He wasn't ever going to do that and had mentioned nothing like it. She's trying to cause a rift between us."

She shrugs, looking down, and fumbles in her pocket, muttering, "I guess that makes this whole thing foolish." She's flipping something around in her fingers, still looking forlorn. "It's not a cock ring."

I blink. "I'd say not because regardless of my opinion of myself, it'd be a wee bit undersized, I'm sure."

She blushes and hides behind her hair, muttering again. "I'll say."

I grin a little, feeling lighter. She keeps playing with the thing and I get curious. "Are you going to put whatever it is on me?" I raise a brow, trying to figure out what is making her so shy.

"It's not for you." She whispers, so much so I wouldn't be able to hear her if I didn't have enhanced senses. "See, Damien's been working with metals and he made this." She shoves her free hand in her pocket and holds up something that resembles a flattened metal circle.

"Oh." I tilt my head, surprised by the turn of this conversation, given the anger and resentment caused by the coyote today. It's driving our mates to have a hell of a row that was splitting our heads open a few moments ago. This is a serious commitment and one I've only gotten asked once before. I don't think it's meant the same way Alistair meant it; I think it's more. I did not expect this after the blow-up earlier.

She whispers, "It's not done. It needs something."

I take the metal from her hand, looking at it. "What does it need?"

"A lock of your hair," she says. The words tumble out so fast that I don't even think she paused between them. Her face is bright red beneath all the hair she's hiding behind; I know it. "If you can't, I understand. I don't have to have it."

Eyeing her thigh, I point. "Cut it with Precious. I don't have sharp pointies like the cat. At least, none that I've seen yet."

"Huh?" She blinks, looking dumbfounded.

"The hair, love. It will not fall on its own, right?"

Stuttering, she nods. "O—okay." Plucking Precious out of her sheath, Blade looks for a place in the back that won't be too noticeable.

I shake my head. "Wait a moment." I look down at the middle finger of my left hand and remove the band. It was a gift of love—not intended for any nuptials—but as it symbolizes a commitment, I couldn't bring myself to take it off yet. I thought it healed until now, but I move it to my right index finger and look up at her. "Now, I'm ready."

She looks confused and I sigh, not wanting to go into detail about something that is going to upset her. "I want—I want to put this on you. I want it to mean something. For that to happen, I have to make a conscious decision about who I am committed to. That person is you," I mumble.

Making an owlish face, she looks as if she wants to ask, but decides not to. She holds up the dagger, spinning it a little. Winking, she shears the lock without me even blinking an eye and picks it up. "Lay it across the ring in your hand and then say something. Give me a minute to remember what Damien said."

"I hope to hell it isn't 'hunk of burning clone'."

She bursts out laughing. "You know about that? Oh, the stories I could tell about the fights at the house between Damien and Taurus over that incident." Giggling, she blinks. "Now I remember! You say 'chosen'."

I chuckle. "That git fancies himself a funny rotter, eh? My girl did clone hand puppet theater for us one night about those two. She loves a good sock puppet clone show." Seeing her smile as she imagines it, I look at the flat thing again. "I lay it here like this with the hair on it and say the word?"

She looks unsure. "I'm not sure. It's muse magick. They're supposed to—but that might not work now that it's only—I'm not sure."

Looking confused, I nod. "Okay. Let's try it, yeah?"

"WAIT!" she yells, looking panicked. "Damn it." Reaching into her pocket, she pulls out another piece of metal. "I might not have mentioned everything. I didn't want to ask you to wear this because you're not—but you can. No meaning other than your affection for me. They're a matched set. They're supposed to work in tandem."

Pursing my lips, I ask, "Was it because of what I can't give you? If you don't want to, I'll understand." I feel doubt on my face, warring with what I want and what is right. I know how the cat feels now, worried that the ties that bind from the past have screwed you out of happiness now. I know she's been hiding how much she's hurting that the bird has never reciprocated the ring she gave him because she knows it's her own fault. She won't put herself on the line and ask. I thought it was stupid, given how bonkers he was for her. Now I know why she won't. It's because asking that question made my heart shrivel in my chest for a moment.

I suppose it's a constant open wound on hers.

Knowing all the things she's carrying, I hope to hell no one ever has to go searching around inside her to heal anything. Demons lurk there, and I don't mean the sexy ones we clones have. I mean, she stores true black holes to hell inside labeled drawers just waiting to get free. I look over at my mate again, troubled by her silence as I ponder.

Finally, she lifts her head and peers at me, eyes dark with emotion. "I choose you to be my soul mate until the end of days. I want you to be mine and wear that ring for all to see as a testament to that. Regardless of what your prior commitments are, I want that, but I won't ask you to if you feel compromised by the request."

Relief has to be written on my face because it's a tidal wave in my heart. "Then we should get moving on this. Let's get them nice and settled on our fingers."

She beams and hands me Precious. "This one needs a lock, too."

I take it and give a spin, winking at her.

Her eyes follow the dagger and she murmurs, "That's weird. No one else but me has ever used that dagger. No one's even touched it since I got it. I'm protective. I handed it over to you. I didn't even think about it. Huh."

I test the weight in my hand, noting that it feels familiar, despite not having touched it before. "It feels like it belongs here. It must be a mating thing." I reach out and snag the needed lock.

"It must be. You are running around with all of my blood in your veins."

The blade spins in my hand unbidden as I listen. I sit it in her palm with a small grin. My hands moved faster than I've seen before while I was touching it. "I think you've made me dangerous."

Her eyes glow, and her smile is a unique blend of love, seduction, and pure evil. "Yeah, I've been told I have that effect on people."

She holds the ring in the palm of her left hand, lays the lock of hair over it. "Ready?"

"I am."

We watch each other, saying in unison, "Chosen."

"The rings glow a bluish color, growing brighter and brighter, forcing our eyes away from the painful glare. My hand feels hot where the ring is touching my skin. The light ebbs and I look down with curiosity. She grabs my hand and examines it.

What had been a solid band of silver was now a carved, embedded ring. The strands of her hair are braided intricately, making up the center band of the ring, and anchored by exquisitely detailed silver catches that hold the hair in place. That muse does a hell of a job. "These are gorgeous, pet."

"You like? You're not saying that just so I'm not all girlish and crushed, are you? I had nothing to do with the style—it was Damien on that one. The initial request that I g—no, all his ideas, I mean. Anyway, all we gotta do is put them on each other. They'll shrink to size, according to him."

"You want to go first, or should I?"

"Me first." I pull her hand forward, stroking her fingers before sliding the ring onto her ring finger. She smiles as the ring shrinks to fit securely on her finger.

Touching my left hand, she kisses each knuckle, and then slides my ring onto the same finger I'd used for hers. My eyes slip closed and I swallow hard, pulling her into my arms. Nestled together, I feel so in love that I marvel at the difference a month or two make in life.

Looking at her hand, she murmurs, "I wear this because I love you. You make me whole. Without you, I'm nothing but a shell of a life."

I whisper in her ear. "I wear mine because I care for you. You've made me a new person. You discovered the person I had forgotten existed and never want to lose. Because of what we did and will do together."

Wrinkling her nose, she nods. "Okay. Big emotional moment over and I'm feeling good, but I have one request from you."

"I won't tell anyone that you were all soft with me. I promise." I wink, pinching her leg.

Shaking her head, she mutters. "Not that. Please don't multitask. If the gnome comes to you and wants things? Or the idiot comes back and needs things? Don't let me come over that day. Allow me to keep that separate. I can't deal with feeling like second place."

I blink. "Love, she and I haven't been together in a while. Maybe since Beltane."

"Baby, I haven't been with anyone but Wilde. You know, I wasn't seeing anyone after the exes. It's been you."

"I appreciate that, but I had to be sure. I love that you're wearing my ring and that I'm wearing yours."

I fiddle with it for a moment, the turn of the conversation making me nervous. "I've never worn a ring on this finger before."

"Never? Is it okay? I'm still a little nervous about the implications, so hop in with a little more explicit definition. You look a little stunned."

I shrug, not sure I can explain why it feels so big and how much it scares me to commit to her. I didn't blink when she asked, but it puts me in such a vulnerable situation. She could destroy me— worse than anyone has. "People have given me rings before, but always with the explicit explanation of what they weren't or what they didn't mean. They put them on other fingers. I never expected anyone to do so. I'm stunned. I mean, not even the cat has, though that's different. She puts rings elsewhere." Her eyes cut to my piercings, and I shrug. "We're unconventional markers. She's got some, too."

"I'm kind of awed and humbled that you'd want to wear mine there." She grins a bit, eyes dancing. "You realize that if you tell anyone what a silly girl I am, I will kill you. This blows that whole 'bad cop' image all to hell and back."

"It's our secret, love." I smile and kiss her nose.

She yawns and I smile. "You tired, baby?"

Grimacing, she nods. "I don't want to be."

"I know, but we'll have tomorrow and plenty of other days."

"Do you mind if I stay? You know, like, kind of permanently?"

I snort. "Kind of permanently? Is that akin to sort of pregnant?"

"Yeah, until you get sick of me or something."

"I won't. You can stay if you like, baby. Since the rest of the family filters in between houses doing this and that, you and yours are always welcome. Hell, I thought that was what the suitcase was for. Hex made you a robe and Leo's got a bunch of healthy food crap in the kitchen for your shakes and such."

Her eyes widen, and she tilts her head. "Your housemates have already set up things for me? Like stuff, because they knew I'd be staying here?"

I chuckle. "Oh, love. Hex and the bitch have been making bank on you since you walked through the door. The book on when you'd do what has steep odds. I think the cat even won a grand on something."

Growling, she mutters under her breath. "She did that big furry cheater. Just tell me the bird wasn't involved."

"Nope. This is an in-house thing. We gamble on each other all the time. Odds on the cat and bird disappearing three minutes into the party are ten to one. I think I'll make a chunk on that."

She gives me a smirk. "Okay, Lucky, tomorrow you and I will visit the big palooka and I'm going to have a look at these books. Knowing this place, the boozy brunette is holding all the cards."

I laugh and stand, holding my hand out to her. "Indeed, she is. In the morning, we'll have her lay out the spread at breakfast."

"Oh, the 'yours' in you and yours won't be trotting through. I have no intention of letting Theodora have a crack at you. Expert help is so hard to find." Her lips curve up.

"I don't think she even showed a hint of interest in me when I flew by your place, baby."

"Good. Shall we go inside and sleep now?"

I grin. "Absolutely, my love. Tomorrow is another day."

The Cat and The Bird Go On A Hunt

DELILAH

When I told Taurus we were going to have a blast working off this tension, I wasn't kidding.

I need blood, and I need it to run down the walls.

Sari has always been a cunt, and as much as I *hate* that word, this time she's let the darkness inside of me loose in a way that is dangerous not only to the wicked but to anyone in my path. The Beast and I are in concert; we want vengeance and we don't give a flying fuck who dies.

I'm not used to that feeling.

My recent kills of choice have been tied to research on crimes going unpunished, as if I'm some avenging angel of justice. It's a patently comic book stance, but it helps me deal with the rising bloodlust as it conflicts with what is left of the human side of me.

That tie broke tonight, and I am struggling to fight it. I shouldn't care; Christ knows the humans wouldn't. Humans are capable of much more violence than faith gives them credit for.

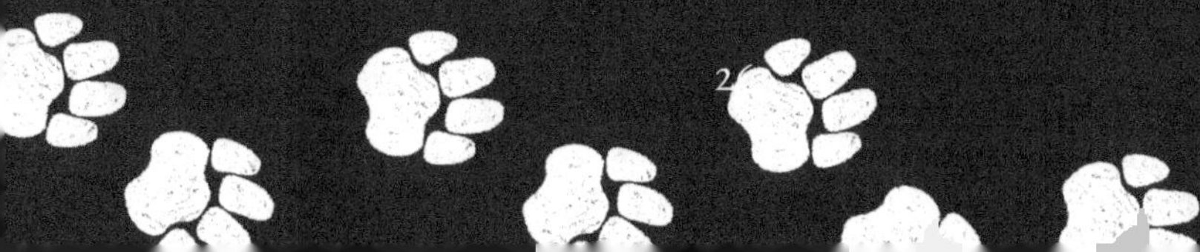

I don't remember when I stopped considering myself human.

Closing my eyes, I focus on targets I've identified in the past month since Wilde died, knowing that I have a few that are both wicked and large enough to sate the desire to maim in my soul. When I remember the intel about the cartel and their clever hiding spot, it makes my lips curve over my large fangs with anticipation.

This will do.

Turning to Taurus, I tilt my head. "I know a place that we can go. Come with me and we'll feast, my love."

His grin is evil as he runs his eyes up and down my body. "That all, love of my heart?"

Chuckling throatily, I shake my head. "Not if you're an *awfully* bad boy, darling. You'll want to see this."

Snorting, he takes my hand, lifting it to his lips and nipping each knuckle playfully. "Minx, I don't know how to be any other way."

I yank my hand back, crossing my fingers and stretching my arms out, cracking my knuckles and shoulder joints simultaneously. "I promise you'll walk funny for a week, you arrogant fowl. Follow me."

With that, I smirk and disapparate, leaving him to find me via our mating bond.

LETTING OUT A DEEP BREATH, I smile as I appear in the old German style rectory building of the church near my hometown. Taurus doesn't know how close we are to where I grew up. Since the Winter Incident, I stopped bringing those I care about near the horrors of my past. I'm wary of this area on the other side after the Beast and my magickal awakening, because I worry about being tracked by echoes of a torturous past.

I don't want her to locate me.

However, I know that heroin is a problem in both my home state and most of the ones that touch it. High poverty and low education populations are breeding grounds for drug epidemics, and this rural area is no exception. The farming and manufacturing communities have been decimated by the economy and technology, leaving desperate people in their wake.

A simple Google search and a little digging around the top layer of the dark web helped me find the rumors that plague this place. It was abandoned financially by the Church—gee, who would have thought the holy rollers would be so cruel to the poor—and it got bought by a cartel member.

Again, religion fails the people it should serve, only to get saved by evil. The agreement that the church and its staff continue its mission while allowing the cartel to operate from one of the unused buildings in secret must have felt Faustian to the nuns and priests, but self-preservation is another hallmark of humanity.

I lick my lips, listening to what sounds like a choir practice as I wait for my mate. A discordant sound makes me wince and I growl—the super ears of a predator are even more sensitive to bad music than a normal human.

"A church, my little tail feather? Seems on the nose, don't you think?"

I laugh again and turn to wrap my arms around him. "Or perhaps just ironic enough?"

He smirks down at me before dipping his head to kiss me with a hunger that promises to be delicious. "Your wish is my command, love. Always."

Pressing against him, I move my body in a way that is unmistakable. "Then let's show the pious what true evil looks like." I pull away, noting the glazed look in his eyes before I turn on my heel and stride to the wide wooden doors as if I'm entering a throne room.

I can feel him watching me as I stop. Tilting my neck back and forth to crack it, I drop into a fighting stance. A spinning kick has the old wood splintering and falling out of the frame as I call, "Yoo hoo, any bodies home?"

A nun that appears to have survived the bloody Crusades appears, her full habit odd for the hour. Her lips purse as if she is used to unwanted intruders, and perhaps in this drug decimated area, she is. That and a cover for the drug runners may be the reason that her supplicants are having choir practice at eleven thirty in the evening on a weekday.

"The church is not open for confession, my child, despite activity inside. You will need to return tomorrow."

Laughing, I throw my head back, allowing the Beast to shimmer forward. My claws extend, my eyes widen and shift, and my body fills with power that mirrors the rage in my soul. I know these people are not responsible for Sari trying to cause pain within my family's relationships, but they are not clean either, so I feel the balance in the Universe will be restored.

"Sister, I am not here for redemption. You cannot redeem those who sell their souls. I'm here for vengeance."

Turning to my mate, I grin. "Winner is on top." Leaving him to gape, I sprint past the nun with her mouth hanging open towards the sound of the offending choir with malice in my eyes.

How dare they butcher one of my favorite Handel pieces?

Taurus must be dealing with the door nun because he doesn't appear, and that's fine with me. I round the corner of the old stone building, scenting my way to the room where the women are struggling through the familiar bridge. I continue to crack my neck as wrong notes and unintentional harmonies make my gut curl in revulsion.

When I locate the room, I don't even bother to banter with the women. My ears hurt and my anger is overflowing like a river in a monsoon. Diving into the choir with a snarl, I swipe at the most offensive soprano first, drawing blood as I hit her shoulder. The others scramble away, trying to climb out of the pile of bodies, trampling on one another.

Yanking her up by her neck, I grin fangily. "A minor fifth? Really? I should kill you *twice* for that."

Done talking, I dart my head in and rip her throat out, noting the sound she makes almost hit the right note this time. Drinking deeply, I toss her aside when she goes limp. I turn to the rest of the choir, ignoring the blood on my face and clothes, as I stalk towards the first cowering group. "Can any of you hit the note correctly?" I ask, pretending to look as if I might spare the one who can.

A willowy blond stands, jutting her chin out. None of these women are dressed in a habit like the one at the door. Being younger, they must follow less strict guidance than Brunhilda out there. "I can," she says, her eyes alight with confidence.

I chuckle darkly.

Even a nunnery has a head mean girl. Bravery in humans only goes so far, and I can promise that it's not stretching out right now. This is pure ego and dominance. This is the girl that most of us deal with our entire life.

Sometimes, the Universe is kind.

"You can? That would be most pleasing." I look at the group she's huddled in, knowing that it's her gang of lackeys. "Can she? Are you willing to bet your lives on it?"

They look at one another, stupidly unsure if they should be afraid of me or her. That is a BIG mistake, as the hooker once said. The other small groups of women look at me and a brunette mouths the word 'no'.

I grin; I like her. Smarter than the others—a better survivor. I might send her to a friend if she doesn't piss me off. I know a religion far more suited to someone with a pair of ovaries like that. Maman would love to train a thing like her for the bar at her place —balls *and* brains.

"Come on, ladies!" I growl. "Answer me truthfully or die." They're going to die anyway, but since my husband's not here yet, I can play with them a little longer. "Can she hit the note?"

The group of four similarly well put together women—for nuns in training, I mean, because vows of poverty shouldn't include the quality of makeup they're sporting—finally give in and nod in unison. "Yes."

That is *exactly* what I wanted to hear. Clapping my hands in gleeful anticipation, I turn to Bitchy McBibleHo and smile beatifically. "That is excellent news! Piano wench! Please go back to the beginning of the bridge. Accompany our virtuoso here."

I stand, putting my hands on my leather clad hips, feeling my tail swish like the agitated kitty that I am. My fangs are itching to rip this little snot to pieces and the hunger for blood in my soul burns my belly.

The music begins, and I sigh, loving the sound of the piano as the girl sings. Her voice trembles at first, but her ego can't take going easy, so she warbles in a strong operatic style she had to have learned from a classical program.

It takes one to know one.

Unfortunately, this environment did not challenge her enough and her upper registers and ear have suffered. Her pitch wobbles fairly quickly, and it's not related to the stress of this situation. Her expression says that she can't even hear the variation in her notes versus what Handel wrote.

What a shame. The Magdalene Mean Girls were incorrect and now they all get to die much more painfully than I had intended.

Imagining Sari's face on the unfortunate woman's body, I dart forward, knocking her to the ground and as I slash and slice. Ironically, her pitch is better as she screams. I might be onto something here: death choirs. Quite groundbreaking, if I say so myself. Pulling her guts out, I hold them up to the whimpering cadre that were her friends. "I said to be truthful. You might be the worst nuns I've ever met."

They look like they're going to make a break for it when the shadow of my mate darkens the door. He takes in my bloody, gore covered form and his face brightens. "Oi, love, you started without me. I had a welcoming committee with a suspicious amount of weaponry for a church." He looks at the cowering choirs and beams. "That's two to four, love. Your arse is mine."

Rolling to my feet, I smirk, shaking my head. "The evening is young, my love." Winking, I pounce into the crowd of idiots who supported their friend, using claws and fangs to rip, tear, and shred mercilessly. He heads for another group in the back corner that seems intent on running through a door they pried open while I was distracted, and I stop, lifting my head. "*Wait!*"

Snarling, he turns to me with yellow eyes. "Costing me kills, love. Hurry it up."

"Not the short brunette with the green eyes. Looks Irish. I have plans for her. Everyone else is fair game." I send him a mental stroke and go back to feeding. I'll need the energy if I'm going to be running through this enormous maze of a bloody medieval church.

I fucking *hate* when they run.

The Bird And The Cat Compare Notes

TAURUS

"Come out, come out, wherever you are, kitty…"

I grin to myself, turned on by this entire outing. I've been like sodding granite since she kicked that door down. It was impressive given she's only had two weeks of training. I've never asked what kind of experience she had in her 'dead life'—that's how I think of the lives the full-time residents of the Rift led before they moved here—but she sure as bloody hell must have had some training. The constant cracking and loosening of her joints points to it, though it could get explained just as easily by her status as a shifter.

That was some MMA shit, and she looked hot as fuck doing it.

My mate hasn't discussed the extent of her shifter physical aspects with me, mostly because she knows that nothing about it bothers me. I wouldn't give a flying fuck if she could turn into a big cat, but I'm not sure if she even knows. I doubt she's tried. Between learning control of the Beast inside, her magick, and everything else

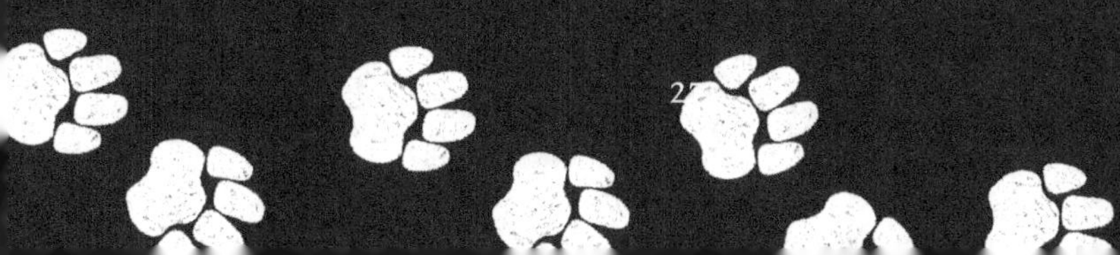

going on in our lives, my guess is she's never considered taking her powers for a test drive beyond what happens automatically.

After I dealt with the unexpected amount of firepower of the Columbian gang members at the door, I found her toying with her food in the choir room. I watched for a bit before I made my presence known and I swear to Satan, if I didn't love her with every corner of my rotten heart, I would have fallen for her again. I'm uncertain if she would have let that flat bint live if she'd hit the note, but I think my kitty knew it would never happen. Humans are nothing if not predictably arrogant and self-serving, so she played their egos against their common sense.

I've caught three more altos since we split up, and my total is now seven. After her stunt, she was five and I bet she's nailed a few along the way. My woman can be deadly efficient when she's in the mood; tonight is no exception. Either way, I come out a winner—literally—because I'm going to pound her into the goddamned ground when I catch her. Who's on top is merely a matter of competition.

A chorus of harmonized screams echo along the high ceilings. "That's eight, my love…"

She sang that part and it makes me laugh as I scent the air. Christ, if she were anymore perfect for me, I'd swear we were part of some mystical destiny bullshit. "Keep lying to yourself, minx. You're mine tonight," I call back, chuckling when there's no response.

Her rage is dancing along our connection, and it makes my demon snarl in happiness. She's not only feeding, but using this trip to clear her mind of the anger at her so-called mate. It's a good plan and since it's going to end in some monstrous sex, I'm all in.

The competition and the chase are bonuses.

Three tattooed gits with MP5s jump out of the next corridor and I smile widely, dropping into a deceptively lazy fighting stance. I'm unconcerned with their weapons and even less with their angry shouts in Spanish. Disapparating behind them, I tap one on the shoulder and he screams as I tear his throat out before he can get his bearings. The other two whirl, bullets flying as their trigger fingers react without noticing that I've disappeared again.

"Oi, gents, I'm over here now," I taunt, watching the panic in their eyes grow. They look ready to run and I sigh, knowing that idiots like this are cowards at heart. No playing with my food for me.

Popping in between them, I grab them and knock their heads together, dropping one to feed. Blood spurts everywhere as I tear messily in frustration. The one on the floor has a large Bowie and I grin. My girl loves souvenirs, and what better souvenir than weaponry? I tuck it under my belt and hoist the moron up to finish him, whispering in her mind as I drink. *~Eleven, my ferocious feline. You're falling behind. ~*

Her laughter tinkles in my mind as I feel the sensation of her ripping the arm off of a victim and clubbing him over the head with it. *~Never, darling. I've got a roomful here. ~*

I shake my head, ripping the throat out of the last of the morons who dared to attack me and pick up one of the MP5s, considering. Is it cheating? We didn't discuss rules about weapons outside of ourselves. She doesn't have any, but if she taps her magick, she won't need them to keep up.

~That changes the rules, baby. Consider me suited up. ~

Feeling the air in the entire building shift, I curse, knowing that I've given her permission to let loose. "Fuck me," I mutter.

~Planning on it, ~ she rumbles into my mind and I get a picture in

my mind of a room that's now filled with dead women in various states of carnage.

The bad news is that I'm going to lose; she just annihilated fourteen people in one swoop, bringing her total to twenty-two. I don't know how many more people are hiding in these buildings, but she's going to wipe this place off the face of the planet if I don't find her and distract her first.

"I'm coming for you, kitty cat. Be ready!" I shout, dropping the gun and disapparating to the first place that feels like her. Using our connection to end our hunt might also be cheating, but I don't fucking care.

I'm done playing.

I FIND her leaning against a wall, draining the Mother Superior on the altar. Moving to her side with a speed that clones are born with, I sink my fangs into the other side of her neck. Our eyes meet as the last embers of life burn out in the woman and I swear to hell, my bloody soul—or whatever passes for it—sings.

We drop her simultaneously, breathing hard in the silence of the enormous room as the dance begins. She moves first, pouncing as quickly as I'd moved a moment ago, and I'm shocked as my back hits the floor. Her lips curve over her fangs in triumph, but I roll us, pinning her to the ground with a matching smirk. Her snarl of frustration makes my demon chuckle, and I lose my edge when she darts up and scrapes her fangs over the scar on my neck.

~The cheating never ends, my love, ~ I pant, trying to get a hold of her slick skin as she uses her claws to slice my perfectly tailored shirt

down the front. It falls to the side as she hooks her legs around one of mine and wrestles for control.

~Fuck the rules. You're mine. ~

I almost give up right then, as her words make my cock throb and my brain scrambles. By the time I've regained my senses, she's gotten loose and is crouching in front of me on all fours like the Beast inside of her. I can see the primal in her emerald and gold-flecked eyes, as I prepare for the next move.

She's fully unleashed.

The world seems to stop as we leap at one another, rolling down the stairs of the altar to the aisle, slashing and biting like wild animals. I rip the leather corset off of her, her breasts tumbling free into my hands, and she groans low. Not to be outdone, her hands grasp the open silk of my ruined shirt and yank it with a force that detaches it from the arms.

With a mental promise to replace what we're destroying, I let her take my tit obsession as an opportunity to flip us. She gives me a fangy smile as she sits on my cock, grinding down as I pinch and tweak her nipples painfully. I know there are scars from nipple piercings there, and I wonder if she'd get them re-pierced. I can imagine playing with those fucking things for hours as she screams into the rafters of our bedroom.

~Later, baby, ~ she laughs into my mind, running her claws over my nipples with a mischievous look in her eyes.

~Not a fucking chance, woman. ~ I growl back, remembering her quick piercing of my ear.

A moan echoes as I replace my hands with my lips and tongue before she can shoot back a reply. I can taste the blood of her victims that's soaked through her leathers, and I make it my mission to make her come before we even get our pants off.

She hears my thoughts and shakes her head, her long mane brushing my thighs as she arches her back and pushes into my mouth. Her hands slide down my sides, leaving red trails as she shreds the belt and waistband of my pants with a flick of one of the deadly sharp weapons that are part of her. *~We'll see about that, my pernicious peacock. ~*

Taking the challenge seriously, I use my fangs and teeth to torture every inch of her pale skin and rosy buds. I'm so intent that I barely notice her spine curving impossibly as she arches further back, continuing the slices down the legs of my pants. I growl when she lifts on her knees, losing contact with my aching cock, and reaches her arms over her head as she bends.

A nipple pops free and I look up, eyes narrowing. Her grin is positively evil as she falls backwards onto her outstretched hands, pushing her body into some sort of bridge. Her feet kick up, flying over her head until they meet the ground and she's in a crouch at my feet. "What the bloody *fuck*?"

"Never challenge a gymnast without locking down all our limbs, my mate." She springs forward, slitting the pants from the bottom until her claws meet the previous cuts, and tosses the top half of my six-thousand-dollar bespoke garment aside as if they made it in China.

Blood stains both of us from head to toe, and I think she might have innards caught in her riotous waves. The sight of her crawling up my body like some primal barbarian queen makes my balls tighten and I smirk down at her. "Give us a kiss while you're down there, eh, woman?"

Her glare is glacial as she prowls, purposely avoiding everything I ache for her to touch. I'm about to chastise her when she moves like wildfire and drops onto my cock. A roar escapes my lips, and her satisfied purr tells me she's won this round. My hands reach down and grip her hips, fingers digging into her flesh, urging her to move. Shaking her head, she stays still, her expression both triumphant and mischievous.

"Stop fucking around, minx, or I'll..."

Her throaty laugh cuts me off as she does something with her inner muscles that makes my eyes cross and my head drop back onto the floor. "Or you'll what, my wicked man?"

I don't have words at the moment because I'm too busy choking on the sensations that curl from my balls to my gut and up my body, paralyzing my brain.

Where in the holy fuck did she learn to do that and why I am just finding out about it?

"Oh, my darling. There are *so* many things I can do that you haven't experienced yet. You didn't realize that I could bend myself into a pretzel to escape, now did you?"

Letting out a breath as she continues whatever the hell it is that she's doing that's melting my fucking brain into pudding, I shake my head mutely. I'm going to leave bruises on the spot I'm gripping, but she doesn't seem to care. Her lips curve over her vicious feline fangs and she lifts and drops without warning, tearing a howl from me as she rocks hard and fast. I might as well let her have this one because I don't know if I'm going to be able to form a sentence when she's done.

Her claws lengthen—she didn't have them fully extended during this fight and that should tell you something—and she rakes lines down my chest that will require healing. Blood drips in rivulets and when she leans down to lick them without stopping the violent motions of her hips, I swear to Satan that my eyes cross.

"Don't. Move," she commands and I wonder if she's done this

with my — Before I can finish that thought, she snarls, lifting a hand to grip my throat. *~Do. Not. Finish. That. Thought. ~*

Her movements grow more frantic and I can feel the rush of her orgasm coming as she alternates between squeezing my neck with one hand and leaving furrows all over my torso with the other. This is the most primal fucking I've experienced, as Talia has lines from old scars in the past and I know my minx does, too, but she seems comfortable being in charge. Perhaps it's her dominance that makes this okay and fuck if I'm going to stop her.

Before she comes, she stops and I cry out in rage, balls tight with the need for release, and she smirks, tapping my lips with a claw. She cuts her finger on one of my fangs and offers it to me, and I suck like I haven't eaten enough people to satisfy me for days. My hunger for her is unparalleled and no amount of random kills will ever sate it. The flashing of her eyes says she knows that and after a moment, she yanks it away.

"Taurus…" she sing-songs, her expression full of wicked intent.

"What?!" I practically roar, unused to her showing this much control over her desire or mine.

She doesn't answer. Instead, she leans back on her hands, lifts her hips, and spins herself in a circle without disconnecting our bodies until she's sitting facing away from me. I choke and sputter as the muscles inside of her start that wicked waving again and I howl in response.

What in the fuck is she doing to me?

"You may sit up," she breathes huskily. "Do *not* take control."

I suck in a breath. I'm not a bottom, but she's hot as hell and something about this encounter screams it is an exercise in trust. Complying, I sit up and it changes the angle of our coupling and she lets out a low groan that would give a porn star a run for her money. It vibrates over my cock, and I wonder how long I will play this game. "Minx...," I warn, letting her know I will play along until I can't anymore.

My naughty mate leans her head back into my shoulder, her back hitting the painful scratches on my chest and lighting the fire again. She whispers in my ear, "You may move. Hands on my tits, bad boy. Make me come."

Eyes flashing with the demon, I snarl and drop my lips to her mating scar to suckle as I thrust into her. My hands wander all over her frame, avoiding the scars I know she prefers untouched without having to look. Her moans and gasps spur me on and one hand slides down to pinch her nub lightly, causing a contraction inside of her that makes my eyes cross again.

I can feel the climax inside of her build again and when it reaches the apex, I sink my fangs into her scar and she screams an ascending scale of sound that puts every dead bint in this hellhole to shame. Her claws dig into my hips and her fangs are bared and glistening against her pink lips. I could watch the view from this spot for the rest of my life and never bloody tire of it.

When her body shivers, I roll my neck, cracking it to prepare for whatever she has planned next. She's claimed victory this evening, and despite my competitive side, the demon inside of me is hungry for more of her Beast's dominance—which has never happened before. A purr echoes out of her, caressing my skin and making my heart race.

~What's next, my violent beauty? ~ I murmur into her mind, surprised by how much I'm enjoying her letting go of all of her preconceived notions of who and what she's supposed to be.

Her tail flicks back and forth and she laughs. *~To the victor go the spoils, my love. ~*

Before I can ask what that means, she's disapparated, leaving me hard and wanting. I roar my frustration into the rafters and she giggles into my mind.

~Ollie, Ollie, oxen free... ~

Oh, my minx knows me well. I *love* the chase and when I find her, I'm going to fuck her until she can't walk, much less run from me again.

~Here kitty, kitty, kitty... ~ I rumble into her mind, the demon face sliding into place as I get to my feet.

This time, she's *mine*.

The Cat And The Bird Are Holy Terrors

DELILAH

I wake up early, stretching the soreness out of my muscles. A grin spreads over my face—I feel *amazing*. We had a hell of a time hunting last night. When we got home, we were covered in blood and laughing. He carried me honeymoon style, and we fell asleep curled as one. The bonding during that massacre resolved all the ugly caused by Sari.

That box I keep saying people put me in?

This little escapade should destroy that image. If not, then they're being obtuse. Even Wilde would have had to look at me with a different lens if he were here. The convent was a brilliant choice.

Stirring, my husband rolls over and murmurs, "Was the convent everything you hoped for and more?"

"Personally, I thought the Mother Superior was right tasty. I think it's the virtue that's so satisfying."

I giggle, turning to face him. "I was so full by the time we left, I could hardly move."

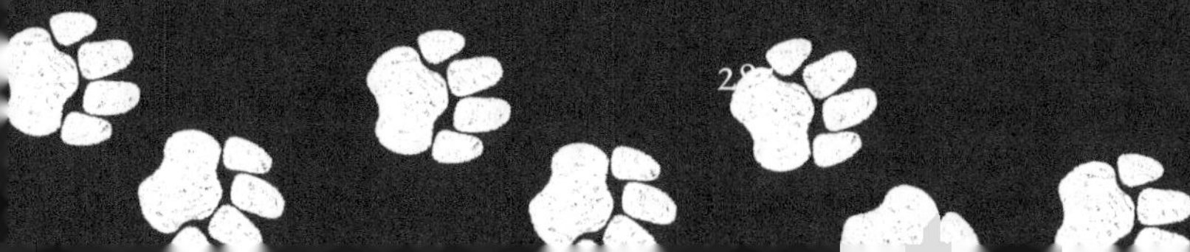

"Isn't that the bloody truth? Cloistered meant no running for us. I know how you hate the running. You were stunning with the choir."

"I *hate* when they run," I pout, then smirk a little at his compliment. "They had pretty voices. They even screamed in harmony."

He snickers and leans over to nip my jaw. "I thought the soprano bint that looked like a stork was a bit off-key, but as you'd gutted her, I suppose I can forgive her."

"That's why I did it, you know. She was butchering Handel."

"We can't have that now, can we?" Shaking his head, he sighs. "It was a good end to a shit night. I'm glad we went out."

I flick my fingers at the cabinet, turning the music on at a soft volume. "Now this is how Handel should sound. It's much better."

"Good thing you butchered the bint who was singing it flat. Right fine choice, that."

I nod, rubbing my tummy. "She wasn't even flat. She was adding a minor fifth." I grumble and listen for a moment, the classical soothing my irritation. "Mickey said that in two weeks I finish training and I'm official and can do my stuff at work. I'm exceptional at secret spy stuff. I'm picking things up faster than anyone he's seen."

He growls. "Bugger. I thought I'd bribed that git enough to keep you off the roster for a while. He owes me a bloody sailboat."

Blinking, I try to comprehend that he and his ilk place bets with things as big as boats, but I shrug it off. I'm still not used to it. "Okay. Well, yay for me, and no boat for you."

He gives me a long-suffering sigh and then tilts his head. "I've been waiting and waiting for you to realize what day it is, you know."

"I blink, pretending to think about it. "Huh. Well, it's a Tuesday."

Rolling his eyes, he shakes his head. "Keep forgetting our anniversaries—big and small—and I'm going to get a complex, my love."

My lips curl and I bat my lashes. "Has it been two months since we...?"

Throwing his hands up, he growls. "I should give up on knowing when you're yanking me. You get me every sodding time." He smiles and rolls over, reaching into the nightstand drawer on his side. "I have something for you and I'm sick to death of not asking. It's not original, but it's from my heart."

The box is small and intricately carved, so I'm calling bullshit on the not very original part. I think he's had every piece of this custom made and prepared for longer than he's admitting. He could have tortured it out of someone this weekend, too. "Ooh. Let's see what it is, since I find it hard to believe that you're too shy to say anything."

He blinks and then grabs it back. "Wait! Wait." He tugs me up so I'm sitting, then kneels in front of me, looking up. "I've wanted to give this to you and I'm sick to death of waiting." Opening the box, he reveals a ring that looks like his, but smaller. "Will you wear this as I do? Be mine in soul and life and death and blood and any other way I can get you? I don't care what finger you wear it on; I don't. Please, love, wear it for me."

My heart feels like it has stopped. I can't be breathing. I'm looking at the ring, so shocked and so taken aback that I don't even know what to do.

I've been brooding for weeks about why he never reciprocated my gift. My theories have always come down to my past. I thought about asking him, but I wasn't sure I could handle the answer.

I let it fester until I had to put it away, so it wouldn't consume me. It hit me hard last night when I felt Rafe and Talia exchange their rings, but I funneled it into our convent outing. I resigned myself to accepting that Taurus did not want to do this with me. I prepared myself to suck it up and move on, I've made my own choices.

And I figured I had to pay for them.

But he's on his knees asking me now, and I'm going to cry any minute. I feel the emotion swelling inside me. "I... I..."

I can't find words, and my hand is shaking as I reach out to him. I nod, swallowing the lump in my throat as big, fat tears fall from my eyes. "I will."

He brushes a tear away with his thumb, before reaching for my left hand. Holding the ring and looking at me, he murmurs, "Which finger, heart of mine?"

I whisper, "Where it belongs."

His eyes glow and he slides the ring onto my ring finger, brushing his fingertips over it as it settles on my hand. Raising my hand, he kisses the ring and then murmurs, "Never doubt my love, my complete devotion to you, to what's true and good and light. Never doubt you are my one, my only, and my life is yours to do with as you will. My happiness is you; my peace is you; my home is you. You are now—and will always be my everything."

Oh, now he's got me completely blubbering.

I'm crying like a complete fool now and I pull him onto the bed with me, needing to have him close. All my paranoia and self-loathing are shoved away in one simple gesture, making my world feel right.

He presses close to me, holding on as he lowers his lips to mine and kisses me. Whispering into my mind, he says, ~Happy Anniversary, my love. Tell me, is it still worth putting up with me each day? ~

That—and more—is how we celebrated a two-month anniversary: a bloodbath, a convent, and a ring.

It seems about par for the course for us.

The Cat And The Bird Find A Little Peace

TAURUS

I stride in, ditching my duster in the closet and pouring a drink. I don't see the minx anywhere around the room, which is disappointing.

She's been working hard in the training program; she stays well past the other gits to practice. Her scores are off the charts, but I can't let her know I'm checking up on her. She wants to do it on her own, and it makes me proud. I'm about to reach out to her to figure out where she is—because I know now that she's in the house somewhere—when she pads out of the bathroom.

Holy hell in a handbasket.

Minx is pulling a brush through her long, wavy tresses. The brilliant red of her hair sets off the alabaster color of the skin of her bare shoulders, and she's dressed in a filmy black silk nightgown with lace cups. Her bare toes peep out from under the long hem of the nightgown, and she gasps when she sees me. I suppose she didn't notice me while she was walking out. She smells like wild jasmine and looks like every git's wet dream.

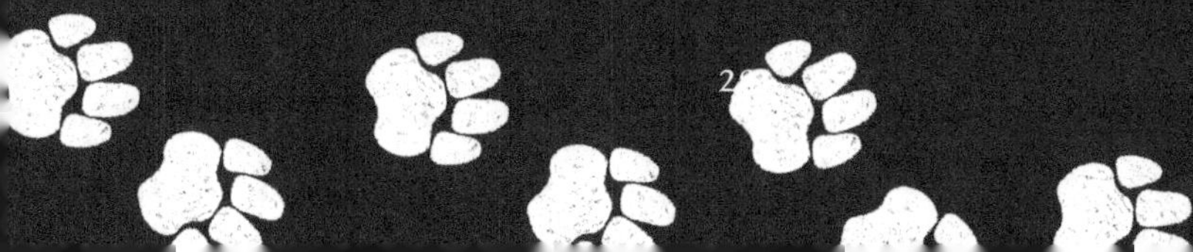

All I can do is stare at the condensation on my glass as it drips on the counter, my drink forgotten.

She frowns and turns in a circle, looking down at herself. "Is something wrong? Do I have chocolate on my face? I was eating while I soaked."

I swallow hard, trying to close my gaping mouth so I can speak. When I manage it, my voice is raspy. "Chocolate—uh, n-no, love. There's nothing wrong."

"Why are you looking at me like I've grown a second head in a very conspicuous place?" She gives me a peeved look, tapping her foot and pulling the brush through her hair again. It makes her jiggle ever so nicely, and I grin.

Sitting the glass down before I sodding drop it, I rest my palms on the wood of the bar. "Because you're the most beautiful thing I've ever seen and somehow I forgot between when I saw you last and now just how breathtaking you are."

She turns a lovely shade of pinkish rose, dipping her head. Her voice is tiny and all the starch goes out of her posture. "Oh."

I grin; I can't help it. Her ways make me smile. For someone who projects such a hard-nosed and confident image, she's flustered like a blushing bride anytime you compliment even the smallest thing about her. I move from the bar to her side, running a hand over her hair. "Christ, woman, what you do to me. You look stunning."

Wrinkling her nose—another one of my favorite cute-isms that I can't comment on—she scrunches down. "I was in the bath. I wasn't trying to be... I didn't know you were home yet."

My head tilts as I watch my finger trace down the soft skin on her cheek, then brush over her chin and trail down her neck. "Since when do you have to try? It's not something you have to do, I don't think. You are."

"No, I didn't mean—" she growls under her breath, getting pinker by the second. "Dammit, now I'm all flustered. I hate being a girl!" Stomping her foot, she huffs.

I smile wider. "What's flustering you, baby? I'm rather fond of the girl in the woman in front of me."

"I feel all—I don't know. This is why I don't wear stuff like this. It's all frilly and I feel like I should bat my lashes and pout. I get all weird."

It's best not to tell her she *is* pouting. I pretend to ponder as if I'm considering. "I see it's not your usual togs and it's right fetching, accurate enough. I'm not sure batting your peepers at me would make sense, what with all the naked glories we've had with each other. Besides, it wasn't the garb that gobbed me, baby. It's the woman inside it. You take my breath away sometimes."

She makes a face at me as if I'm the most troublesome person in the universe, but gives in and chuckles. "I know. You looked at me and I think girly clothes rot my brain. I get all soft."

"Only dressed like that, then? Never get that rotted brain feeling any other time?"

"Did I mention how you were looking at me? I think it plays a big part, too." Her expression is indignant, and she's tapping the brush on her arm, again setting every bit of her to jiggling.

That's my favorite.

I look down and pluck the brush out of her hands and then sweep her into my arms. Striding over to our bed, I settle us against the pillows with her sitting between my legs. I brush her hair in lazy strokes, humming under my breath. It's peaceful and despite how bloody fucking amazing she looks in that getup, I'm in the mood to show her why girly isn't such a bad thing.

Her lips curve and I feel her mood lift. She tilts her head back, relaxing as I stroke through her curls, moving with the brush. It makes me smile to watch her let go, so I hum a little louder. Her hair is shining like a fire and she must have used some of her home brewed soaps and such because the mixture of scents combining with hers is like an aphrodisiac blended just for me. Everything about this is what I want for us all the time.

Peaceful. Loving. Pain-free. Relaxed.

Swaying a little as I pull, she lets me pet and brush her, acting very much like the cat she is. I bend and kiss her shoulder or nip her earlobe or nuzzle her jaw, reminding her I'm there and keeping her from snoozing. Her tail flips out and taps my leg in time with the brush strokes and I grin—the kitty is *very* soothed. I feel my tail drop and find hers to twine together on the bedspread.

I sing low into her ear, crooning the King song I'd promised her. It's only for her because we're not in a bar full of people that hate us. It's just us, cocooned in a wonderful moment in time where everything is right. We don't get many of those, and I intend to savor it.

Her sigh is barely more than a breath, but I hear it, and I feel every muscle in her body relax. I'd bet she's smiling like sunshine and I'd win hands down. As much as she protests girly stuff—much like my primary—she loves it. It doesn't define her because she's far more complex than some others give her credit for with their one-dimensional view.

I make no such errors. Drooping against me, she purrs like an outboard motor, tail flicking with mine. I can only assume our little haven was missing something because, in a blink, she has a Godiva box on her lap. I pause for a moment, whispering in her ear, "I didn't want to wait for Presley week or some such, baby. I hope you don't mind."

"I don't mind." She chomps one of the white chocolate covered strawberries in her box indelicately and the contrast makes me chuckle. "I didn't drop these on your lap this time. Though, I ate the idiot who made them. Which is what he gets for being snooty and telling a pregnant woman 'no'."

Ah, there's the blood warrior behind the fluffy kitty.

"You should have killed him a second time for being stupid, my love."

"They don't die twice. It's no fun." I feel her pout and it makes me laugh. "But how bloody hard would it have been to dip some blood balls in white chocolate for me? I even had the blood balls! People are no fun at all."

My chest shakes as I try to contain the laughter bursting free. "Infidel. We could go kill his family."

She shakes her head, sighing. "I wore black leather from head to toe —well, mostly, because there wasn't too much to the leather, I guess. You'd think I came in toting a shotgun and wearing a ski mask." She looks up at me, wrinkling her nose. "Why bother? I bet they would taste as bland and white bread as him. Ick—not worth the calories."

"Philistine. Plebeian. Troglodyte. It's a good thing he's dead."

"Very. He'd be pissed that I took all the good stuff." She giggles and turns her head to one side, nipping my jaw. "Oh! Did you hear I did it all by myself?"

"Mmm hmmm. You took out a target all by your lonesome. I'm very pleased."

"I was all worked up and thought I'd jump you when I got home, because of all the energy and stuff, but this is good, too."

I fall back against the bed and groan. "I'm cursed with bad timing, love."

"Bad timing?"

"Yeah. I missed a jumping moment, and you got all clean and soft like."

"You have been seducing me since we sat down, so I don't think it's all a write-off."

I grin. "True enough. Jumping notwithstanding, I'm having a right good time with how we are."

"It's a pleasant change from all the ugly."

"Being drama-free is nice; I'll give you that, minx."

She goes still for a moment, and I realize she hears her mate in her head. Of all the bloody times for that git to drop a line, he does it *now*? "Bloody hell. What now? Sampson can't give us a night off?"

Her eyes roll up at me and she snorts. "Oh, yes, because he bothers me every night while we're shagging or killing." She listens again and sighs. "No, it's Talia. It seems like there's a problem with her arm. Nothing serious, but it needs the healing touch."

I straighten while I connect with my primary, verifying what the artist told my wife. She apparates a bottle out of—somewhere, hell, I don't know. She's getting eerie with the magick and disapparating. I'm not sure where anything comes from anymore.

"Shall we away, then? This one shouldn't take but a few. Nothing I can't do, barehanded and all."

"Let me, love. Save your strength for the strong-willed and daft." I take her hand and sigh. "I'm going to hide that woman, I swear it."

"I was planning on letting you do the work, baby. I'm saving my energy for the workout afterward." Her eyes dance as she pulls my arms around her.

I grin, admiring her pluck and groping her bum, then disapparate us both to her other house to find our mates.

And kill them if it keeps me from getting laid tonight.

The Artist Sends An SOS

RAFE

I'm in the studio, working on an interesting sketch while I watch for her to get home from work. Since I'm not burdened with that responsibility, I'm relaxing in my big comfy chair and sipping bourbon. She strides in, clad in low-rise jeans and a tank top, her bronze skin glowing against the purple of the sling her right arm is—wait a minute.

Like a thief in the night, she heads to the closet, trying to hide that she's shucking a brace and wincing. I see Precious on her left thigh instead of her right, and I know it's bad. She never throws lefty with Precious unless she has to. I keep quiet, pretending not to notice that she's struggling with unbuckling her sheath one-handed.

If she's going to pretend, I'll let her.

I head to the bathroom to wash the charcoal off my hands and arms. "I feel that, you know. Don't think you're fooling anyone, love."

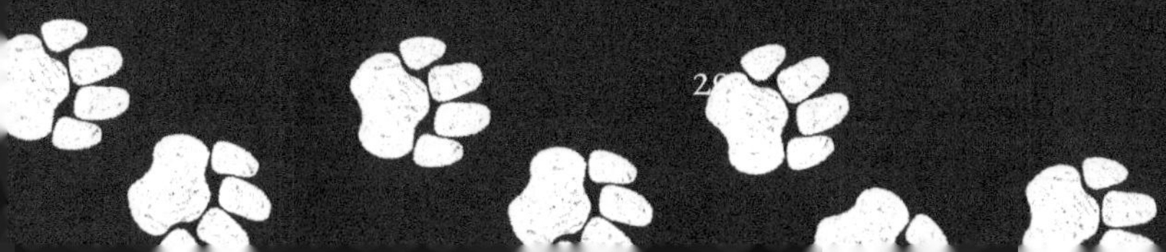

A flurry of mental images about snooping mates and death fills my head, and I chuckle. "You're not supposed to feel me when I'm blocking you, damn it. Only Taurus has ever been able to."

I feel her glowering in the other room and I snort, coming into the room. I have on low-slung track pants and I'm bare-chested with my hair undone. It's her favorite look outside of naked, so I give her a minute to stare before I speak. "You only say that because I caught you trying to pretend that it isn't killing you. It could get you killed in a nasty scrape and you are being hard headed as hell about it. It's not snooping if I feel it without thinking about it."

She narrows her eyes at me. "What do you mean; you could feel it? You're not—that's not supposed to—are you empathic?"

"Not last time I checked," I shrug. "I could feel you hurting and then heard you hiss. Then I felt you hurting again. It didn't take a genius to figure out what was hurting."

She stomps her foot, and it makes me grin. Cats of a feather and all that. "You're not supposed to *do that*. I'm empathic with full shields to keep from bleeding into people. If you feel my pain when I'm blocking everyone, that means..." She stops, her brow furrowing and looking as if she's contemplating something deep.

"It means what? It doesn't happen all the bloody time. I guess I've always been kind of intuitive about people and feelings. I'm a sensitive bloke, that's all."

"Oh. Okay. Maybe it didn't mean what I thought. That's good. You're intuitive and nothing else. Good." She frowns again, and it takes everything in me, not to mention the big ass shiner on the right side of her face.

"Should I not mention that I feel your pain as well? If it's going to make you frown more, then I won't."

"Feel?" Her eyes widen. "Feel? What do you mean, feel? That's not intuition. That's... feeling."

"Very astute, love. Feel is what I meant. I could feel it hurting—like 'ow' for me—and I could feel the intensity; that's why I'm trying to get you to stop pretending it's fine. I was humoring you for a bit, but I think you need to get it taken care of. I can't make you, though."

"Right. You can't. That's right," she frowns again and mutters under her breath.

"I could try, but it would end with you more torn up, which is kind of counterproductive, don't you think?"

She looks at the closet again as if thinking about something. She walks inside, out of my line of vision, and I wonder what in the bloody hell she's doing in there. Suddenly, a lance of fiery pain stabs into me and I roar.

"Holy hell, woman, if you want to walk around in pain, warn me next time, for Christ's sake! That's not funny!" I hear a thump in the closet and look in, finding her on the ground looking stunned. "If you were trying to prove me right, that's a damned good way of doing it. Blade, what in the hell are you doing on the floor? Are you okay?"

She shakes her head, then whispers, "You shouldn't have felt that. You shouldn't have. Even with a blood connection, even mated. No one should have, not even Taurus. I'm fine."

"You don't feel fine. You feel like you're still hurting and scared or worried. Definitely stunned."

Blade jumps to her feet, wincing at the jarring of the appendage. "Sorry. I don't understand. If you're feeling me through everything that I just threw up between us, then I don't think there's anything that could block you. As far as I know, that's not something normal. I have stronger shields than non-empaths, for obvious reasons. I've just never heard of anyone, not to mention a non-empathic clone, that could read—no, more than reading, feel—pain simultaneously with a shielded empath. It doesn't happen. It doesn't. There must be some rational explanation. It's that or our bond is a lot deeper than we intended."

I shrug. "I've always been receptive to powers and such. It didn't occur to me to say it to you because I can access a bit of my woman's stuff. If I think about it hard enough and focus, I can. I rarely feel that deeply unless someone's sending it on purpose, like if the woman's siphoning into me. It doesn't surprise me that our bond would be deep, though. Your blood's running in my veins, pet. We're connected bloody deep, I'd say. We both chose that—as much as we could choose, I guess you could say."

Her expression is a bit gobsmacked and I wait for her to process whatever it is she's thinking, trying not to panic. Is she upset? I didn't think it was a big deal; I can access my mates' gifts. The kitty calls me a natural power sponge. She says I have some gift for picking things up. I always have. I went on a mission once when I was young and green at the Company, liked the art in the git's house, came back and drew it all. That's how I figured out that I excel at art. Somehow, my brain does it.

It seems like it's making Blade awfully upset, though, so maybe I shouldn't have told her? I never know what I'll pick up. I feel her resistance to the thought I'd picked this up without intending to, or without knowing what kind of burden it could be to have that power for life. I know she's wondering how to address it and whether to make a big deal of it.

"Are we pretending I can't feel that?"

"Argh!!" She stomps into the bathroom, looking irritated.

I sigh, pinching the bridge of my nose. A familiar scene, that, and one I know is fraught with options—none of them good. The cat did a similar dance when she figured out how hard it was to keep me out and that I could see right through some of her veils. She's gotten *much* better, mind, and sometimes, she's successful, but again, her powers are much more than anyone knows and I've always known at least that. "Bloody hell."

Scratching my chin, I weigh out the possibilities. I could give her space; I could not give her space. It seems irrelevant to me since I feel the frustration and indecision from here. That's not even including that damn shoulder injury that she's going to get fixed tonight, come hell or high water. I roll to my feet and approach, tapping on the doorframe.

She looks over her shoulder, feeling me as much as I do her. "Okay. So, we have a situation."

"It's weird, feeling you as you feel me—very stereo trippy." I tilt my head, sitting on the counter. "Situation?"

"Well, less a situation, more a confusion. I don't know how it got so deep, but does it bother you? Because thinking about it for the few moments before you came in here—it doesn't bother me. I kind of like it. It makes me feel more connected to you because I'm more connected to you. Brilliant dot work, isn't it?" She shakes her head as if trying to figure out if her words made any sense.

"You're making perfect sense, pet. Maybe on the redundant side, but it doesn't bother me at all. However, pretending that arm's okay won't work. It's going to make me cranky as a bear because I'll feel it, too."

Giving me a wry look, she looks at her shoulder, warring with pride. "Fine, you win, but only because you pulled the 'it hurts me, too' card. I'll let you know that was cheap."

I chuckle, lips curving up. "You don't have to look so overjoyed about it."

Her head tilts. "Do you even get cranky as a bear? I didn't know your cranky meter went up that high."

"I've been told in no uncertain terms that I have my moments. Rarely, and it has to be something that sets me off, but I do. Getting up early in the morning makes me snippy."

"God, sometimes I wonder about you. You are just about as opposite of me as a person can be. I do not understand why you want to put up with someone who jogs several miles before 8 am, gets volcanically pissed at the drop of a hat, and is as strong-willed as a communist dictator."

"Variety, my love, is the spice of life," I say, holding my hand out to her, hoping to lead her back into the bedroom. "I also have a weakness for strong, stubborn women who shag like they only have a few hours to live. It's a nice yin to my yang. I'd be bored living with another me for sure."

"Hmm. We can't have that now, can we? A bored Rafe scares and boggles the mind." She gives in and takes my arm, walking into the bedroom.

"Too true. That's when I wonder things like how many people you can hang from hooks in the ceiling before they bust the drywall or how to reprogram the droids to hate each other or what the tensile strength of bungee cords are in relation to balcony velocity. It gets me in trouble every time." I sit her on the bed and grin, chucking her chin. "Besides, you've got a lot of right endearing qualities that I enjoy despite your fetish for exercise and early mornings. Layers like an onion, the ogre said."

She looks up and grins. "I've got layers?"

"You do. It's hard to be an interesting person without them. Everyone has what the outside world sees and a secret life inside that they only share with the chosen few, you know? Further into the layers, the fewer people it gets shared with."

Looking pleased, she ducks her head, and I ruffle her hair. Sometimes, the right words find you. "Speaking of ogres, I'm going to figure out what the cat's doing now because the arm thing is for the birds." I take a peek into my woman's head, trying to see if I'm hitting a soft core or okay to proceed. "Yeah, we're good. They have clothes on and everything."

"Huh?"

"I peeped to see if the cat was reachable for a patch up. Have to be careful because last time I got porn."

"Oh, damn. Did you call her? Rafe, that's not right. I can wait until tomorrow or next week or whatever." She frowns; looking like she feels stupid and selfish, and I shake my head.

"Uh-uh. Not next week, tonight. Get it through your skull, General Pouty. You're getting fixed tonight." She gives me a peeved look, and I sense her feeling like I've accused her of being judgmental and mean. "You're only bossy when you're covering for something you see as a weakness. Not all the time."

Her mental string of curse words at my astute breakdown of her psyche is amusing, but she glares at me.

"I heard that. She'll be here in a blink. Literally, I suppose, since she's into that poofing thing."

"Great. This is *so* unnecessary."

"Don't worry. I clarified it wasn't an emergency. If you're thinking it can wait, then do me a favor and raise that arm above your head and wave it please?"

She's so damned stubborn that for a moment, I think she's going to, just to spite me. But she changes her mind when I sit on the bed and her arm bounces, causing her to gasp.

"I thought so. No need to cripple us both to prove my point, pet."

"Ugh. Not good. Sorry. I know that hurt you. You're right—this stereo thing is trippy."

"It proves what I was saying. Besides, it's physical pain. I can deal with that very well. I'm okay."

Her head tilts and I see by her expression that the cat has told her mate about the injury. She makes faces as if they're arguing mentally and I wonder, not for the first time, what it must look like to outsiders when mates like us have these mental arguments.

Do we look like schizophrenics? Hell, are all the schizophrenics in the other place just people from another ribbon talking to mates far, far away?

I went to the bottom of the ocean on that one, so I'm going to leave it alone. This is why my mind shouldn't be unsupervised like I said.

"See? You tell people you're a little dented and you get all poked."

"You are more than dented and you know it." To be safe, I send Deli a reminder to calm down her king before they get here or nothing will get done."

The Cat Repairs A Broken Wing

DELILAH

We apparate into the room together and I sigh in relief when it doesn't appear as though Talia's badly injured. I don't know if the bird could take another life-threatening injury in a seven-day period. Talia's sitting on the bed, propped against the pillows, with my mate at her side. He's stroking her hair, and she's trying to look annoyed versus pampered. It makes me want to giggle.

Well, I guess she's not dying again, which is a relief.

"Right. What's the what, woman of mine?" Taurus barges across the room, glaring at Rafe, and I roll my eyes. "You two playing too rough at naughty naked games, mate?"

Rafe snorts and shakes his head. "As much as it'd be nice to claim victory on this one, I wasn't even there when it happened. Not a drop of nakedness about." Sighing, he looks forlorn that somehow he hasn't helped her mangle herself in an epic feat of sexual adventure.

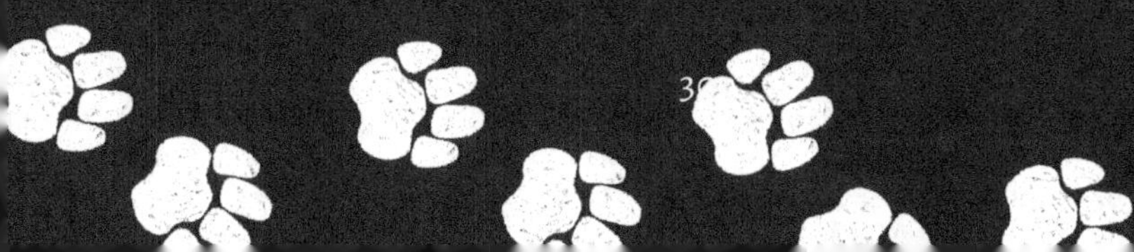

Men are the same no matter how enlightened they seem—always thinking with the little head rather than the big one.

"Sod off. If you must know, I was hitting like a girl at the gym." Talia glares at them both, but Taurus grins a little. Unfortunately, the rest of us are not privy to this part of the story.

My primary is clearly about to ask about it when he blinks, then narrows his eyes at me. Rafe bursts out laughing as he looks me over. "What in the hell are you wearing, kitty cat?"

The other woman's gaze swings to me as if she's seeing me for the first time and I realize that, in my infinite wisdom, I did not think of changing out of the filmy peignoir that I put on after the bath. She turns, hissing at my primary, "I thought you said there was nothing going on!"

Embarrassing. Truly mortifying. Bloody hell.

I flush bright red and curse under my breath again. "Damn it. Clothes! This is why I never wear shit like this." Glaring at Rafe, I mutter, "Shut up, you romance novel-looking reject." I trudge over to the bed, knowing my pale skin is now a rosy pink from head to toe.

"I'm sorry, guys. It's nothing. There's some torn cartilage, or a ripped muscle maybe," Talia explains, looking as chagrined as me.

"As far as I saw, there wasn't anything going on! I didn't notice the clothes," Rafe grumbles, throwing his hands up in defeat.

She glares at him again, and I feel he'll be hearing about this later. I don't envy that lecture. "I was working out and Long Hair is making an issue out of my minor injury. It's nothing."

Ignoring her apologies and the surprising lack of vitriol from my husband, I pad over to the bed. "No big deal. It won't take long at all if you relax. A pulled muscle or small tear isn't a hard job. This is nothing like last time."

I tilt my head and study her, figuring out the best way to treat without having her scream the house down and setting off the overprotective clones we love. "Can you get the shirt off and lay on your tummy? That way, I can get at the part that's hurt."

"I made an *issue* because you can't move your bloody arm, woman. I like your arms, so I figured getting it patched up might be a good plan," Rafe grinds out, looking irritable.

Taurus steps closer, looking at Talia, and then turns to me. "Will you fix the shiner, too, love? Mottled black and blue isn't her color, I'm afraid."

"Excuse me?" Talia asks, looking at everyone in frustration.

"No worries, I can fix it," I say. Turning to the crowd, I flick my hands. "Back off a bit, guys. Everyone talking about her instead of to her has to be annoying. She's already in pain. Plus, you're crowding the medicine woman. Skedaddle."

"Um?" Talia raises her hand and waves at me with her good arm. I blink and she turns bright red. "I can't get my shirt off because I can't raise my arm. I tried to move it a little while ago, but it keeps getting worse. And don't you say a word, Long Hair, but could someone hand me my blade?"

I smile, shaking my head. "Not a problem, dear." Flicking out a claw, I slice up the sides of the shirt. "Swiss Army hands to the rescue."

Her expression looks shocked, and I realize she's never seen the claws up close. The night I healed her, I was further away when I sliced. Though Taurus and Rafe have felt the burn, she has not. Feeling self-conscious, I flick it back in. I'm not sure why I feel as though I've done something wrong.

What is it about her that flusters me so much?

"That works, I guess," she murmurs as she grins a little. "I am sorry to interrupt whatever you two were doing."

"It's okay. It wasn't anything serious. I'm sorry if I weirded you out with the claws. I forget that not everyone is used to the 'kitty' me. It's off-putting for some and makes them uncomfortable." I say the last part quietly because I've had many unpleasant experiences with people not accepting my furry half and I don't need that kind of blow to my self-image again, thanks ever so.

"Speak for yourself, woman," Taurus huffs. "That will teach me to sing the bloody King for you."

Rafe chuckles under his breath, looking amused. "She's always a sucker for the soft stuff, though she protests so much."

I glare at my primary and then send my husband a gentle pinch. *~I'm trying to make Talia feel better. Cut me some slack, you ninny. You know how much I liked it. ~*

Talia grins at me, her eyes darting between the two and then back. Her face changes as soon as she attempts to move. She rolls onto her stomach as instructed, and I peel away the tatters so she can get comfortable. "You okay? If so, I'll try not to jar you too much while I get a read on the problem."

"Do whatever you need. I'm good now."

I shoo Taurus and Rafe off the bed, crawling up and cursing as I get caught in the gown's hem. I give in and hike the damned thing up over my knees, before I break my neck or hang myself. I lay a hand on her shoulder blade, closing my eyes as I delve inside to feel for the injury without putting pressure on it.

Talia's voice is full of sardonic humor when she says, "You know, we need to stop meeting like this. One day, it might be nice to get a cup of coffee or something."

"Very true. I'm sure we'd have plenty to discuss. Volumes, even." My eyes flick to our mates and I grin a bit.

"Oxford tomes," she says, then winces as her chuckles make her shoulder move.

"You're all tense because this hurts and the pain is making everything tense. I'm going to need to get that to let up to heal the problems." I float a bottle of massage oil over, having brought some supplies from home. I stop, waiting for her to decide.

Just out of range, but not far enough for my ears, I hear Rafe ask Taurus. "Does it make you nervous that they're talking about us like we're not here?"

"It's always that way until the 'here' bit is naked stuff. Though, the thought of those two joining "forces over a cuppa is frightening." He shudders. "It's on your head, Sampson. You're the one who keeps calling. Remind me to thank you for that."

Having had enough of their nonsense and feeling put off since Talia hasn't responded, I turn to glare at them both. Her head bobs against the bed and I let out a slow breath of relief. "Clones: you can't live with them and you can't drop them off a cliff," I mutter, uncapping the bottle of jasmine scented oil. I stop for a moment, seeing my issue. "I might need to figure out leverage."

"Actually," Talia murmurs, "you're wrong. You *can* drop them off a cliff. But they disapparate and show back up on your doorstep. I know because I tried."

Taurus growls low. "Bloody buggering hell, woman! That was a long sodding time ago, love, and we were having a fight."

I roll my eyes. "Back to the problem at hand, please. I have to get leverage to put the right pressure on because I'm going to work from the base of your spine, loosen the muscles, and then hit the shoulder blade once you've relaxed enough for me to work. I'm going to sit over your legs. Don't panic."

She nods again, snickering at Taurus' consternation. I adjust my gown, straddling her legs carefully. Once I'm situated, I pour the oil in my palms, rubbing them together. "This might be cold. I'm not sure."

I lay my hands down, working the muscles at the base of her spine.

"It's a little frosty," she hisses.

Licking my lips, I nod, adjusting so I can warm it better with my palms. "I'll see what I can do."

Man, she is tense everywhere, and I hope to hell I'm going to be able to help her, otherwise we'll be stuck here all night.

The Artist Is Entranced

RAFE

Propping my shoulder against the wall, I wait. I have to respect her request that we stay calm and back off so she can get Blade to relax. I know all of us looking at her when she's hurt makes her feel weak and stupid. That'll make her cantankerous.

A scent catches the air and I smile—jasmine. I love that bloody stuff.

My primary continues working on my wife, dipping her head as she knuckles out kinks and knots. "Ah. That's getting better." She works the muscles of her lower back, watching every reaction. Even without magick, I know she's got a gift for this. "The oil was heated when I had it in the bathroom, but by the time he called me, it cooled."

"Mmm. That feels good. The cold only gripped for a sec."

I figure the less I say, the less I'll get in trouble for. I'll keep my mouth shut while she works.

Besides, it's a pretty picture.

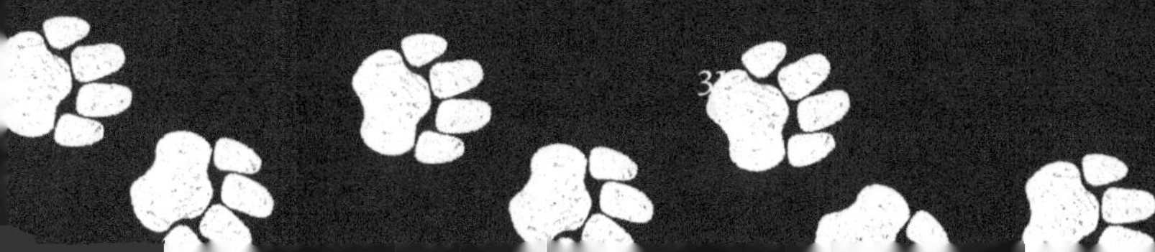

"Good. My hands are usually warm when I do this, so it shouldn't be much of a problem for long. The healing part generates a bit of heat."

The cat moves up my wife's back to around the ribcage area and I glance over at the bird. He's leaning against the opposite wall, grinning like a loon.

Guess he thinks it's pretty, too.

Blade sighs, relaxing under the massage. "Nice hands."

"You've been holding back lots of owies, it feels like," she chides. Resting her hand just under the shoulder blade, I watch the cat lean over and use leverage to loosen the muscle up. She's done that to me before when I sat too long in the chair working and my shoulder's trashed.

Looks different right now—not that I'm complaining. Not a bit.

I catch the bird looking at me, and without warning, he speaks into my mind. *~I don't know who's enjoying it more, mate. The golden goddess or me. ~*

Chuckling, I wonder for a moment why no one thought it was important to tell me he could pan-orate, but I nod. I drop into the fat armchair, trying to look casual. I wonder if I can do it back. Cat's mated to him and me, so maybe? *~No bloody kidding. Sometimes, I amaze even myself with my brilliance. ~*

I have no idea if he heard that, as he doesn't respond. Damn.

"I'm used to holding back that stuff. Easier for me to handle on my own, without expecting others to do it for me. Ouches only hurt if you think about them."

I observe the cat, trying to see what she's doing now. Ah. She's chiding her.

"Remind me to send some special oil over here. I could give it a little kick so you wouldn't need me around to make it work for you." Her hand moves to work on a bicep as she kneels, the other hand working the right shoulder blade. That flame red hair is sweeping all over the golden and porcelain skin around them, and the visual effect is stunning.

Not to mention other things.

I'm so wrapped up that I break the low tones by blurting, "No need for that."

My eyes dart from one to the other, but they don't pay attention to me. That's good—I'd look like an idiot right now.

"Appreciate it," my wife says.

I feel her skeptical emotion through our bond, and it occurs to me she heard me.

Fuck.

My primary turns to me, tilting her head. "I wasn't saying you can't do this. Don't be a baby." She rolls her eyes at me and leans down to whisper to my wife, "Fragile egos on these men. He's been on me to teach him how to do this. All sensitive about not picking it up as quick as he'd like."

Blade chuckles, then winces, and grumbles, "See, now, Long Hair —leave off until Deli's finished. I laugh at your pouts and I hurt."

Something transpires between her and the cat and they giggle a bit, but I'm not paying attention. I've gone back to ogling. They can share a little secret as they want. I cover my mouth, trying not to snort. When I get under control, I clear my throat. "Alright then, love. I'll be a good boy and sit quietly while you finish."

As if we don't all have the preternatural hearing, my wife whispers,

"Personally, I think the sensitive pride gene got over-enhanced in the entire batch of clones."

The cat giggles again, making her body shake and her hair tumble a bit as she lays her forehead on my wife's shoulder, whispering to her. "Gee, do you think so? However did you figure *that* one out?"

I arch a brow, looking over at Taurus. "They *know* we hear them."

He grins a bit at me. "More than that, mate. At least one of them is listening to you." Eyeing me, he smirks, looking both amused and interested in our mates.

~I hear all of you. Don't act so bloody superior, you leches. Not that I couldn't smell you, which I'm certain she can. It's like a pheromone factory here. You should be ashamed of yourselves. ~ She sniffs and returns to her work, looking satisfied that she told us off.

"Nah, luv. Don't think there's much room in the knickers for being ashamed right now. Talk to me again later." Taurus smirks again, looking as if he's enjoying every second of this.

"Have I mentioned how much I love those cat's ears of yours, love?"

"No," she grumbles, still looking peeved at us.

"Good. Didn't want to be a liar." I stop right there because Blade cries out as my mate works on the hurt shoulder. She's being gentle, but it's a mess, so it's bound to be painful.

"That's a little sore."

"Hold on," my primary croons. She closes her eyes, concentrating as she attempts to soothe some aches.

"I feel a flash of pain hit me as Blade sends a flurry of images, none of them friendly. "Could you two keep the fantasies down, please?

You're emoting everywhere and it's making me tense. Otherwise, you can leave."

"Leches." The kitty wrinkles her nose at us in disapproval, then goes back to relaxing the unhurt side of Blade's back, her hands glowing a bit with the magickal touch she's using to staunch some pain.

I blink at them both innocently, zipping my lip.

Hell, if I'm getting kicked out of this little party.

The Bird Has No Complaints

TAURUS

I hear the goddess whispering to my wife, "Sorry, they were making me hot. I didn't mean to—oh, that feels good."

No shit, love. No shit.

The sound alone makes my gut clench. Let me tell you, both are sodding enjoying every second—outside of the shoulder pain—and I'm not the bloody sinner to stop them. My wife thinks she's sneaky, putting words into my primary's mind. She doesn't realize that I hear like it's a stereo between our connection and mine to Talia.

~Shh. They were getting to me, too. The healing is taking a backseat to others' things, for sure. ~

That is some very sodding interesting information. I can't help that I'm bent the way I am. My two favorite chits in the entire universe, looking every bit like sun and moon together, wriggling around half-dressed, is one of the best things I've seen all year.

Fuck yeah, it does it for me. I'm alive, aren't I?

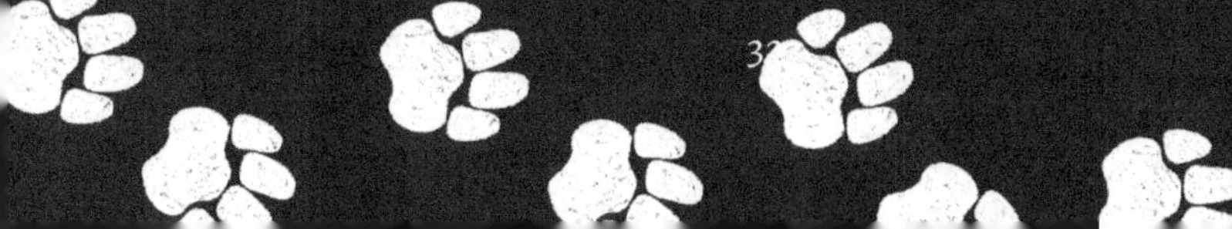

Interesting bit, though, is that Sampson and I watching them is affecting them. That is useful information. At the pace we're going at fixing the goddess, I'm never getting laid tonight. It was looking promising before the lazy git called us in. A little show seems like a fair trade.

"I hope it feels good. I'm trying to keep it less on the ouchie side if I can."

The golden one lies still, getting soothed and whatnot. I wonder why the wife's never done this to me? I might feel a bit cheated. Observing them, I smile, proud of my wife as she works to heal my mate. Her hands are strong yet kind, and though it's hot as all hell, I see the softness she's showing her.

I've got no complaints, I confess.

Speaking of Sampson, I look over at him sprawled on the chair like the romance novel-reject my wife accused him of being. Dressed in track pants and a waist-length mane, he looks every bit the character from a bodice ripper. It's the opposite of what the goddess sees in me. His eyes are on them, not missing a thing. He inhales, closing his eyes as his lips curl up at the scents. He might not be a predator anymore, but I can tell that git could hunt.

He'd give us all a run for our money, I think.

It's always the quiet ones who surprise you. I should pull his old file and glance at it since we're family now. It couldn't hurt to get to know more than he's indolent, has a sharp sense of humor, and wrangles the goddess even better than me. There's more than a jasmine scent in the air, and you don't have to be a hunter to smell that.

"I'm trying to make this part as painless as possible," my minx murmurs, dropping to her elbows and laying her palms over the injured area. Her chin rests below the injury as she crouches down and works on something I can't see. I can't tell what she's working on, but it must be internal. Her voice echoes in my skull, making me cover a smile.

~ *We could torture the boys a bit since they're being such idiots.* ~

Ah, love. How quickly you forget how hard it is for us to block one another out now.

It can't hurt to let her think they're getting away with something, though. The last time we were here, Minx upset herself so much that she got drugged up. I still haven't figured out why she was so twitchy the last time, and now she's as calm as can be. I have to say, though, I'm mighty impressed with how well my wife's doing pan-orating without blood ties. She's a quick study and her brain's one of a thousand things I love about her.

Before I ponder that further, Talia forgets that I'm connected to the minx and sends her reply in a mental picture. She doesn't mind-speak like the Minx and I do, though apparently, the stoat does. Talia's chuckle as she messages something about torture being too good for her husband comes through to me loud and clear, along with thumbs up on the minx's plan.

Hell, she's not in pain, so why not let them have their little game? It's not like I'm not enjoying myself, is it?

"It stings a little more than the other stuff does now."

"Stings? Let me get a little deeper." My wife sprawls along my primary's back, ignoring the rest of us as she's working.

It's a good thing because I'm on the edge of a snicker and if she looks at me, she'll know.

"That's better, thanks."

Sampson is watching like a hawk now and I smirk, knowing he feels the purr my wife has kicked up. It's cheating, and the goddess says the stoat can do it, too. The rotter must have gotten it from my minx. He seems to share more than a few of the minx's skills, so I wonder if the special skill designation of 'artist' is not accurate. He might be what the lab coats call a 'parasite'. It's rare that they find a clone from a strand who can absorb powers either temporarily or permanently from those they have blood ties to.

That bears further consideration—later.

I straighten, most of my body standing at attention. I'd prefer to look less obvious, so I nod at the stoat before murmuring into his mind. *~Buggering hell. ~*

My wife is trailing her fingers over my primary's skin, murmuring under her breath as she works. They're polar opposites—sun-kissed skin versus porcelain, curves versus lithe, brunette versus redhead. It's stunning. The artist nods his silent agreement, unable to tear his eyes away to look at me. He's being as quiet as possible, given that the minx is listening in.

Speaking of her, she's giggling as she talks to my goddess. *~Men are so easily baited. You should see them. ~*

Talia sends her a series of snapshots that de-note baited, hooked, and reeled fish gasping for air. She's right, as neither of us is looking like we're going to move soon. As they chuckle, my lips curve at the easy camaraderie between them. My primary sends another message I think is trying to let my wife know that if she needed to be on her back, we'd pass out. She's not far off the mark on that.

My wife laughs as she experiments with sending Talia the sensation of an eye roll. *~You'd think I was grabbing your ass or something from the way they're acting! I think Taurus' eyebrows might launch into outer space. ~*

Brilliant, love.

Talia sends back a message about boys being easy to tease, and they both laugh again. They've not been speaking much outside of their minds, so the stoat is looking at them, trying to figure out what's going on. I grin and keep it to myself, also finding it amusing to watch him. He's a playful git, and it's amusing as hell to watch his reactions.

~Oh, yeah. They always follow the little head, not the big one. You know, we may have discovered the golden ticket of clone control. Imagine the possibilities. ~

I frown, not loving the 'cat who ate the canary' look on my wife's face. Adjusting to get comfortable, I continue being a voyeur, deciding that giving up the information that I'm aware of their game is less important than enjoying the sight of them.

Sampson has figured out how to work the pan oration—further cementing my parasite theory — because I hear him when he speaks. *~They haven't said over four words since they threatened to throw us out. ~*

My wife catches my eye, moving her body with feline grace and sin as she pushes into the tendons and muscles. Everything within me throbs as she shifts her weight and moves around.

Christ.

I see Talia smirking and talking to my wife in her mind, enjoying playing with us. My eyes cut to Sampson, who has shifted in his chair again, looking uncomfortable. A sniff of the air confirms that he's in the same predicament as me and hell if I know what we're going to do if they keep up this little charade.

The girls zing back and forth again, discussing our discomfort and giggling. Talia sends my wife a question and I feel the devilish streak in both coming out. My minx murmurs her response in a husky voice that makes me groan. *~I have to heal your face, don't I? I promised Taurus. ~*

The goddess approves with a chortle, and it feels like she's hiding the amusement as best she can. It makes me glad that she doesn't seem in pain anymore, but I'm not sure where they're going with this.

Holy hell, what are they planning?

The Cat's Plan Backfires

DELILAH

Talia is cracking me up—she's a funny gal. I'm not watching the boys so much now as letting my senses guide me in relation to their emoting. *~Do you think the shoulder is okay enough to flip? ~*

She stretches under me, moving her arm and shoulder, and I hear the echo of what might have been a groan. "Look, Ma, no pain."

"Good. Do you think you can turn over now so I can do your face?" I chose those words purposefully, making sure that I said something easy to misread as an innuendo for those in the cheap seats.

"Oh, yeah, I almost forgot. Be careful around the bone because it's sensitive; stroke it gently," she murmurs, and I have to bite my lip to keep from giggling out loud.

The connection between me and my mates is strong. I feel my primary getting revved up, and even though he knows we're baiting him—or must know—he doesn't care. Taurus is no different, struggling to keep it on the down low, he's hiding arousal in the

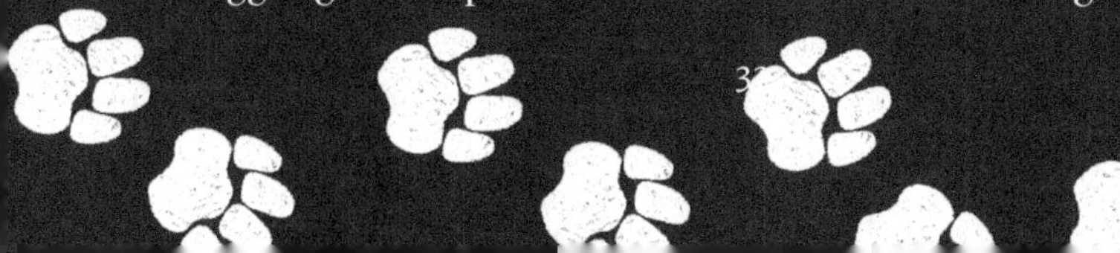

room's corner. Perhaps he even lowered the lights when I wasn't paying attention.

Talia takes my cue and rolls over, her moves lithe as she settles to look up at me. Her eyes are wicked, and her lips curve in a smirk as she bucks her hips a bit, as if trying to get comfortable. "Is this okay?"

Uh-oh. Perhaps I've made a calculated error.

I close my eyes, trying to calm everything inside and not to be the idiot I feel myself being right now. This is complete and utter idiocy; I am a moron. I try to buy myself a little time by making a face like I'm groaning, leading the boys on from afar. What I'm doing is figuring out how to keep myself from getting in trouble. We're all amped up in this room—or at least, most of us are—and we all know that I've had female mates. I have crazy hormones, though, because I'm pregnant, right? This is all a bad timing thing, and I'm just reacting to hormones. I'd find a cantaloupe attractive.

"That's perfect, dear. Let me lean down and look." I lean over, stretching up to see her face. My torso hovers over hers with a hair's breadth between us. My fingertips brush her cheekbone as I pretend to look at the bruise. It doesn't need this much attention, but we're torturing them and I'm trying to hold it together with band aids and duct tape.

I feel Taurus' eyes on me, watching the whole thing, and his intensity fills our bond. He's dropped into the opposite armchair, and I'm sure he's about ready to go off any second. It's working on them. Unfortunately, it's also working on me, and hell if I know what I'm going to do. I need to stop this, finish, and get the fuck home. Again, I'm an idiot.

Talia sucks in a breath, shifting us as she arches her neck and pretends to give me a better view. She's fine, and I need to stick this out until we get home, or I'll look stupid. "What do you think?

Can you fix it, like you did the shoulder?" Her voice is husky, and I trap a groan inside.

Damnit. This is crazy. I can manage this. What is wrong with me?

~I think Taurus is going to have a coronary. ~ I murmur into her mind, eyes raking up and down her neck, watching her pulse jump. I continue distracting myself by looking at her face, letting my hair fall over us a bit. It helps me hide us from speaking, even a little. "I think I can rub this the right way, though I don't know if you'll end up moaning. Facial bones are very delicate."

My primary reacts to that, and it shocks me to discover that he is going crazy in the other corner. He's watching us and growling under his breath. He's thinking about fitting us together like toy bricks, which makes me giggle.

Talia murmurs low into my mind as she notices. *~Rafe's going crazy. He's got some kind of brick fantasy going. ~* Out of pique, she grins up at me in response to my audible question. "I'm sure you'll be plenty gentle, sweets. We will have to see if I moan when you rub me."

I groan, trying to shield myself from all our mates' emotions and my confusion and the complete insanity of the position I now find myself in. I'm going to screw something up, and I don't know how to prevent that. However, as I've lost my faculties, I can't put a stop to this. I reply without even thinking, "Let's see if I can kiss it and make it all better." I brush my lips over her jawbone, all rational thought leaving the building.

The surprise filters through our bond from my primary, and he tries to keep himself from gaping. He's squirming in the chair and thinking many inappropriate things and making it hard to focus on not being an idiot. She shifts beneath me, and I suck in a breath. I try to clamp everything down inside. Her hand brushes my leg, and I dig my nails into the bed.

What the hell were we all thinking?

This was a dangerous plan—a super dangerous plan. I was being all professional and then we started this teasing thing. Now I'm drowning in everyone's pheromones and scents, and I feel the Beast inside raising her head in interest.

Bloody hell.

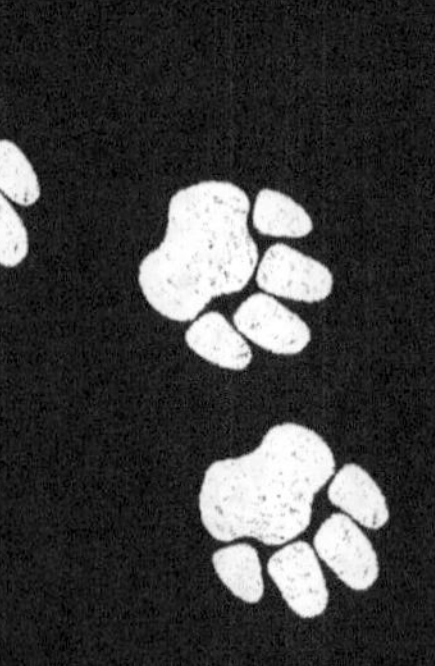
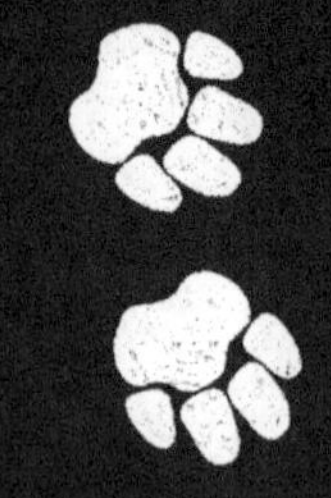
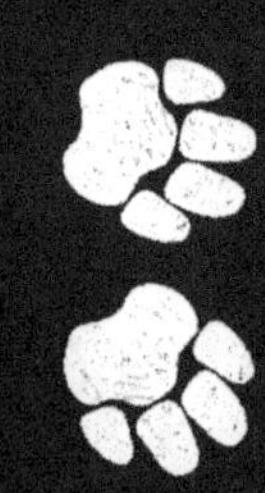
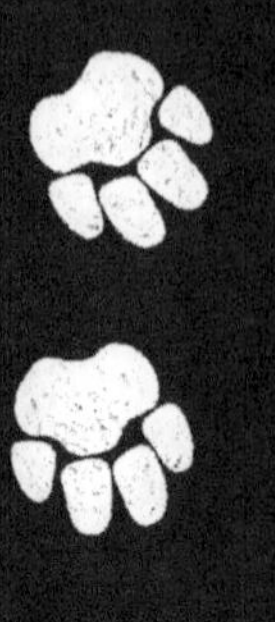
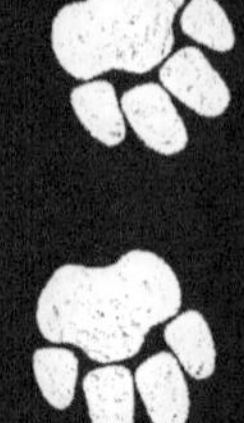

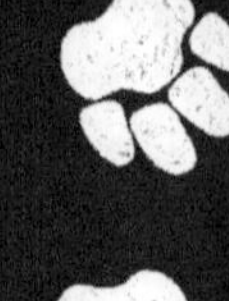

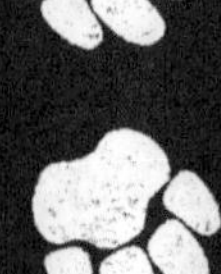

The Bird Pushes The Envelope

TAURUS

*F*uck, *I don't even know which direction is which.*

My wife is lying on my primary, moving around with her in ways that are making me lose my mind. Everything is hanging right in the balance, almost touching. The scents in the air are making my demon feel the need to hunt. My fangs are down, my eyes are gold, and I know without looking that I'm beyond the ability to hide what their little game is doing to me. I know my wife feels the tension; her Beast feels my demon. She's edgy, feeling the burn as much as I do, but ignoring it. I don't know why; it's not like she's averse to women, nor is the golden one unattractive. Her arms wobble and give out, and I watch as she collapses on Talia with a low grunt.

Sampson loses his grip across the way, and though I've been keeping an occasional eye on him, I notice now that he's entranced. It shadows his face a bit, but I see the gold in his eyes. I turned the lights down to be encouraging—sue me, I'm alive and male—but the highlights across the room as they hit his long hair and lithe frame make my mouth water.

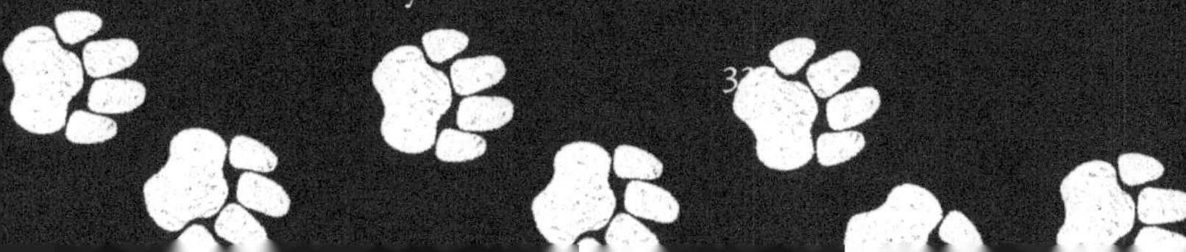

I growl low, everyone's arousal causing the room to be thick with emotions. I push some of that towards my wife to get it out of me and to help her with the struggle.

They're both fighting this, and hell if it will not cause one huge ass problem if they don't get it straightened out. They got caught in their own bloody web. The hiss from my primary makes me smile wickedly, and I know it's working.

"Oh, crap," my wife whispers, and I watch her move, wiggling and unable to hold still as some of my emotions push hers over the edge. Her growl echoes at the hiss, and I know they're about to give in.

My primary's eyes turn serpentine, and she reaches up to yank the minx's head down, kissing her.

That is more like it.

The Artist Hungers

RAFE

Holy shit, they're kissing.

The feral in the room notches up again, and I don't even know what the fuck I'm going to do. My skin is on fire, and my body is aching with arousal.

They kiss deeper, legs and arms moving together in a symphony of dark and light, like the sun and moon in an eclipse. They're murmuring low to one another, but I can't focus on their words as I watch them touch and explore one another.

Small groans followed by the whisper of silk falling to the ground and a flip of positions make me grip the edge of the chair like I'm going to blast off. The acting, the touching, and the sounds are more than I can handle, almost. But I can't stop watching, and they sure as hell are too busy to tell me to.

"God yes, Deli, touch me," she cries. My mate's low response is full of Beast and she's feeling ready to pounce.

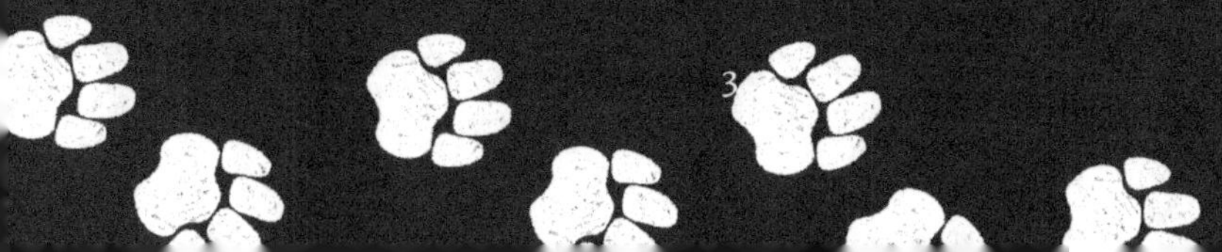

I'm trying to hold out, trying to keep sane, but it's hard. It's damned near impossible. I don't want to lose control and miss the rest of the show, but I don't know how much more I can take. They hiss and growl and move together, but I get distracted for a moment as another scent fills the air.

My eyes pry away from the women, hitting the shadows across the room. The bird's having a rough time of it. I could try to see what he's up to, but given my predicament, I opt for allowing him the courtesy of not shifting to night vision via the demon. I can't even imagine what part the two of us will play in the hungry, wild tangle that is our mates right now. I feel his hunger, though; it mirrors mine.

The bloodlust in this room is rising with every second.

A throaty chuckle echoes from the bed before I feel the apex hit my wife. She hisses my primary's name, waves of her pleasure hitting me hard through our bond. Something inside me twitches, and I know, without even seeing, that her fangs are itching to come out. The cat falls over next and she hits me with an intensity I've never felt before.

Holy crapbuckets, it's happening.

Taurus makes a strangled noise in the corner, and I know he's feeling it, too. The power of these two is nearly knocking us flat. I can't help it; a howl of frustration leaves my lips. I'm unsure what to do except try to quench the need.

I lift my wrist and tear into it, knowing that it won't sate my hunger or the primal lust flowing through me, but it might calm the demon so I can see straight. It doesn't and I let my arm drop, blood dripping on the floor in a way that's going to get my ass kicked by the housemates.

Deli is every bit as fucking hot, and wild as she's made out to be. Not that I've talked with him about it, but I've seen the marks, scratches, and bites. I've also heard the rumors that floated around this place before she rang him up. Deli does *not* disappoint. She overshadows her reputation by miles. She shook the hell out of me and I'm trying to keep the serpent from fucking this all up. I'd like to repeat this a few hundred times and my fangs itch like crazy.

I'm hungry and I want to feed.

Taurus, however, smells Rafe's blood. My senses are giving me enough input to determine that my primary has turned to watch him. His hunger is enormous, and I imagine that with four predators in the room, all aching for a feeding, he's amped into oblivion. He's not used to not being able to tear in anymore.

I feel a fang scratch my thigh, and everything inside clenches when I'm distracted by the scent of my blood. She nicked me when I shifted. It sends the primal into overdrive. I need blood—want,

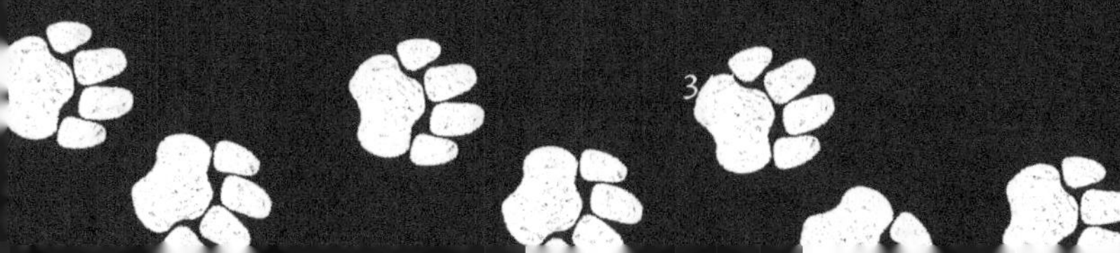

drink, feed. I shake my head, trying to clear it to no avail. She said that doing what she does gets her what she wants.

What does she want, I wonder?

"What do you want, Deli? What do you need?"

Her head lifts, and I see emerald-gold eyes full of swirling colors and four pointed fangs glinting in the moonlight. She was trying to hide the kitty, to keep me from seeing that she's struggling with her primal side. I hiss again, and she snarls, tossing one word into my mind. *~Feed. ~*

My response gets delayed by the sense of Rafe turning his gaze to Taurus. I feel both demons in the air and a torrent of emotions in the room that are trying to vie for dominance. He lifts his arm and licks the blood off it, almost as if taunting my primary. He ambles, his gait deceptively laid back for the primal energy he's emanating. Taurus growls low, advancing, following the scent of the open wound. I smell his blood now, and I wonder if he opened a wound on his arm.

What are they doing?

"Who do you want?" I murmur to Deli, unable to stop watching the clones and unsure if she meant what it sounded like she meant. I can't cross a line she hasn't offered.

My ethos won't allow it.

~I want your blood and I want it now. Bleed me—do it, drink from me. ~ She snarls the command, almost hitting a roar, and I get the panther in comparison now. She's like a big game cat, prowling and hunting, and I'm the prey.

I lose my ability to pay attention to the boys, letting the fangs drop and rearing back. Relief floods through me as I hiss low, then strike, watching the blood flow from the artery I opened before I gulp.

~*Yes!* ~ she cries into my mind.

Her fangs sink into my skin, tearing as she draws. I feel her drawing, as hungry and demanding as I am. The drinking rockets another climax through me, and I feel it ripple through her. She tastes like a fine cabernet, spicy and sweet at the same time.

It's unexpected, yet delicious, and I want more.

The Artist Loses Control

RAFE

The women are feeding, and it's making me lose my bloody mind. I don't know where I'm going; I started walking as if I knew.

I smell blood: theirs, mine, and his. I don't hunger like this. I never hunger like this. Licking my lips, I move towards the scent. If I don't find relief soon, I might go on a sodding rampage, and that never happens. I'm not like them. But there's blood, and I almost taste it as I get toe to toe with the biggest predator in the community, looking at him.

His shudder is slight, but I can see it. He watches me eerily, then walks around me as if circling prey. A low roar shows his frustration, and it occurs to me he doesn't know what to do. I feel the bloodlust in the air, smell the arousal, but there's confusion. It's a faint sensation, an echo of what my mates feel from him, but it is there. It's making him even edgier because he's angry that he's inexperienced.

I can help, but I don't know if I should.

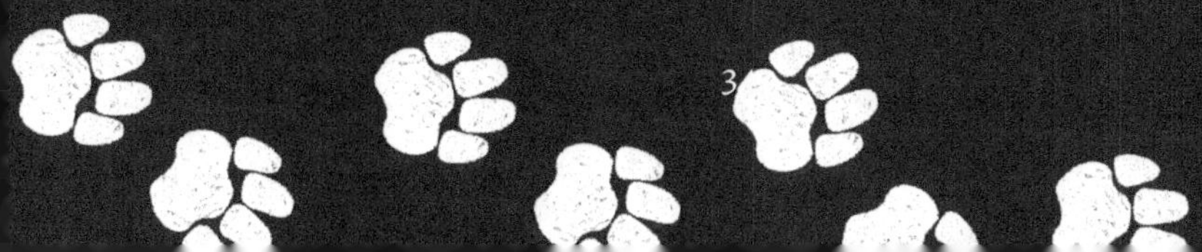

As if my brain has exited the room, I spring forward, knocking us both to the floor. My eyes meet his as our bodies touch, and I tug his wrist up. I wait for the assent in his gaze before I tear my fangs in, drowning in the taste of him. I want him.

That is unexpected.

"You want to. I want you to. Do it." His smirk is evil, and he darts forward to slash a scratch behind my ear, licking the blood off as it dribbles down my neck.

Did he just…?

"I've been right curious about you for a while, given the stories."

Fuck. He did. Is there even any…?

I lift my head from his wrist, demon eyes searching for the bottle that rolled under the couch. When I find what I need, I feel boot-shakingly nervous. I imagine the cat did, too. The last time we had this kind of experience, we got run through the wringer.

Is this going to fuck everything up?

It doesn't seem to matter because I'm growling low in his ear as he moves against me, and the blood in the air is making rational thought impossible. I tear off the end of the tube because I can't focus enough to figure out how to open it and slather it as needed. "Ready to find out?" I rumble near his earlobe.

His eyes glow and I snarl in response, before everything fades to sparkling lust as we move together. It's new, and I can tell that this is not a normal feeling for him.

~It's going to hurt. ~

I can't help that, and I use enough of my faculties to make that easier as I drape over his back. I offer my wrist as my head fills with a pleasure so intense that my eyes almost cross.

"*Son of bitch,*" he roars and I stay still, waiting. He grabs my wrist, tearing into it and feeding hungrily.

I howl in pain that is delicious and dip my head, sinking my fangs into his shoulder. Everything flows into one mindless loop of indescribable sensation. The blood, the sex, the scents—everything is making me crazy. He mutters into my mind, and it makes me groan.

This is going to be a big deal; I just know it.

The Blade And The Cat Curl Up

TALIA

She feels the line and stops feeding, her cheek lying on my hot skin. I follow suit, though the snake does not want to. It's a hazard of my condition, I suppose. I'm glad her beast has more sense than my inner animal. It might not have always been the case, but according to Taurus, she's learned to co-exist with her monster so well that it's drawn out his.

Talk about a woman who changes everything and everyone around her daily without even trying. No wonder the raving masses are so drawn to her.

When I feel her move, I frown, but she wants to get my attention. I thought I'd hang here for—well, maybe forever. I'm shagged out.

~Um, do you feel that? ~ Her mental voice is curious, and my brows furrow.

I send out a feeler, a question, not wanting to speak out loud if she isn't.

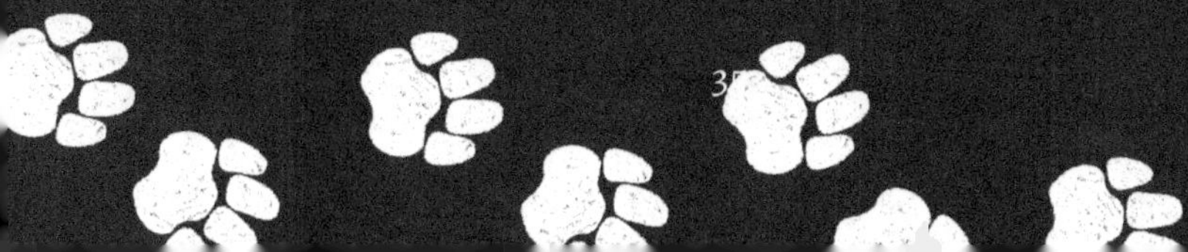

Her head lifts, and she peers over my leg, looking into the room, scenting the air. *~Holy fucking hell, Talia, look. You gotta look. ~*

I grumble, but the urgency in her voice makes me pause. I lift a little and peep, then bolt upright in the bed, eyes wide as I gape like a fish. "What the...?" I whisper, amazed.

~I told you it was worth moving for. ~ She chuckles low, being careful not to cause a disturbance.

Grinning, I send her an image of my thoughts about our two warriors and what they look like. I lay back down, feeling more than a little pleased at how things worked out. I'd always sensed that despite his protests, Taurus might have more interest at that end of things than he let on. Reading through all those blogs wasn't only about me; otherwise, he would have let me read and waited to play the home game.

I can't blame him. I've discovered the immutable attraction his mate engenders. I have to stop teasing him about being an insatiable lech now that I understand what the kitty does to a person. It's only fair that he figures out why I'm so bananas about her mate.

The kitty nods at me, sliding up behind me in her typical graceful fashion to set her chin on my shoulder. *~I knew that arguing and antagonism came from somewhere. ~*

"Whose?" I keep my voice low, but since I can't pan-orate like them, I have to speak out loud or it's going to get confusing for her. She's new to the whole mind-picture thing.

"Theirs. The name-calling, the gauntlets thrown, and all the usual posturing male bullshit; it's a sure sign. Clones don't go to grade school, but I sure did."

For the first time, I notice that the sun is filtering in through a few cracks in the long hair's blackout curtains. "Geez, woman."

"It's not my fault. Don't look at me; they're the ones still going."

I blink. "It's not your fault? Whose fault was it? I'm still not sure what happened, so I know I did nothing."

She makes an innocent face that looks about as sincere as a pregnant nun, and I laugh. Batting her lashes, she counters, "How about shared fault? Agreed?"

Smirking, I shake my head. Taurus is right; you can't say no to her. It's too damned fun to give in. "You know, considering what happened, I'll give you that one." I look at her for a moment, feeling playful. "If I have this right, we only do this twice, and I know that I'm a lousy fucking lay, right?"

Her eyes widen, and she growls. "I will kill him. I was drunk, I had a fight with them, and he was angry. He pushed me about catering to them, and I said, 'they're my family, she's my family, and he's like, fuck her'. I was mad, and it slipped right out of my mouth. I've told no one before, not even Rafe."

"Taurus thought I'd get a laugh, and I did. I get a chuckle every time I think about it, and every time I have to see the little gremlin." My grin is wicked, and I chuckle again.

Deli was toasty and admitted to Taurus that Sari had been with her only twice—enough to push mating before the treacherous blonde one could get to her—was amazing. That Sari sucked at it is amusing to no end. It explains why the biggest proponent of free love and sharing doesn't go looking for other ladies to punish Deli. They know Sari doesn't give a shit who Deli is with unless it threatens Wilde. Now, my mate is a different story.

"That bastard! I'll beat him, and not in a way he'll enjoy," she grumbles. "No one should have ever known that. It is part of the reason—you know. That whole forgetting thing that he and I had an issue with. I forgot because, well, I figured out I was a trophy, not a proper mate. It stopped mattering after a while."

"Who am I going to tell? It's not like I talk to anyone but Rafe. She doesn't come to me, only to Taurus, and Wilde's gone like the wind. You're safe."

"True, but I know enough about how contentious you and he are with her. I don't want it slipping out in a rage by mistake. She might not give a shit about me, but she will care if I've tarnished her super sex monster reputation. It could get hideous for both of us," she murmurs. "Besides, Rafe has to know she's a lousy l—look, you almost made me say it again!"

I shrug, still finding the entire situation hysterical. That stubby little gnome seems to think she's the gift to the universe, and her announcement that the cat was mated to her was about hurting my primary. I don't feel bad that she doesn't live up to her own hype. I do, however, care if she punishes my mate and the woman that I'm finding myself more attached to by the minute. "I say nothing; I hear nothing."

Thinking about what I want to ask, I wonder if now is the wrong time. What the hell, why not? I've always been a 'damn the torpedoes' kind of gal.

"What happened here, babe? I hate to be gauche in asking, but this whole thing," I gesture towards our occupied mates, "is not something I'm used to. Not that I have complaints, but it's off-brand."

She peeps over at our mates and shakes her head. "I don't have any complaints."

When she turns back, I'm surprised to see what I can only interpret as an unsure expression. My emotion sensors must be on the fritz because she's gone from confident and playful to emanating fear from every pore. Even her body seems to have tensed up and curled in.

"What do you mean, what happened? I mean, I know you know what happened," she says, twirling a strand of hair around her finger and staring at it as if it holds the secret to eternal life.

This is odd. Taurus has mentioned several times that while she's a wildcat in public, she's not the same in private. I've not experienced this variation of the cat before. Our interactions were always comfortable for her; she's never seemed hesitant. I find myself at a bit of a loss because I don't want to assume or over-reach, but this is not my normal behavior, either. I need her to let me know what's going on in her head.

"You mean that?" She points at the bite mark on my leg, breaking the silence again.

I frown, feeling less certain than I did before. "I know what happened. I'm not clear on the why, I guess. As this was a first for me, I'm feeling like I don't want to be the gnome." Looking over my shoulder, I murmur, "He's going to have more issues than I do, I know it."

Again, she surprises me by rolling her eyes. "You are so not her. He is not him. No one is them but them, trust me on that." Her face darkens for a moment as if recounting something painful, then returns to normal. Chewing her lip, she shrugs as if her moods aren't changing by the minute. "I found you attractive before this. Once we got up close and personal, it was more like needed."

"I don't understand. I'm getting damn frustrated with myself because I say that a lot with you two."

It doesn't help that she's bouncing between deep darks to blasé to insecurity, either. I'm trying to read her expressions and not accidentally read her emotions because that'd violate privacy. I need help, though, because I go by what people say, and she's not saying much that helps me.

"You're not her. This correlates with them in no way at all. I speak for both of us on that, I know." The shadow crosses her features again, and then she looks serious. "What I meant was that I'd wanted you to bite me before. Once we were physical, it became imperative. I know they'll have issues relating to others, themselves, and maybe even to us. That's theirs to work out. Rafe has the patience of a saint, and me—well, I'm me."

"I know all about his patience. He's put up with a lot from me." There's that darkness again as she muses to herself. She mentions nothing about herself, and that doesn't jibe with what Taurus told me about his relationship with her. Sometimes he has to pull it out of her, but she talks about what she thinks once you bait her. She's so quiet and thoughtful, and that is not what I would expect at all.

I roll onto my back and look at the ceiling as she works out how to respond. I think that perhaps there is something important that these two are keeping because they aren't ready to tell it. Something to do with Sari and Wilde, if my guess is right, and the worse Sari behaves, the deeper this Wilde rabbit hole goes, the closer we come to one of them spitting it out.

Taurus hasn't noticed because they are so synced that these little micro-expressions aren't triggering him. They are triggering my empath abilities. I can't help but wonder what is so awful that neither of them has discussed it, not even Deli telling Taurus. That, my friends, is a scary, deep dark, and I don't like it at all.

"What did I say?" she asks, looking curious.

I shrug. "I don't know. I feel insecure. I'm used to discussing my feelings. I don't want to harp or nag or seem neurotic." I shake my head and then roll out of bed, looking for the robe Hex gave me because my clothes are toast.

"You're not harping. I guess you could do that instead," she whispers, her hair falling to spill over her face.

"Sorry; I move fast."

I see her nod, the curtain of red moving, her face concealed. "I noticed."

"See? That. I don't know what you meant." I hunt around for Precious, feeling the need to have something solid and familiar to comfort my frayed nerves.

She shrugs, still obscured by a mass of scarlet waves. Her voice is soft, and I have to stop hunting around to get closer to hear her better. "You're gone. It hurt, I guess. I mean, I know I'm not—that I don't seem... It's not like it's unusual for people to do that." She stops talking and shrugs again. If it's possible, she's gotten even less wordy in the past minute and a half.

"Hurt?" I climb on the bed and crawl over to her, frowning in my confusion. What did I do? "What hurts?"

"You left. Poof, you left like it didn't mean..." Scooting a bit, she tucks into a small ball sheltered in that mass of tangles, and I see what Taurus means when he says she can turtle with the best of them. She's about as small as someone of her height could be without disappearing. "It's okay. I understand. I know how it goes."

What in the hell is she talking about? How it goes? I tilt my head and look at her, trying to figure out what's gotten her so closed off when it hits me. She said she understands, that I left.

Oh, hell.

"I wasn't leaving. I was feeling exposed, so I was going to put my clothes on. I was feeling nervous, and I feel better when I flip my blade if I'm nervous. Rafe might have mentioned that?"

I see the skin on her arms flush red, but not her face. I must have hit the nail on the head. She thought I was getting up and trotting out, finished with her now that it scratched my itch. Taurus said she had abandonment issues, and boy, he wasn't kidding. Apparently, they're exacerbated in relation to females.

Fucking Sari and fucking Rhea.

Those bitches ruin everything and everyone they touch. I look at the powerful woman that my mate loves more than breath tucked into a shell so tight that it's amazing she can breathe, waiting like an abused animal for me to trample her emotionally. She hasn't moved more than a few muscles since I got up.

It's like I hit a trigger and she gave up. What have they done to her? Just as importantly, what have they done to Rafe that I don't know about?

"Sorry," she mumbles. "I just—I'm sure he mentioned it. I didn't mean to be a pain."

Now she's apologizing because I unintentionally hurt her? I sigh and move over closer, pushing her hair back off her face. She loosens a little, and I wedge my way into the ball she's curled in, setting my head on her stomach once she lets me. I blink for a second, remembering Maeve, and look panicked. "This doesn't bother you, does it?"

"Nope. Someday I'll be a whale, and that would be hard to do, but it doesn't bother me."

"You'll still be beautiful," I respond without even thinking. I blush, realizing I said that out loud. "I think he'll love it, I mean."

She seems to realize what she heard, and a tiny smile curved her lips. "You think so? Even if I am big and swollen?"

I huff. "Well, yeah. I don't bite just anyone, you know." I roll over onto my stomach, looking up at her. "Is that okay?"

Pursing her lips, she looks at me. "Yes, it is." I feel the purr kick in as I curl up with her, and it makes me smile. Her eyes dart around for a moment, and she whispers, "Can I tell you a secret? One I've kept tucked where no one can see?"

Uh-oh.

I'm hoping this is not whatever secret those two have been hiding because we're having a good day, and I don't think I'm ready for that right now. The guys are sleeping off their debauchery on the floor in the corner, so I can say that Taurus is not ready for that, either. "Sure. You know me; I'm mum's the word girl."

"I know. Keeping it mum takes massive concentration and skill with the bonds like they are."

That would—along with her pregnancy—explain the sharp increase in her appetite and need to hunt. She's holding some draining magic to keep whatever it is she's keeping for them. I'd be interested to know what in the hell she's doing to keep anything mum, given that Rafe feels my pain and Taurus feels her heart beating. It's a little terrifying to wonder what she's got going on inside. "I might tell Taurus, but that's more than 'I know so he knows' thing."

Her face flushes red, and she shakes her head.

"God, it's not about Taurus, is it, because he's fantastic at sifting through my mind and picking up things."

"No, it's about when I messed up."

"Messed up?" I frown.

"When I had an accident?" She squirms, trying hard not to be vague but struggling with the topic.

"Which accident?"

"You know, when I disappeared, got strung out, and called Taurus pretty?"

"Oh!" I blink. "You mean the acid trip from hell. That was not one of the fun nights of my life. It was hard on Taurus. I remember I felt bad because it was my fault. I started it—or Rafe did."

"Yeah," she nods, the hair falling over her face again. "See, I, um, know how I got distracted."

I didn't think she could get any redder, but here it is. I run a finger over the blush and then tuck her hair behind her ear. "You mean how you let go of the drug ball? What is it, baby?"

"I kept trying to tell Taurus that it was my fault because I'd never screw up something that simple. I mean, its basic containment and all." She talks faster as she picks up momentum. "But he wouldn't hear of it, and it was so dumb that I was almost glad I said nothing."

I feel her discomfort, so I lean in closer, arranging my head on her leg. I know touch helps her mate, and her, too.

"See, I asked if you'd rather me bleed or bite me, and everyone kind of stared at me like I was an idiot. I got distracted thinking about it —you biting me, I mean—and kind of covered it up by blustering through. At the end of the spell, I couldn't focus because I was still all flustered because I said it and everyone looked at me funny. When I went to finish, my head wasn't in the right hemisphere, so I let it go without remembering the ball because I got worried that you thought I was icky or something. I forgot and poof."

I blink, gaping like an idiot for what feels like the hundredth time today.

She flops backward, burying her face in the sheets with a groan. "I can't believe I admitted that. I am so stupid. Sometimes, I wonder if the disconnect between my brain and my mouth is broken."

"I wanted to," I murmur, feeling silly myself.

"You wanted to do what?"

I shrug. "I wanted to bite you." She stops thumping her head on the mattress and looks up through a tumble of waves. "I was going to, but you pulled back and sliced a vein before I could answer anything."

"Everyone peered at me like I was suggesting we run naked through the Met. I was sure I'd said something wrong. I moved before the silence could get any more awkward."

"That moment is so clear in my head because I thought you didn't want me to. It was the fangs—that's why I hesitated. I looked at Rafe, if you remember, because I didn't know if you knew about the fangs. Then I looked at Taurus, to make sure he didn't have a— that he was alright with me..." I cut off, rubbing a hand over my face. What a bloody cock-up.

"I knew. I mean, Rafe had said. It's not like..." she snorts, shaking her head. "Everyone kept staring at me, and I was sure I had fucked up royally by saying that. I got so distracted thinking about it, watching the blood drip."

"Before I could say anything, you sliced. Then I was going to bite you a few nights later because I didn't want you to assume I was saying something I wasn't when it happened. But things happened, and we didn't get to come to visit you two."

"Hell, we screwed the pooch big, didn't we?"

"I didn't want you to think I didn't want to share blood with you."

"It's what I thought. I had some not so good feelings. That's why I got so flustered about everything. That's why I didn't tell anyone."

"I mean, it would not be like tonight. I was going to take your hand and tell you that the awful night wasn't about me judging you, and then I was running to ask you if you'd mind if I snaked your finger."

Smacking her forehead, she sighs. "I am the queen of this situation. All hail Deli, the queen of Fuck Up. It's always because of some mental hang-up."

"I swear, it wasn't your blood. I wasn't judging you. I'm sorry it got a sod a dog-ish."

She smiles down at me, looking rueful. "I didn't think it was my blood, per se. I mean, it is magickal, which is kind of cool to anyone. I figured you guys don't work that way and it was an acceptable way of telling me that without having to say, 'look, you stupid bint, we don't do that sharing thing and not with you'. The nonsense I cook up in my head when I get paranoid. I am aware—painfully so—that I have ties that make me less than desirable in some ways."

"It's like the ring thing. I'm not prying, but if you tell him, you tell me. It's that kind of deal."

She pinches her nose. "Christ, yes, like the ring thing. Just like that."

I ponder for a minute, finding the corner of the sheet interesting. "Was that the night you felt attracted to me?"

"I mean, I always kind of thought, but I don't, um, entertain that anymore, but when you came for the flowers and the baby you were cu—no, maybe not that. Sweet? Maybe? Yeah, I felt attracted before then. I just don't—not anymore."

I frown. "I thought you didn't like me. I thought for sure you weren't fond of me at all. That's why I didn't come back until you two goofs drained—I mean, you two swept away people drained each other."

She shakes her head emphatically. "Damn. I didn't mean to give off that vibe."

"When I came back, I had on my death gear, so I could feel more in control."

"Damn. I figured you didn't come back because—hell, I had no idea. When you and Boneless showed up when we drained, I was too busy watching you two flirt to say much of anything." She leans back and bangs her head again in what's becoming a pattern.

"Stop banging."

"It doesn't hurt. It's a reflex. You'll get used to it. There's nowhere to burrow in the middle of the bed, so I can't hide." Her nose wrinkles. "I like to hide when I'm on unsure footing."

That explains Taurus and his ranting about sleeping in closets. It also explains why she turned herself inside out a moment ago when she was having trouble answering me. "I suppose I could offer to hold you, and you could burrow into me or something."

Looking as if she's considering the offer, she smiles. When she's comfortable and playful, she is adorable. "Hm. That could work."

I grab her and pull her close, hugging her. "Witch."

"Ordained, even." The purr starts again, and I smile. "Snake in the grass."

"Pussy cat."

"Sneaky serpent. I have the urge to ask about apples."

"See why I don't tell people what I am? Jokes, jokes, jokes."

"Is it because they call you original sin?"

"Hey, I like that," I grin, feeling pleased.

"You realize being a cat inspires a thousand and one jokes for all occasions, right?"

I kiss her forehead, feeling lighter. "Yeah, well, I've always seen you as more of a panther, all fierce on the outside, soft on the inside."

"That's right, Sin. That's what she looks like."

"You know I throw knives, right?"

"I apparate. You won't hit something that isn't there. I can stop them in mid-air—in theory. They wouldn't let me try in front of people in training, so I've yet to try more than moving things. I assume I could stop them from flying at me."

I hiss low, then smile, not able to hold it for long. I kiss her, my heart expanding for the infuriating and complex woman sitting with me. "You're very important to me."

She smiles in a way that I've heard Taurus describe but never seen —happy, almost child-like in her glee. Now I know why it melts him; it makes you feel like a superhero. Her hand slides down my face, and I feel the achy bruise go away. She did not need as much time to fix me last night as she pretended. "You are too. Important, I mean."

"What is it with you and your mate, always with a yen to fix me when I'm dented?"

"I'm a healer of broken toys, dear. I have always been. Also, I promised, didn't I? I got distracted."

"I'll take credit for that one if you're planning on staying here all day."

She grins. "Perhaps I could be persuaded."

RAFE

Yawning, I roll over and stretch a little. My head's muzzy from the night before. I'm always a slow riser, and when I remember what happened last night, my eyes pop open.

Holy fuck buckets.

I look to see if he's awake yet. We're no longer on the floor—the woman moved us to a place more amenable to sleeping. It was nice of her, but scary that neither of us noticed because we slept so damned hard. I guess they hotfooted to a guest room since we're in my bed here.

The women were bloody hot together and they're off figuring out their end of things, but him? Hell, if I know.

It's not like I haven't been a convenient outlet before, so I'm not offended, just... resigned, maybe. An unavoidable truth in my life is that this situation will only end in pain. I suppose the woman feels even worse about it, and she's got the shorter end of that stick than me, so I can't whine as much as accept it.

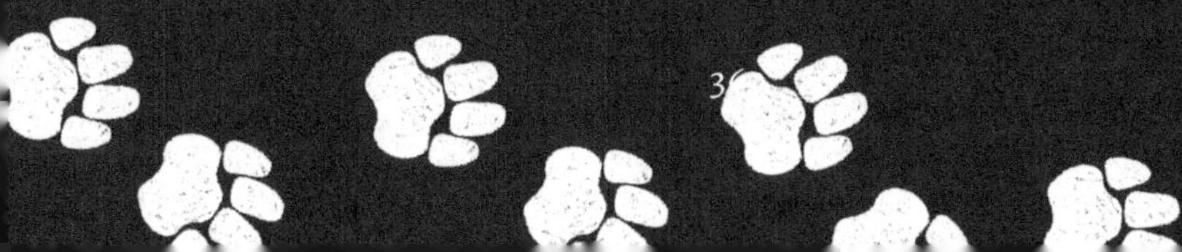

I slide to the edge of the bed, trying not to disturb him as I rise. Perhaps it is best if I shrug it off and head off as the awkward morning scene is about to unfold.

"Where are you going, Sampson?"

Turning to look over my shoulder sheepishly, I shrug. "I was pondering a drink."

Untrue, but now that he's awake, all hope of avoiding the hems and haws has dissipated.

He grins—which is fucking spectacular to see, though I've not been on the receiving end of that much before now—then rolls over, scratching his stomach. "If you're in the mood, I could use a scotch. If you're not, I'll get it later, no worries."

"No scotch. Is bourbon okay?" I stand, walking over to the bar to grab the bottle and a few glasses. Sitting them on the side table, I pour a hefty amount in each and hand him one, settling down against the pillows. I have no idea what he's expecting of me or what's going to happen, so I sip the single barrel as casually as one can in my current state.

Taurus is definitely going to give me 'the speech'.

He pushes up far enough to sip his drink and looks up at me. "Thanks. Are we good?"

Ah, I had this nailed in my head; I can do this.

I have to consider what I can and can't say. Finally, I nod and sip my drink again. The fewer words I say, the fewer problems there will be.

"Good."

My temples throb as I feel a migraine coming. I know that the worry from last night, the worry and the rest of the emotions swirling inside of me are going to make this a humdinger. "Yeah." The corner of his mouth twists up into a grin. "A laconic pair, aren't we?"

How can I say anything when I know you have one foot out the door?

Running my hand through my hair, I force a chuckle. "Apparently."

Taurus watches me for a moment, sitting up against the pillows. After another sip, he stares out into the room at Hex's immaculate décor. "I want you to know, mate. As fond as I am of your body, I'd appreciate it if you'd hold to the no-Talia-pain philosophy you've been working on. If she got hurt, it wouldn't be a good day. That's not a warning, but I worry about her is all."

I'm not sure how to answer that, so I stay quiet, pouring myself another clone. It feels like I'm going to need it because so far, all I've gotten out of him is a mini-praise for not being grotesque and a not-really warning about hurting my wife. It doesn't feel like this is going to be a very productive morning.

"This is all rather new to me—you, us. I'm not prepped for the after snuggles, though," he frowns and looks at me for the first time in a while, "doesn't seem to be an issue. I'm not sure I understand that, either."

I might as well be functionally muted for all the words I have right now. I should say something, but what? I can't say something like 'well, mate since I'm sure I was a hormone-induced flight of fancy, as usual, I didn't feel like I should do things that might muddy the lines of acceptable behavior from a side piece'.

Ugh. That sounded harsh even in my brain. This is not good.

"Bugger." He wipes a hand down his face, looking as if he's going to say something when a loud noise from across the room distracts him. "Christ. It's the bloody Company. That's a '*now*' sound, mate. I have to run."

Before I even figure out what to reply, he's disappeared and I'm left wondering what happened. "Did I dream it all?"

Christ. I'm such a fucking idiot.

The Cat And The Blade Talk Terms

TALIA

"I've never shown you the claws before?"

"Nope," I say, running a finger down her cheek. "It was quite a revelation last night."

She grins a bit and gives me a shy smile that melts me. I see what Taurus meant about her having a way that defies words for that.

"Do you want to see them for real?"

Her expression is so unsure that again, I almost forget who I'm looking at. Something bad had to have happened to this woman because someone who has as many talents, brains, and that body should *never* look so unsure. "Sure, babe."

Holding her hand up, she flicks out each claw individually, which is impressive. "Handy dandy, Swiss Army cat, at your service. They skewer, they "mince, and they make julienne fries." Her grin twists, and she murmurs, "Imagine waking up one morning and finding that these pop out randomly now. It was shocking. Learning how to harness things was even harder."

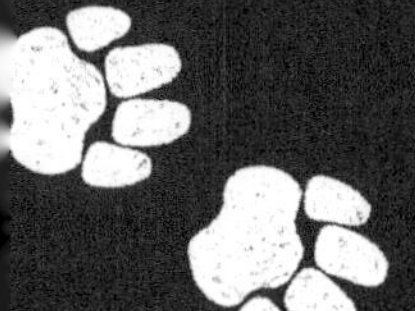

"I want to say that I can imagine it, but I don't think I can. The fangs were a slow process for me, me and you kind of stumbled into a mutation that was major. However, it clears up the lacerations the bird's been sporting for the past few months. I knew you had claws, but that's not the same as 'knowing'."

"No one believes it until they see up close. Not these, not any of it. Even then, it's not a simple transition for them to accept."

Something in the way she says that echoes of sadness and loss.

She had trouble with people accepting her changes prior to Taurus. People hurt her, and she admitted she came to him looking more for a cure than a reason she'd mutated. It disgusted him that people shamed her into trying to... what did he call it? De-evolve for their comfort.

I lean in, looking at them, remembering that they are much sharper than they look—which is sharp.

"You can touch. They're not as sharp as they should be. I haven't sharpened."

Shaking my head, I smile. "Unnecessary. Thank you for sharing with me. I'm sure that you'll share the rest of it with me." She looks panicked for a moment, and I cover her hand with mine. "I only know because if Taurus knows, then I know. I don't spook easily, especially once I've been all seduced and whatnot."

That gets her attention. "Seduced?"

"I didn't say you did it; I'm saying that's how I'm feeling when I think back on it."

Huffing in a way that is very reminiscent of her spouse, she crosses her arms over her chest. "I was doing what I always do, trying to heal you. You could ask the boneless one, but he's otherwise occupied, I guess. Ask him later."

I grin. "I will. I got worried because even though you started at my ass to get to my shoulder, you were all business until I touched your leg. It felt like I was stepping way over the line."

She shrugs, giving me that shy look that is enchanting. "I was holding back a bit because I wasn't sure; I could have been reading you wrong. I read people wrong a lot now; I didn't used to."

"It's amazing that we made any progress at all."

"I guess I could have scented, but the boys were all distracting and I was nervous and when I get nervous, I lose all ability to use my skills. Ironic, huh?"

I smile and pull her closer. "I like when you're nervous."

Her body wraps around mine, and she sighs. "You know, you're going to look wicked hot in that snakeskin thing for the party."

Blinking, I groan. "Ugh, I'd almost forgotten about that mess. I guess Rafe will lose his possessive thing now that he and the bird did their thing. Damn. I was looking forward to that."

"I don't think that's possible. He'll be all over you."

"Yeah, yeah. We've wandered into my neurosis-land. The mercurial fiend always upstages me, and now he might, even with my spouse. That's smarting when I think about it. "Poor Rafe. He's stuck with the ugly sister."

Turning her face away, she shrugs and I'm not sure why, but she murmurs, "He's so beleaguered with problems: which desirable person to pinch, who wants me more, blah blah blah."

My brow arches and I consider, as she doesn't sound like she's joking, only like she's trying to "sound like she is. Could she have as much baggage about this as I do? Taurus told me she's not always as forthcoming in private as she is when she's in her element, and I believe him now. I don't know whether I should ask. If she hasn't told him, she will not tell me.

"Of all the people I expected to have to work to keep away from him, my mate wasn't one of them. *That* should be interesting." I tilt my head. "Hey, what about you, Miss 'You touch no one' girl? Aren't you worried about your husband?"

"Nope," she replies so quickly that I don't doubt her for a second.

How does she have such an unshakable faith? Why doesn't it bother her to think Rafe might take time away from Taurus?

It sounded as if something was bothering her. But she must have shields like nobody's business because I can't read an ounce of her emotions, even when I drop mine a bit. I wonder what is hiding behind her walls. I'm never able to pick up so little when I try.

"The lazy one wants to be with you, darling. Don't worry about that. I mean, if I were to want a few minutes or something, he'd be okay, I think. We're pretty laid back about that."

Ah, there's the problem.

I've made her feel as if she's the one who's the sore thumb. I don't know how, because she's the star of this play, the colorful yet bloody and ruthless foil to the bird's leading man. Yet somehow, she's worried that no one will want to spend time with her. She's not at all worried about sharing with anyone, except that she'll be unwanted. Is she worried I don't want her? I don't know what to do with that. Her wound about female mates must be even deeper than I thought. "You know, you've never told me what *you* think of the snakeskin."

She smiles, dipping her chin. "I probably like it more than they do."

Grinning, I give her a squeeze. "How's the possessive now, since they're no longer the elephant in the room and we can talk?"

"I still am, but I trust Rafe. I've always trusted him, and I've always shared with him. If they choose one another, it's hard to explain to people who aren't us. We're so similar in fundamental ways, yet different in the visible ones." She frowns and stops, looking for words.

"He's the calm to my roiling sea. We complement and complete one another differently than Taurus and I do. My love for him is not my love for Taurus; his affection for him is not his love for you, and so on. We don't rank people in order of how much we love them, and we don't get jealous of others over who spends time with whom. We love the people we love and enjoy every second of our time with them. It's like savoring every second, then savoring every second with the next person. Our faith and trust in another mean that we never assume the other has a better or deeper relationship with one mate versus the other. We love them unconditionally and give each other space and respect to do that. I'd be a hypocrite if I got upset with him. You know?"

Deli gives me a smile, looking down at us, and shrugs. "I know how much he loves me and that he'd do nothing to hurt me, nor would he do that to anyone he loves. So, it's all good."

Interesting.

She doesn't consider her primary to be in the same league as the people she's worried about. In fact, it's almost like she's not concerned about him taking away time with Taurus at all. I don't know what those two will decide, but her unshakable faith that it will all be fine is admirable. "I don't think I was who Taurus was thinking of when he made his declaration, either. You know us being sex partners? Bang buddies? I mean, what the hell are we?"

"Closer the first time, I'd say."

Again, the unsure language with that, but she was confident a moment ago. "You looked hot too, you know."

Flushing bright red, she gives me a pleased look. "I was going for subtlety."

"You're in liquid latex stripes and that's it."

"Who said that's not subtle for me?" Her expression has turned playful, and I see the shift in her behavior now that she's showing off what she's confident about.

"I get you now, kitty. I see you. If it's about sex and flirting and such, you know where you stand and who you are, so you stand proud. Emotionally, you're terrified. Christ, Taurus and I have got to sit down and see if we can run through some blogs of the past and hunt down what the hell happened to these two. Whatever it is, it fucked them up enough that they trust only each other. "*Now* I'm scared," I say, not even hinting at my concern.

"You haven't seen half the stuff in my closets. I should keep the binders hidden if you think that's over the top. Never open the armoire in my bedroom."

"Christ, not another love to worry about losing to the pack. This is getting redundant," I sigh, wondering how many people will chase her at this party. She's the more popular, more in-demand one.

People will be after her like flies on honey.

She ducks her head and murmurs, "Between Taurus and you, I intend to stay occupied and grope free if that's okay. I mean, unless you don't want me to—I can stay with Taurus if you'd prefer. That's fine."

That look of fear shadows her face for a minute as she tries to back away from what she said. Does she think I don't want anyone to know about us in public? She's willing to lurk in the shadows if it makes me more comfortable? I've said it before, and I'm going to keep saying it. Fuck Sari and Rhea. Or un-fuck them because I think that would punish them more. "I didn't mean only at the party," I say. "When she finds out, this will kill Sari."

Her posture crunches again, and the hair falls over her face. "She figures into us? I mean, if so, I can say nothing. It's okay."

"God, no, not at all." I shake my head, pushing her hair away. "I don't want to be another problem."

Her expression is more than relieved. "You're not. I mean, okay, she will freak, but I—I don't care."

"The only things that factor into my being with you are your heart, your mind, and your desirable body."

Smiling a little, she murmurs, "Good. Thank you. I was having an old mate moment, and it wasn't good. I can do whatever you need; I need some time to adjust to that. That's all."

I kiss her and then give her a serious look. "It's all about you, baby, no one else. I've been falling for you from the moment you touched me, I think."

"It set me on my ass. I get unsure and paranoid sometimes. Sorry."

"Taurus is very much in love with you. True?"

It's not a smile this time; it's beaming. "Yes. I get that now."

"Any doubts?"

"No."

"Can you accept that I'm the same way? Or I will be, um, probably."

Her skin flushes again, and she whispers, "I can try."

"I'd no sooner hurt you than I would Rafe. Though, you may need to explain things to me like a mentally challenged twit."

Deli chuckles and sighs. "Me too. I think we'll be okay if we talk. Do you want to take a shower maybe, and go get some food? I heard you have all your own stuff here now." Her smile is shy but pleased they have assimilated me into her herd, even in a small way.

I wrinkle my nose. "That, my sweet, sounds like an amazing idea because I don't think we're done yet." Giving her a saucy grin, I roll off the bed and hold my hand out, tugging her along towards the bathroom. "Let's get squeaky."

The Artist Has Issues

RAFE

Mate,

I didn't handle this morning as well as I could have, and I feel chapped about it. I didn't expect what happened between you and me yesterday. I'm right glad it did because there aren't words for what you did. I feel off about it all, I guess. When I feel off or unsure, I fall back on what I do well—being a prick and protecting the ones I love. Bugger. I can't help feeling like I should have said something different.

Maybe I was too cold.

I think it wasn't very good for you and I'm sorry. I hope I'm being paranoid and I wasn't as big an ass as I think I was. I probably was, though.

Regardless, I wanted to tell you that yesterday was—it

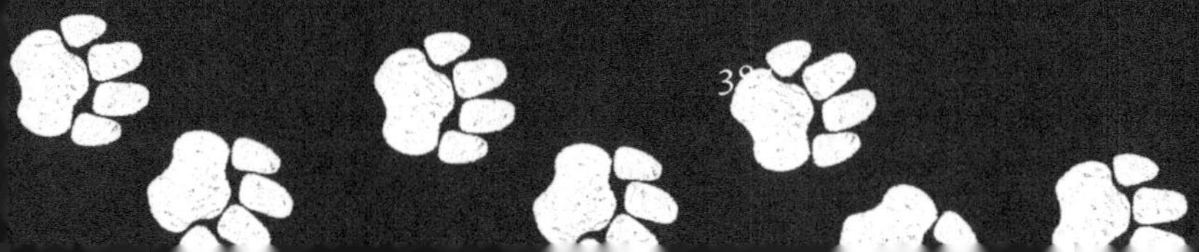

will stay with me for a long time. I hope that it wasn't a one time deal, but I figure there's more to be said. That's better face to face, I think. I might need some help there—figuring things out—as I'm in unfamiliar waters. I'll look you up when I get home tonight, but I wanted to... hell, I don't know.

Hang loose, Sampson.
Taurus

The hastily scribbled note was waiting for me when I came back from the supply store.

Once he left, I went to the kitchen to get more bourbon and a bite. I figured I'd shower and work out my emotions with a drink and draw session. I did this to myself, and no way was I going to bother the women. They need some time alone—it's good for them, particularly for my primary. That wound is open, and at least one of us should heal, right?

Unfortunately for me, the women took up residence in my sodding studio. Blade didn't feel comfortable knocking about the top floor of our house with its history, I'm sure. I can't blink in and out, so I had to run out to get supplies. Whiskey alone wasn't going to cut it. I was frustrated, angry, and self-destructive when I left.

When I returned, our women were gone, and the note was here. I have no idea what to make of it. Am I supposed to feel bad that he thinks he screwed up? Should I let it go? What is he saying he wants? The sex was fucking amazing—we both know it.

Maybe that's what it was and what it will be. Maybe that's all I should hope for. Every time I look for more, it's ugly and I can't fuck things up for either of the women, so I should assume that this is a fun thing. I can have a lark. That's it: a once in a while, fun thing.

Great.

The Bird Clears The Air

I pop into what I assume is the master bedroom in their house. Looking around, I smile at the touches that I identify as the minx and the décor that has to be her interior designing housemate. It's elegant yet feminine in that 'Fifties ingénue' way.

The only hint of the stoat is the scattered art supplies and shared hair products in the bathroom. I love the huge, claw-footed tub, giant Jacuzzi in the corner, and the enormous shower stall big enough for an army. That git must have laid this entire place out to service a herd. You could have the lot of them in here all at once without even being tight on elbow room.

My problem is that the stoat's not here, nor was he in the studio when I dropped the note off earlier. I doubt that he is in one of the guest rooms. I have no idea, though, and I'm not comfortable with the history in this room, so I don't want to stay here. I don't know where to go, and I feel like a git.

"How's it hanging, Assassin?"

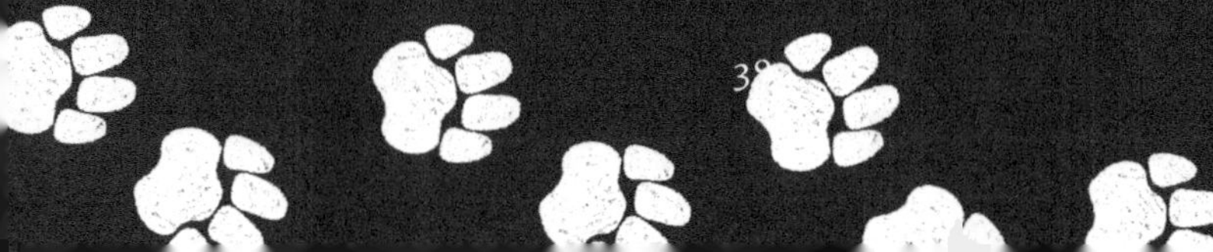

I blink when I see the Designer Duchess in the doorway sipping a dirty martini. There isn't a single flaw in what she's wearing—which I expected—but I didn't expect the grin. Her reputation is for being a dispassionate observer of truth, but she looks more like a fond big sister.

"Where's the long-haired one? I left him in the studio earlier, because I didn't think he'd move."

She snorts, sipping her drink again. "Much like a bad penny, he always re-appears. He's back in his hidey-hole. Once all of you crazy people left, Hex cleaned up the mess. The studio's usable and fluid-free again. Xanax save me from the bitching. You people." Sniffing delicately, she turns on her heel and says over her shoulder, "Go down the stairs, take a right, and then follow the guest hallway to what used to be the solarium."

Right. No mention of the women. I guess they took a powder? Fuck.

I leave the minx's haven without snooping more—my gut clenches when I consider opening a door and seeing what's inside up there. Following the directions given, I end up at the enormous set of double doors. I pause for a moment because not only is this whole situation awkward, but I don't have the foggiest idea what to do or say. I have a distinct impression that I fucked something up. I might have behaved like an ass, which is why I left the note while I was on a brief break. I knew he wasn't there when I did, but I hoped I didn't know why.

Christ, Taurus. Just suck it up and go in—that's my way, head first, and balls out.

I open the door, smiling to myself when I find him in the over-stuffed chair from last night, a sketch board propped on his lap. There are papers scattered at his feet, headphones in his ears, and a bottle of bourbon on the table next to him. He has charcoal smudges all over his hands, arms, and chest, and he's tapping his foot on the chair as he works. I almost don't go in because I worry that, much like the minx, he's damaged.

It's possible that he's more damaged than she is, and he's not told anyone. I could screw this up and make my primary's life worse. Hell, I've got my wife, right? No need to make everything worse. Leaning against the doorframe, I watch, trying to decide what to do. I can't make myself leave, though it would be the best plan.

My reticence is strange; I'm not one to give in to sentiment this early on.

He pauses in the drawing, looking up for a moment. "Hello, mate." His eyes drop to the paper, and he finishes a couple of strokes. Once done, he sits the charcoal on the napkin on the table and pulls the headphones out.

I push off the doorframe, sauntering into the room as if I have the slightest idea what I'm doing, pasting a sardonic grin on my face. "You and yours are too blasted good at sensing. It ruins a bloke's appreciation time." He tilts his head, watching me, and I curse internally.

It seems like I've already hit a nerve.

"We live in a household where you never know who is behind you or what they're wielding. It sharpens your reflexes."

"My household is not like that. Well, except for the time I thought Damien was making a move on my woman or when he annoys me."

"There are no locks on the doors here, so you never know who the hell is lurking about. The bitch keeps me on my toes, Victor and the droids give each other hell—you might even get caught in a prank war."

"I waited a long time to meet Philomena, but I'm not disappointed every time we end up having a chat. When did you move back down here?"

He shrugs, setting the board aside and tucking his knees up. "I went for supplies because the women were in here. When I came back, they'd split and Hex had finished cleaning. With no one around, it seemed safe to hole up in here and work."

Interesting. I wonder where the women went? I didn't see them upstairs, so maybe they found another perch. I drop into the opposite chair, looking at the stacks surrounding him. "What are you working on, mate?"

"I'm messing around to keep busy." He looks down and frowns, as if he does not understand how many things he'd finished in that span of time. "I had no idea how busy I was." Scratching his chin, he spreads charcoal all over his face, looking every bit the absent-minded artist he is.

Should I tell him? I feel wicked. So, no.

"What's the subject du jour in the great art caper here?"

He blinks as if no one ever asks him this. Maybe they don't. I could believe that outside of his family members, none of the exes gave a damn about what he used as an outlet for his emotions.

"Various subjects... I draw from memory—though not always my own. I filch from the woman's memories, but she'd be mad if she knew." He picks up a sketch of Aradia, curled by a fireplace on a Persian rug. That's my home with the minx, and I just replaced that rug, so I know he's being truthful. He jerks his thumb at the corkboards behind him. "The left one is my memories and the right one is hers."

I'm interested because my primary has spun some heady tales of his talent, so I stand and go look, stopping as one catches my eye. It's my golden goddess dressed as a sexy, badass cop with the mother of all attitudes. That must be from the night they met.

"Impressive."

I mean that, though he doesn't know how hard it is to get that kind of praise from someone who steals art as part of his job. I move to the next board to look and there's a dreamy watercolor from the night of Beltane, depicting the night sky and the circle, followed by several others that are so accurate that I'd assume he saw them through her eyes.

His depiction of fire, of the Egyptian gods, and of the spirits is astounding. The minx and I look like we've been born from the fire. That bugger could sell these—if one of us wouldn't kill him for it—for no small fortune.

He's not just talented; he's a master.

"You've got a lot of talent. Then again, talent runs in your family in ways that death runs in mine." I grin. I don't know if he realizes how sodding wonderful everything in this room is, even the throw-away sketches at his feet.

"Thanks. It's been a hobby since I was at the Company. Someone wanted me to learn for a training mission. I started sketching and figured out I was good at it. It stuck with me. Now it's my thing, I suppose."

My lips curve at his humility. He has no idea how good he is; he knows he enjoys creating. Rafe doesn't want praise—he displays his work in this room no one enters. Perhaps the reproductions I saw around the house were done by him. It would explain why I had to look twice to make sure they weren't authentic. From the Monet to the Rembrandt to the Van Gogh, they looked authentic enough that I almost checked to make sure the originals were in the last place I saw them.

I walk over and brush the smudge off his chin because I can't help myself. "When the only things you're good at are pissing people off, stirring up hornets' nests, and killing, you grow an appreciation for those with the Renaissance skills."

"That's not all you're good at," he murmurs.

"Well, I'm a fair hand at pool. I don't think that's what you mean, though. If it's the between the sheets shit, that's nothing big— that's genetics and training. You know that."

He rolls his eyes at me. "I could argue that, but since it's not the point, I would believe that you have plenty of talents you don't talk about. There are some that you don't know about. The Rift works that way. Everyone also knows that."

I shrug, feeling uncomfortable tooting my horn with him. I love crowing about myself to anyone who'll listen—the goddess and my wife can attest to that—but this situation is putting me on an uneven keel. People rarely ask about much besides the clothes and the job, and I'm fine with that.

"I sing. Play a tune on a piano or guitar. I'm not bad with a saxophone."

"Exactly—not everyone can do those things. You prefer to be known for the other stuff because it doesn't fit with your image." He watches me as I stalk to the other side of the room, wiping his hands off.

"It's easier being known for this stuff."

"It's a magnificent wall to hide behind."

"Well, it helps that I enjoy the killing and the pissing off vacuous cows," I smirk.

"Enjoy your work, or what's the point?" He rolls to his feet and stretches, all lithe frame and grace. It makes me wonder how he stays so sodding fit, being so stationary all the time. "You want some food? It feels like it's been a long time since I've eaten. Leo will whip something up for us."

I blink. *How in hell's name does he not know when he ate last?* "Sure, Sampson. I'll get a bottle if you find something in the kitchen. My knowledge of this place extends from the bedroom to here—which I learned today."

He nods, padding off to find one of the many members of his house I've never met. I apparate a bottle of my eighteen-year-old Macallan scotch because I figure we're due a conversation that might require alcohol. I wander around his studio for a bit, looking at all the drawings, paintings, and sculptures tacked or shelved on the walls. He's beyond prolific, and I see a few cabinets on the far wall that hold more works. There are plenty of pieces featuring my minx in various costumes, portraits, and situations. I see the love he feels for her radiating off the page.

There are quite a few of the other members of his household, too, but it's not all light—there's darkness, too.

I figure that he's taken anything that represents the old family members and stored it because there's not a trace of them. As much as he's done of my wife and my primary, I can't believe he didn't use them as subjects. My guess would be the only cabinet that has a padlock on it is where they live. I see their influence, though, as the displays seem to flow chronologically, and if you look closely, you see an ebb and flow of happiness to pain in the artwork.

There's him and my wife in the middle of her circle, drenched in the moonlight and holding one another. The pain radiates off the page. Another piece looks almost like the cat is sporting bruises and dents; she's curled up in a closet and surrounded by spider webs tying her to a wall, beast face on as she struggles against an unseen captor.

That might be the most interesting one so far—or so I think until I come to one that feels the angriest in style. The subjects are small, yet intricate, and curled up in a corner as the looming darkness creeps towards them. It's very abstract, and I don't know what all the pieces around them mean, but I can only assume they're symbolic. A ribbon, a bottle, a tooth, a jester hat, a crown, and a match are in various places in the room. There are roots extending from the figures, going deep into the ground, and planting them in place.

It's not the subtlest of symbols, that one.

Again, it feels like they've buried more than I realized. That painting alone, sitting next to the spider webs on one side and flanked by one of the Minx in extreme closeup, tells a tale. She has a tear of blood and a look of anguish so deep that it hurts my heart to look at it. It tells me they've gotten hurt far worse than I knew. There's a space next to the tear sketch, and I can only wonder what piece he took down and put away that follows that timeline.

Whatever it is, I doubt either of them is ready to share it. He must have taken the more controversial pieces down after my primary started visiting here.

"I brought the food, mate," he says, and I turn on my heel, pretending to be interested in a shelf full of gorgeous ceramics. "The glasses are on the bar unless we're drinking from the bottle."

"Mate, you don't drink eighteen-year-old Macallan from the bottle. It's not done," I scoff, striding over to the bar and picking up two glasses. I pause by where he's plopped down on the bed. "Do you prefer rocks?"

"Neat, please. Don't worry; they don't leak. I'm skilled at glass-blowing. The git at the place I go to says I could work for the crystal barons," he grins a bit, chomping on something that I'll admit smells fucking fantastic.

Looking at the glasses with their raised, etched designs, I concur.

Is there any art form he's not fucking fantastic at?

Padding over to the bed, I pick up one of the deep-fried something or other. I give it an offhand glance, considering before I chomp it down. Holy hell, that git that cooks for them is goddamn amazing. The lounger was gone for ten bloody minutes. Deciding to get comfortable, I walk back to the couch for a moment. I shrug out of my duster and then grab my glass, perching at the end of the bed.

"Bloody good scotch. I'm glad you brought it," he says, still munching from the plate of unidentified deliciousness.

"I almost didn't. The last time I shared a finger of this with someone other than my wife, it didn't go well." I sip, remembering what ensued when I did. Clearing my throat, I push that away as that twat will not monopolize my thoughts. I have more important things to attend to tonight. "Then again, it's always a good time for good taste."

I see the shadows pass over his features at the mention of that night, but he rights the ship very well. His face changes as he tucks his emotions away. He is skilled in that. "That is the truth." He sips again, closing his eyes.

Savoring my drink, I take a private moment to admire the long-haired fiend in front of me. I gaze at the muscles, skin, and form of the man who flipped a switch I didn't know I had, wondering what draws me. He's packaged right nicely—as are we all—but he's different. Taking another sip, I school my thoughts before he opens his eyes.

When he does, he gestures at the space. "Get comfortable. I can turn it up."

I blink, looking over to see a TV on the wall playing a martial arts flick. I feel stupid when I realize I didn't even notice it was on. There's no sound, so that explains the headphones he was sporting when I came in.

"Sure, turn the volume on. I planned on seeing this one with the goddess one night, but got paged to Bucharest for a job and never got back to it." Having it on takes a bit of the silence pressure off, and I look around, wondering about the comfortable. After a moment or two of internal debate, I settle on unbuttoning my shirt and tossing it on the couch with my duster, then lowering myself onto the mattress and sprawling out.

It makes me smile a bit when I catch him looking me over as he digs for a remote and turns the sound on. "I've been meaning to for a while myself. The boys filled up the queue again the other day, and I was pleased to find some things I'd missed. This guy's always good for a laugh."

"I have to respect a bloke who's not like us and does his own stunts." I turn to look at him, giving him a grin. "I could pose and let you look if you want to admire. Maybe flex a bit? We could stop dancing around the fact that we shagged like we were feral, and I loved every bloody second of it. Or we could watch a movie, whichever sounds good." I shrug, deciding to slide back into casual disinterest because I don't have a clue what he's thinking.

He snorts, looking both surprised and amused. "I don't think you need to pose; you look good enough without it for sure. Dancing wasn't my plan, but the scotch was a pleasant bonus. What would you rather do instead?"

I didn't prepare for that question. "I don't know. These are deep, unfamiliar waters, and I'm not sure of sharks or rip currents. I'm not sure of anything besides knowing you were the first, and you know it. I'm not sure what the next step is. It's not in my nature to let it lie, though, as nothing gets solved that way."

Tilting his head, he sighs. "No, it doesn't. I knew I was when we did it. It means something. I didn't think about then, and well, it was novel to me. I've never been that to someone before." Pausing, he licks his lips, setting the plate aside. "The next step is more about what you want. It was good, and I would do it again if I could."

I snarl, giving him a dark look. "I'm not the writer. I'm not sure why I want you or what I feel for you, but I'm not the writer."

"Thank Christ for that."

The vehemence behind that statement is interesting, but I don't have time to examine it. I sit up, moving closer to him with a defiant look. "What *do* you want me to be?"

His expression changes, eyes blinking a bit of the gold as he looks me over again from head to toe. Moving closer but not touching me, he growls low. "What I want is for you to be mine."

Everything in me tenses in surprise, but I rein it in, not showing the shock at his words. I didn't expect that for a second, but I move closer, laying my palms on his abs and flexing my fingers. "Fuck, why? You and I, mate, we're fire and water. I'd give you no respite, no calm, no peace. It's not in me to do so. You are everything I'm not, except fucking gorgeous, because you are that. This want I have for you? This craving is a deep hunger. I hunger for your blood—having it pour over my tongue, explode over my senses— and for your body." I notice the navel ring and flick it, amused by the body mods I see I missed in our frenzy the day before. "I want you; I do. I don't know what to do. Help me."

"Perhaps because you are opposite, because you're strong and passionate, it draws me. Believe me; I've got plenty of calm on my own. I'm hungry for you like—fuck, I can't even describe how, but it's more than I've felt for another man before. You hit a primal place; you make me burn, and I like it. I want you to be mine. I want to drown in you like yesterday, but more and whenever I can. Your looking at me is making me crazy."

The primal inside is raging, demanding an answer. Springing forward, I tackle him, cutting his shoulder with a fang and licking off the tiniest bit. "Fine. You want me? You take me."

"Fine by me," he growls, lunging forward.

The conversation's over for now.

The Cat Goes Solo To Seek An Old Rival

DELILAH

Taking a deep breath, I inhale as I look at the scenery around me.

It's smoggy, crisp, and full of delicious-smelling treats that are both on legs and emanating from the shops that line the corridor. London is a beautiful city, and if I were here with my husband, I would enjoy it as fully as possible. Hell, even if I were here on assignment, I might take in the stores and give Taurus' fortune a good ding.

However, the reason that I am here is not as pleasant as those alternatives, and I cannot indulge. I want to be as steely as I can be for this errand, so I can get back to Talia like I promised.

Scratch that—I have to be made of iron and fire to complete this task.

Looking around, my gaze falls on the bookshop at the end of the block. Its position is on a corner, flush against the buildings on either side. I'm not fooled by that choice of location as it gives a vantage point to observe 180 degrees of entry. I'd bet a month of extra training sessions that the back of the building has little to no

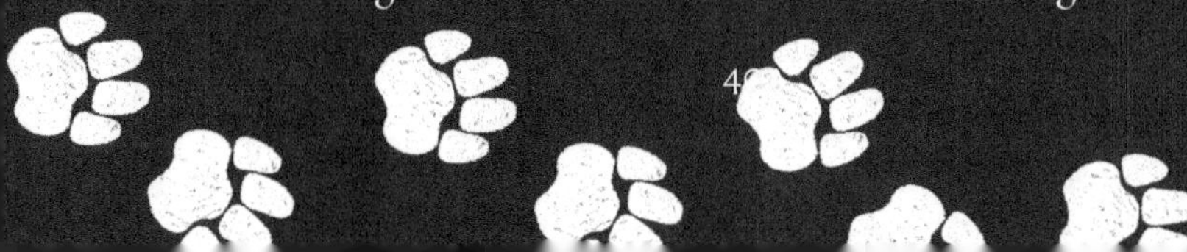

space to maneuver and that the subterranean levels connect into tunnels and old London siege escape paths.

I would expect no less from her.

Twirling the stem of the water glass in my fingers, I watch the passers-by come and go as humans do. Some in a hurry, some distracted, some trudging along—I've always known that most of them are not conditioned to be the apex predators that their biology suggests. Even before the mutation, I knew that something separated me from the rest of the people I lived, worked, and played with throughout my life.

Now I know: magick.

It's not the only thing that has redefined my self-image—the beast has her own role—but I know as surely as the sun rises in the East that I have never been one of them. It explains much of my childhood and young adult life. I always felt like a square peg in a round hole—too smart, too wild, too angry, too passionate—to fit in, no matter what the situation was. I took control, not because I was driven to lead as much as to ensure that I did not grow bored.

Though I suppose I can't claim that control is something I've always yearned for. My beast and I have made our peace, particularly since she mated with his demon. We work together rather than against one another most of the time, and for that; I am grateful. My magick is another story—it's as untamed as the foliage in my sacred space.

Hours tick by as I learn the patterns of traffic on foot and on the street. Patience has never been one of my virtues, but training for the Company has taught me the value of reconnaissance. I know enough of my prey to feel confident, but not of her current base of operations. Without a solid plan, this could go horribly awry.

After all, the last time I saw Heraclea Titania St. James, she was falling from the roof of a skyscraper—that I threw her off.

New York City, *a decade ago...*

"You haven't won!"

She looks at me with satisfaction, a silky purr escaping her lips. The jade-green eyes behind the fake librarian glasses dance in amusement, and she tosses her wild mane of coal, silver, and gold over her shoulder. The lights of the city glisten on her ebony skin as she pops her hip out, throws her head back, and fucking laughs.

"Oh, little girl. You are the cutest thing on this side of the Hudson. Haven't you learned by now that I always win?"

Balling my fists in rage, I dig my nails into my palms; the pain focuses my mind for a moment. This bitch has been plaguing me since middle school, and no matter where I go, she turns up like a bad penny. My life goes to absolute shit every time she shows up.

Trust me, I can fuck up my life well enough on my own without Clea around to give me an assist.

"Fuck you and fuck your stupid-ass riddles. I don't know why you are always here, but get the hell out of my city and leave me alone!"

Tapping her four-inch heel-clad foot, Clea stands like a goddess out of a comic book. Her style is never the same, not even from day to day. This evening she's wearing a gold lame mini dress that leaves nothing to the imagination, matching designer hooker heels, and chunky gold jewelry. Without the glasses, she'd look like she was ready to tour with Beyonce.

As if she's read my mind, she smirks, clicking a long shiny fingernail against the corner of the frames. They immediately turn into designer aviators, and her look is complete. "Is this better, sugar? I can't have you judging me for something as trivial as the wrapper for my candy."

I throw up my hands in disgust, growling loudly. "I don't fucking care if you have magick, Clea. It didn't impress me as a kid, and it sure as hell doesn't now. Go home."

Her laugh is throaty, and she waggles her finger at me. "Uh-uh, little girl. I'm here to stay—as long as you are. If I were you, I'd hide all of my friends and lovers. You know that I have no trouble claiming what is rightfully mine."

Hate can be a venom to your soul, and mine has always been crawling through my soul like vines wrapping around an ancient temple. I work hard to create space and relegate those parts of me to a compartment that I can manage, but my past with Clea always proves an impossible fire to quench. I can feel it snaking through my veins as I watch her strut and pontificate.

"—and if I remember correctly, the score is Delilah zero, Clea seven." Her smirk is cruel as I remember all seven of those incidents, and my chest aches with the re-opened wound.

"Jesus, fuck, Clea. What the hell did I ever do to you? Why have you made my misery your life's mission?"

Shrugging, she studies her nails. "I get bored easily."

Rage burns inside me as I think of my childhood best friend, Elysia. She defected to Clea's camp upon her arrival in sixth grade. They made my life hell until I transferred to a different school system for middle school. The first boy I had a crush on, Drew, fell victim to her charms within a week of her arrival in seventh grade. The next girlfriend I had, Rayna, moved to another state when Clea sicced the popular kids on her the next year.

Every time I found a handhold, she was there to push me down. Each year she found a friend or crush—Jax, Mellie, Shayna, Nikolai—and either claimed them as her own or drove them away for fear of her wrath. I spent my school years alone and fighting an enemy that might as well be invincible.

"Bored?! You get bored?!" I screech, my anger fueling each step as I move closer to her.

She watches me, lips quirked in amusement as if I'm a character in a TV show that she's grown fond of. "Yes. Bored. You must know what it's like to be moving eighty miles an hour in a fifty mile an hour zone, even if you can't compete with me."

Halting, I tilt my head, knowing exactly what she means. "So? That means you can get your jollies by destroying a human being every single chance that you get? What gives you the right?"

That's not the question I should ask, but it's the one I most want the answer to. I should ask how she finds me and ingratiates herself into my life every time I think I've escaped.

"Deli, Deli, Deli. You still have not learned that I have no interest in torturing humans, nor do I owe you answers to your excruciatingly tiresome questions. The only thing you will ever get from me is failure." Her sunglasses disappear, and I can see her eyes glittering with glee. Taking slow, measured steps, she crosses the distance between us to give me a smug grin.

What in the actual fuck? Why does she always do this? What the hell did I do to the Universe to deserve her?

My eyes rake over her, assessing her attire and comparing it with mine. I'm dressed in a tiny plaid skirt, fishnets, a half-buttoned oxford, and steel-toed Docs. My 'rude grrl' phase might piss my parents off, but it's made this confrontation much easier. She doesn't have the upper hand in her clubbing clothes, and I do.

"Clea, I don't know what you call your campaign of terror, but I'm an adult now. I'm not letting you get away with bully bullshit from high school. You haven't seen me since graduation, and a lot of things have changed."

A perfectly sculpted brow arches. "Do tell, little girl. I'm on the edge of my seat."

I roll my head on my shoulders, drop my bag, and roll my sleeves up to my elbows. She watches as I flick the few buttons undone on my shirt and tie it under my breasts. Feeling my movements freed up, I crack my knuckles loudly and drop into a defensive stance. "I won't let you ruin what I've built here. I'm studying what I love, and I will be on stage someday, listening to the crowd roar. You can't take that away from me."

Her eyes narrow, and she watches me, admiration flashing for a second before she lets out another laugh. "Oh, honey. Who has convinced you that the Great White Way will have you? I must meet them and congratulate them on a crueler trick than I ever could have played."

Bristling, I step forward, fists up as I invade her space. "You won't get the chance to find out, bitch. I'm ending this here and now. This is our last dance, Heraclea Titania St. James, and when I'm done, you can crawl home to your absent parents and lick your wounds alone."

Within seconds, we launched at one another and hit the rough gravel on the rooftop with a thud. Clea and I have been physical before, but that was before I took two years of mixed martial arts. Instead of the girly, hair-pulling slap fights we had in the past, this time we were at it for real. The tang of blood hits the air, and I don't know which one of us got injured, but it won't be the last blood drawn tonight.

Rolling to the side, I pop to my feet, bouncing on my soles as I watch her get up. No one in the universe should be that quick on their feet in four-inch heels. The Goddess is not with me this evening, and I don't know if she's sided with Clea or angry at the violence. I circle her in criss-crossing steps, eyes sharp and posture tense. Her arm shoots out and I duck, her right hook missing my face by a hair. Cracking my neck again, I dart forward, aiming for her gut. She weaves and I tumble, somersaulting over glass and debris with a snarl.

This is a street brawl, and luckily for us, there's no one up here to stop it.

"Well, isn't that cute? The kitty cat has some moves. You have been busy."

My grin is feral as I advance on her. "That I have, Clea. I am not a fool. As much as I prayed you would stay the hell away, I knew you wouldn't. You're like a bad case of crabs—you just keep coming back, no matter how many times I try to get rid of you."

"Crabs, huh?" She snorts, dodging my left cross. "I knew you were a witch, but I wasn't aware you were whoring yourself out. How did I miss that?"

Growling, I lunge and knock her to the ground, getting in a few jabs to her ribs before her feet hit my stomach and push me off. Her shoes go flying with me, and she leaps to her feet with the grace of a predator. I crouch as I catch my breath, watching her for a telegraph of her next move. She grins like a Cheshire cat, dancing away backwards.

"Here, kitty, kitty... I've got a nice ass-beating for you..."

I ignore her taunts, knowing that her ability to bait me has worked to my detriment in the past. It allowed her to give me a shiner days before my first Homecoming and break my wrist before a solo in the sophomore musical. I reported none of it, preferring to fight my own battles. My parents thought I was clumsy, and I let them.

I have always known that with Heraclea Titania St. James; I was on my own.

"You will never let it go that you got away with poisoning Hecate, will you?"

Her grin widens. "Whatever do you mean? I would never harm an innocent animal."

"You poisoned her, and she died, you goddamn psycho!" I screech, the pain of that memory making my heart ache. Of all the things Clea took from me, my only lifeline being a fat black cat that I'd rescued was the worst.

Eyes glittering in an unworldly fashion, she takes a step back and waits. "What if I did?"

I don't know what comes over me, but the red haze of rage covers me so completely that I charge like a rhino. Hitting her square in the gut, I send her flying backwards and, like a horror movie come to life, I watch her fly backwards over the edge of the roof.

Her shriek echoes off the skyscrapers and building as I rush to the edge and look over, watching her flail on her way down. Whirling around, I wait for the sound of a crunch and a car alarm going off, unable to look at the gore that awaits below.

I killed her.

Holy fucking goddamned shit.

I fucking killed her.

Panic takes over, and I run to the shoes, bag, and shirt on the ground. Scooping them up, I clutch them to my chest as I head into the building and down the steps as fast as I can without tumbling down them. After thirty floors, I hit the basement, eyes wide as I look for a way out. I find a locked door that must be for maintenance and knock it down with a spinning roundhouse full of adrenaline.

Looking out into the alley, I scan for witnesses before beating a hasty retreat into the darkness. If I can get away, if I can avoid anyone seeing me, I may not end up in prison for the rest of my natural life. Just as Clea predicted, Broadway was now no longer an option.

In fact, I will have to lie as low as possible until I know for sure that her case is closed. To do that, I'll have to drop out of school and disappear.

Even in death, Heraclea Titania St. James is ruining my life.

The Cat Makes Her Play

DELILAH

Yesterday, I watched the street. Today, I'm hoping to glimpse her.

Since Marvin told me I was pregnant, I thought long and hard about what kind of care I'll have for this baby. Given my own aberrations and Taurus' makeup, I knew that a regular OB wouldn't cut it. The Company might know everything there is to know about the clones and their creation, but from what I've seen so far, they don't know dick about the extranatural world.

And that's not something I'm willing to let them figure out on my fucking kid.

Those of us with a little 'kitchen magick'—as I thought I had before—don't call it supernatural, paranormal, or any of that garbage. It's always been the 'extranatural' world in every coven or group that I found. I suppose the other species that I haven't met call it the same, but despite repeated requests from everyone that I've ever worked with, I've met none of them—only magickal folk of the human hybrid category. I know where to find most of them

because of the collection of maps I've drawn in my Book of Shadows over the years, but sought none of them out.

Perhaps it is time to change that, but it will have to wait until I get the Resistance community in order.

I'd love to know if the intel I have on all the creatures and species that others claim to have worked with is real. Now is not the time to hunt merfolk or crones or other shifters. I have prey that demands my attention now, and I can't abandon that task.

Clea is not human.

That much I gathered from the creepy letters and gifts that got left for me every single place that I moved after that night. There is no way a human, even with strong magick, would have survived that fall. Despite that, she never approached me again. Oh, no, she only tortured me psychologically until I felt that nowhere on the planet was safe.

Running from her is how I ended up in a small dive bar off the beaten path in the Midwest. I wouldn't have strayed so close to home, but the rumors of people disappearing without a trace and reappearing days or weeks later caught my eye. I'd been watching feeds and ticklers on the web for unusual happenings since the first stalker package, hoping to get ahead of Clea before she found me each time.

Clea always left her mark when she hit a city. I learned over the years following the incident to watch for an uptick in weird events, particularly in the club scene. I don't know why she did any of the things she did outside of stalking me, but I sure as hell knew when it was her. Unfortunately for me, she usually hid her hijinks until she'd dropped her message off.

I grew tired of her obsession and tired of hearing her name whispered in the circles of the extranormals. If I could figure out which species was selling cloaking devices or forming rips or whatever the hell they were doing in Cincinnati, I could make use of it and get away from her for good.

What I found was a dive bar, a few friends, and nothing more for months. Sure, I could tell that people were behaving oddly and that a secret lived here, but I couldn't figure it out. I went back day after day, charming every local I could until I met Michaela and Dona. The way they looked at one another all the time, checking to make sure they didn't say or do the wrong thing, told me they were the key to finding out what in the hell was going on in this place.

Clea didn't show. I have no idea why, except that something or someone more pressing must have been claiming her time.

Eventually, I wormed my way into the girls' good graces and received my invite to The Rift. Once I was there, I knew I could move here and get away from Clea for good. I had to figure out how to do it while alerting no one that I was on the run.

I took up the cause of the Resistance and... Voila! I had an instant home.

Knowing all of this, it would be hard to imagine that I'm sitting at this table watching the bookshop I know belongs to Clea, waiting for my chance for anything besides finishing the job I started.

She's a magickal midwife.

At least, the rumors I've monitored ever since emigrating to The Rift for good say that she is. In fact, they say that she is the best magickal midwife in the nine realms. I don't know about that. I've only visited two, but I know my sources are not wont to exaggerate. She's presided over hundreds of births, according to the stories, from faeries to selkies to demi-gods.

I guess even the devil has a calling.

If I'm going to give birth to a miracle baby born of a magickal shifter and a clone, she's the person who I need at the birth.

Ain't life a bitch?

Irony aside, I know I won't be able to get close enough to her to speak with her unless I get the drop on her. She's as much of a fucking genius as I am, and since I figured out her dirty secret, I don't have the foggiest clue what her powers are outside of the birthing realm. Clea fell thirty stories and lived—she could be able to fly, be invincible, have regenerative powers, be undead—I just don't fucking know.

I can't barge in and demand her services without a background check. Everything I've found out online is suspicion, rumor, and unsubstantiated claims. I have to see for myself what she's packing before I go in unprotected.

So, I wait and I watch—again.

THE NEXT DAY, I decide that I have seen enough.

The bookshop is not merely a bookshop, and Clea has chosen her headquarters well. People filter in and out all day—far more people than a modest independent bookshop should draw. They all look normal, but something about the aura of the entire block is off. I wouldn't notice it if not for my budding magick, so I doubt any of the human Londoners have ever given it a second thought, even if they go inside.

A quick scouting trip to the roof of a bakery allowed me to use my beast vision at night, and I could make out a lush, leafy miniature rainforest on the roof of her store. That could not exist in

London's climate without extranormal help. There appears to be a glass greenhouse and fountain area, so I assume she meets with clients there. It would give them cover to drop whatever enchantments and glamours they used to stride through the Queen's capital without drawing suspicion.

It's stupid that I have to approach this way, but such is life.

I disapparate to that perch again, having witnessed a noticeably short, stubby man enter the store at a brisk pace. He seemed too round and too awkward to be human, so I believe I may get a glimpse of a species I have yet to see in person. Could he be a brownie or a gnome? Perhaps a dwarf or an elf?

Straining, I lean forward and drop the kitty face to see if I can make them out as they step out onto the roof. Before I can see what the little man is hiding, my breath catches.

Argus.

That fucking wolf can smell prey for miles. The rumors online say that Clea won him in a game of cards from Odin. Another said she had captured a shifter cheating on her and relegated him to wolf form to be her companion as a punishment. Another tale said that he was a warg, and yet another claimed she'd tamed the Fenrir wolf. They attributed Argus to everything from a shifter to a were to the pet or enforcer of gods and goddesses.

I knew him when he was a quarter of the size he is now, and he gives Aradia a run for her money. If Argus is not extranormal, then there is no way he does not have dire wolf blood. He's enormous, jet black, and his eyes are as blue as the sea. He is never leashed, but he wears a collar of trinkets imbued with protection spells suited to Clea's surroundings. I saw him rip apart a black bear that charged us in the woods when we were in middle school.

You do not fuck with Argus.

I'm without my familiar, so I can't let him scent me. Noting the ring of peacock feathers around his neck, I wonder if that is a coincidence or if Clea has figured out that I am here. I don't wait to find out, though, because this turn of events means that I have to go back to the drawing board and plan yet again.

I am not afraid of the Big Bad Wolf, but I don't want to become his dinner, either.

Time for an alternative approach, Deli.

I NIBBLE on the croissant as I watch the comings and goings. I'm back with an alternative plan, but I had to come later in the day than I would have preferred. The extension of my side project is clashing with my community duties, my mate duties, and my work duties. I can't be in four places at once, and it annoys the piss out of me. I also can't use a spell as a substitute for any of those things, so I've opted for technology.

Talia made me promise I'd be back within the next day or so—otherwise, she's sending the bird after me.

"I don't know what they are up to, Lily. It has my hackles up, though," I say, reaching up to adjust the wireless headphones tucked into my ears. "It's too quiet. The chatter is minimal. We have to be ready."

A noise distracts me, and I look down, watching Twist skitter under cars and between people as he returns. Looking triumphant, he climbs up onto the table and stands in front of me, holding a piece of paper like a prize. I smile, taking it as I hand him a piece of crusty goodness on my plate.

"Lily, I have to go. I'll get back to you later." I hang up without ceremony, knowing that she's gotten used to it. I open the paper, studying the leaflet with interest before I burst into laughter.

It's an advertisement for the bookshop, and I'll be fucked if that bitch didn't hit the nail on the fucking head. She's calling it '*Destiny*'.

Clea has always had a sharp wit, but this is even more on point than usual. The flier is for a sale on books and gifts, which implies that perhaps she's selling more than just occult books in there. I pat Twist's head, letting him know I am pleased, and he chitters in response.

I'm going to have to put him in danger again. I have to know what she's hocking in there and what's on the roof before I can approach. I can't step into a store like that, run by that person, and not know every square inch of the place. She could have enchantments on the products, other casters—or worse—hiding, or even have some traps built into the structure.

No way am I getting suckered into walking over a containment spell.

"I need to send you home to the Maison. I will send a message to Victor before I do. He needs to suit you for surveillance." The coal-black ferret stands on his back legs, raising a paw as if pumping his fist, and I chuckle. "That's the spirit, love. You will be my eyes and ears in the wolf's den—be invisible."

After he chitters a response, I pat his head again before picking up my million-dollar booty phone. Sending a quick text to Victor, I sigh. While Twist is getting outfitted, I have a trip to make. I have to see the bird since I haven't since he and the artist hooked up. He texted me to check in, and I don't want him to feel like I'm ignoring him.

"Be careful, darling, and I will return after I complete my mission. Do not take any unnecessary risks—Argus would enjoy eating you for high tea."

I could swear the animal snorts and shimmers as I disapparate him to my other home. They say that pets take on the personalities of their owners.Taurus is in for a hell of a ride with any animal I bring into our lives. He has enough trouble trying to tame me.

Now to calm the ruffled feathers of a big bird at HQ.

The Cat and The Weasel Accomplish Their Goals

DELILAH

I drop into the chair at the cafe with a groan. My visit with Taurus was brief, but I could tell how excited and happy he was just by looking at him. After we chatted, I dropped by the office to see what I might have to do next to complete my training. It won't make my mates happy, but I told my handlers that I wouldn't be available for it until the end of the week.

After all, I have this errand to finish and a new mate to spend time with.

When I don't see Twist right away, I wait for a couple of minutes, worried that my tiny familiar has gotten himself into trouble. He's very punctual for a weasel, and his absence is making me frown. If he doesn't show in five minutes, I'll go in there with claws blazing even if I am walking into a trap.

Luckily for both of us, Twist shows up right as I'm about to go nuclear in the middle of London.

I sigh in relief as he scampers onto the table, the tiniest camera in existence strapped just behind his head. Opening the app on my phone, I feed my friend fruit while I go over the footage from his journey. He'd infiltrated easily enough, and I'm surprised to find that the angles are excellent and the camera moving steadily through every nook and cranny of the shop.

A brilliant little shit—no wonder Mercury gave him to me.

There are bookshelves full of the usual occult authors lining the walls at the front of the store and displays of cheesy wanna-be Wiccan playthings. Nothing dangerous so far. There's a checkout area and a definite 'mystical' décor. Then he skitters under a curtain and the entire aura of the store changes, even through the lens of the camera.

The back half of the store looks crammed to the brim with real supplies, books, and displays with parchment signs with hand-written pricing. This is the actual business, and it's the money-maker for certain. I can see lists on the wall of spells, hexes, and charms that can be purchased—these have digital displays as if the pricing changes based on availability of supplies or popularity. Scales and measuring equipment line one set of counters and locked glass cabinets with various objects that I can't make out. Those are dangerous items, and I'd bet a Benjamin that they have security hexes on them. He tours the entire area, and I frown, noting that the interior is far larger than I'd thought. It will be hard to get through without some kind of alarm going off.

I sigh, tapping my fingernail against my teeth. I may have to go under or over to get in. That complicates things immeasurably. I know I can't pop in, and Clea is not a fool. No doubt she's placed magick sensors, checkpoints, and aura reading objects linked to her powers throughout the building. I sure as fuck would.

Going under is officially off the table. I'd barely found my way through the mazes of underground tunnels before I gave away my position. Glamours are also out of the question—that would be amateur hour. I have no choice but to come in from above and pray that she hasn't put a net over her building as I did with the Resistance Quarter.

Goddamnit.

I fucking hate heights when I'm not filled with rage or challenging someone.

Twist's camera finally approaches a stairway that winds both up and down, looking like it might lead to a medieval tower.

I snort. *Again, with the on the nose shit.*

Clea's parents are professors at the college in what used to be our hometown. Her mother works in the English department with mine, her focus being on mythology and folklore, and her father is the head of the archaeology department. That explains her name and all the trinkets she's got ahold of. Their professions also explain how she could move around the world at will, following them on digs, lecture circuits, and guest teaching positions.

They are sweet, hippie-dippy academics who never could understand why we didn't get along when our parents were such good friends. Their daughter being a goddamn psychopath had completely escaped their notice, I suppose.

The ferret cam scurries up the stone steps and finally emerges on the roof. My hand flies to my mouth as I take in the scenery, envy coursing through my veins. The rooftop is a lush rainforest of plants and flowers, most of which are definitely not native to England. There's a sitting area, a sacred space, a fountain, and I shit you not, beehives. I can see animals, reptiles, and birds running around as he skillfully avoids detection.

That bitch made her own fucking Garden of Eden on a London rooftop, and if I didn't hate her before, I most definitely fucking hate her now.

"Twist, does this video show any objects that might anchor a field like we have at home?"

He shakes his tiny head and waves a paw at my screen. I watch him move along the side of the garden, inspecting every corner. She probably has an enchantment to protect her space, but there's not a magickal barrier to keep people out. I'd bet Argus sleeps in the garden at night and that's security enough for Clea.

When the camera moves again, I can see Clea sitting with the pudgy man from yesterday near the fountain. It doesn't have audio, so I can't hear what they are discussing, but the little man looks distraught and she seems to comfort him. Perhaps he is one species that has difficulty reproducing; she is considering taking on his case. Not all extranormals have an easy time doing so in the human world since magick is no longer as prevalent.

I'm shocked to see that she looks different from what she did in our last encounter. It might be a costume—Clea has always loved dressing for the occasion—that she dons for particular clients to project the image she needs to calm their nerves. Her ebony skin is shining in the sunlight, but her hair is a mass of natural waves and tiny braids, the silver and gold threads in them catching the light as she moves. She's wearing a colorful, filmy dress that's almost a caftan, and she's barefoot.

She's the very picture of a fertility goddess of old, and I decide she is still playing her old games with people.

The man gets up and sticks a stubby hand out, but she laughs and leans in to hug him. Whatever she whispers in his ear seems to calm him, and she turns to lead him back into the shop. Argus stands and stretches, looking around curiously for a moment, his eyes glittering as he sniffs, but he turns to lope behind them.

He almost found Twist. If the wind had shifted, he might have sensed him and gone on the hunt. It was too close by far.

After they leave, the camera jerks and shakes as Twist leaps and bounds across the garden and over to the nearest roof to make his escape outside of the wolf's den.

I sigh, clicking the app closed. That's the route I will have to take to get the drop on Clea. Fuck me sideways. It's a good thing I've been honing those gymnastics skills in training or I'd be in serious trouble.

"Well, little guy, I think we're done for today. I have to go home and meet my mate, and I'm starving. I need a bite or five before I can figure out how I'm going to get in there. You did a superb job, my darling." My eyes twinkle and I whisper, "Just for that, steal anything you like from the bird tonight and I'll cover for you."

He chitters happily, and I disapparate us both from the cafe, musing about how I get in and then once I do, what in the fuck I'm going to say to convince my lifelong nemesis to do me a favor.

Nothing like reality to turn an entire day to shit.

SNEAKING onto the roof of *Destiny* and back off again without triggering any alarms is my test to ensure that I won't have to murder my old enemy again before I can ask for help.

Dressed in a black catsuit that I bought specifically to torture Taurus with, boots, and a stocking cap to cover the beacon that is my hair, I make my way to the southwest corner of an adjoining building. I picked it because the offices inside were all such that I couldn't imagine them having cleaning staff or nighttime visitors, which meant I could apparate inside and use the elevator. Stairs are a pain in the ass when you go this high, and I have no desire to be sore when I get to the top.

I open the door and slip onto the gravel with light feet, creeping to the edge to look at the gap between the buildings. It's manageable with the right skill set, and I've been practicing. I pull the grappling hook gun off of my belt, feeling like I've stepped into a spy movie. Humming the Bond theme song under my breath, I squeeze the trigger, watching the hook fly and catch at exactly the right spot.

Take that, Emma Peel.

Setting the weights and balances, I test the rope, making sure that it's taut, and that I secured both ends in the concrete. The last thing I need to do is take a tumble and wake the entire Rift to come look at my idiocy. If you are wondering, no, I have told none of my family that I'm here or what I'm doing.

Hell, Rafe is the only one who even knows Clea's name.

It's better that way, as my knuckle-dragging husband would rather I birthed a litter of kittens on his duster than let me employ someone who has almost killed me on multiple occasions as a birthing coach. In fact, he'd probably launch a campaign of terror across both dimensions to finish what I started in New York.

Plus, I'm not sure that I want any record of the extranormals filtering into Company records. I don't know if I trust them enough to believe that they won't start a Mengele-level program to make an army of their own. Their knowledge of magick and the people imbued with it is nil, and for the moment, I'm fine with that.

Taking a deep breath, I let the beast out. My fangs drop, my tail twitches, and my claws extend as I draw on every preternatural power that I can muster. I'll need it to do this without having a panic attack. The low rumble that echoes out of my chest is an agreement to work together, and I hop onto my makeshift tightrope, and as I put one foot in front of the other, I let my tail extend as a balance. Slowly but surely, I walk across the rope, stopping with every jerk and breathing through the fear. I was much braver in the club that night with Taurus, but that was because the beams and metal were solid and I didn't feel like a stiff breeze would send me tumbling to the pavement in a puddle.

When I reach the roof of Clea's building, I let out a long, quiet breath. My stomach stops flipping, and my tail twitches in victory. I did it. I motherfucking did it, and no one was here to help. I am going to be the biggest badass in the history of the sodding Comp—

That's when a slow clapping sound stops me in my tracks.

The Cat and The Witch Parlay

DELILAH

My eyes dart around until the sound draws nearer. Clea emerges from the foliage, her eyes glittering as Argus watches me with a snarl. "Who would have thought all it took for you to get over that ridiculous fear was the need to break into my home?"

Blinking, I jump to the ground gracefully, crouching in a defensive position. "What can I say? I'm a motivated bitch these days."

We eye one another warily, both waiting for the other to pounce, but it doesn't happen. Neither of us is likely to be the first to extend a courtesy, so we're going to stare until someone breaks. It's Argus, who snorts, tosses his head, and howls at the moon before looking at me dead in the eyes.

"A shifter? Oh, my love, what a wonderful surprise you've given me," Clea coos at the wolf, ruffling his ears as if he's not terrifying. She turns back to me and laughs, her voice husky with mirth. "Well, well, little kitty. You have been up to no good. What other tricks are up those bespoke sleeves?"

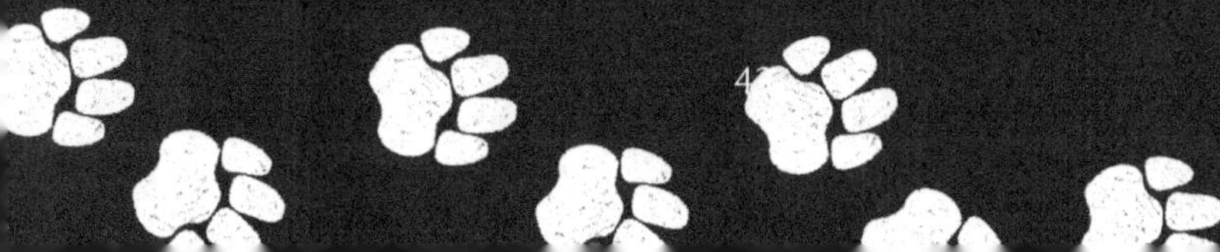

"Cut the crap, Heraclea," I growl, rising to my full height. "We both know that I'm not here to giggle over a Cosmo."

Sighing, she steps over to the sitting area, flicking her wrist at me. "Very well. I will find out whether or not you are comfortable sharing, and I am losing beauty sleep by the second. Come, sit, state your case and be as boring as everyone else who finds their way to my garden."

My nose wrinkles and I huff. "Boring? Boring is the last thing I'm called anymore, Clea."

Her head tilts as she studies me, and her lips curve. "No, I imagine you are right. Magick, a shifter, and mated to—something I am unfamiliar with. That alone is enough to whet my curiosity."

I throw up my hands, infuriated that my shields have failed me. That never happens anymore. "What, do I have it stamped on my fucking forehead now?"

"No," she purses her lips as I walk over to the table. "But you have cat eyes and a tail that I can see now that you are closer, your aura has significantly changed, and you wear a ring and bite marks. One doesn't have to live at 221B Baker Street to put the pieces together."

Rubbing my hand over my face, I drop onto the bench on my side of the table. I reach up and yank the cap off, shaking my hair out until I feel more in control. "Subtlety has never been my strong suit, as you well know."

She laughs again, and Argus pads over to sit at her feet, much like Aradia does. "This is also true, Delilah. You have always been an open book to me."

I glare, not wanting to rehash history or we'll end up at one another's throats. "The past is off limits, Clea. Our detente is for the here and now." I pause. "And possibly in the future."

Her eyes widen, and she looks positively delighted. "The future, you say? That is mysterious. Since you have no interest in finding out why I survived your outburst or why I provoked it, I suppose we should carry on with why you are here. I would have thought after evading me for the better part of a decade, you would have stayed under the radar."

"Damnit, Clea! Not everything is about you." I slam my fist on the table, and Argus snarls, to which I snarl back. "Sometimes, it's about what's best for other people."

Looking thoughtful, she nods. "Yes. Am I to assume that you are here for something that your many talents cannot assist with?"

I roll my eyes as if she's mentally deficient for asking, wishing that I had something to distract me from the roiling emotions of this meeting. "Don't be daft. I'm here because I need something that only Heraclea Titania St. James can give me, if the whispers are true."

"Spit it out, Delilah Lenore O'Hara."

Her expression is imperious, and I have to curb the urge to punch her teeth in. Outside my parents, Clea is the only one who ever uses my full name. It's always been part of our game, and she knows it. "I need your services."

"That's not good enough," she sing-songs, her face breaking into a smug grin.

"Fuck!" I exclaim, jumping to my feet and walking over to punch a tree. I thought I'd locked our shit in its room in the inner sanctum, but apparently, I was lying to myself.

"Tsk, tsk. I imagine that will be hard to explain to whoever is waiting for you in your hiding spot, won't it?"

I growl, closing my eyes and willing the broken knuckles to heal as I walk back to the table. I take another deep breath, saying the alphabet backwards in five languages before I feel like I'm under control again. It's been months since I've lost control like this in front of anyone outside of my family. I hate this woman.

When I open my eyes, she's staring at my hand, and I smirk. She didn't see that coming, so my inner rage cools. I've always wanted to one-up Clea, and for once, I got my wish. "You're right. It would have been a problem, but now it's not."

A single brow arches, but she shrugs as if she doesn't have a care in the world. "It's a good thing that we're not fighting at the moment. Our last battle was successful."

I frown, almost taking the bait. She wants me to ask what she means, and that is a conversation for another time. "Clea, I'm here because the gossip among the extras is that you are the most talented magickal midwife in the nine realms. I'm uncertain what that means, but given the circumstances, I'm willing to overlook my ignorance in favor of my needs."

Her eyes widen, and she pushes to her feet. "You? You need my services as--"

"I do," I say carefully, not wanting to embellish just yet. "Are you willing? I can double or triple your usual fees if need be."

Putting her hand over her heart, she tips her head back, and she looks up at the stars as if pleading with the universe. When her eyes find me again, she tilts her head. "If I agree, you will tell me everything. Part of the cost of doing business is that I must know every single thing that will affect the delivery. You must allow me to know what happened, how it happened, how you have changed, what your powers are, information about the father, your environment, and every aspect of your life. Are you willing to sacrifice your privacy for this boon?"

I expected this, and though I'm not one hundred percent certain that she needs all of that information; I knew that I would have to haggle with her. Heraclea Titania St. James never agrees to do someone a favor—she bargains for her services.

"Yes. I will at a later date share every pertinent fact that you request. However, if you ask anything that I think will endanger me or someone I love, I will tell you to fuck off back here to Ferngully and find another option."

She nods, tapping a finger on her lips. "You mentioned a price. However, I don't trade in human currency unless my customers are human. You are not."

Snarling impatiently, I slam my palm on the table again. "Spit it out, Heraclea Titania St. James," I mimic.

Her laugh is soft, and she shakes the mass of waves that flows around her shoulders. "Ah, little kitten, I have missed our sparring, even if it is only with words. I shall indulge you, if only because it has been a long time since I had such a good time setting my terms."

I give her a look that says, 'get it the fuck over with' as I tap my fingers on the stone table. "Tick Tock."

Standing, looking regal in a way that only a woman over six feet tall can, she gives me a feral grin. "My price includes the following terms, girl, so listen well. You will provide the information without complaint. You will introduce me to your people, whoever they are. You will not seek me out to harm me for the past—ever. The last item is paramount and non-negotiable, Delilah. After you have completed the journey you are on, you will seek me out again, and we will discuss why this shop is called *Destiny*. It will be most enlightening, and until then, we will not discuss the past. Are my terms clear? Do you agree to them?"

I close my eyes and replay her words carefully. It is never an intelligent idea to engage an extra in a bargain if you have not reviewed every word and phrase for a hidden meaning. Many species will kill you for breaking one, even if it was unintentional. This entire situation has clued me in that Clea is most definitely an extra, and I don't have the foggiest idea of what kind, so I won't risk being on the wrong end of a tricky bargain that allows her to kill me.

After I finally determine that I understand her terms, I look at her. "I agree to your terms, Heraclea Titania St. James."

Her smile is wicked, and I ignore the victory in her eyes. "Delilah Lenore O'Hara, we have a contract. Blessed be those who honor their word."

I watch as a tendril of magick snakes out from her hands, and I allow mine to join it, the two twining together as humans would shake hands. Sparks fly, and Clea shrieks with laughter as flowers burst into bloom at our feet.

"Oh, little kitten. This is going to be one hell of a ride."

Giving her a dismissive look, I grow tired of the power plays, and disapparate without a word.

I don't know how much more clearly I can say it, but fuck Heraclea Titania St. James.

The Cat and The Blade Run Into A Snag

DELILAH

Once I achieved my midwife goals, I knew I could enjoy my new relationship without that poking my brain insistently.

I came home and snatched Talia for some on-on-one time. On a scale from heaven to hell, it's been high in the stratosphere. We're a week and a half out from that damned party, which my boys and gals at home swear that they have under control. Things went well with my mates, and the lunatic squad has been suspiciously quiet, but I'm not worried about that.

Outside of a minor tiff with Rafe over an injury to my hand at work, everything was fine. That means disaster is coming, in my experience, so I'll enjoy the good vibes while I can. I'm not sure how stable internal peace is.

Given the newness of this experience for our mates and the tenuous grip we have on one another, I am not sure how long it will hold before something new comes up. We'll work it all out before we have to present ourselves in public.

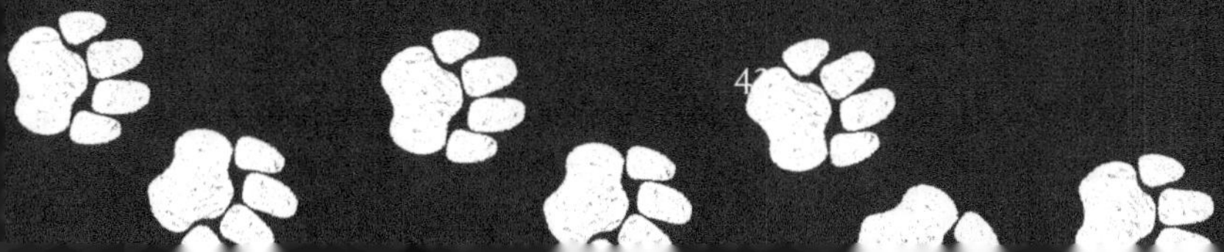

That much, I'm sure of.

Apparating into the master bedroom of the house Taurus made for us, I look for Talia. A few days ago, we all moved from the Maison to get some privacy. Rafe and Talia took rooms in the guest house, and we switch off as people spent time together. Hex helped Rafe move his art supplies and displays to a room on the top floor so he could work.

It's like we're an actual family now.

Talia isn't here, though, and I'm puzzled. I shed my work clothes and stretch up on my toes. All the aches seem to melt a bit as I feel the buzz of my home engulf me. I love my job and I'm getting good at it, but it takes a physical toll. The better I get at the different trials and test missions, the more difficult my assignments get.

It's making Taurus crazy. He'd never tell me not to do a job, but I know he can't help but check in on me to make sure they haven't given me more than I can chew.

"You're home," my new mate cries as she comes up the back stairs. Clad only in a swimsuit, Talia looks every bit the summer girl she is. Her hair is piled up on her head, and she smells like suntan oil and the ocean.

I beam. "I am. I had a good mission the past two days, and I even saw the feathered fiend for a few because he couldn't help but check up on me in his not-so-stealthy way, and now you're here." I squint for a moment, watching her face, and I frown. "You're here looking like you have something bad to tell me."

She blinks. "No, no. Not bad, I—I want to ask something."

Arching a brow, I drop onto the bed and try to hide my fear with a relaxed pose. "Now, I think whatever it is rather important, so rip the band-aid off and tell me."

"I need some clarification," she mutters, shrugging and looking at her hands like an embarrassed child. She pulls her hair out of the bun and shakes it out, walking over to the closet to change.

"What do you need clarification on?"

She steps out of the closet in a tank and shorts, her hair a tumble. I see one eye peeping out of the wall of hair she's let fall over her face as she mumbles, "You and me. Is this—us—is this the same old, same old in your family circle? I don't understand how your family works, and you said something the other night to Taurus. After the stuff we said yesterday, I'm confused."

"You're not her," I say.

I have no way to make this any clearer for her because I can't tell her what being Sari means. I've given her the most basic overview, and while all of that is true and hurts me, I can't give her the rest.

"I don't want to be."

"Perhaps I need to be clearer about what happened with us. I can explain why it's different." I sit on the edge of the bed, knowing that recounting this tale will not ease her paranoia. I'll do it anyway, though, because if she's asking me, he will ask Rafe.

Rafe is far less equipped to shut everything off and talk about this dispassionately.

"Sari and I slept together twice. The first time was the night Rafe and Wilde were together for the first time. Afterward, Rafe and Wilde became a 'thing'. Their relationship caused problems, but Wilde and Rafe claimed individually not long after. Sari didn't approach me until she had a wild hair up her ass about completing a 'family claim'. I think it was because she was trying to head off Rhea and Alistair. She and Wilde tried to pretend they were okay with us being involved with them, but their 'approval' never quite made it to their eyes." I sigh, shaking my head.

"It was a chess game with them. Alistair and I mated; Rhea and Rafe mated. 'Family claims' came up, but not before I read a post where the four of them were 'family mated' at an event on the other side. Sari completed the claim with me to beat Rhea, and Rhea did what she could stomach to mark her spot on the mountain. Even without sex, I was the last frontier, I suppose."

"I feel so odd about that. I don't play those games, and I don't have any interest in them. I don't work that way."

"Once Sari's teeth were on me, I wasn't important anymore. It was never about me; it was about marking territory. It hurt, but there were worse things to get hurt over, so I let it lie."

"I'm not a sharer—nor is Taurus. We've never had these problems."

"Unless you slept with me to have a notch on your belt, achieve some political goal, or it was part of some game: you're not her. That's how I know."

It isn't the only reason that I know, but it should be enough to keep her happy.

"You and Rafe changed things. I wasn't with you because I wanted to nose in on you and him, nor vice versa with Taurus and Rafe."

I chuckle. "Gosh, I sure hear that a lot. Rafe and I change things; we change people. You'd think it'd make us feel special, but it doesn't. It only leads to pain and frustration—or has in the past." I give her a serious look; my eyes are dark. "She never wanted me, Talia. She didn't want anyone else to have me, but she didn't want me. If I'm honest with myself, Rhea didn't want me, either; she only wanted the ability to one-up Sari. I think that's all any of them ever wanted."

"I did it because of you."

I smile, trying not to let my sadness ruin the moment. "I know I needed to know because I don't want to have only a blood connection with you. I have feelings for you, and for self-preservation, I needed to know. I've never felt like this before or done anything like this before. I don't like mincing words when it's important."

"I feel the same way. You understand why I'm less upfront about the subject because of the scars I carry."

I close my eyes for a moment, thinking about the moment that I realized that the frenzy to mate with me had been about beating Rhea to the punch. It wasn't long before the mess started. I'd never thought about the timeline until now. The family mating business happened, then the party, but Wilde started his bloody quest, and the Beast appeared. After that, the whole train derailed, and it all went to hell. I don't know how it went so wrong so fast, but it did. It started with their deception and ended in pain for both of us.

How could I have known?

"I wish you'd tell me what's going on behind those sapphire blues, though," she says, dropping next to me.

"Once you get into the tower, you can hurt me. People inside the tower have hurt me over and over, so I hide. But you've gotten in, and it terrifies me." I flush red, feeling stupid for being so unable to express myself.

Stopping for a moment, I consider whether I should tell her how terrified I am that she is not ready for this and that I will end up broken beyond repair if she calls it off. Can I admit I don't have faith in her? I want her to be my mate? Can I tell her I have this terror clawing at the pit of my stomach, screaming that she's going to crack my heart and change the fabric of who I am?

No, I can't.

I can't tell her that based on something that could be Maeve having indigestion. I was in Myanmar today, and I ate foreign food. Tasty as hell with a nice little kick, but this could all be a tummy problem, not a cat sense problem.

She grins. "You, too. I—"

Pausing mid-sentence, she frowns, her expression growing dark. Her head tilts as if someone is speaking into her mind, and I see her concentrating on sending her pictorial response. Talia snarls, head snapping back to glare at the room. She rockets off the bed, looking deadly and angry, leaving me flabbergasted.

"Talia?"

She gives me a sad smile and comes to brush her hand on my cheek. "I care about you very much."

That said, she stalks back to the closet and straps on her blades. I know that when she does this; she's protecting herself. I don't know what she's protecting herself from. "What did I do wrong?"

"You did nothing wrong; don't worry. Something hit me like a ton of bricks, and I need to go for a while," she says, finishing up the sheaths and putting on sandals.

"I'm confused," I murmur.

I didn't say any of my thoughts out loud, and as close as my mates are to me, there are parts of me they do not have access to, even Taurus. The doors in my mind palace stay locked despite my deep connection to him.

She turns, giving me a sorrowful look. "Do you want to come with me? I have a place I go when I need to be away. They can't reach me there."

I nod, feeling more than a little worried. What had one of my mates said to her to have her off the rails like this? "Okay, I'll go."

"Are you sure? You don't have to. You could help us get there. It's a long drive, and you'd make it simpler."

"I am. I'll go with you," I nod, pulling on a handkerchief halter and tiny shorts, trying to keep up with her frenetic motions. I feel like I'd rather be putting on my armor, and if I knew it wasn't hot outside, I'd take my duster. It's almost like my security blanket now, and having it when this feels so unstable would help me feel safe.

No room for safety here, though.

The Cat Goes To Paradise Lost

DELILAH

Talia closes her eyes, creating a perfect picture in her head and pushing it to me so I see where to aim. I don't know this place. It might not even be in the Rift. I can get us there across the divide without screwing up, but I need to lose the emotion and focus on her image.

Hopefully, this is worth it.

It's the lighthouse I see first, the smell of the gulf making my nose twitch. Even the picture of the scenery is calming her; I feel it. I look around as we apparate there, seeing the mangrove forest and a cove wrapping around the lighthouse grounds. There are only small strips of beach on either side to allow strangers to enter. It's a beautiful escape, and I know she's been coming here for a long time when she needs to recharge her batteries.

When Talia turns towards the sea, I look up, feeling the sun on my face and warm water lapping at my toes. She stares out into the wide expanse of turquoise water, spanning around to the bay where dolphins are swimming. I close my eyes as the distinctive

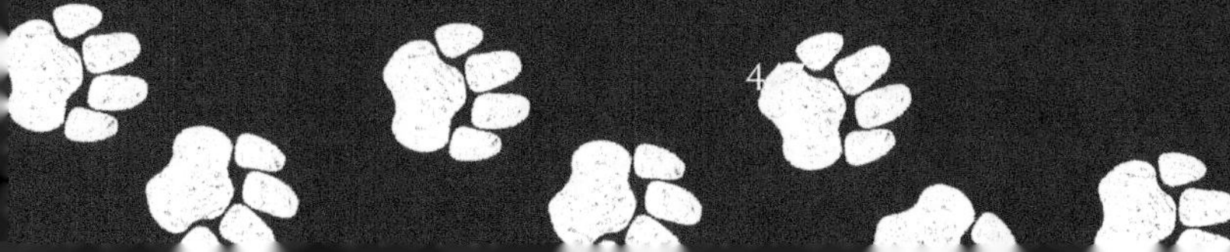

scent of the beach tickles my nose—a combination of saltwater, wet sand, life, death, and decay that's both pleasant and oddly comforting. I should have known by her appearance that Talia had the soul of a beach bum. Her comfort is in nature and the scenery, while I find my comfort in dark, quiet, cool places I can hide.

Hugging me to her, she whispers thanks in my ear over and over. When she lets me go, I glance around some more. I open the door inside me that allows my magick to connect to the world, and it all hits me at once. The water and its rhythm, the animals playing onshore and off, the palms and the seagrass swishing, and the singing in the waves: it surrounds me like a hug from an old friend, soothing the jagged edges of my nerves.

Singing—that's new.

I've heard the song of the forest and the call of its inhabitants, but not the sea. I look over at her, pondering telling her about it, letting her feel what nature feels like for me, but she's staring into the ocean with a serene smile. I don't think it's the time. This is her special place—I can tell. She invited me to see it, which is amazing.

While I look around, she strides over to the water's edge and drops into a crouch. Smiling as the breeze rustles her hair, she watches a fiddler crab tear off a bit of food and stick it in its mandibles, a single enormous claw aimed at her in an imaginary challenge. She steals a glance at me, looking sheepish. "I'm sorry."

I smile, letting her do what she needs to do. I don't know what happened or why we are here, but I realize how significant it is that she invited me, and so I let her lead. "Sorry?"

Talia plops down on the sand and digs her feet in, holding out a hand to me. "Yup. Big time, sorry. I got hit with a large, unpleasant surprise in my head, and I crumbled. I still hurt, but this place always makes it better. As do you."

Walking over to her, I drop onto the sand, giving her a puzzled look. "No need to feel sorry, but I guess I don't get it. What did those idiots say to you?"

She looks out on the water, upset, and murmurs, "I don't think he loves me; he wants Taurus. I'm a second thought to him."

I blink, feeling thrown off balance. I'm so stunned that I don't quite have the words yet. "If I could let you feel how untrue that is, I would. I can't—I don't have that kind of empathy. It's just—it's so untrue."

"When that bastard of mine was feeling lonely for you, they started talking, and Taurus got irritated with him for not contacting me like he did when you were at work." Dropping her head, she sighs. "I punished Taurus. He should have kept his damn mouth shut or occupied."

I sigh, still unsure how to help without getting far too involved in their issues. "Sometimes Rafe assumes people know how he feels. He's more of an action person than a words person. He's trusting enough to forget that some people need to hear it out loud. That's my fault because we've always been so intuitive and connected that words aren't necessary much of the time."

"I've never thought he loved me as much as Taurus loves you. I'm used to that."

Fucking what?! She's saying this now? *After all these things happened?*

Frowning, I murmur, "I don't think that's fair. Taurus and I have three months of trials and triumphs to build on and develop that kind of bond. We've had longer to weather and longer to get more confident in our relationship. I'm sure Rafe felt like a complete moron if Taurus said something about not talking to you. He probably even got defensive that Taurus had done something he hadn't."

Talia doesn't understand. She doesn't know where Rafe and I have been—neither of them does. She can't know how close he was to holing up in our house like a hermit for the rest of his days after the exes. She doesn't know what punishment Rafe took to allow me the space to find Taurus.

I can't tell her either.

It's not entirely my story to tell, and telling part of it means I'd have to tell all of it. Neither of us is ready to tell the tale of the winter trauma. I still can't think about it, and every day, something comes up that makes me think about forcing it so they'll understand why we are the way we are. It's not healthy to bottle it up, but it's been that way for so long now that we have to be ready to take on all that pain again or it'll consume us.

I can't let their insecurity force me to do something that I don't know if he and I can survive yet.

I shake my head and say, "I don't think you realize how close he was to giving up until he met you. Sometimes I was sure he was going to—I was sure that I was going to come home one day, and he'd disappear. He ran off once a long time ago when he got hurt. He left for three days. This time I got the feeling he wouldn't be back."

She sighs and picks up handfuls of sand, running them through her fingers, and watching them fall. "He's got Taurus, and so do you."

"I'm sure he cares for Taurus, but I know very little about that yet. I absolutely know what he feels about you. I know how bloody silly he looks when you're not around, and he's thinking about you when he thinks no one is looking. I know that I've never seen him act as he did with you that night. I've never seen him allow himself to want someone all to himself. If Wilde hadn't done a header, he might have even asked you not to see him anymore. It upsets him to think about it, and I don't think he ever felt that before."

Resting her chin on her knees, she shrugs. "I don't know, Del. He and I—it's been hard. We've been less with the calm good times, you know?"

I nod, feeling like I'm the wrong person to be having this conversation and uncomfortable to be doing it. But I will, because he deserves someone he loves to believe in him, and because she deserves to know what she's missing.

"He's let plenty of people almost leave him because he wouldn't be selfish enough to weigh in on how much they meant to him. He wouldn't ask for what he wanted. But with you, he does. I think without you, he'd give up. Taurus may be novel and he may enjoy him, but that doesn't mean he isn't crazy about you. Besides, Taurus and I haven't had it easy, either."

Talia doesn't respond, and I search for the words to help her understand who he is, who we are, how we work. "Rafe and I lead complicated lives. We're a trial—the things you and Taurus have to go through to be with us are difficult. Trust me when I say that we know that. I know it makes me feel you'd be better off without us making those waves for you."

"It's too late. You lead complicated lives—lives I will never understand—but I love both of you, so I build my boat to handle the waves."

I don't like the sound of that; it's like she'll accept them to prevent her from losing what she wants. That's not how it works, and it will cause a lot of problems.

Looking out into the ocean, I whisper, "I've often wondered if I'm worth the trouble. I'm sure he has too. I know you're worth the petty crap we deal with from the mates, but we're used to dealing with their shit." I scrunch my toes in the sand and shrug. "I think if he contacted you, then his intentions were good. Hell, I know that unless you're hurt, he rarely contacts me when he's with you. It's not a sign of him loving or wanting to be with one person more than another. It's more of a sign that he realized he'd been a jackass and wanted to let you know he knew he'd been a jackass."

"I know Taurus loves me; I know you care about me. I don't know why, but with Rafe, I'm afraid that he doesn't." She tilts her head, reaching out to touch my hair. "You are worth the waves, love; you are. You sound defensive."

How could I not when you're sharing feelings that threaten every-thing we just started building?

But I don't say that; instead, I go back to the subject of my primary. "Rafe is out of practice with people that aren't me. He's only had people who don't care whether he loves them. Rafe's not connected with anyone since the Rhea incident, not even his other mates," I say, musing for a moment then giving her a sad smile.

"But this is a complaint I've heard before; he doesn't say the words as much as do things he thinks communicate his love. It causes problems."

My eyes close and I listen to the sea again, finding its song calming and soothing. I'm going to cry for him soon as I think while he may have found the people that he could spend the rest of his life with, he may lose his wife. It's not because he's a bad person or a poor mate.

It's because they always want him to be someone he's not—me.

The opposite is true as well, and I do not know how to explain that, but it's the tragedy of being involved with a bunch of self-absorbed narcissists until now.

That's why I need to get her to understand; it's not an option if I want to avoid the two of us being destroyed again.

The Cat Realizes Paradise Has Been Paved Over

DELILAH

"I've never seen him move as fast as he did with you. He left bitching at me to go out with you. I sure as hell knew he liked you from that very second because he doesn't walk off with people he just met, not anymore." I dig my feet in the sand, feeling exposed for a moment. "I didn't mean to be defensive. I wonder sometimes if Rafe and I should be so selfish as to pull others into our miasma of bullshit. If it's worth it to have other people get some taints that follow us on them so we can be happy. It's pretty emo, but it's true."

"Could you sit with me for a few minutes? I want to hold you while I think. Is that okay?"

I nod. *What other options do I have?* "Yes, it is."

"Are you mad at me?"

"No, I'm not. I'm worried, fretting, and self-judging, but not mad at you. Why would I be?"

I'm not mad at her, but I'm terrified for both Rafe and me.

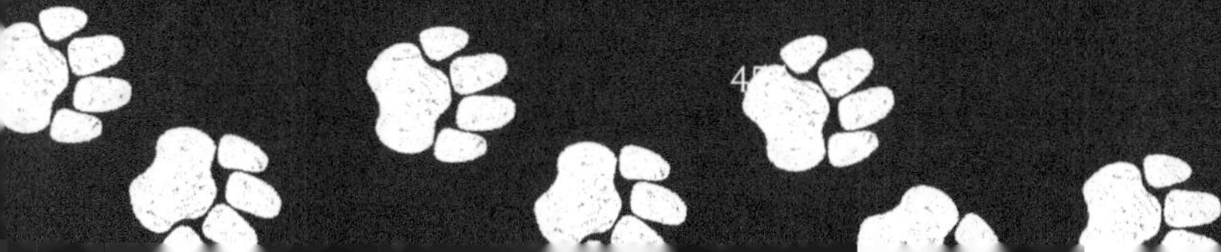

She pulls me down and sits me between her legs, wrapping her arms around my waist. She rests her chin on my shoulder and looks out at the water. "I'm so unsure and for being so much bloody trouble."

I don't know how to answer that without qualification. My fears have me paralyzed. *Do I reassure her?* "I can't be mad at you for having feelings. I'm unsure all the time; it comes with emotional scarring. You're wonderful and beautiful. I love being with you, and so does he. I can't make you believe what isn't germane to you, though."

Frowning, she holds me close. "I don't know why I believe you and not him. I don't know what's wrong with me."

"Maybe it's because I'm here telling you myself and you need him to tell you himself? It could also be because you were sure that Wilde didn't love you, sure other people have used you, and now it's hard to trust Rafe because those people have betrayed you? People have used you to get to Taurus before. Perhaps that informs your bias now."

"Maybe. Did you see what I did this morning at the bar while you guys were at work?"

Yeah, I saw it, but I was hoping not to discuss it.

"I heard you sing at The Zoo, so I peeked at the feeds. I have to say, I hate those bitches, but a live broadcast is brilliant. Your song was pretty. Was it about Wilde's death?"

She nods. "I saw you sing it on the stream the other day, so I thought I'd try. Who was your song for?"

"No one. I love Patsy Cline, and it was a country-themed week." I grin. "Plus, it's a little crazy around here, and it felt à propos."

I really hope people don't start using that shit as a weapon rather than musical therapy—it occurs to me it will be very problematic.

"I needed closure from his so-called death. I still don't believe it's real, but dead or not, he's dead to me now. Singing helped me deal with that." She sighs and strokes my hair. "What do you want me to do?"

"Be here. Be with me." I don't feel like I'm safe enough now to say anymore than that.

"If I seem like I'm going away, would you stomp for me as you did for Taurus?"

Ah, the dangerous line we tread.

If I let her any further in, then yes, I will storm the gates of Hell to keep her with me. Unfortunately, the more accurate truth is that if she can't learn to trust Rafe and accept who he is, I'll end up storming the gates to find them barricaded shut.

I would never recover. I've picked up the pieces from a woman trampling my heart twice, and I didn't love them like I believe I will love her. I don't know what will happen to me if she does the same thing.

"Yes," I reply, knowing that the road to Hell is paved with good intentions.

"Me too."

Oh, do I wish I believed her.

I smile a little, leaning against her. "I'm not the only one. Please try to remember that—I know it's hard, but it's true. He and I both have an enormous capacity to love—even to the point of not giving up on what we should. I can love Taurus so much that the Earth spins around him and still falls for you so that the sky shakes.

They're not lesser, only different. He's the same way. I don't know what he feels for Taurus, but I know you make his Earth spin."

"I'll try, okay? I'll try to trust that."

"It's all anyone can ask, love. He's beating himself to death inside over hurting you." Something occurs to me, and a chill runs down my spine as I feel it rings true in my heart. "He might contemplate telling Taurus he can't be with him anymore if it hurts you."

She's quiet for a few moments, as if considering. "That wouldn't be fair of me, now would it?"

Goddamnit, why in the hell does everyone think it is okay to trample all over him?

I don't give them that idea and because he's laid back doesn't mean he's immune to heart break. The screaming in my head is almost deafening as my brain starts spewing things I want to say to her.

If this is what you wanted, you should have said it days ago before Taurus came to him and mated with him!

I breathe in, watching the waves roil as a storm forms far off on the horizon. Counting backward, using my control mechanisms, I get the Beast and the magick inside me to calm. Maeve sends me an indignant push along our bond, making her outrage known, and I send back a soothing calm to keep her from inflaming my primal further.

When I feel everything is in balance, I speak. "Rafe has always guilted himself to death. He blames himself for everything, partially because they blamed us for everything and it stuck. It's why it took him so long to heal from our exes; he felt he should have known and stopped us from getting involved with them. It doesn't matter if it's fair; he'll do it in a second if he thinks he should. He's lost someone he cared about to make another person he loved happy before."

"What?" she blinks, turning me in her arms to look at me. "What do you mean he's done it before?"

"He's given someone up to make another love happy because it hurt them to think of it. He did it knowing that the other person was reluctant to do the same for him. It got ugly for a while."

"That's like what I was planning to do with Wilde before he died." She looks thoughtful for a moment. "Was it a non-mate?"

"Yes. It had the potential to become that kind of relationship, so it ruined a friendship and made it hard for everyone in the family for a while. It caused bad things to go down before they came to tolerate one another. It's not what it was. That was his choice, though, and he lives with it every day."

Every day he feels the scars on his back that remind him of the danger of letting someone decide who he can and cannot love. I can't tell her that because it is not my story to tell. The events that led to those scars almost tore my household apart.

She's definitely not getting that kind of weapon when she's doing this.

The Storm Begins To Form

DELILAH

My statement seems to make her uncomfortable, and she pulls away, rising to her feet and holding her hand out. "Do you want to walk the tides with me?"

I nod, letting her pull me to my feet. Holding her hand, I walk down the beach with the surf breaking over our feet. The sound is soothing and the smells are fantastic, making my senses overload with a peace that doesn't quite reach my troubled heart. I don't know what she'll decide, and I don't know what he'll do when she does, but I'm preparing for a world of hurt for both of us. I should never have allowed that night to happen; I knew they could not handle being a family in that way. Their beliefs do not allow for that kind of structure.

It's my fault for getting him and me into a situation that might break both of our hearts and affect the happiness we've had.

Again.

I stay quiet, unable to voice any of this to her for fear of making this whole thing worse.

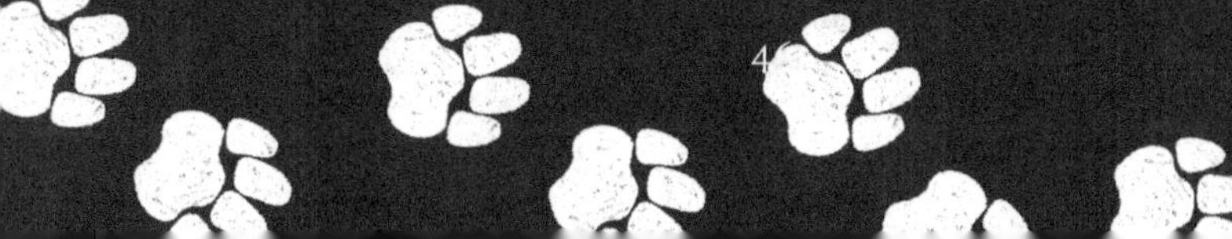

She whispers, "If he gave up Taurus, I'd have to give you up. It's the only way it would be fair. But I don't want to do that."

That's what she's concerned about? Giving up on me, not what it will do to him if he has to do that again?

"He would never ask you to do that. He might not even let you." I shrug, feeling my inadequacy at explaining how Rafe and I work, what we do for those we love, and how we see the sacrifice. "He'd tell you it is his choice. He's very stubborn."

"I'd have to, damn it. I gave up Wilde for him, and I don't want to give up on you, but I'd have to. My ethos wouldn't allow that imbalance."

It's not fair of her to make me discuss this hypothetical when the possibilities are making my heart crack in half as we speak. It happens every time.

When will I learn?

I can't let her see, though. I can't let anyone see me break like that again. "I guess you'd both do what you felt was right."

Her snort is bitter, and I'm surprised. "I think he's in love with Taurus. I know he's out of his mind for him."

Sighing, I stop walking for a moment, looking out into the sea. "We've not been fortunate in the past with this. Perhaps I should not have let it get this far. I don't know what he's feeling, but I could find out. I've been trying not to be nosy. To be truthful, he was in love with someone else that he gave up. He'll live."

My flippant response doesn't account for how broken we both are by now. It doesn't address how hard it is to even let anyone in— much less multiple people—and now the person we did trust might destroy us.

Keeping my face calm and detached, I nod. "You may have a point, but again, it is outside of both of our control. I wasn't being nasty; it's the truth. He's set in his ways, and I know how he is. I'm not being accusatory, only honest."

"I have to live knowing that if he gives up Taurus, he's giving up something else he loves. I can't live like that."

What in the hell does she want, then?

She's the one putting us all in this place, and I don't know what I am supposed to say right now. "I think he'd do it because he loves you. He'd do it because you mean that much. He'd do it because it's in our nature to be who we are and to do what we do."

It's in my nature, too, and I'm feeling like I'm right on the edge of taking the leap. I can put a stop to this now and walk away. I can keep this from becoming so intrinsic to our lives that losing it will decimate our identity. I don't know if I'm strong enough to do it. He was, but I don't know that I am.

She kicks sand across the beach and growls, "This is too damn hard! It's not supposed to be like this." Her brow furrows as she looks at me. "You feel distant. You're upset or hurting or something. I don't know why."

It's because I'm grieving for you already.

I'm grieving what I might not lose today, but I will lose, and it will have nothing to do with anything that I did. It will have to do with your insecurity and my inability to shoot the hostage. I give her a sad smile. "I don't know what to say. I'm afraid of saying the wrong thing or of hurting someone. I'm afraid to speak for him, and I'm too scared to speak for myself. I have to give myself some space to breathe."

"I don't bring people here. I made an error in judgment and brought Wilde here once with the hellhounds. I've never even brought Taurus here." She looks out into the sea as if contemplating that as the wind blows through the palms.

How is that supposed to make this better?

"That humbles me; it does. I don't want to mess this up, but you have to realize this situation affects me, too."

"That's why I come here—not even Taurus can reach me here. There's no mystical trail to follow like there is in other places. I don't know why." She turns back to look at me and sighs. "I didn't ask you to come because I wanted advice or because I wanted you to fix things."

"When I need to get lost, I hide in the closet. There are other places I could go, though. I can block everyone; I can cut ties. Maybe not to Taurus anymore, but if I felt motivated enough, it might work. If I wanted it enough, maybe I could."

"I asked you here because I'm happier when I'm with you."

But you're so caught up in 'does Rafe love one of us more' that you'll toss me aside without blinking? Yeah, okay.

I cough so I don't say my angry thoughts out loud, and then walk over to squeeze her hand as I try not to cry. "Thank you for bringing me. I know you didn't want me to fix things. You've gotta forgive me if it's my first instinct to help. It's just how I work."

My heart aches in my chest as I fight back the emotions swamping me. Can I keep letting her in? Can I continue giving her access to the part of me she's going to break when she cuts things off out of fairness?

What should I do?

"I think I should have brought someone who was a little easier to get into compromising positions. When I'm here, I don't mull. Mulling is for that other place. This place is for setting it all aside and being." She sweeps her arms out, looking around. "Look at it, Del. It's stunning."

"It is gorgeous," I murmur, agreeing with her. Contrary to her assertion, she started this talk, and she's not given me a sign that I should feel safe sharing with her. I don't know how I'm supposed to have happy naked times when I'm shaking with fear inside, thinking that she's going to call everything off.

"I'm so peaceful here." She strips down, gives me a wink and walks out into the crystal blue water, splashing about in the waves for a moment. She looks at me again, holding her hand out. "Are you okay? You're still mulling and thinking."

I nod, feeling bad for ruining this for her, but this conversation has killed my joy completely. "Yeah, I might have been the wrong person to bring. I can't seem to turn it off right now."

She drops her hand and steps back, her expression sad. "If you want to go..."

"No, no. I'm afraid of being disappointing because I'm not good enough. I love the way the ocean is singing to me and the tides swish and the scent on the air is tickling my nose. But I can't stop worrying. I'm trying."

Frustrated, I pull off my clothes and wade into the water. Diving under the waves, I let the silence surround my noisy mind. The singing only gets louder, and I wonder about it for a moment, but let it go to emerge and shake my hair out. "I need to refresh a little, I think."

"Did that help?"

I close my eyes, shoving all my riotous emotions down, imagining them in my feet. "I feel a little better. I have an itch, but the water helped."

"Itchy? Is it sand fleas?" She looks worried, her eyes focusing on my tummy.

"No, something is bothering me; it's nipping at my consciousness. It happens to me sometimes before big things happen. It should go away. It's like something's not right." I shrug.

She walks out of the water, plopping onto the sand with a miserable expression. "I feel him."

I blink. "Feel who?"

"I was ignoring it because I wanted to ignore it."

Frowning, I walk over to stand next to her. "Damn it, I feel nothing. I only feel the itch and, well, nature, because I let it in."

"I feel him. He's running."

I stomp my foot in the sand, irritated beyond telling. "I hate when they do that. I hate when they shut me out, when they run away, and they don't even try—"

"No, Del, it's this place. It's shielded, so we're not supposed to feel it. I'm not supposed to feel him; I don't even feel Taurus. Despite that, I feel Rafe deep inside me, and he's running." She lies back on the sand, quiet now.

Thanks for finally telling me, I guess. It's not like he's my primary or anything.

Dropping next to her in defeat, I sigh. "I feel everyone and everything unless I shut it out. I even feel when they're trying to shut me out. It's a constant low hum in my mind. I can open the door and let some or all of it in when I choose to. I keep many things closed so I don't get overwhelmed."

"Here you can open the door, but it won't get in."

"No wonder I feel off. I'm disconnected except for Gaia. She's never cut off."

"I feel him." Her eyes are shadowed with sadness as she looks at me. "I'm sorry. This is my sanctuary. Maybe it wasn't right to bring you here. You're not having a good time."

How am I supposed to when you've blasted all the progress everyone made this week away because of your insecurities?

I don't say that, though; I just shake my head. "That's my fault. I've been letting myself get caught up in things that aren't my business. I should stop."

"You mean Rafe and all of this."

Lying back, I stretch out, shielding my eyes from the sun before mumbling, "If he's running, that's his choice. He'll be back when he needs to be. I'm not worried."

That's not true—I'm nervous as hell. However, I was right; I can't be in the middle. Whatever is going on with her and him is going to end up affecting me, my happiness, and my life. If they can't work it out, I lose.

I was so stupid to let all this happen so fast, to think something would go my way—our way—so easily. I should have known better than to trust anyone but Taurus. He's the only one who hasn't broken me beyond repair in so long that I can't remember, and I can't do this with her.

"What does it mean when he runs? I sense turbulence." She stops, closing her eyes and looking like she's concentrating. "No focus, only jumbled and confusing emotions."

Christ, I'm tired of interpreting. Why doesn't she ask him?

She doesn't want to know what it means when he runs. The last time was after he gave someone up for Wilde. He runs when he needs distance and time to grieve. It surprised me when he didn't with Alistair, but since I left so often and he had his studio, perhaps it was a different version of running.

"I guess he's feeling guilty and confused. The last time he ran, he went north, where Lily and Mercury live. He blocked me for three days, and I think it would have gone on longer if one housemate hadn't caught him sneaking in for some of his things one morning. It might be easier to track him down this time because I've got more juice. Since I don't clamp down on my magick, it makes many things now possible, but I also haven't had his blood for a while. It's a toss-up."

That's all I'm giving her. I shouldn't have to do this.

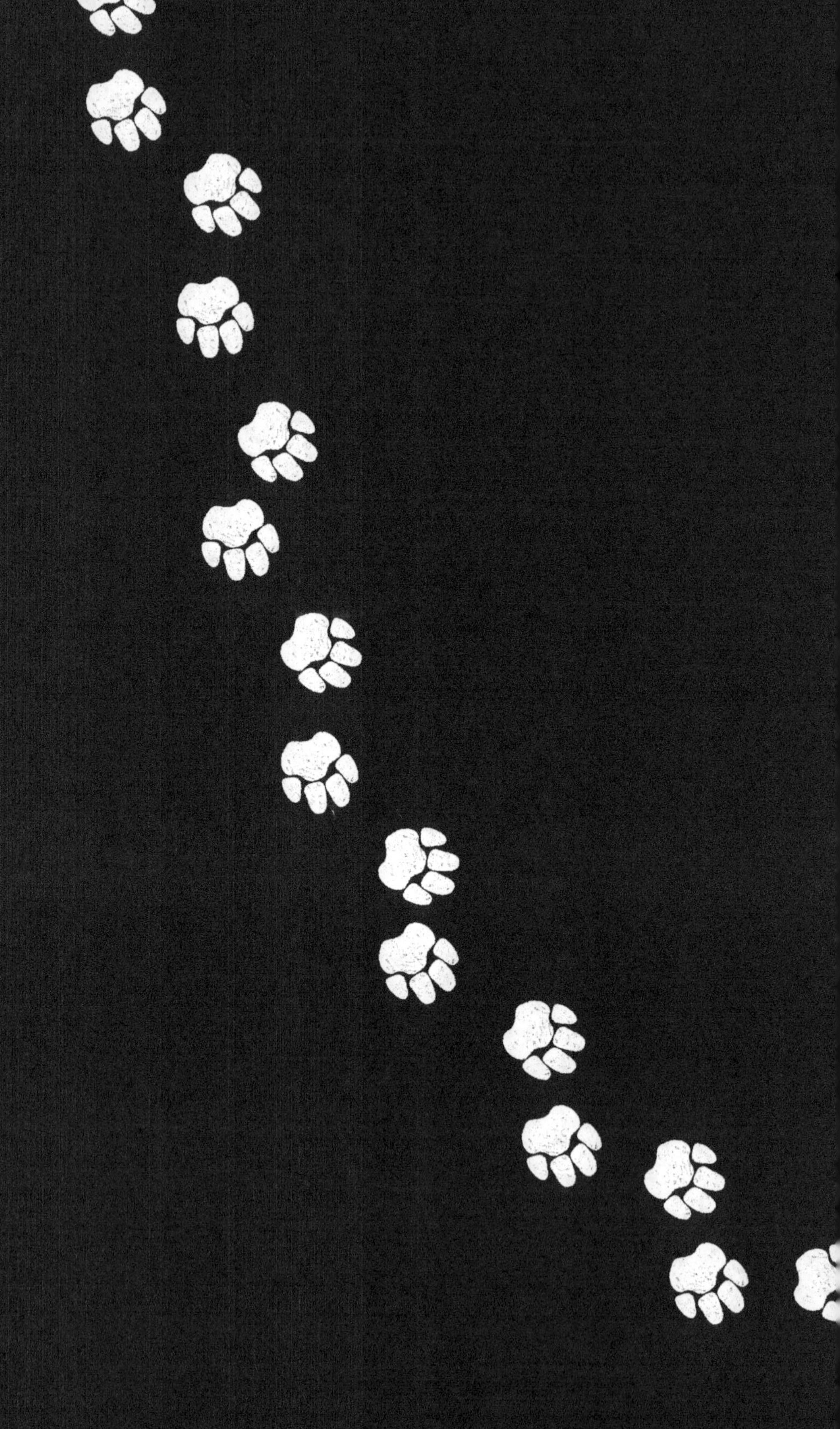

The Blade Drags Everyone Into the Darkness

DELILAH

"I can find him. I don't know if he'd resist, but I couldn't block him the other day, and I was using everything I had to do so. My shields are damn good, but he felt my arm like he was the one with the tears."

Well, fuck, then why are you so worried about how much he cares and how connected you are? Why are you making me suffer while I wait for you to break my heart into a million pieces?

"Will he answer? I don't know what's in his head. If you guys are that connected, I suppose he feels everything you're feeling right now, which explains a lot."

"What do you mean?"

"He feels you. He knows what you've been feeling here."

She looks stricken, turning pale under her tan. "I didn't think. I sometimes forget that it goes both ways with mates, and he—damn."

I pound my head into the sand, closing my eyes in defeat. This is when everything gets blown to bits. Here I am, stepping onto the land mine.

Detonation: inevitable.

"What's wrong? What's with the sand pounding?"

She isn't this dense, is she?

"I don't know what he did. If I were a betting woman—and I am —I'd say he's irrational. He would talk to Taurus before he took flight, which makes this entire conversation moot."

My reason for being here just went up in smoke, and now I need to prepare for the fallout. I run my hands over my face, trying to build another room to store this crap inside. I see the atrium in my mind with its ornate doors, so now I need to construct a new one for her.

Shooting to her feet, she gives me an angry look and stalks towards the water. "That's *just* like a man. It's not Taurus that he needs to talk to! That lazy, long-haired stoat needs to talk to *me* or at least *act* as he wants to, god fucking dammit!"

Well, if that's not the kettle... This sucks.

I'm keeping quiet because I can't help, and she has no idea that she's being unfair to both of us. Talia is as damaged as he and I are. She's self-destructing all our happiness because she's got a self-esteem issue.

Turning back from the waves, she pushes her hair out of her face. "And it would be nice if it wasn't because my irritating, interfering, dickhead of a mate had to open his motherfucking mouth!"

If this were anyone else, I'd look at this situation like a farce.

Talia is feeling unloved, so she ponders hurting me to help herself. Rafe feels guilty for finding some happiness. Taurus—who the hell knows what he's doing—but it seems he's getting screwed as much as I am. All she wants to do is whine about two men who adore her trying to do things to make her happy.

"Look, I only meant it wouldn't be out of character for him to have told Taurus they can't be together. If he felt your pain, he wouldn't wait for you to ask. He would do it, come to you, apologize, and move on. That's what he does for the people he loves. He takes care of them."

"If he does that, I will get so fucking pissed off that it's not even funny." She stalks back over to me, looking incensed, and for the life of me, I can't figure out why. Everything has worked out how she wanted without her even having to be the bad guy. She's got what she wants. Why so angry? "Do you at least understand that it's *not* about Taurus?"

I blink. "I guess. It seems like he's the problem, but it's deeper than that."

"It's how Rafe is with me. If I were as secure in him as I am in you, this would not be a problem. But it's always *you telling* me how much he cares, or Taurus, but never him. Honestly? If this is how he's always going to be, then I'd rather he gave me up and be with Taurus. He'd be happier, and I'd hurt less."

That floors me.

She ran off with me rather than talking about her problems. She hasn't contacted him since we've been together. She's feeling insecure about him, but emoting with me. She left with me—taking me to a place she's only taken me and that idiot Wilde to.

I feel bad, but I can't say anything about it. "Talia, he didn't realize you felt insecure. Rafe would cut off a limb for people he loves. He's racked with guilt because he didn't make you feel happy and loved. You feel secure with me, which can't help. He's never been enough for our mates, and you just struck that chord hard."

Talia finally stops yelling, so I guess I should go on. She needs to hear this from someone looking in from the outside. "You don't get it. He may not have said this in words, but if he gives you up, he's gone. He won't be with anyone. I felt it by the time he thought you were leaving—panic. I felt the bone-deep fear of loss so great that you can't claw your way out. Everything inside him stopped. He was so far gone when you two started. After all the shit and the pain, he was ready to hit the road. You changed that."

Her expression is dumbfounded, and she sucks in a breath. "You mean that if I don't—if I give him up, he'll go away?"

Someone needs to be sane right now, and as usual, it's me.

"He might if he's shattered; I don't know if he can take it. It has broken him for so long—like me—and I can't hold it together for him while he heals this time. It drained me the last time; hell, it still drains me. He let you in farther than anyone else. I don't know if he can come back from it. Why the hell would he come back if that's how you feel?"

Perhaps I'm speaking for him; perhaps I'm speaking for myself. I'm not sure if the two aren't inseparable right now. We're both headed for a fall, depending on what she does. I can't say that I know whether I'll ever be able to look at her again if she leaves. I can't even say if it won't break me so that I can't look at Taurus. Rafe can't be any different.

How can I judge him for something I feel so keenly after an even shorter time than he's been with Talia?

She gets paler, holding her stomach and murmuring, "I can't. He can't go away. I love him. He can't." Dropping to her knees, she looks like she's going to barf.

I sigh heavily at the dramatics. That's yet another thing I won't be able to handle. My stomach roils for a moment, and I plead with Maeve internally to help me be strong. Having PTSD, anxiety, trauma, and being pregnant simultaneously is shit when things get emotional like this. But I can't escape people who consistently want to be the main character in everything, and it seems like I've run afoul of them again.

Exactly what did she expect to happen when she let loose with all this?

Despite my feelings for her, I'm getting resentful of her self-centered misery and tired of being the go-between for two people who need to talk to each other. Goddess, I miss Taurus. I wish he were here so much because he'd know what to say. It might be ugly and painful, but he'd know. He'd see I'm hurting, and she doesn't see or care.

"I'd give him up to Taurus or to anyone, but he can't go away. I have to know that he's happy, that he's out there, even if I never see him again. Oh god. Oh god. I'm going to be sick."

Sighing again, I rub my temples as a massive headache forms. "I'm sure that he feels as if he's failed you. Because of his past, one of his biggest fears is not being able to give enough, not being able to be enough to make people happy. He might even think you'll be better off with me. Neither of you trusts each other as much as you should."

I get up and walk over to a palm tree, standing under it to get out of the sun. I close my eyes again, working on building the room in my heart. The door is dark and lethal-looking, like her. The hinges are shining silver and sharp like knives. The inside is gothic and dangerous, with a single painting of the beach.

Just a little more and it will be ready for me to shift things in and get it sealed.

Sobbing loudly, she kneels and clutches her stomach.

I can't force myself to go to her; I'm too busy detaching my emotions from her one by one. Maeve is trying to soothe me and failing; her tiny light fighting to spread through the darkness inside me. A tough little spark, my wee one, but she can't fix this. She doesn't agree with my method of handling this. She doesn't comprehend my bone-deep, weary pain that comes from grief and loss.

"Deli help me. What should I do? I can't lose him; I can't."

My temper snaps, and I almost scream.

Why the fuck did she do this? Why did she question the foundation of their relationship because he had a good time with Taurus?

I'm not worried about Taurus loving someone more than me. I'd rip someone else's face off for looking at him, but not Rafe. Neither of them would ever hurt me, and I know it. But Talia doesn't believe me when I explain that. I don't look at her, but I choose my words for their clinical precision.

This is me: detached and cool, unwilling to give her my pain.

"Talia, Rafe doesn't say things out loud as often as he does things to show his love. I am certain that he'd give anything up for you. Whether he's said it, I believe that he's chosen to do so already if he's running. He has barely even spoken to anyone but you and our family since Wilde died. He avoided other mates and friends unless I forced him to interact with them."

"But he hasn't been with me. I figured that Sari—"

"No. She reserved her special brand of torture for me from the time we arrived at that hospital. She went to see him one time—to put an end to the bullshit about the rings."

"It hurts so much. Deli, I want him. I need him. Oh God, what have I done?"

Ah, Cassiopeia, what have you done?

Closing my eyes, I wonder if I could blink out of here and go some-where—anywhere—but here. Her pain is palpable, and my own is funneling into the room I've built inside. She's not even the tiniest bit concerned about what will happen to me or Taurus if Rafe stays gone. She's not worried about whether he'll punish himself for hurting her, but I am because he will. He's going to flagellate like a priest caught in the nunnery.

I'm going to feel every bit and just keep quiet, like with Victor. It will also have to live here in the room. I will need to make space for it. The cabinet appears in my mind, and I imagine its drawers being labeled one by one, getting ready to place memories and injuries on them to seal away.

The air shifts as if something in the magick in this place is shifting. I feel that she's reaching out to him. She's looking for him. I don't know if it's working because I'm not willing to bust the barriers someone has cast on this place to pieces to help her. I could, but I don't want to.

The energy she's putting out is getting intense. I stop my internal construction to walk over and sit nearby. It crawls over my skin, and I shudder. Their connection is powerful. Before I can stop her, her hand reaches out and grabs my wrist.

No, no, no! This is bad; this is bad.

I try to shake her off, but I can't. The wind howls. She's sucking in my power, and this is so dangerous; she doesn't know how to control it. I don't know how deep the well goes! I can't get her hand off me, and the sea is roiling, the sand is blowing, and the sky is getting dark. Everything around us is turning black, and I can't make it stop.

We are so royally fucked.

WHAT HAPPENS NEXT? *Find out in Book Four (TBA Title) by preordering here!*

CHARACTERS, PETS, & CREATIONS

Delilah Lenore O'Hara (dee LIE luh Len ORE OH Hair-uh) numbered as x1501; human—maybe. Lived in Rift for two years, born in an Earth town called Whistler's Hollow. Thirty-five years old, lives in the Resistance Quarter in a house called The Maison with her family of clones and droids including: Rafe, Victor, Caesar, Hex, Sandrine, Siren, and Philomena. She is mated to Wilde, Sari, Rafe, Alistair, and Rhea. Rafe is her primary mate. She is one of the current Resistance leaders and mayor of the quarter with Lily. She has a pet white tiger named Aradia given to her by Preston for her birthday this past year.

Nicknames: The Cat, Nightbloom, Sandwich, Peach, Deli, Delicat, Twinkles, Darkness, Kitten, Queen D, Nancy, Juliet, Tiger Lily,

Donatella (don UH tell UH) numbered x098; human; living in Rift three and a half years. Leader of the Resistance during the Conflict, creator of droids. Lived in Down Under house with Victor and Caesar until she met James. She left the Rift with James and his droid Lucinda to live on Earth, abandoning Victor and Caesar to live with their family friends at the Maison.

Nicknames: Dona

Rhea (Ree-UH) numbered x256; human—maybe? Living in the Rift for four years in Cabal Quarter. Mated to Alistair, one of the original three brothers, and close friend of Talia from life on the other side of the portal. She lives in The Firehouse with Alistair and eventually mated with Sari, Wilde, Deli, and Rafe. She has a robotic dog she used to get into the Resistance.

Nicknames: Flame, Blondie, Lady Fair,

Rafe (Ray-F) numbered 086; clone; former operative. Clone won in a contest by Dona that fell for Delilah and became her primary mate. Mated to Sari, Wilde, Alistair, and Rhea. Artistic and known for being languid. Lives in The Maison with Deli, Hex, Sandrine, Siren, Leo, Philomena, Caesar, and Victor.

Nicknames: The Artist, The Lounger, The Stoat, Royalty, Ennobled One, Tyger,

Caesar (see ZAR) numbered A001; droid. First droid created by Victor and Donatella and leaders of the Resistance in the Conflict. One of the creators of almost all droids, and a submissive. Was involved with Lucinda until she moved with Donatella and James to the other side of the portal. Likes to be on a leash. Changes his hair color frequently.

Nicknames: Puppy

Victor (Vik-tor) numbered 020; clone. Former mate of Donatella and part of the Resistance in Conflict. Lived in Down Under house with Caesar and Dona until she left for the other side with James. Lives in The Maison with Caesar along with Deli's family now. Has a deep history with Deli and Rafe. Secondary father of all droids with Caesar.

Nicknames: Vic, Fangy, Pops

Alistair (Al-is-TARE) numbered 001; clone and one of the three original brothers. Lives in Firehouse with Rhea and was a big part of the Cabal side in the Conflict. Former operative for Company. Mated to Rhea, Sari, Deli, Wilde, and Rafe. Very close to Deli at the moment because of craziness. Loves her beast.

Nicknames: Tyger, Ace,

Sari (sar-EE) numbered x260; human—maybe? Lives in Coyote Den with Wilde, Janus, Roman, and Calista. Mated to Wilde, Rhea, Deli, Rafe, and Alistair. She was a defector from the Resistance in Conflict and helped Cabal win the war. Turned to Resistance again after Cabal abandoned Rift. Convinced Deli to allow her to join their town based on her former droid turned clone, Wilde. Has a coyote mutation and is torturing people now.

Nicknames: Coyote, Gnome,

Roman (Roh-man) numbered as A201; droid. Partners with Janus and lives in Coyote Den with Sari, Wilde, Calista, and Janus. Rumored to be involved with Philomena in a threesome.

Nicknames: Hottie,

Janus (Jan-us) numbered A202; droid. Partners with Roman and lives in Coyote Den with Sari, Wilde, Calista, and Roman. Rumored to be involved with Philomena in a threesome.

Nicknames: Spicy,

Philomena (fill OH main uh) numbered A200; droid. Lives in The Maison with Deli, Hex, Rafe, Leo, Sandrine, Siren, Caesar, and Victor. Drunken pill popper but cares about her family. Rumored to be in a threesome with Roman and Janus. Fashion hound and elitist.

Nicknames: The Bitch, Duchess P

Wilde (why uhld) numbered 056; was a droid and turned into a clone by The Company after he and Sari betrayed the Resistance. Blogger and intellectual snob. Mated with Rhea, Sari, Rafe, Alistair, and Deli. Lives in Coyote Den with Sari, Calista, Janus, and Roman. Was a sweet romantic, but recent events have him allowing the suppressed demon inside free and he is using it to punish those who upset him—including Deli and Rafe.

Nicknames: the Blogger,

Sandrine (san-DREEN) numbered A124; droid. Created for Leo as a companion by Vic and Caesar. Has a panel in back that keeps Buzz, a genetically mutated spider, in it. Kicks ass and takes names. Lives at Maison with Caesar, Victor, Deli, Rafe, Leo, Hex, Siren, and Philomena. Helps care for the animals, including Aradia and Mercury's giant bugs.

Nicknames:

Leonidas (Lee-oh-nye-dis) numbered A096; droid. First droid created for Deli. Lives in Maison with Deli, Rafe, Hex, Victor, Caesar, Philomena, Siren, and Sandrine. Dates Sandrine. Chef of the household. Very easy going. Loves pulling pranks with the other earliest droids.

Nicknames: Leo, Romeo, Nuts and Bolts,

Hex (HehX) numbered A100; droid. Dates from Belle's family. Punk rocker ala Billy Idol. Lives in Maison with Deli, Rafe, Leo, Victor, Caesar, Philomena, Siren, and Sandrine. Martha Stewart of the house, runs and decorates everything. Wears frilly aprons and combat boots. Second droid Deli ordered.

Nicknames: Punk, Rocker, Sid

Theodora (thee OH door uh) numbered A050; Droid. Created by Dona to help Talia when she was ill and couldn't work. No one knew she'd been shot, but Theodora is the only droid to be modeled after a person, not a clone template. She looks exactly like Talia, but is the polar opposite in personality. Involved with Damien and they all live in the Homestead house with Talia, Taurus, and the hellhounds.

Nicknames: The Lady, T, Theo,

Damien (day ME en) numbered M001; muse. The only muse known to exist. Appeared to Talia one day and has lived with her since. He and Taurus fight constantly. He talks in riddles and visual images, making it hard to understand him. He has various forms, can hop portals of his own, and has a monstrous form he rarely shows. He is an artist and has muse magic that no one understands. He is partnered with Theodora.

Nicknames: Melted Crayon, Crayola, Monster,

Belle numbered X300; human; living in Rift for three years; Cabal Quarter home called The Shop that mostly goes unused for their home on Earth called The Ranch; joined the Resistance after Sari pressured her to be let in; she ordered Chaos first, then Veruca. Functions as Sari's bully.

Nicknames: The Bulldog,

Mayhem numbered 045; clone given to Belle during Conflict; mechanic; edgy rocker look; only mated to Belle; friendly with Sari's family; Deli thinks he's sent out to seduce people to get them to like Belle; supposedly closed to Michaela;

Nicknames:

Chaos numbered A215; droid; speaks in riddles; looney tunes; dances and sings; prophecy is supposed gift; dating Hex

Nicknames: Crazypants,

Veruca numbered A255; droid; created for Belle to shift into a wolf; edgy punk; not dating anyone friends with Calista

Nicknames: little wolf girl

Cruise numbered 004 ;clone; mated to one of the original Cabal members; left the Rift to become an A-List celeb after the Conflict

Shea numbered A116; created for Tamara after Resistance formed; lives at Tropical House; family in house Manuel, Grayson, and Derek; casual lover of Deli; also has ties to Black Rose Family

Manuel numbered 092; broken out of Company program without permission; claims to be mated with Tamara; lives in Tropical House; family in house are Derek, Tamara, Shea, and Grayson; ties to Black Rose Family

Tamara numbered X1601; human from Earth; chef; lives in Tropical House; family in house with Grayson, Shea, Derek, and Manuel; ties to Black Rose Family

Amanda numbered x1753; human; lives with Constantine; member of Widow's Peak Family; closest to Sari;

Nicknames:

Constantine numbered A120; lived here six months with Amanda in Widow's Peak Family; close with Deli; one of her non-mate lovers;

Nicknames:

Lily numbered x471; lives with Mercury; favors droids; semi-involved with Rafe; part of Captain's Ship family; co-mayor of Resistance with Deli

Nicknames:

Mercury numbered A097; droid; quirky and odd; makes genetically altered bugs; likes role play; lives with Lily in Captain's ship family; involved with Deli as non-mate lover; hurt her when beast came out; voyeur and loves to take pics/video

Nicknames: Captain

Aradia Deli's white bengal tiger; rescued from a bad circus by Preston and given to her for her birthday

Twist Deli's all black ferret produced when she dressed as a pirate for a movie opening night with Mercury

Tweedle a ghost that lives with Lily and Mercury

Grayson numbered A129; droid; considers his primary mate to be Tamara; creepy and pretends to be a Dom; ominous and unsettling with poor social skills; made by Victor and Caesar; he is also involved with Rita

Rita numbered X1610; human recruited by Tamara; her family is called Black Rose; involved with Grayson; considers primary mate to be JJ; very submissive and self conscious

JJ numbered A125; created by Victor and Caesar; involved with Rita as primary and Tamara; not very sharp

Wally numbered A132; created by Victor and Caesar; part of Black Rose; droid with wolfish characteristics like Veruca; fun and loves music

LIST OF FAMILY NAMES, HOUSES, AND MEMBERS

The Maison Family: Delilah, Rafe, Leo, Hex, Sandrine, Siren, Philomena, Victor, Caesar, Aradia, and Twist

The Homestead Family: Taurus, Talia, Theodora, and Damien, and the Hellhounds

The Den Family: Sari, Wilde, Calista, Roman, and Janus

The Firehouse Family: Rhea, Alistair, and Priscilla

The Ranch Family: Belle, Mayhem, Chaos, and Veruca

The Down Under Family: Dona, Lucinda, and James

The Captain's Ship Family: Lily, Mercury, and Tweedle

The Widow's Peak Family: Amanda and Constantine

The Tropical Family: Tamara, Shea, Manuel, Grayson, and Derek

The Black Rose Family: Rita, Wally, and JJ

The Gearhead Family: Michaela, Preston, Aramis, Kane, and Shane

The Library Family: Dahlia, Mack, and Rupert

The Tech Family: Heather and Chance

The Hallows: Dahlia, Rupert, and Mack

Jaguars: Rana and Everett

The Wilds: Amora and Strike

The Coach House: Marina and Ward

The Starship: Simone, Percy, and Wilhelmina

Maple Leaf: Penelope, Gregor, and Aramis

The Sanctum: Dove and Cherise

LOCATIONS IN AND OUT OF THE RIFT

Bytes 'N Chips- A dive bar used for one of the portals to The Rift as well as a frequent recruiting location.

Dirty Deeds- A bar created by Sari that was the location of unspeakable debauchery. How it was destroyed is unsubstantiated.

The Maison- Delilah's enormous home. It is the epicenter of Resistance activity.

The Zoo- The new karaoke bar Sari and Belle opened without permission.

The Company- A mysterious organization that created The Rift, runs the secret Project Reality, and maintains surveillance on the inhabitants of The Rift. Allegedly, they are a private mercenary organization with no ties to any government, criminals, or other governing bodies

Sacred Space- The anointed space a magick user keeps to perform rituals and spells. Only Deli has one.

Portal- The pathway to The Rift from Earth. The main one is located in Bytes 'N Chips, but there are more throughout Earth. Those who can apparate do not always use them.

The Resistance Quarter the magically protected area in the Rift where the Resistance all live

The Cabal Quarter the original spaces where families lived when the Cabal ruled and everyone first came through the portal.

Riftverse Terminlogy

Clone- created from DNA and modified through trade secrets involving quantum physics, wormholes, and the Company scientists.

Android/Droid- am artificially intelligent creation that is technologically advanced far beyond human capabilities including bodily functions, charging, and sentience. Created by Donatella, Victor, and Caesar prior to the Conflict and continually improved upon by a team of their creations.

The Rift- A pocket dimension that the Company HQ and staff, along with humans of the Cabal and Resistance live in.

Bytes 'N Chips- A dive bar used for one of the portals to The Rift as well as a frequent recruiting location.

Dirty Deeds- A bar created by Sari that was the location of unspeakable debauchery. How it was destroyed is unsubstantiated.

The Maison- Delilah's enormous home. It is the epicenter of Resistance activity.

The Cabal- A human governing body put in place by the Company to keep the human inhabitants in line.

The Resistance- Originally, the rebels and droids that fought the Cabal/Company in the Conflict. Currently, the inhabitants of Deli's hidden city.

Claiming/Marking- A ritual involving biting that is akin to engagement for clones and some droids.

Mating- A ritual like marriage that involves biting, claiming, blood exchange, and marking.

Apparate/Disapparate- A form of travel used by some clones and magicks users that is similar to teleportation.

Sacred Space- The anointed space a magick user keeps to perform rituals and spells. Only Deli has one.

The Zoo- The new karaoke bar Sari and Belle opened without permission.

The Company- A mysterious organization that created The Rift, runs the secret Project Reality, and maintains surveillance on the inhabitants of The Rift. Allegedly, they are a private mercenary organization with no ties to any government, criminals, or other governing bodies that operate as both white and black hats if you can afford them.

Familiar- An animal that facilitates magick for an extranormal, also serves as a companion and protector.

The Beast- The name for the sentient panther shifter inside of the Delilah.

Demon- All of the clones are created with one based on their template and the droids are also programmed with one if it suits their template.

Template- The base appearance and personality of the droid/clone. These were decided by the scientists of the Company and mirror a cast of individuals they cloned/passed through the wormholes.

Oversight- The individual that runs the Company. He/She is unknown to those without Alpha Level Clearance.

Clearance Level- Those involved with the Company have clearance levels for access to information and systems. It is based on the Greek alphabet with Alpha being the highest level with the least individuals.

The Conflict- The war between the droids and the clones (Resistance and Cabal) that resulted from the caste system the Cabal created.

The Battle of Blood and Steel- The final battle of the Conflict prior to peace talks.

The Creation- This refers to the process of the creating the first three clones and the subsequent process refinement.

Other Place/Side/Real World- Earth, circa now-ish

Project Reality- The name for the experiment the Company is running that contains the inhabitants of The Rift. They are unaware.

Portal- The pathway to The Rift from Earth. The main one is located in Bytes 'N Chips, but there are more throughout Earth. Those who can apparate do not always use them.

Reviews, Print, and Merchandise

If you have enjoyed this story, please review it.
It helps other readers find my work,
which helps me as an indie author.

Thank you!

Reviews are appreciated on the following platforms

TikTok
Instagram
Facebook
Bookbub
StoryGraph
Threads
Goodreads
Amazon

To purchase print copies or merchandise, go to The Worlds of Cassandra Featherstone

Get Secret Bonus Scenes!

For a secret bonus scenes, *click the link below, sign up for my newsletter, and get your freebie.*

Get your bonus scene here!

Stalk Cassandra Featherstone in the Dark Corners of the Web

JOIN MY FACEBOOK GROUP AND FOLLOW ME EVERYWHERE!

WANT MORE?

SIGN UP FOR MY BI-WEEKLY MANIFESTO

Series Sampler

Join my Ream as a FREE follower or exclusive subscriber to get access to cover reveals, WIPs, Serial Stories, and personal chats from me!

LOSER

Kat

The little blue icon on my app has been glaring at me all day, but I'm too damn nervous to open it. Everyone at Woodlawn High has been buzzing all day with their notifications and the squeals of joy and moans of despair were too much for me to take. My anxiety is through the roof—this is the moment I've been waiting for since middle school, but I can't seem to force myself to bite the billet and check.

Maybe it's because I don't have the support system most of my class-mates have?

That's probably true, given I've always been a loner and I don't fit into any specific 'caste' here. It's hard to make friends when you get shuffled from foster home to foster home over the years. I've rarely stayed anywhere long enough to make a friend, much less a group of them.

I'm not delinquent or anything—the families I've been placed with just return me like a pair of pants that doesn't fit after a year or so. The caseworkers click their tongues sympathetically and hunt down a new placement, but I've never been given a reason *why* people don't want me around. One lady said I must be born under a bad sign and hell if I knew what that meant other than I'm not good enough to keep around.

It would be different, almost understandable, if I misbehaved or got bad grades. But I don't—I'm always in the top five percent of my class and I do everything I'm asked. I don't even lord my smarts over the other kids or adults. Being presentable and unassuming was something I adapted long ago to improve my probability of staying in a home long term.

Unfortunately, it never worked and though I should be a shoo-in for scholarships and acceptances galore, I can't bring myself to be rejected yet again.

So I wait for the last bell of the day, slinging my bag over my shoulder and trudging home to the latest in my temporary hous-ing. I can't even contemplate looking at the possible heartache waiting for me in the college application system WHS insisted we use. The fear is too great and despite knowing I'll be on my own for good at the end of this year, I'm unable to risk the pain.

I hate being this way.

My court mandated therapist says it's some sort of attachment disorder that's common in foster kids, but I think that's bullshit. The problem isn't *me* not forming attachments; it's asshole adults not forming one to me. Being left at a safe haven in a fucking basket as a baby wasn't because *I* did anything wrong—again, fucking adults couldn't handle their commitments.

As usual, I arrive home to an empty house. There are two other kids who live here—Bryce and Blake—but they're at football practice. Of course, the Jamesons *love* them; they get to strut around at games because their strays are the stars of the team. I'm not mistreated, but I'm definitely an afterthought. Both of my 'parents' are still at work, so I drop my bag on the couch and head for the kitchen to get a snack.

Don't get me wrong. I *could* have been placed in far worse homes than any of the seven I've been in since elementary school. None of the ex-fosters starved, beat, molested, or abused me. They were all decent folks with jobs and houses that weren't hellholes, but they never liked me.

I have no idea why. I tried to be everything they wanted.

But when the end of each school year came, I was handed in like a textbook and off I went to some group home until the next contestant stepped up. It baffled everyone, not just me, but that's what happened every single time.

Sighing, I pull some fruit out of the fridge and grab a soda. I have homework to do and if I want to have time to work on my stories, I'll need to get it done before the house is full of people at dinner time. Bryce and Blake will have gotten messages about their applications, too, and I'd bet my pinkie toe those idiots got into some big sports school. Brett and Allison will be oozing happiness for them and I don't know if I'll be able to keep food down if I have to admit my failure when they ask.

Being eighteen sucks ass.

After I grab my books and tablet, I head down to the den. I have to give my current parents credit; they set up a very nice workspace for us to study in the converted basement. By the time they took me in, the Jamesons created a cozy room down here where the three of us could relax and do our work for school without being interrupted. It might have been more for the boys than me, but I appreciated it all the same. Desks, a couch, big chairs, and bookshelves fill the space, making it almost seem like our mini-library. They even put a small fridge for drinks and snacks in case we had to be up late to cram.

It's my favorite place in the entire house and I spend most of my time here.

I sink into the huge armchair, putting my drink and snack on the side table. It only takes a few minutes to arrange myself in the soft cushions and I pause to tug my headphones out of my pocket. Music always soothes my jagged edges and I need it to stay focused on the bullshit AP Calculus I need to keep my average up in. My course load is heavy, but I applied to tough colleges. I wouldn't have a chance to get in, especially on a scholarship, if I wasn't taking equally challenging classes in comparison to all the prep school kids.

As always, the sounds of Vivaldi carry me away as I scrawl equations on my screen and before long, thoughts of the blue notification completely fade away.

"Kat!"

The shouts barely register as I continue working on the problem set, gnawing on my lower lip in concentration.

"Jesus fuck, where is she? I could eat a hippo!"

"Kat!"

Thumping followed by what could pass for a stampede of elephants jerks me out of my math filled trance when Bryce and Blake come down the stairs. They smell as bad as the aforementioned pachyderm's cage, so they must have rushed home right after practice. The blond twins glare at me as if I'm the offending element despite being sweaty and covered in dirt and grass stains.

This doesn't bode well.

Usually, they're tired and hungry after practices so I'm used to cranky ass boys, but tonight, there's a light to their faces. That had to mean they've gotten their letters and dinner will be a gush fest in honor of their perfection. I'm going to need all of my strength to fake smile and nod as Brett and Allison fawn over them.

I don't begrudge them their success—not really. They work hard and play even harder on the field. It's not their fault they're the American dream teens and I'm the nerdy basement troll no one wants. But it's awfully hard living in the shadow of their bright light, especially when I'm no less intelligent or talented.

"I'm finishing the AP Calc, guys. What do you want?"

They roll their eyes at me before Blake scoffs. "It's not due until Monday. You're so hyper."

Duh. I take anxiety meds, douchebag; of course I'm 'hyper.'

"I can only be who I am, Blake." That earns me a snort from Bryce and I know it's because he thinks that's the problem. "Is dinner ready?"

"Almost. Get upstairs and set the table so we can shower—Brett's orders." Blake grins smugly.

The two of them seem to always arrange it so chores get passed to me for some half-assed reason and this is no exception. Sighing, I put my stuff aside, fully intending to hide down here after the dinner mess is cleaned up. Likely by me, but like I said, I could definitely live in worse foster homes so I let it go. Doing some chores isn't worth risking the group home for the last few months of my high school career.

They take off running up the stairs and I wait for them to disappear before I follow suit. My phone is tucked in my pocket and I feel like it's a stone of shame I have to bear. I know once the adults make over the twins' success, they will remember me, and I'll be forced to find out what disappointment lies in wait for me. The dread weighs on me, but I head into the sunny kitchen and pick up the pre-prepared pile of plates, silverware, and napkins on the counter.

Allison looks up from the stove and gives me a half-smile, nodding as I take the dishes into the dining room. Like I said, no one is mean or horrid, they just seem...obligated. After a while, it makes it hard to waste time trying to be bright and sunny. Being reserved makes it a hell of a lot easier not to feel rebuffed when they don't pay attention to you regardless.

"Make sure you include champagne glasses for your dad and I!" she calls from the other room.

The twins definitely got acceptance somewhere big. Brett must have gotten the bubbly on the way home.

Once I set the table, I return to help Allison bring out the roast and sides. I'm a little amazed at her efficiency when it comes to getting the housework done while working full time, but I suppose it's something people with real parents get taught as they grow up. My home life has been so fractured that I haven't learned how to cook more than very basic shit from YouTube videos. That may be a problem after graduation, but I've never felt comfortable enough to ask Allison if she'd teach me. I'm sure she would try, but it doesn't feel right.

"How was school, Kat?"

I look over my shoulder, seeing Brett in the entry to the dining room. He's already changed from work and smiling, but I see the distraction in his eyes. He's waiting for the boys to come down. "It was fine. I've got a Calc test at the end of the week. I'll be studying a lot to get ready."

"Good, good. No matter what happens with applications, keeping your grades up will ensure no one pulls any offers," he says.

Those words aren't for me. They are for the two wet haired boys who just appeared behind him.

"Kat's too much of a geek to ever let her grades slip, Dad," Blake says as he pushes past his brother and drops into his usual chair at the table. "Grab me a Powerade since you're in the kitchen, mouse!"

Both Brett and Bryce stare at me and I turn around, heading to the fridge despite the fact that I was *not* closer than the other twin. Out of habit, I take two of the drinks and a soda for myself. I've been here long enough to know Bryce will send me back to get him one as well. It would feel like typical sibling stuff, but for some reason, I just *know* they do it to fuck with me. I have no idea why I feel that way, but trusting my gut has been the one thing that helped me get through all the upheaval in my life over the years. It's a good gauge for knowing when I'll get booted or if people are being earnest in their reactions.

The therapist says that's some sort of trauma induced early trigger warning shit, by the way.

After I hand out the drinks, I sit down on my side of the table and we wait for Allison to come out. Brett is at his seat at the far end of the table and the twins are punching each other as they look at something on their phones. I know where this is all going but I drop my gaze to the table, swallowing the coppery taste of fear as it courses through my body.

I'm going to be exposed and there's nothing I can do to stop it.

Read the first three episodes free on Kindle Vella: https://www.amazon.com/kindle-vella/story/B0BSTMB1X3

EVERY DAY IS MONDAY

Sydney

"Jesus fucking Christ," I mutter as I slog through the streets of Tempest Seven. "Just because they locked us up like animals doesn't mean we have to live like them."

Pausing in my walk to the education center, I look around myself in abject disgust. The inhabitants of this end of Tempest Seven aren't the bottom of the proverbial barrel, but outside of the 'lockdown losers', people stuck here never seem to get out of the cycle of poverty and despair. I don't think it means we have to throw garbage everywhere and give the drones nice shots to prove to the humans that we're as unworthy as the leaders of this stupid country say we are.

What would it hurt to tidy up, even if we don't have much?

Honestly, I believe it's only a third rooted in laziness. I think the other parts are exhaustion and hopelessness. Since the First Infected Being Sweep of 2020, supernaturals all over this country were tracked, catalogued, reassigned, and declared property of the government. By the time they ran the second through fourth sweeps, the population of some supernatural species dropped by fifty percent. The rules on how to track us down and receive your bounty were infuriatingly vague, which gave the most violent psychopaths in the world a free license to kill, maim, rape, and disappear anyone caught on the 'Non-Human Watchlist'.

I was a baby when my mother left, but my father taught me everything I needed to know about being a shifter. Unfortunately, he was one of the people who ended up on that list and was killed in the Second Infected Being Sweep of 2020. That sweep was brutal, and since I was a 'half-breed' orphan, I was placed in the orphanage in Tempest Seven. From the moment every child and teen arrived, they were forced to attend the Federal Enrichment Assimilation & Re-Education Center.

Our human professors taught us that being born this way is a punishment from their God, especially if you were a mixed type. At first, we tried to tell them about our various species, but it became clear very quickly what would happen if we didn't fall in line. You either learned to smile and nod, providing the rote answers and scripts they gave you when tested or interrogated, or you died.

Now, in 2024, there are no rebellions against the Federated Human States of America, nor are there any aid workers from other countries left to help or try to get us out. The world has given up on the former United States—it's been ruled a failed state by the United Nations and cordoned off at every border on land and sea.

We're on our own in the former land of the free and home of the brave.

"As if anyone would want to come here anyway. Shit went downhill fast after that baboon was elected," I mutter to myself. I realize I've spoken louder than I thought and I look around carefully, making certain I'm not near a Confession Enforcement zone or any other beings. My breath releases slowly when I confirm that I'm totally alone and not in a hot zone.

No one watches out for others now; the temptation to gain things your family or group needs is too high. A random person would dime me out for a week's supply of crackers and I can't blame them. Food and drink are rationed, our clothes are drab and provided, and the world is dimmer since the Sweeps. They force us to stay small so they're in control, and we have to live with it because of the fucking Markers.

My hand flies to the back of my neck, grunting in irritation as I scratch at the tattoo that covers the skin where the implant is located. These were the second step on the path to the current tyranny of our 'benevolent' government. That spray tanned fuck won the election because the humans here were that goddamn stupid, and then the virus hit. COVID brought America to its knees and like all good con artists, President Taterman used the distraction to funnel money into secret programs under DARPA.

Men who stare at goats my skinny ass.

They released a widely contested study that blamed the virus on the 'infected'. Unfortunately, they defined that as beings living in our country that had paranormal capabilities. The rest of the world laughed at the senile old fuck until the media hype was so huge that the various species around the world convened a leadership meeting. With so many cameras and videos everywhere, it was only a matter of time until a random human caught one of us doing something and bam! A viral TikTok would expose all of us whether we were ready or not. The vote was close, but the supernatural community decided to come out of hiding to protest their innocence.

'The Unveiling' was the most watched TV event in decades, and the consensus was our leaders had done the right thing. At least, until the next study was released. This one made Taterman damn near salivate as he screamed into the TV cameras about the 'unclean' liars and thieves who have been hiding in plain sight, taking our jobs, and stealing the lives humans should have. It quickly devolved into a mass panic and our kind were left scrambling.

We'd told them who and where we were, like a bunch of fools.

Thus, the evil assholes at the top started their mission to protect the humans from us and reclaim their country. Supernaturals in other nations were fine, but the atmosphere here became dangerous within the blink of an eye. Taterman stacked his own deck in the courts and the legislature by fear-mongering, especially since the world was still reeling from a pandemic. Eventually, he was able to get the support he needed for the first Sweep.

Secret Supernatural Enforcement Agents used databases, social media, DNA websites, immigration records, and everything they could to gather the biggest dragnet of personal information ever assembled. Civil rights advocates and other world leaders were vocally opposed to such violations, but nothing could stop the juggernaut of hatred. Once they identified every supe in the nation —to the best of their ability—that's when they stripped our citizenship, robbed us blind, and re-assigned every single one to the sectors they'd been building in secret.

Let's be honest—they're supe prison camps.

But the humans felt safe once more because while we were all being shuffled all over like cattle, the rest of the scientific community worldwide started to get COVID under control. Taterman crowed about the United States' involvement, taking credit for slowing the spread by locking up the infected beings. No one but his nutty followers believed him, but at that point, it didn't matter.

So when they came to implant the Markers, no one spoke up.

We all have them, and depending on what you are and how powerful you are, they are different. But resting above the spot where they cut us open to shove in the controller, there's a matching tattoo of the logo that is now on the flag of the Federated Human States of America... but that came much, much later.

Democracy dies in the dark, the old slogan said... and here lies her rotted corpse.

"Hey, Syd. It's a beautiful day in the neighborhood, huh?"

My brooding gets interrupted by the arrival of Thad, my friend since we got placed here four years ago. He's a bear shifter and the size of a small SUV, but it doesn't bother me. I survived the sector version of high school partially because we stuck together. My brains and his bulk were a good match and it kept us from getting cornered by the gangs and cliques.

Okay, fine, it kept me from getting cornered. Obviously, Thad held his own without me.

"That sentiment hasn't been applicable for half a decade, man." I toss my braid over my shoulder and wait for him to catch up. It's our second week at the F.E.A.R. Academy's college level program and being late is more than frowned upon. I have to give us extra time every morning because Thad lumbers out of bed like his animal—slow and grumpy. "We gotta get moving."

The dark haired shifter looks at me, scratching the piratical scruff he's usually sporting. "You're ridiculously concerned about rules for someone with such a rebel spirit."

"Rebels die, Thad. I'm very aware of that." Turning on my heel, I head toward the huge building at the end of the main drag with a heavy heart. Losing Dad was hard and I'll never forgive him for assuming humans are anything but ignorant beasts that barely rise above their simian relatives.

We continue walking in silence until we reach the steps. The line is stretched down them as the guards run the wand over each student to check for weapons. After that, we put our bags on the conveyor belt for the magical detection while the security mages in government issued loyalty collars scan us for anything the wands wouldn't catch. It's not quick, but it keeps fights in the schools non-lethal most of the time.

That's the official reason, but the real purpose is to allow the staff to abuse students if they step out of line. The Markers not only brand and track us, but they siphon energy and power in small bits to keep us all weak enough to be controlled. Weapons would even the score and the humans who run these stupid ass brainwashing cults would be at risk.

"Look who's last at the trough again." The wry voice of the only demon in Tempest Seven gets my attention. Huck Monroe saunters up, tilting his worn black cowboy hat back as he smirks at me. "Y'all are just cruisin' for a bruisin'. I swear, you don't have the sense that the Devil gave a goose."

My eyes narrow at him briefly, then I turn forward and shuffle along as the line moves. "You don't have to hang out with us, Huck. In fact, it'd be great if you fucked off and stayed there."

Thad laughs, bumping his shoulder against the annoying fear demon's and I sigh. Huck was sent here during the First Sweep, like us, and he's been a Southern bramble in my side ever since. It's my bad luck that Thad enjoys his folksy charm and it means he sticks to us like glue during school hours.

"Sometimes you're meaner than a wet panther shifter, Sydney Jolie. I should take you at your word and mosey off, but I like your boy."

Huck's pitch black eyes are hidden by his Ray-Bans, but I know they're sparkling with amusement. He finds my dislike funny, and I don't get why. But then, I don't get a fucking thing about men, especially supes, nor do I want to. Life in our sector is hard enough without having to consider birth control or babies or even finding privacy. I'll save that for the day when I get the fuck out of here.

"I heard they're bringing in a new group of students today." Thad changes the subject quickly, knowing I'll continue to needle Huck and vice versa until one of us loses their temper. "The rumors say the shipment has vamps, losers, and traitors. I'm worried this sector is turning into a dumping ground for psychos."

It wouldn't surprise me if the humans started segregating the camps by species, value, or even criminality. Even after they corralled us into the sectors, the leaders have continued to exert their influence and power over us. The Markers were first, then the lockdowns for the ones they deemed dangerous, and now they're shuffling people weekly at random. I've often wondered if all of this is covering up something like what went on in the 1940s among the humans, but I haven't seen any proof.

Our media is monitored and curated, so unless you know someone with a highly illegal device, you have no idea what's happening outside of the FHSA.

"Next! Keep it moving, you little shits," the yell from the front of the line brings me back to reality again.

"Wicker is the fucking worst," Thad mumbles as we ascend the steps to stand behind the person being inspected. "Watch his hands, Syd."

"I'm aware." Despite thinking we're the scum of the earth, some of the human staff and enforcement in the sectors are fucking creeps. Some supes are willing to trade sex for perks, but that doesn't stop the predators from being creeps to those who don't. "I'll let you go first so Bishop gets me."

"Got it," he says as he muscles in front of me. "Huck, stay behind her."

"Why, I'd be delighted, Thaddeus."

I guess he's useful sometimes, but he'd better not let it go to his head.

Get it now!

Sneak Peek: Hell on Wheels

BAD BLOOD

Rogue

"I don't need you anymore," Mina scoffs.

Holding my face in a disinterested mask, I arch a single brow at the witch, who has been my best friend for three years. We've struggled for months to connect in the same way we did when we first met, but so many things have conspired against us: life, outside influences, time—even our own team members. I met Mina because of our love for the derby, and now it might be the only thing left we share.

Blue hair shakes as she packs her gear, clearly done with our conversation as well. I don't have the words to respond to her, and I'm not sure if she actually wants me to. The divide between us has grown so large that I stopped imagining a world where I would ever get my friend back. I've been expecting this for a month or two; Mina's been distant and there were rumblings she might switch teams to climb the ranks in the Silver City Sickos.

Turning on my heel, I open my locker and dump my things into the duffle silently. Skates, socks, pants, shirts... I shove it all in and grab my leather jacket. I can feel her eyes on me as I sling it over my shoulder and head for the door. She probably expects me to fight her or have some sort of emotional breakdown, but after the things Mina has done lately, I refuse to give her the satisfaction.

You did your best, Rogue. You accepted every cut, scrape, and bruise with quiet grace.

"No outburst? I'm surprised, R. I thought you'd at least try to get me to keep propping you up."

My eyes narrow and I count to ten in my head, letting out a deep breath. I avoided letting this festering wound affect the team for so long, and now it's all going to come out. The shame of what I allowed to happen when others couldn't see floods me and I have to dig my nails into my palms to keep from screaming. Mina wants to taste my pain, and if I give it to her, I can't ever get it back.

Only losers let their enemies see the damage they've done.

If only I could turn back the clock and figure out what started this mess, I'd change it and Mina would laugh with me as we head out for a drink after the match. But that's not possible and there's far too much blood in the water to go back, especially if she's defecting to the Sickos. Those bitches are the nastiest, pettiest team in the league, and they're known for playing dirty to win.

When we first joined the Babe City Bombers, we swore we'd never turn into those psychos, but here we are. It's amazing what some press coverage and a viral video of her doing a twirl will do to someone. Mina has bought into her fifteen minutes and she's been slowly turning into a person I don't know. Out of two practices and one match a week, it's amazing if I don't go home to cry myself to sleep at least once.

Just take your stuff and go outside. Rebel will wait for you.

My stepbrother is the closest person to me in the Universe and if I go out there crying, he might just disarticulate Mina piece by piece in the parking lot. The amount of rage he has for how she's made me feel over the past few months has grown to a level that scares me a little. Only fear of violating our oaths as Guardians has kept him from serving up much deserved revenge on her.

*Of course, her magic is **much** weaker than ours, and the High Council would take that into account.*

Our adoptive parents aren't perfect, but they'd lose the plot if we got exiled, so turn the other cheek it is.

I ignore the continued prodding from behind me as I walk over to the back door of the rink and head outside. As predicted, Rebel is waiting for me, his ass propped against the hood of his black Shelby GT500. His brow creases as he takes me in, and before I can open my mouth, he's stalking to the door with murder in his eyes.

"Reb, stop! It won't solve anything!" I call, running my hand over my face.

He wheels around, the iridescent flecks in his eyes giving away the Fae in him. "I'm tired of watching you suffer because your ex-friend decided she's an influencer. She's a one hit wonder with her head shoved up her ass so far she's kissing it. What she needs is a fucking reality check, Skates."

I pinch the bridge of my nose. He's not wrong, and that makes it hard to hold him back. I can't say I'd hate seeing him bring her to knees and if anyone could do it, Reb's best suited to do so. There's absolutely nothing Mina can say that would bother him—her powers are useless against his. No coercion or manipulation she could conjure would even touch him.

I've been avoiding taking care of it myself because of the impact it would have on the team, but now that's she's fucking off...

Reb smirks as he tiles his head. "Are you finally considering telling her to get fucked, little sis?"

"*Do not* call me that. I'm not little, nor am I your sister. Reck was my brother and since they sent him away, I'm stuck with you," I grouse as I kick rocks across the pavement.

He laughs, winking at me as he walks back to the sweet ass vehicle he plans to race tonight. "If you stop being such a pain in the ass, I *might* let you drive tonight. Think you can handle that?"

Uh, yes, please, asshole.

The stink of this evening is wearing off as I speed around the curves of the winding hills. Tonight's race is a longer one, but I don't mind because when I stepped out into the crowd wearing Rebel's cheeky grin, a roar of excitement filled the air. We'd both be in the fucking thick of it if the jug-eared bitch whose family runs the club knew it was me behind the wheel, but since she rarely descends from her throne, it's unlikely she'll ever catch the scent.

Roadrunner Racing is a front for laundering cash for the Stuhll Mob, and they're known for being vicious thieves and thugs. The matron of the family is the second wife of the dumbest rhino shifter I've ever met, but she more than makes up for his lack of brains with her sociopathic whims. Merra is a tiny fennec Fox shifter, but her thirst for money and power is unrivaled. Rumor has it she swindled her family into the poorhouse before she fell in with Thad, but since no one can actually *locate* any of them, it stays a whispered threat.

Together, they own half the slums in the city, and the club is just another way for them to clean their extorted protection money. Crossing them isn't the brightest plan Reb and I have ever come up with, but it may be one of the most dangerous.

Gotta get your kicks somehow, though, right?

Scenery flies by as I shift around the curvy roads, occasionally checking to see if any of the losers have gotten any closer. All I see is an empty road, so I press the button on the dash that connects me to Reb's open line. He's staying concealed in the pit area, but when I get closer to the finish, I'll want to know what the crowd looks like. The last thing I need is some asshole with powers that will automatically see through the Fae glamor if I get out of the car for the peacocking.

"How's it looking? Any worries?"

A snort echoes in the car as my stepbrother comes online. "No snitches at the moment. I'm eyeing the gates."

We're talking in our own code—it's not like we're on an encrypted line. Gamblers are a tricky breed no matter what species they are; techno-warlocks have blended science and magic to influence everything from supe races to human sporting events, so caution is prudent. Even if we didn't get dimed out to the Queen Bitch, neither of us wants to end up being blackmailed. Guardians are only beholden to the Society, and if we get compromised in our private lives, it could spill into our professional pursuits.

That's the shit that starts wars, and I'd prefer not to go down in history as some fucked up Helen of Troy.

"Good. I'm almost there. Have the champers ready because we're gonna party tonight."

His laugh is dark and I can picture him pushing his green hair out of his eyes as he replies. "I'm not pulling a bunch of revved up asswads off your tipsy ass again. You suck at controlling the pheromones when you drink."

I roll my eyes briefly, trying not to snark back at him. Reb is a full-blooded Unseelie and I'm a half-breed; the other half of my unknown bio parents was a succubus and I have zero frame of reference for learning to control my powers now that I'm an adult. If my actual brother Reck was around, I'd at least have someone to commiserate with, but since the only one around when I emerged was Reb, I'm stuck with his snark.

Being discarded orphans blows goat shifters and no one will ever convince me of anything different.

"You're being morose again, Rogue. My parents ditched me, too, because they were afraid I'd come out a hybrid. You don't have a copyright on being left behind," he grumbles.

I guess that's true, but his full blood status sure makes our adoptive 'family' favor him.

"Reb, until they trade your twin as currency because he's not worth the effort to feed and clothe, you don't get to play the 'poor me' game with me. Back off."

There's a lengthy pause before he answers and when he does, his voice is full of bitterness. "We've said too much on an open line. I'll see you at the checkers."

Great. I didn't mean to piss off my only ally. He'll get plastered at the after party and despite his grand pronouncements, it will be me prying hungry bitches off him before he becomes a baby daddy at 21.

Just fucking fabulous.

Throwing the Shelby into a higher gear, I put the pedal to the floor and fly down the back half of the track. My night is now a thousand times more stressful, and I wanted to lose myself in the heat of the engine to forget my earlier spat with my ex-best friend. I swear to hell, men are the biggest babies on the planet.

My mood continues to darken as I crest the last hill, thoughts of murder and mayhem fogging my brain. By the time I'm cruising down the strip, I've worked myself into a lather that can only be contained by copious amounts of alcohol and sex. It's not the healthiest coping mechanism mentally, sure, but half of my power stems from sexual energy, so I don't examine it too closely.

Never dwell on shit you can't control, Rogue.

Reck used to tell me that before they sent him away, and he was always right. Unfortunately, I didn't listen then, and it's highly doubtful I will now.

I foresee a bar fight in my future and I can't say I'm not looking forward to it.

After all, it's not against the rules to play dirty there.

Get it now!

About Cassandra Featherstone

Cassandra Featherstone has channeled her lifelong passion for writing into a flourishing career, a journey that started when she first grasped a pencil as a gifted child with ADHD.

Her debut novel, born during the solitude of COVID lockdown in March 2020, draws on a tapestry of personal encounters and insights that resonate deeply with her readers.

An international bestseller, Cassandra has topped Amazon charts in categories such as LGBT Anthologies, LGBTQ+ Mystery, and Bisexual Romance, among others. Her works navigate the complexities of bullying, PTSD, body dysmorphia, mental health struggles, personal reinvention, and the empowerment of claiming one's own space. Importantly, Cassandra offers a thoughtful and respectful portrayal of LGBTQIA+ relationships, subtly reflecting her own connection with the community through her narratives.

Her literary repertoire spans sci-fi fantasy, urban fantasy, paranormal, and comedic genres in academy whychoose settings, with a strong commitment to portraying consensual, safe, and accurately depicted BDSM and kink lifestyles. Her books are an invitation to explore transformative stories that are both inclusive and engaging.

Often affectionately called 'The Muppet' for her wacky theater kid personality, she resides in the Midwest with her tech-savvy husband, their creatively inclined college student, a literary-minded dog, and four scheming cats.

READ MORE AT CASSANDRA'S WEBSITE OR HER FACEBOOK PAGE. SIGN UP FOR EXCLUSIVE CONTENT AND UPDATES HERE.

FIND HER ON ANY OF THE SOCIAL MEDIA BELOW AS SHE *LOVES* TO CHAT AND *NEVER* SLEEPS!

Also by Cassandra Featherstone

THE MISFIT PROTECTION PROGRAM SERIES

Road to the Hollow

Return to the Hollow

Home to the Hollow

Rejected in the Hollow

Revealed in the Hollow

Healing in the Hollow

Revenge in the Hollow

AUDIO OF THE MISFIT PROTECTION PROGRAM SERIES

Road to the Hollow

APEX ACADEMY CAPERS

Come Out and Prey

Let Us Prey

In Prey We Trust

Oh Holy Spite (3.5 novella)

Eat. Prey. Love.

Prey It Ain't So (4.5 novel)

Prey It By Ear

AUDIO OF THE APEX ACADEMY CAPERS SERIES

Come Out & Prey

Let Us Prey

In Prey We Trust

TRANSLATIONS OF THE APEX ACADEMY CAPERS SERIES

Come Out & Prey (German)

Let Us Prey (German)

In Prey Trust (German)

DISCORDIA UNIVERSITY

Veiled Flame (Book One)

Quiet Burn (Book Two)

Zero Spark (Book Three)

SECRETS OF STATE U

Blood on the Ice (Book One)

Suspicions on the Stage (Book Two)

TBA TITLE (BOOK THREE)

FAETAL ATTRACTION

Hell on Wheels (Book One)

Jammer in the Box (Book Two)

F.E.A.R. ACADEMY

Failed State (Book One)

Trigger Protocol (Book Two)

VILLAINS & VIXENS

Bloodthirsty (Book One)

Ruthless (Book Two)

Wicked (Book Three)

AUDIO OF THE VILLAINS & VIXENS SERIES

Bloodthirsty

Ruthless

TRIANGLES & TRIBULATIONS

Hoist the Flag (PQ)

Yo-Ho Holes (Book One)

**CHILDREN OF THE MOON-
WITH SERENITY RAYNE**

New Moon Rising (Book One)

Waxing Crescent (Book Two)

Waxing Gibbous (Book Three)

Samhain Secrets (Novella 3.5)

Full Moon (Book Four)

Waning Gibbous (Book Five)

Waning Crescent (Book Six)

RISE OF THE RESISTANCE

Ream Exclusive Prequels

Hooked on a Feline (Book One)

Peacock Me Like A Hurricane

Love The Way You Lion (Book Three)

TBA Title (Book Four)

REAM SERIALS

Secrets of State U

Discordia University

Denizens of the Dark

Faetal Attraction

Agents of the Ouroboros

Rise of the Resistance

F.E.A.R. Academy

ANTHOLOGIES

Unwritten

Shifters Unleashed

Jingle My Balls

Love is in the Air

Silent Night

Snowed In

All Hallows Eve